JAMES W. HUSTON

FALLOUT

**AMERICA'S NEW
TECHNO-THRILLER TOP GUN,
NEW YORK TIMES BESTSELLER**

JAMES W. HUSTON

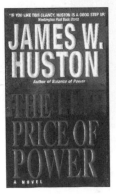

**"GIVE JAMES HUSTON
AN A-PLUS."**
Ft. Worth Star-Telegram

Resounding praise for the bestselling novels of
JAMES W. HUSTON

BALANCE OF POWER
"This military thriller hits the ground running . . .
Huston handles both battle and courtroom with
skill. The pace is fast and the suspense is gripping."
Chicago Sun-Times

"A fun read with interesting characters . . .
Huston's geopolitical thriller debut is a winner."
San Francisco Examiner

THE PRICE OF POWER
"A remarkable adventure story . . . told in page-
turning urgency . . . A suspense-laden tale of
power and glory, of risk and consequences."
Newark Star-Ledger

"Clever plotting, sharp dialogue, and
sustained suspense . . . Huston succeeds
with this tense legal and political thriller."
Virginian-Pilot and Ledger-Star

FLASH POINT
"Lifts off with a vengeance . . . A page-
turner that will definitely cause you
to burn the candle at both ends."
Wichita Falls Times Record News

"Superb action . . . Huston's third
military thriller is also his best."
Kirkus Reviews

Also by James W. Huston

BALANCE OF POWER
THE PRICE OF POWER
FLASH POINT

Available in hardcover

THE SHADOWS OF POWER

JAMES W. HUSTON

FALLOUT

AVON BOOKS

An Imprint of HarperCollinsPublishers

AVON BOOKS
An Imprint of HarperCollins*Publishers*
10 East 53rd Street
New York, New York 10022-5299

Copyright © 2001 by James W. Huston
Excerpt from *The Shadows of Power* copyright © 2002 by James W. Huston
ISBN: 0-380-73283-1
www.avonbooks.com

First Avon Books paperback printing: June 2002
First William Morrow hardcover printing: July 2001

Avon Trademark Reg. U.S. Pat. Off. and in Other Countries,
Marca Registrada, Hecho en U.S.A.
HarperCollins ® is a registered trademark of HarperCollins Publishers Inc.

Printed in the U.S.A.

10 9 8 7 6 5 4 3 2 1

For Don Chartrand

FALLOUT

1

Iran-Pakistan border: Midnight, 3 March 2002

"Hafez," the older guard said. "Someone is coming."

The headlights working their way down the rutted road two miles away were not a welcome sight. The two Pakistani border guards were standing their usual night duty on Pakistan's mountainous border with Iran. They both knew they weren't there because of their skill as guards. They were there because they had failed in their duties elsewhere, and the only place left to put them was an obscure border in the mountains on a rutted road in the middle of the night where one vehicle a night might come through loaded with chicken feed.

Hafez sat up in the drafty wooden shack warmed only by a glowing electric space heater that was inadequate against the biting cold. He breathed in loudly through his nose, trying to stretch while pretending that he hadn't been sleeping. They both had scruffy beards and wore mismatched Army uniform pieces. "I know," Hafez said harshly as he stood. Even though he was younger, he outranked the older soldier. Hafez was in charge of the border crossing until they were relieved in three hours. "We will inspect him completely," he said.

The older guard groaned. "What for? There is never anything. Why bother?"

"Think about it! Why would a truck come through this checkpoint? We get shepherds, traders, refugees, but not trucks." Hafez sniffed against the cold. "Not many anyway."

The older guard looked at him, then at the truck, now half a mile away. It started to snow softly in the darkness. The floodlights pointing out from their guardhouse toward the truck highlighted the snowflakes. "We do get trucks; five or ten every month. What difference does it make anyway?"

"It is our *job*," Hafez answered as he threw back the sliding door and put the strap of his assault rifle over his shoulder. He stepped in front of the truck that had pulled up to the bar that defined the border between the two countries. The Iranian border guards two hundred yards away had waved the truck out of Iran without so much as a comment. Hafez put out his hand for the truck to stop. He shook as a chill rushed through him. "Right here," Hafez said in Urdu.

The driver stopped and rolled down his window. "Good morning," he said in Farsi as he handed Hafez his passport and the truck's documents.

Hafez shook his head as he took the driver's papers. He didn't understand Farsi. He looked at the older guard behind him. "Iranian."

On top of a large hill between the border and the high mountains behind it, Riaz Khan lay on his belly on the cold ground and cursed as he studied the border scene through his night vision binoculars. "They are stopping the truck," he said to the men behind him, who could not be seen from the border side of the hill. "This was supposed to be the easiest crossing point," he said as he glanced back at one of his men.

"That's what we were told."

"You had better be right."

At the border, the older guard nodded, completely uninterested.

Hafez looked at the truck, then leaned into the floodlights so he could read the documentation. "Where are you going?" he asked the driver, again in Urdu.

"I don't understand," the man said in Farsi.

"You speak English?" Hafez asked.

"Little," the driver replied.

"Where are you going?" Hafez asked.

The driver's face soured. "Everything is in the papers."

Hafez didn't like that response at all. "Get out of the truck," he ordered.

The driver looked up at the falling snow, reluctantly grabbed his coat off the seat, and slid to the frozen ground. "What did I do?" he asked as he threw on his heavy, soiled coat and jammed his hands into the pockets.

"I didn't ask you about the papers. I asked you where you were going. Do you not know where you are going without looking at your papers?"

"Quetta," the driver said. He spit on the ground, partially in contempt of the guards, but ambiguously enough that they couldn't accuse him of it.

Hafez knew Quetta, a distant Pakistani city. "Why?"

"Because they told me to go to Quetta. Why do you think I'm going to Quetta? For vacation?"

Hafez looked at the truck. It was a Russian-made stake truck that had seen better days. The diesel engine idled roughly. The back of the truck was full of random scrap metal exposed to the elements. "What is in the truck?"

"Scrap metal."

"Where are you coming from?"

"From the Aral Company in Kazakhstan."

Hafez studied the papers in his gloved hands. "You are driving a piece-of-shit truck from Kazakhstan to Pakistan, all the way through Uzbekistan, Turkmenistan, and Iran to deliver scrap metal?"

The driver hunched his shoulders. "If you think it is stupid, tell the one who is paying me to ship it. Now I must go. My penis is going to freeze off."

"I don't care about you *or* your frozen penis," Hafez said, stepping in front of the man. "Pull over there," he said, pointing at a dirt spot to the right of the road.

"Aaaaaah," the driver protested.

"Move your truck over now," Hafez warned, "or you will *never* pass through this country."

The driver held his tongue. He climbed back into the cab. He forced the reluctant transmission into first gear and moved the truck to the side.

"Get the machine," Hafez ordered the older soldier.

The older guard protested in Urdu, confident the driver couldn't understand them. "What is the point? We have *never* found anything, and if we drop the machine it will break and they will make us pay—"

"Get it!" Hafez ordered.

The older guard mumbled as he walked to the storage shed behind their guard shack and took out the American instrument they been trained on. It rarely got used. He carried it to Hafez and held it out. "Here."

On the hill, Khan had seen enough. He couldn't hear what was being said, but he knew by the gestures of the guards that his plan was on the verge of collapse. "Let's go," he said angrily. "Get your weapons ready." Khan and the men with him ran to their two trucks and raced down the dirt road in the dark with their lights off.

"You do it," Hafez said at the checkpoint. "I'm going to watch this driver. I don't trust him."

The older guard turned on the machine and watched the needle as he walked around the truck, ready to find nothing so the inspection could be over and he could go back to the warm shack. Directly above the VU-meter on the instrument was a small plate that said in English, A GIFT OF THE AMERICAN PEOPLE. He watched the needle as he turned the corner to the back of the truck. Suddenly it jumped to life and bounced around the lighted dial. He looked closely at the indicator, then at Hafez, who was standing by the cab of the truck with the driver. He motioned with his head for Hafez to come to the back of the truck.

Hafez frowned in concern and started walking to the back of the truck. "Stay right there," he said to the driver. He joined the older guard. "What?" he asked.

The guard simply looked at the meter on the box. Hafez followed his gaze, realized what it meant, and stepped away from the truck. The older guard followed suit.

"Twelve hundred milliroentgens per hour!" Hafez exclaimed. He ran back to the front of the truck. "What is this?" he screamed at the driver. "What are you doing? What do you have in there?" he asked, pointing to the scrap metal piled in the back of the truck.

Hafez turned and ran to the guard shack for the phone as the two unlighted trucks rounded the hill and headed straight for him. He stopped and watched the trucks come, then looked back at the older guard, who was standing stupidly next to the truck staring at the VU-meter on the instrument. The driver was inching away from the truck. Hafez stepped toward the oncoming trucks and took his assault rifle off his shoulder. He didn't like the way this was developing.

Khan and the others came to a skidding stop fifty feet from the truck. The men jumped out of the trucks and pointed their weapons at Hafez. Khan yelled at the driver in English, "Get in the truck! Drive on! Now!"

"No!" Hafez said, aiming his rifle at the truck driver. "Get away from the truck. It has radioactive material on board and is being confiscated!"

The driver looked at Khan and Hafez and slowly moved toward the truck.

"Stop!" Hafez screamed.

Khan lowered his assault rifle toward Hafez and fired.

The bullets hit Hafez and drove him back. Hafez fired into the sky as he fell down screaming.

The driver ran to the door of the truck and climbed into the cab.

The older guard stood motionless, holding the machine, unsure what was happening or what to do. He finally moved behind the truck, dropped the instrument, and unslung his assault rifle. The others with Khan began firing at the older guard, but he was too far behind the truck to be seen clearly.

"Drive!" Khan yelled.

The driver threw the gearshift forward into first and started the truck moving. The older guard aimed for the tires as he fired. The four tires in the back of the truck were immediately shredded by the high-speed bullets. Two of Khan's men dropped and started firing under the truck, which continued to roll away from the checkpoint with the driver hunched down, trying to avoid the bullets flying in the darkness.

Hafez rolled over. Blood ran from his stomach wounds. He was determined not to let the truck escape. He began firing at the truck and the driver from the ground. Three of his bullets hit the fuel tank, which exploded, breaking the truck in two just behind the cab and rupturing the heavy containers in the back of the truck underneath the scrap metal.

"Let's go!" Khan screamed.

"We must get the material!" one of his men yelled.

"It is too late! Get in the trucks!"

Hafez and the older guard continued to fire furiously.

Khan and his men jumped back into their vehicles and raced away from the burning truck.

The driver jumped out of the cab and began to run as the entire back end came off the ground from the explosion of the extra fuel tank behind the cab in the back. Before he had gone five steps, he collapsed to the ground in a heap, dead.

Hafez and the older guard lay motionless on the ground near the burning truck. Just like the driver, their bodies had surrendered to the gamma rays coming from the weapons-grade plutonium in the middle of the raging fire.

2

Lieutenant Luke Henry—Stick, as he was known—kept his desert-camouflage F/A-18 pointed straight up. He pushed the throttles into afterburner to sustain his climb. As he reached twenty-five thousand feet, he pulled the engines out of afterburner and pulled back on the stick, flipping his jet onto its back, flying straight and level but upside down. He looked up through his canopy at the earth. There were airplanes everywhere. F/A-18s, F-14s, and F-5s. The camouflaged F-14s and F/A-18s were being flown by TOPGUN instructors like Luke and were simulating Russian fighters. It was the graduation strike, where the TOPGUN student class led a strike on a target east of Fallon, Nevada, that was defended by TOPGUN instructors and actual Russian SAM sites.

Luke checked his fuel and pulled down toward a student F-14 that was tearing in supersonic. Luke waited until the F-14 passed directly underneath him, pulled down hard, and quickly locked up the F-14 with his radar. The F-14 knew it immediately.

The F-14 came out of afterburner and turned hard to meet the threat which the two men in the F-14 thought would be directly behind them. He waited for the right moment, then saddled in on the Tomcat from directly above. *"Archer,*

Archer on the F-14 turning left at fifteen thousand feet,"
Luke transmitted on the radio. The controller conveyed the
bad news to the F-14 on the students' radio frequency. Luke
watched the F-14 hesitate for a moment, then perform a slow
aileron roll, an "I'm dead" roll, and exit north.

No students had reached the target. They had failed ut-
terly in their mission, which wasn't uncommon in the graduation strike. It was a hard target to get to when defended
aggressively by instructors who weren't holding anything
back.

Luke checked the clock. He transmitted, *"Knock it off,
knock it off."*

All the airplanes in the fight rolled wings-level, slowed to
a reasonable speed, and headed for Fallon Naval Air Station
fifty miles away. They joined up in sections of two or flights
of four, depending on who was around and who had enough
fuel to wait for others.

Luke turned his F/A-18 toward Fallon, and one of the student F/A-18s quickly joined on his right. Luke glanced over
and recognized the airplane and helmet of Mink, Lieutenant
Rob Stoller. Good student. Aggressive, eager, and capable.
In spite of the fact that Mink had gotten killed in the graduation strike, Luke thought he'd done a good job in the school.
Luke nodded to him.

Stoller transmitted to him on the secondary radio, *"Stick,
you up?"*

"Yeah, Mink."

"How about a photo op?"

"What would you like?" Luke asked as he checked his
heading and fuel.

*"I want me and your airplane, with those purple moun-
tains in the background,"* Mink said, pointing to their right
with his head. *"I've got a wide-angle lens."*

Luke looked past Mink to the mountains and nodded. He
tapped his forehead and pointed to Stoller, indicating he had

the lead. Mink nodded, tapped his forehead, then his chest, taking the lead.

Luke pulled back on his throttle and crossed under Stoller's plane. He came up on the right side and flew a close wing formation on him. Stoller dug his expensive camera out of the map case in his cockpit. He held up the camera and pointed it at his face covered with a mirrored visor and oxygen mask, and tried to get just the right angle to ensure that Luke's airplane and the mountains would be in the background. *"Almost got it,"* Stoller said, but he was right-handed and he was trying to take the picture with his left hand to get the perfect angle, to achieve the kind of picture you might see in *Aviation Week & Space Technology*. He couldn't even get his finger on the right button and hold the camera.

He took his hand off the stick and held it with his legs as he adjusted the camera and removed his gloves. He set the camera on autofocus and finally was ready to take the picture. He had taken his eye off the horizon and had inadvertently commenced a slow left roll.

Luke watched with annoyance as Stoller continued to roll to his left. He had rolled nearly forty-five degrees before Luke alerted him. *"Watch your roll,"* he transmitted.

Stoller looked ahead and suddenly saw he was rolling over to his left. He quickly grabbed the stick and threw it to the right to level out. But his movement wasn't as smooth as it should have been. His right wing swung down rapidly.

"Level out!" Luke warned as he saw the wing coming and tried to bank quickly to his right to avoid it. By rolling right he threw his left wing up to meet Stoller's dropping right wing. Their wings collided, with Stoller's right wing hitting hard on the missile rail on the outside of Luke's left wing. Stoller's right wing crumpled and folded in half, causing his airplane to roll sharply right, into the dead wing.

"Shit!" Luke yelled inside his Hornet as he pushed the nose of his airplane down hard and right and tried to get out of the way. As soon as he was clear of Stoller's falling airplane, he pulled up to get on top of him and began a gentle left turn to stay near him. Luke looked over at his left wing with terror in his heart. *"Mink! You got it?"*

Mink's voice was strained and high. *"Negative. I'm missing half a wing! I can't stop the rolls!"*

Luke could tell that he wasn't going to recover. Luke was at ten thousand feet above the desert, and Mink was passing through seven thousand feet. *"Eject! Eject!"* Luke yelled.

Mink heard him and tried to read his altimeter. Then he realized it didn't really matter how high he was. He had no chance of recovering control of an F/A-18 with half a wing bent up. He reached between his legs and pulled the ejection handle.

Luke watched as the canopy came off the falling Hornet and silently drifted away from the jet. The rocket motor on the seat fired, and Mink came hurtling out of the cockpit into the dry desert air. The Hornet spiraled downward and slammed into the desert floor.

3

The ramshackle building stood at the end of a nearly impassable dirt road outside of Peshawar. Most of the men crowded into the room were accustomed to much more desperate conditions. Riaz Khan had known both a life of deprivation and a life of privilege. He lived in both worlds in Pakistan. The people he worked with were mostly privileged, but those he identified with—those he planned to die with—had never owned anything of value and didn't care whether they ever did.

Khan was desperate. His entire plan had turned on getting the material through the border. And now the man who had helped him come up with the most dramatic scheme to embarrass all three of his enemies at once, was about to abandon him. He was the one who had brought them inside information from India. He could stop everything just by withholding his approval. "You *cannot* cancel your part—"

"You have left me no choice," Shirish said in a quiet, authoritative voice. "I told you that we had a small window of time. You said you could get the material through the border. You have failed."

"No," Khan replied, trying not to explode. "No, I didn't. Mahmood did."

Shirish turned and regarded Mahmood behind him. He looked around the room, which was full of Pakistanis except for himself and the tall Russian. "It doesn't matter to me. These are your people. You can divide blame as you see fit." He shook his head in complete frustration, the kind that grew from knowing that someone else would hold him accountable somehow, and it was completely out of his hands. "What you do is now up to you. I can no longer help you."

"Yes!" Khan roared. "It will still happen! We will get to the United States. We will not fail!"

Shirish smiled ruefully. "You said you had an *inside track*! That you could get your men into TOPGUN. You couldn't even do that. Then this border incident! You have brought the attention of the entire world down on our heads! My country does not want that kind of attention. Our help must be withdrawn—"

"Mahmood!" Khan yelled. He balled his hands into fists and glared at Mahmood, a man much smaller than himself, with the soft hands of a politician, the man who had embarrassed him in front of the world and, more particularly, in front of Shirish, the Indian intelligence agent whom Khan had convinced to help them. Khan's face was barely perceptible in the shadows as he hissed at Mahmood, "You promised you would get us into the TOPGUN school. You had your man in place in Washington, you said. And you promised the material would make it through the border. You promised the guards would be no problem. I was almost killed just trying to salvage your plan. Now our friend here," he said, pointing to Shirish, "is about to abandon us because of our incompetence. And who could blame him? We have shown him nothing," he said in exasperation. "We may not be able to do any of it, because of you!" he went on, pointing at Mahmood's chest—Mahmood, who was trying to say something but whose mind was failing him.

"We have here," Khan said, gesturing toward the Russian, "the one who was going to turn the plutonium into a weapon that would have put us in front of the world." Everyone in the room knew who the humorless Russian was. He was the one who had come out of nowhere to help them. The men thought it proved that Riaz Khan could get anyone to do anything for the cause, even a Russian nuclear scientist. "All he needed was the materials. And you *failed* us!"

Mahmood was petrified. He knew Riaz Khan's reputation. "How could I know that the *one* border guard in all of Pakistan's mountains who was not drunk would decide to stop this truck? How could we know?"

"Always an excuse!" Riaz paced. He looked at the Russian. "Is it possible to get more? Can it be done?"

The tall Russian looked grim and shook his head slowly as he considered. "The material from the border is gone? There is no way to get it?"

Khan replied, "I told you. The truck blew up. The border guards shot at the tires and hit the gas tank. The whole truck went up."

The Russian suddenly went pale, understanding the implications for the first time. He knew that the attempt to get the plutonium across the border had failed, but no one had told him there had been a shoot-out and a conflagration in the process. He dreaded the answer to his next question. "Were the containers with the plutonium broken?"

Khan thought about it for the first time. "How would I know? We never got close enough to the truck to see the containers. For all I know they weren't even on the truck."

The Russian rubbed his forehead. "Has anyone tested you for exposure?"

"Exposure? Exposure to what?"

"To radiation," the Russian whispered. He quickly went to the corner of the room and took a small electronic device out of a box. He turned it on, crossed to Khan, and put a microphonelike device up to Khan's chest.

"What are you doing?" Khan asked, frustrated with such odd behavior.

"Checking for exposure."

Khan watched as the needle jumped. The Russian frowned. "What is it?"

The Russian looked grim. "Who else was there?"

Khan pointed to two others who were nearby. The Russian checked them.

"I'm afraid you have been exposed to radioactive material."

"So what?" Khan said dismissively.

"So you have radiation sickness."

"I feel fine."

"Based on the levels I just saw, you will almost certainly be dead within a year."

"What?" Khan exclaimed. "What did you say?"

"You have been damaged by the plutonium. I told you not to get too—"

"We didn't do anything! I never got closer than fifty meters to the truck!"

"That is close enough, given the right circumstances. I'm afraid there is nothing you can do about it."

Khan looked around the room, at the others who had heard everything. "Then we move up our timetable." He paused as he absorbed the idea of dying in twelve months. He asked the Russian, "Is there any more material we can get through your contacts?"

"Our best chance would be Berdsk, but even that would be difficult. Oziorsk and Miass also"—he shrugged—"but better than those that would be Almaly and Olar. They are in Kazakhstan, right on the border with Kyrgyzstan. But after the border incident . . ." He frowned. "I don't know, I think we must wait at *least* six months—"

"See!" Riaz screamed, outraged. "See!" he fired at Mahmood. "It cannot be done now! We can*not* wait six months. Six months!" He laughed. "Six *more* months, because of your incompetence! All the borders of Asia are being watched with ten times the attention they were before! Nothing will get through!"

"We must be patient, Riaz, if the—"

"No! You heard it! We have no time to be patient. We have *been* patient. It is time to *act*."

Mahmood lowered his voice in desperation. "I will *not* have you ruin this. There is too much at stake."

"You said it would all be in place by now, Mahmood. I believed you! Everything else *is* in place. I have taken irrevocable steps, and we must act now or we will never be able to. Do you not understand that? Are you so stupid?" Khan asked. He turned to one of the men next to him holding an AK-47 as if he had held it every day for years. "How many men can you send over the border?"

Mahmood interrupted. "No, Riaz! We must do things in order—"

"Shut up!" Riaz yelled in his native Pashto, the language of the northern frontier provinces, a language no one like Mahmood would ever understand.

The armed man said to Khan in Pashto, "He has done nothing for us."

Khan agreed. "He had his chance. He brought us nothing except the international attention that we did not need. And now he has killed us." He looked at Mahmood like a serpent. Khan's huge, muscular neck was red with anger. "We do not need him. I know who his contact is in Washington. We can bring other pressure to bear." He and the armed man exchanged a knowing glance.

Riaz turned suddenly to Mahmood and grabbed him by the throat with both meaty hands. He lifted him up off the floor and held him, choking the smaller man. "No more waiting! No more promises!" Riaz screamed in Urdu.

Mahmood's eyes bugged out in surprise and terror as he tried to free himself. He began flailing his arms, trying to grab the ferocious hands that held him. His feet kicked vainly for something solid to give him leverage. His red face began to turn pale. The other men watched casually as Riaz lifted the man higher so everyone could see the life drain from his face. Mahmood's feeble struggling lessened as his arms fell slack against his side. His hands twitched and his eyes rolled back into his head. Still Riaz held him high, as high as he could hold him. Finally Mahmood was still.

Riaz tossed him aside like a sack of meat. Mahmood's head cracked against the stone floor as he landed in a heap in the corner of the room.

Riaz looked at the man he had begun addressing earlier. "How many men can you take across the border into Kashmir?"

"Two thousand," the man replied softly, unmoved by Mahmood's death.

Khan considered. "One week from tonight begin the infiltration. Gradually. They must not be detected. Remember. You are not to attack. That will come later. You are there only to be ready, and to recruit others. It will be some months' time before the attack, but it will come."

The man nodded. "We will be ready."

Riaz pointed at Mahmood lying in the corner. "His failure has made it impossible to do what we had planned. Now we must do something different." He looked at his subordinates. "Don't worry about the details. You just do your job, and I promise I will do mine. I will get there, and I will do it." He looked at the Russian, who was unable to speak from watching a man he knew murdered in front of his eyes. "I need to talk to your friends in Russia."

The Russian continued to stare at Mahmood's purple neck with clearly visible handprints and at his buggy, open eyes. Two flies had already begun circling the body. "They are not my friends."

"True. They do nothing out of friendship." Riaz smiled. "It is always for money. Or power. I can identify with them. They are my kind of people. I need to talk to them."

The Russian scientist nodded, trying to ignore what he had just seen, trying not to throw up. He had never wanted to leave

Russia. He was comfortable where he had been, working in a laboratory at the nuclear weapons plant at Trekhgornyy. He was content, until he got laid off from the plant. They had no more money to pay him. He'd tried to find other jobs in Russia, but there was nothing, and certainly nothing that would allow him to use his training, his Ph.D. in nuclear physics from Moscow University. The local Mafia had offered him a job as a driver for more than he'd been paid as a scientist for the state, when he had the job.

He had refused. He knew he would never work for the Mafia. But then they had come back, offering him a position overseas, working in his field, helping them "solidify a relationship," as they had put it. And he would be paid in gold, five times what Russia had ever paid him. He couldn't resist.

Khan crossed over and stood in front of the Russian, looking up into his blue eyes. "You need to tell your friends to get me more material. Within a month."

The Russian tried to hide his fear. "It is impossible—"

"I am sick of that word!" Khan screamed. "It is *not* impossible! They did it once, and they can do it again. Security in Russia is terrible. You've said so yourself."

"Terrible, yes, but not nonexistent!" the Russian protested. "And getting it here would be doubly impossible."

"We cannot wait!" Khan insisted, looking at Shirish.

Shirish replied, "We have only one more time we could do it. One and only one."

"When?"

"October."

The Russian knew he'd be the next bug-eyed corpse lying on the floor if he didn't come up with some alternative. "You are doing it the hard way," he said cryptically.

Khan looked at the rest of the men in the room, who were shifting their weight restlessly. He returned his stare to the Russian. "Oh. Really. You have an easier way and have just not told us about it."

"I have only now thought of it," he said, looking straight ahead, over Khan's head.

Shirish stepped closer and listened with interest as the Russian spoke in English.

"What might it be?"

"You want to do serious, permanent, irreparable damage to the Americans with little risk?"

"Yes," Khan answered slowly. "Obviously. That is the critical first step in our plan. You have known that!"

"You should listen to the Americans more. They are so open, so honest. They hang out their laundry for the entire world to see. If they find a weakness of their own, they have hearings. There are groups in America that do nothing but point out their own country's weaknesses and faults. Such a weakness has been exposed for years. It would do much more damage than that nuclear warhead you were hoping to rescue at the border. And the rest of your plan could remain the same."

Khan was intrigued. "We could do this from TOPGUN in Nevada?"

"Oh, yes. With ease."

"And it would do as much damage as a nuclear weapon?"

"Perhaps not quite as spectacular, but equally deadly."

"It must be too hazardous."

"Far less dangerous than trying to smuggle a nuclear warhead into the United States."

Khan turned away and walked toward the window. "I have no interest in biological killing. It is—"

"It isn't biological."

"What, chemical?"

"No. You need to carry nothing hazardous at all."

"And you think we could do this with ease?"

"If you get to TOPGUN, you could do it."

Khan pointed to the table where several air navigation charts and some papers lay. "Show me," he said.

* * *

LUKE sat in the instructor's ready room at TOPGUN across the table from Lieutenant Quentin Thurmond, Thud, the only black instructor at the school and Luke's best friend, who was eating a glazed doughnut as he drank coffee.

Thud spoke with his mouth full. "So what the hell happened?"

"Mink was trying to take a picture. He rolled into me. I tried to get out of the way and our wings hit. His came down on my Sidewinder rail, and his wing just broke in half."

"Shit, man," Thud exclaimed. "That's not your fault."

"Yeah." Luke lost focus as his mind drifted. "Except Gun gave me the Big Dark Look."

They both knew what that meant. Commander Rick Beebe, the TOPGUN commanding officer—actually the training officer, the N-7, of the Navy Strike and Air Warfare Center at Fallon, Nevada—was legendary for his looks that could wither the weak. When he gave you a look, it usually meant something worse was coming.

"Mink just gooned it up."

"Yeah, but I'm the instructor. It's always our fault. He's going to board me."

"What?" Thud exclaimed. "Why?"

"To be sure I'm fit to continue as a TOPGUN instructor," Luke said with irony in his voice.

"You've got to be shitting me!" Thud cried. "You have got to be friggin' shitting me!"

"Nope. He just told me."

"About what?" asked Lieutenant Commander Brian Hayes, the Intelligence Officer. He was close to both of them and felt perfectly comfortable injecting himself into any of their conversations. He flipped open the pink doughnut box. His face showed immediate disappointment at finding it empty. "Who took all the doughnuts?"

"Some thief," Thud lamented. "Believe that?"

"I didn't even get breakfast," Hayes said.

"Stick's getting boarded for that midair," Thud announced.

"You're kidding me, right?" Hayes asked as he walked across the room. His right knee and foot insisted on turning in just slightly. It was barely noticeable; Luke and Thud could tell that Hayes was doing everything he could to hide it. Hayes had been recently diagnosed with multiple sclerosis.

"Nope," Luke said, still stinging from the announcement. He tried to be his usual optimistic self, but he was so embarrassed by the fact that he was getting boarded, he found himself reddening every time he mentioned it. It was eating him alive.

"That's bullshit," Hayes said. "We ought to board the Skipper," Hayes said, quickly glancing over his shoulder to make sure Gun wasn't around. "Probably just a formality."

"Yeah. That's it," Luke said. "Just a formality. That's why I'm grounded until they get it done." He stood and filled his coffee cup.

Thud was speechless. "Don't worry about it. It'll pass. No problem."

Luke looked at him as he drank. He knew Thud was just blowing smoke. And he knew Thud knew.

COLONEL Yuri Stoyanovich sat behind his desk in the dimly lit, dilapidated building that was the headquarters of his regiment, the 773rd IAP—Istrebeitelnyi Aviatsionnaya Polk, Fighter Aviation Regiment—and ignored the loud knock on the door. Command of one of Russia's premier fighter regiments was an honor. But it was a pain in the ass, too. The airplanes were easy. Well, perhaps not easy, but easy compared to the pilots and the difficult times Russia had been cursed with for almost fifteen years now. "Mr. Gorbachev, tear down this wall!" Yes, well he did, and now the Berlin

Wall and the rest of the Soviet Union were mostly rubble. And he was in charge of one of the piles of rock.

Stoyanovich missed the simplicity of climbing into the cockpit of a jet fighter and escaping the problems below. Even now that Russians claimed to be free, they weren't free of difficulties, or of poverty. There was no gas. There were no cars anyone could buy. They weren't even free to get paid what they had earned from the government as pilots. Their pay was always late, if it came at all. The fighter pilots of Russia, the elite of the military, lived in barracks not fit for dogs.

Stoyanovich leaned back and scratched his scalp through his thinning, oily hair. His men, the pilots and the others, took out their frustrations in ways that were often self-destructive. He dealt with a new problem every day. Today the pattern had held true, only it wasn't just another personnel problem. The one knocking on the door was his favorite pilot, a longtime friend and ally, someone he had mentored for more than ten years. He had become a brilliant success— until now. "Come in!" Stoyanovich yelled finally.

A pilot marched smartly into the office. The concrete floor echoed his hard-soled boots. He faced the Colonel and saluted. "Major Vladimir Petkov, sir. Reporting."

Stoyanovich studied Petkov as he tried to decide what to do with him. "Major, you know why I have called you."

Petkov feigned ignorance. "No, Colonel Stoyanovich. I got the message that you wanted to see me, and I came."

"You have no idea?"

"No, sir."

"Did you not think it might be because of your ill-advised journey into town last night?"

Petkov frowned. "I did not do anything noteworthy in town last night, sir."

"No. What you have said is correct," the Colonel admitted. "You did not do anything in the town. I was wrong. It is no wonder that you did not know what I was talking about. Please forgive me." His sarcasm was not lost on Petkov. "Perhaps, then, you would like to talk about coming *back* to the air base, Major Vladimir Petkov. Perhaps you would like to tell me how the automobile you were driving ended up in a ditch, in a pile of horseshit and mud, upside down, with the windows broken and the wheels spinning up into the sky like a fractured turtle—"

"Yes, sir."

"You do remember that, Major Petkov? This has now come back into your mind?"

"Yes, sir."

"Ah. Then, would you please tell me how this happened? What forces acted on you that threw you off the road so suddenly as to cause such a disaster?"

Petkov stared at the floor. "There weren't any—"

"No, there weren't any forces, were there?" the Colonel said, standing, his girth straining against his coarse wool uniform. "The only force acting on you was the one that makes you stupid every now and then, the force that seems to overtake you just often enough to remind your superiors that you cannot be *trusted*."

"I can be trusted—"

"No, you cannot, Major! You drink too much vodka and then do stupid things! Your superior officers have looked the other way for years! Many have come and gone," he said. "I, too, have let it go before, but no more. You have not learned!" the Colonel roared.

"I am sorry to have acted as—"

"Sorry? Do you really think sorry will do *anything* for you?"

Petkov didn't know what to say. He had failed himself miserably. He'd tried to stop, but the base was so remote. Other than flying, he didn't care much for the life he had fallen into. The flying almost made it tolerable.

"You are the best natural pilot on the base . . ." the Colonel said, his voice trailing off in regret. "The best I have ever seen. You earned the wings of a Sniper Pilot earlier than anyone else in the regiment. And well deserved. But your judgment fails you. You fall into self-pity, or depression, and make more bad decisions."

"It won't happen again—"

The Colonel wagged his finger at Petkov. "You are right about that, Major. Very right. Because from now on, you are not flying. You are grounded."

Petkov's face went white. "Colonel," he gasped. "Flying is my life. It is all—"

"I know that, Major. Believe me, I know that. You have instructed many pilots here, you have taught them tactics, you have shown them what this fighter of ours can do. But I can no longer allow a *drunk* to show his bad judgment to the other pilots."

Petkov was stung by the word. He couldn't face the fact himself, and to hear it from someone else, someone he respected, somehow hurt more. "I can go to the rehabilitation—"

"You have already *been,* Major. That is what you talked my predecessor into. That is the game you have played before. It is even rumored that you gained access to your records then and changed them, to hide the fact last time that you had been to the special rehabilitation clinic before. So you bought yourself another chance then. But not this time, Major. You have come to the end."

Petkov knew the Colonel was right. He fought back the sadness he felt. "What will you do with me, Colonel? You have always been a friend to me. You made me what I am."

Stoyanovich paused. It killed him to look into Petkov's face. But he was willing to do what he had to do. "You are being reassigned to security."

Petkov couldn't believe it. He thought the Colonel was

just trying to frighten him, to get his attention. "For how long, Colonel?"

"Indefinitely, but probably for the rest of your career. I'm sorry."

Petkov felt the life drain out of him. His boots against the floor sounded like they belonged to someone else as he saluted and did a smart about-face and marched out of the room as if nothing had happened. But something had happened. The one thing he loved had just been taken away from him forever.

4

Bill Morrissey didn't like the report at all. As the head of the South Asia section of the CIA, Directorate of Intelligence, he generally hated the volatility that permeated the whole region. The report he held in his hands was another in the disturbing trend that was making it an even more dangerous place.

Morrissey carried the report into the office of Cindy Frohm, one of his senior analysts, and tossed it onto her desk. He trusted her judgment. "Read this," he said, sitting in the chair across from her.

She glanced at the title of the report. "The Pakistan crossing incident?"

"Twelve hundred mils an hour. When they took the scrap metal off the truck, they found ten boxes just *shitting* radioactivity. Two of them weren't sealed well, and two more had been breached by gunfire and the explosion. Ten boxes!"

"Weapons-grade," she said.

"Plutonium," he said ominously.

"I'd heard," she said. "Who was bringing it in?"

"Well, if it was Pakistan, you'd think they wouldn't do it on a scrap-metal truck, and you'd think they'd tell their own border guards to let it through."

"Who else could it be?" she asked, confused.

"Maybe Pakistan, but not the *government* of Pakistan."

"*That's* pretty scary." She considered some of the possibilities that flooded into her mind. "We should send someone from the NRC or the DOE over there to help."

"We offered. They were offended."

"They would be."

"I want you to figure out where it was going."

She saved the computer file she was working on and faced Morrissey. "What do you think?"

"Iranian driver, documents showed Pakistan as the destination, but passing through a lot of other countries, too, including Iran."

"Could be anybody. Iranians sure would love to have nuclear capability."

"But he was coming into Pakistan. He had passed through Iran. If this was their game, they would have kept it."

She pondered some of the twisted possibilities. "Maybe Pakistan just wanted to be able to deny it if something went wrong. Plus, we don't really know what happened at the border. Sounds to me like someone knew it was coming and tried to hijack it. What happened to the driver?"

"Big gunfight, but the radioactivity got him."

"And the guards?"

"Same. And if this truck was trying to make a run through the mountains with ten boxes, how many other boxes have gotten through?" he asked.

"Any theories on how they got hold of it?"

"Lots." He sighed heavily from the weight of trying to track the flow of boxes of radioactive material throughout his area. "Most likely, though, is the Mafia."

"The *Mafia*? Russian Mafia? We've never confirmed they have access to any nuclear material. Plus, it was from Kazakhstan."

"Nothing to do with nationality." He shifted in his chair. "The entire Russian nuclear system, like most of their systems, is a wreck. They have guys with Ph.D.s in nuclear physics driving cabs. These Mafia assholes have sniffed out how hungry for nukes some of these desperate regimes are. They're renting them nuclear engineers."

"It's all about money . . ."

"Exactly. Read that," he said pointing. "Then come see me."

LUKE Henry brought his beloved silver Corvette convertible to a quick stop in his garage that looked like a barn. It was the older model Corvette. He couldn't afford a recent model Corvette on a Navy pilot's salary. He climbed out and slammed the door of the car so hard he was momentarily afraid he would break the window that was rolled down inside the door. He walked across the dirt driveway toward his house. He'd given his entire life to the Navy. He had gone to sea, risked his life every day and every night for years flying off a carrier, and now they'd turned on him. Betrayed him for a stupid incident that was unavoidable.

He noticed Katherine's car was still there. She always left on the early-morning flight from Reno to San Jose every Monday to go to work. He frowned. "Katherine!" he called as the screen door closed behind him. "Katherine!" There was no response.

He walked through the house and found nothing but empty rooms. He finally made it to the master bedroom; she wasn't there either. He stopped to listen for sounds. He suddenly heard her in the bathroom making an odd coughing sound. He wasn't sure whether to stand there and wait or do something else. He decided to go to the kitchen to get something to drink. He opened the refrigerator and took out a beer while he waited.

When he had told her three days before that Gun had decided to board him, she assumed, as had everyone else, that it was just a formality. Nothing would come of it. He breathed deeply. Well, something had come of it. And all they had planned and counted on was out the window.

Things had changed a lot since they met. She had been working for a large law firm in Palo Alto, doing corporate and securities work: high technology, cutting edge, dot-coms, IPOs, M&A, VCs, Paige Mill Road. She knew all the lingo. Very heady stuff. As someone two years out of law school, she made four times what he made flying fighters off carriers in the dark. Something out of balance about that, he had thought, but he tried not to dwell on the pay. After all, she worked killer hours and didn't get to fly fast jets. So he figured it was a wash.

He'd been stationed at an F/A-18 squadron that was based at LeMoore Naval Air Station in the central California valley when he wasn't at sea.

They'd met at a concert in San Francisco—Rage Against the Machine. They'd run into each other. Literally. She had stepped on his foot and turned to apologize. Her gaze had lingered just long enough for him to know it might pay to begin a conversation with her. They'd gone out for coffee after the concert, both deserting the friends they'd come with. She thought it was "incongruous" that a Navy pilot liked a band called Rage Against the Machine. That was the word she had used: "incongruous." That's when he knew he wasn't dealing with just another good-looking woman. He wasn't even sure what "incongruous" meant, but he was sure she knew, and he was certainly willing to learn. She told him it was odd, since the machine against which they were raging was undoubtedly, at least in part, the government, those who told others what to do, and he was part of that government. He smiled, then laughed. She frowned, then laughed.

The first thing he'd been required to explain was why he was called Stick instead of Luke. He said that it was because he was tall and thin, but she had used that opportunity to tell him she thought the whole "call-sign" thing was silly, like some fraternity initiation rite. She had called him Luke, but smiled when she said it. He knew she thought that was a funny name, too. Once she found out that he'd grown up in Nevada and was *actually wearing* cowboy boots, the entire thing was even funnier to her. Funny in an inside-joke kind of way, where she was the only one who got to know what was so damned funny, and it was he who was funny, without intending it. His haircut was certainly something she didn't encounter every day, very short on the sides and combed forward on the top.

That first night as they drank coffee, Luke could see her evaluating everything about him. He realized that someone without a lot of self-confidence had no chance with her. But he didn't care a bit what she or anyone else thought about his name, or his heritage, or his boots. If she didn't care for any of those things, fine. Even if she *was* good-looking. So he just held steady and watched her. He thought her small eyeglasses, obviously chosen for their look, were quirky and impractical, and her short, midriff-exposing, spaghetti-strapped top and sexy capri pants were "incongruous"— he'd used the word once he found out what it meant—with her role as a corporate lawyer. And if *anyone* was part of the machine against which the band had been raging, it was probably the corporations that used Third World nonreading slaves to build things no one wanted but were persuaded to buy through the companies' clever marketing campaigns.

She'd loved that and had thrown back her head in beautiful laughter that seemed to bounce off her perfect teeth like musical notes off crystal. He told her that her long, curly blond hair was also not the usual sign of a corporate lawyer, and he insisted on seeing her business card.

They had dated on weekends, when Luke would drive his Corvette to the Bay Area from LeMoore. They would go to Marin County, or Sausalito, or just ride the ferry around the bay. He'd fallen for her more deeply than he'd ever imagined possible. It left him short of breath. The thought of living without her was inconceivable. He knew by the second month of dating her that he wanted to marry her, but it took him another six months to work up to hinting at the possibility to gauge her reaction. She'd laughed again, but it was her encouraging, "what a great idea" laugh, that life is good, and this idea will be part of the wonderful, enchanted life she seemed to be leading. Luke knew he was completely outclassed. She was from a higher plane in almost every way. But she loved him, and he knew it, and he wasn't the kind to catalog all the ways she was better than him. No point. If it didn't matter to her, he wasn't going to let it matter to him.

He had asked her to marry him right as his squadron tour was ending, just as he was rolling to his shore tour. They knew they would have a chance to be together every day. The timing was perfect. Then he got his dream assignment—he was asked if he wanted to be an instructor at TOPGUN. He was thrilled. So was she, until she learned TOPGUN wasn't in San Diego anymore. Fallon, Nevada, he'd told her, and her enthusiasm had evaporated.

She didn't want to leave what she was doing, and after days of agonizing over how to solve the problem, they'd arrived at a compromise. She would keep her apartment in Palo Alto and come to Fallon every Friday afternoon through Monday morning. They had agreed that practicing law in Fallon, Nevada, simply wasn't the same as practicing law in the heart of Silicon Valley, in Palo Alto, California.

But she knew that he was going to stay in the Navy. He was determined to be a commanding officer of a Navy squadron and ultimately of a nuclear aircraft carrier. He loved flying in the Navy and wanted to make it a career. She'd breathed in deeply and said she didn't know how, but she would make it work. They would make it work.

Now he had to tell her that all their plans were being turned upside down.

"You're home," Katherine said from behind him, surprising him.

"Hey," he said. He turned to see her. She looked terrible. Her face was drawn and pale, and her long blond hair was more disheveled than usual. She was dressed in a business suit, but she looked as if she'd been camping. "How you doing?"

She stood next to him and put her head down on her arm on the counter. "Sick."

"Flu?"

"No," she said.

He frowned.

"You sitting down?" she replied.

He looked at the stool on which he was obviously sitting. "Looks like it."

"Morning sickness."

He stood and stared at her, openmouthed. "Seriously?"

"Seriously," she said, trying to smile. "I did the test after you left this morning. I got dressed and tried to get to the airport and just lay on the bed. I couldn't make it."

Luke put his arm around her. "That's unbelievable!" he said, groping for exactly the right words but coming up short. He hugged her.

"Nothing will be the same now," she replied. She looked at his face closely for the first time and saw something there. "What's wrong?"

"I got the board results today." He sat again.

"What did they say?" she said, sitting on the stool next to his.

"Gun's going to put a letter in my jacket."

She knew exactly what that meant. His commanding officer would put a letter, in his personnel file, that would say he'd been found wanting in the evaluation conducted of him relating to an accident. She also knew that no one had a great career in naval aviation after such a letter. It was as effective as a court-martial.

"Why?"

"I didn't exercise enough 'judgment' or 'leadership.' The accident wasn't my fault, but if I had exercised sufficient leadership, I could have avoided it. Believe that?"

"But what could you have done?"

"They say by trying to bank to the right instead of pushing the nose over I caused my left wing to go up and hit Mink's. I should have just pushed over and headed down. I could have avoided the whole thing. But more important, we shouldn't have been doing a photo op on the way back from the graduation hop."

She shook her head slowly. "I'm sorry, Luke. That's just wrong."

"I've got to get out."

"That's completely unfair. Can't you appeal it?"

"Probably some way, but nobody's going to overturn a CO. It's just his thing."

"I'm so sorry."

She pushed her hair away from her pale face. "So now what? Airlines?"

Luke rolled his eyes and shook his head as he stood and put his empty beer bottle on the counter next to the sink. "I'd rather cut myself with glass than fly around in a cylinder the size of a submarine. That's not even flying." He thought about it again, as he had several times during the day since hearing the result of the board, knowing it was what he would end up doing. "If I get out now, I'll never fly fast jets again."

"You could fly in the reserves."

"Not with a letter in my jacket. They'd treat me like a leper—if they let me in at all."

"We could move to the Bay Area and live off my income. You could be a kept man," she said, trying to smile.

"Very funny."

"I'm sure you could find a job in Silicon Valley. You're an EE. If you could stagger in the door of a few high-tech firms, you'd have fifty job offers in a day for three times what you're making *right now*. Just post your résumé on the Internet at a couple of the bulletin boards and sit back and decide which job you want."

"You think I'd get my *own* cubicle?"

"If you're *really* lucky." She got a glass of water out of the dispenser in the refrigerator door. "So what *do* you want to do? We always thought you'd stay in until you were old and gray. It was the only way I'd get you out of my hair occasionally. Now you'll be home all the time. What will I do with you?"

"I want to fly fast jets. Fighters. That's all I've ever wanted to do."

"You just said there's no way."

"Exactly."

She looked at him, not sure how to encourage him. She shrugged as she drank her water. "So that's it? Your life's over? You'll be like Joe DiMaggio telling everybody about how great you used to be for the rest of your life? Maybe you could get a job with Mr. Coffee."

"Thanks for your support."

"Oh, I'm just kidding. Trying to lighten you up a little. Don't worry, you'll find something."

"There isn't anything, Katherine. That's the problem. I know all the jobs that are out there."

She looked at the sadness in his eyes. She'd never seen that before. "Do what they do in Silicon Valley."

"What's that?"

"Just make it up. Figure out how you'd like it to be, then go out and make it so."

"THUD, it's Stick," Luke said excitedly into the phone.

"Hey," Thud replied. "What's up?"

"Doing anything?"

"The usual."

"I need to talk to you."

"When?"

"Now."

"What for?"

"I've got an idea I've got to run by you."

Thud hesitated for only a moment. He would do anything Luke asked. He knew it was reciprocal. He and Luke had formed a fast friendship when they'd met in the training command learning to fly jets. "Want me to come out to Rancho del Luko?"

Luke and Katherine lived in a house that he called a ranch five miles south of the air station. He could have lived in Navy officer housing just off the base, as Thud and most of the other TOPGUN instructors did, but he wanted more room. Ten acres, minimum, as he'd told the real estate agent when they started looking. Katherine had been too speechless to say anything. Compared to living in Palo Alto, it was like living on the moon, only affordable. Luke wanted space, and horses.

"Yeah, if you don't mind. And bring Michelle. I don't want to leave Katherine by herself right now."

"Why?"

"Morning sickness."

"No shit! Is that what you want to talk about?"

"No, it's something else."

"This must be really good. I'll be right there."

THE maître d' handed the two men the large, stiff menus, which they took with the entitlement and ease that came from innumerable political dinners in Washington. One of them was constantly buying lunches or dinners, the other happily receiving them. Receiving them was a violation of the federal rules against accepting gratuities, but Thomas Merewether didn't care anymore. He used to be scrupulous about it, but he was tired of eating at the Department of Defense cafeteria and McDonald's. He loved good food but couldn't afford much of it on his salary. He saw no harm in accepting a lunch now and then.

The other man was equally in love with the political lunch. The idea that he could have the attention of an Undersecretary of Defense for the cost of one lousy lunch was astonishing to him. In other countries where he had served, it would cost thousands of dollars in bribes and trips and mistresses just to get *access* to a highly placed government official, not to mention actual results. But in America, where there were so many rules against everything, getting an official across the line even slightly gave him tremendous power. Everyone knew when they'd crossed the line, and just by crossing the line it was as if they'd already sold you their souls.

Yushaf had known the Undersecretary for several months, since assuming his current position as chargé d'affaires at the Pakistani embassy. He had replaced a man who'd been too timid to make the necessary approaches to U.S. government officials. His predecessor had seen the rules as a hindrance. Yushaf saw them as levers he could use to manipulate people. But time was growing short. Certain forces in Pakistan were now demanding instant results. And demanding them in a way that made it clear that a failure to produce would be catastrophic. Exactly how was left unclear.

"Thank you for your willingness to spend some short amount of time with me, Mr. Undersecretary."

"My pleasure," Merewether replied. "Our countries have much in common."

"Indeed. The United States has been so gracious in providing the weapons and defense systems necessary to protect Pakistan. There was a time, though—too long—when our countries distrusted each other. But when President Clinton honored us with a state visit and insisted on renewed ties, especially between our military—"

The waiter interrupted them. He wasn't about to let them spend ten minutes on pleasantries.

Yushaf ordered a Perrier, and Merewether ordered a vodka on the rocks. They sat back with their menus, and Yushaf spoke. "But I got ahead of myself. How have you been, Thomas?"

Merewether planned to say the usual political thing, to say everything was fine, but recent developments had caused him not to care much anymore. He now derived a good deal of the pleasure he experienced in life by being completely direct and completely truthful, at least when that served his purposes. "Difficult. My wife—my *ex*-wife—has been pounding on me for more support." He reached for the pack of cigarettes he always kept in his shirt pocket, forgetting that he'd decided again to quit that morning. "I've already given her everything I own. She has the house, I have the mortgage. I'm living in a shitty little apartment in Arlington." His eyes crinkled into an ironic smile. "We used to be a two-income family with one house. Now we're a one-income family with two houses. Well, one apartment, actually, like I said . . ." He shook his head. "Who cares . . ."

The waiter placed their drinks in front of them. "Are you ready to order?"

"I'll have the roast beef," Merewether said, handing his menu to the waiter.

"I'll have the tomato salad and the swordfish," Yushaf said. He returned his attention to Merewether. "It is your *life*, and I'm interested in your difficulties." He took out a pack of cigarettes and handed it to Merewether with a gold lighter.

"So how's it going with you? How's your job?" Merewether asked.

Yushaf smiled falsely. "Actually, I am a little disappointed."

Merewether looked up at him. "Why?"

"I thought we had an understanding."

"About what?"

"We're trying to make our military as good as it can be. As skilled as yours. I do not believe that the United States appreciates the threat that India poses to my country. We must have the best equipment, the best training, and be prepared to defend ourselves to have any hope of overcoming the Indian attack which could come any day. They have seven times our population and twenty times our land."

"Shit, Yushaf, India isn't going to *do* anything."

Yushaf's face clouded. "What about their ceaseless pursuit of nuclear weapons? Don't get into an arms race, we were told. But you know what is worse than an arms race between two enemies? An arms race when only *one* country is building. India was building and building. And we could do nothing. Then, when they went public and tested, we had to do the same. And the U.S. came down on us and blamed us for being aggressive." Yushaf smiled. "The Manhattan Project is fine for you when you *suspect* Germany may be trying to build nuclear weapons. But it is different in your eyes when India, a country ten times the size of Germany, threatens *us* with known nuclear weapons. We are somehow supposed to sit there and take it. But I'm sorry . . ."

"No, that's okay. We deserve it. We're pretty two-faced when it comes to nuclear policy."

"But what I was saying is that I thought we had an understanding, you and I." He paused and waited for Merewether to look at him. "You said you would help me get some of our pilots through your training. Your TOPGUN."

Merewether tried not to roll his eyes. He'd heard this pitch before. He'd thrown Yushaf a bone and said he would try to get some Pakistani pilots into the next class that took foreigners. And he *had* asked. He'd been told it was impossible. "It is very difficult—"

"Of course it is difficult. That is why I asked you. You are in the right place to make it happen."

"I'm not the Secretary of Defense—"

"Yes, but you *are* the Undersecretary of Defense. It is up to you if you wish to make it happen."

Merewether stubbed out his cigarette on the bread plate. "It is *not* up to me—"

The waiter placed large white plates in front of them on the crisp linen tablecloth. They were silent until the waiter left the table. Merewether picked up one of the heavy silver forks and played with the spinach salad. He hated spinach.

Yushaf ate his tomatoes in the beautifully presented tomato salad with vinaigrette dressing. He was making great progress with Merewether. He could feel it. He cut one of the tomatoes and began speaking. "Another TOPGUN class has commenced since we last spoke."

"How do you know that?" Merewether asked, annoyed.

"You serve a meal, but you don't invite my country to the table."

"Your country makes things difficult sometimes. You're not always trusted."

"We have had training from your military on many occasions. We have American-made weapons and airplanes, at least as many as you will allow us. We wish to follow in your footsteps in training and maintaining our forces. Yet we do not get the support of your military that other countries with the same commitment have. You do not allow us to defend ourselves."

"Don't get dramatic on me."

"Why were our pilots not invited to this class?"

"There are too many American pilots waiting to get through. They don't take foreign students at all."

"Because we are a Muslim country, no doubt."

"Oh, please. Don't play that Islam crap with me—"

"Perhaps if we were a small Jewish state you would let us attend."

"Where do you get that bullshit?"

"Israelis have graduated from TOPGUN. Do you deny it?"

"A long time ago."

"No, it wasn't. Are you saying it is impossible? It can never happen?"

"Never say never."

Yushaf pressed. "When do you think I should start planning to have our pilots come to America?"

"Don't *push* it," Merewether said angrily.

"I am sorry," Yushaf said, leaning back and putting down his fork. "I don't mean to push."

"Why is this so important to you?"

Yushaf backed off. "It's just that I had heard about the class starting . . ."

"I'll see what I can do. It won't be easy."

"If you are able to help my country, I would certainly do my best to help you as well."

"Meaning what, exactly?"

Yushaf looked innocent. "Meaning nothing. Meaning perhaps whenever you Americans want us to return the favor and train your pilots in Pakistan, we would be happy to accommodate that."

Merewether smiled sarcastically. "I'm sure that would be just what they need."

Yushaf glanced around. "I must get back to the office." He stood and turned his back to the door so he was squarely facing Merewether and no one else could see his face. "Thank you for taking the time to share a meal with me. Please don't forget my request. It can benefit both of us."

"Right, whatever. See ya." Merewether picked up the pack of cigarettes and the lighter. He lit another cigarette and placed the lighter down on the table. It was heavy. He picked it up and examined it. He looked at its bottom. It had an imprint: 18ᴋ. Merewether forced himself not to look around the restaurant as he slipped the lighter into his suit coat pocket.

5

Luke walked out onto the porch of their small house as the sun set in front of him over the western mountains. The collar of his gray fleece was turned up against the chill. He couldn't see Thud yet. Luke still had the newspaper tucked under his arm, anxious to show it to Thud. He unfolded it and sat in one of the wooden chairs on the porch. He read the article again. He stared at the picture that accompanied it. He found himself sweating at the possibility that someone else had already thought of the idea. He felt as if he had to move on his plan within minutes or someone else would surely think of it and jump in front of him, someone better placed, with better contacts, and piles of money.

Katherine came out onto the porch and sat in the chair next to Luke's. She leaned her head against the wooden backrest and put her feet up on Luke's leg. "Is Thud coming?"

"Should be here any minute."

"Think he'll want to get out?"

"It's hard to walk away from TOPGUN."

She nodded and sighed. "The cool air feels good. I've been so hot lately."

"It sure does." He rubbed his hand on her leg. "How you feeling?"

"Okay." She looked at him. "What do you think he'll say?"

"I don't know. It'll probably sound desperate to him."

"It is kind of . . . I don't know . . ." she said, pulling her legs up under her. "Audacious."

"Here comes Thud," he said as he saw a battered Explorer turn into the long driveway.

Thud pulled up in front of the house and turned off his engine as the dust cloud settled around him. He stepped out and closed the door. Michelle got out on the other side. "Hey," Thud said, seeing them on the porch.

They stood up and waited to greet him. "Hey."

"How you feeling?" Thud asked Katherine.

"She was just worshiping the porcelain god again," Luke said.

Katherine ignored him. "I'm okay. Getting better, I hope."

"Michelle had it really bad with Quentin Junior, but she was okay with Alicia." Thud walked up the steps. "I have a theory. It's the sex of the kid."

"I'll have to see."

"I don't agree, by the way." Michelle smiled.

Katherine hugged Michelle as she climbed the steps to the porch. "I'm so glad you came."

"I had to. Luke made it sound important."

"It is."

"You're not selling Amway or some shit, are you?" Thud asked, frowning.

"How did you know?" Luke said as they sat. "I was going to work up to it, but you broke the code right away."

"Can I get you all anything?" Katherine asked.

"Let me get it," Luke offered.

"No, I've got it. Anybody?"

"Coffee?" Thud inquired.

"Sounds great," Michelle said.

"Sure," Luke agreed.

"Coffee it is." Katherine nodded. "I'll be right back."

"So what's up?" Thud asked as he put his feet on the porch railing.

"Look at the sunset," Luke said, gazing toward the distant mountains in the west.

Thud turned to his side and looked. "Why do you have to live out here in the boonies?"

"I grew up in the boonies, dude," Luke replied. "I like to be able to see the sky. To see a hundred miles in every direction. I don't do well when I wake up and walk outside and look at your ugly face next door every morning picking up a newspaper on the driveway in your pink bathrobe."

"How the hell did you end up in the Navy? We get zero space on a ship."

"I've told you a thousand times. They gave me a scholarship. We didn't have much money."

"Why the Navy?"

"I wanted to fly."

"Why not the Air Force?"

"I don't know, I figured flying off carriers would be the hardest thing there was to do in aviation. I love a challenge."

Just then an F/A-18 tore by overhead, heading south toward the restricted area for a night hop. "Sound of freedom," Thud said as they both watched it fly by.

"Nothing like it," Luke said with regret. He stood and held the screen door for Katherine, who was carrying a tray of mugs and a thermos of coffee.

Thud studied the horse trailer parked next to Luke's garage. It was large, white, and dented. "What's with the horse trailer?"

"I got a deal on it."

Thud frowned and looked around. "Hey, Stick, I hate to break it to you, but you don't have any horses."

"One day." Luke sat down again. "I wanted to let you know I'm going to submit my letter of resignation."

"No," Thud protested. "There's got to be a better way, Stick. Ask the Admiral to review it. Everybody knows what a great pilot you are. Gun just had it in for you, for some reason."

"Thud, you *know* that wouldn't make any difference at all.

And if I stayed in, I'd be the coffee mess officer in Adak, Alaska, by next year. You *know* that."

"I don't know that." Thud poured milk in his coffee and stirred it. "There's got to be a way."

"There's no way."

Thud shook his head as he thought about life at TOPGUN without Luke. It would take all the fun out of it. "So now what? Airlines?"

"You've got to be kidding me. I'd rather throw up on a bus."

"Nice," Michelle said disapprovingly.

"Sorry. Inside joke. That's a reference to a test they give you in Pensacola—"

"Whatever," Michelle said, still frowning.

"So? What is it? What are you thinking about?" Thud demanded.

Luke looked at Katherine, who nodded. "Check this out," Luke said, handing Thud a folded newspaper.

He looked at the section on top. "What's this?"

"Read it."

Thud read it, then looked up. "Interesting, but so what?"

"The United States bought twenty-one MiG-29s from Moldova. Did you know that?"

"Sure. Couple of months ago. They're at Wright-Patterson, as I recall."

"Check out the article. Extra engines, parts, and five hundred Russian air-to-air missiles. Believe that?"

"So what?"

"What if we could get our hands on a few of them?"

"A few what?"

"MiG-29s."

"And do what?" Thud frowned.

"Remember when Gun told us there were nine thousand adversary sorties that went unfilled by TOPGUN last year?"

"Yeah."

"What if we had eight MiG-29s and could start our own, private TOPGUN?"

Thud stared at him, then looked at Michelle, then back at Luke. "Are you serious?"

"Dead serious. And I want you to help me."

"How?"

"Start the school with me. Our own TOPGUN School. Our MiGs. What do you say?"

"I've got another eighteen months at TOPGUN."

"Your obligation is up. You could get out now if you wanted to."

"Damn," Thud remarked. "That's the craziest idea I've ever heard. You really think you could pull it off?"

"I just started thinking about it. Took my breath away. No more going to sea. No more commanders telling us what to do. No more getting out and flying for the airlines and hating life."

"Who would you get to fly with you?"

"Former TOPGUN instructors who've gotten out."

"That just might work, Stick. What about maintenance and parts?"

"There's a new company, just formed. Joint venture between DaimlerChrysler and Mikoyan in Russia, called MAPS—the MiG Aircraft Product Support Company. They formed it to convert MiG-29s and MiG-21s to NATO specs and modify and maintain them. They're doing it for Poland, Hungary, and the Czech Republic. I called them. They said they could do the entire thing for us. All the maintenance, you name it. You interested?"

Thud was impressed. "Maybe. Maybe I am," he said. "Where would you fly these MiG-29s?"

"Tonopah."

"Seriously?" Thud asked, surprised.

"Where's Tonopah?" Michelle asked.

"About a hundred twenty miles south. It's in the middle of total damned nowhere. It's where the F-117 Stealth fighters were based until they were disclosed to the public. Now it's just sitting there idle."

"Probably a wreck."

"Nope," Luke said, leaning forward. "It's beautiful. I drove down there yesterday. Absolutely perfect shape. Nobody would be telling us we're coming into the break too fast there. There's not a house within twenty miles of the place. Hold on," he said as he stepped inside the house for a moment. "Here's a picture I took yesterday." He handed it to Thud, who looked at it carefully. "It's harder than hell to find in a car. Just off Highway 6 east of the town of Tonopah, there's this random missile on a pedestal pointing up at the sky and an ominous sign that says TONOPAH TEST RANGE, OPERATED BY SANDIA NATIONAL LABORATORY FOR THE DEPARTMENT OF ENERGY."

Thud handed the photo to Michelle. "The Department of Energy? Why do they have an air base?"

"I have no idea. It probably has something to do with you-know-what . . ."

"Nuclear."

"That's the only interesting thing the DOE does that would put them in the desert that I know about. Anyway, whatever it's for, they're not doing it now."

"How much would it cost to do this?"

Luke nodded. "I'm not sure, exactly. But the U.S. bought all twenty-one MiGs and all the missiles *and* spare parts for forty million. The base is empty. I figure we lease eight MiGs—maybe nine, one two-seat trainer—and the air base. It's got to cost a lot less than buying all of them did."

"So how much money total you talking about raising?"

"I don't know," Luke said, glancing at Katherine. "Maybe a hundred mil."

Thud almost choked. "Dollars?" He laughed out loud. "Are you out of your mind? Where you going to get that kind of money?"

This was the part Luke hadn't wanted to bring up. He knew what it would do to Thud to hear it. It could ruin everything, and would put Luke's credibility and Thud's friendship at risk. "Your father."

Thud stared at his friend as if he had just been betrayed for the first time in his life. "Oh, I get it," Thud said bitterly. "You need me to pimp my father for dough."

"No, I don't. It's got nothing to do with it. I'm happy to go *anywhere* for money. If you know a couple of other billionaires that might be able to fund us, let me know. And if some of them are former fighter pilots from Vietnam, like your father, that would be even better."

"Ain't happening, Stick. We're not even on speaking terms."

Luke looked at Katherine, who wasn't about to say anything. "Yeah, help me with that. Your father flew Thuds in Vietnam. One of the few black fighter pilots in the war. And he holds it against you that you're a TOPGUN instructor?"

"He didn't want me to fly. He wanted me to go into business with him. His multizillion-dollar business. That's why I was a business major. Then, when I told him I wanted to go into the Navy and fly, he did a total meltdown. I don't think his Vietnam experience was all that positive. He always said, 'Don't trust the government! Ever!' Like a mantra. 'Don't trust the government! Don't trust the government!' "

"So *I* can't ask him?"

"I didn't say that. But *I'm* not asking him for anything."

Good enough for Luke. "So what do you think? You willing to get out to do this if we can pull it off?"

"I'll have to think about it." Thud looked at Michelle, who was giving him one of those spousal frowns that says,

"You'd better talk to me before answering that question."

"I'll have to think about it a lot. But it sure sounds like a kick."

"Your father isn't our only idea," Katherine said. "If he isn't interested, I know some other investors in Silicon Valley. We can go to venture capitalists if we need to. This isn't the usual sort of thing they like to invest in, but who knows? Maybe they'll branch out a little."

Thud nodded. "I'll think about it."

"I've got a cross-country scheduled to go to Ohio to check out the MiGs. Want to come?"

"Ops O approved?"

"He doesn't know *why* I want to go to Wright-Patterson. It all looks normal to him."

"I thought you were grounded."

"That was until after the board. Now I can fly until I'm gone."

Thud thought about it. "Why the hell not?" he asked enthusiastically.

PETKOV lay in his bed in his uniform and lined boots and stared at the dark ceiling. He had been on base security for two weeks. The Colonel hadn't changed his mind, and everyone on the base knew it. All the pilots knew he'd been assigned to security for the duration of his natural life, which, they also knew, without flying, wouldn't be long.

He looked at the clock on the table next to his bed. One more hour. He had the night duty again, midnight to eight in the morning. The worst watch of the worst assignment on the base. The only things that happened to an officer in charge of security were bad.

Every morning he'd come back to his room after his watch and try to sleep, while his fellow pilots headed toward their MiGs to climb into the cold morning sky to their freedom. He couldn't explore how he felt, knowing he would never climb into a MiG again. It had been the only thing worthwhile in his life. He had ruined everything else.

Suddenly there was a knock on the door. Petkov rolled slowly off the soft, noisy bed, walked across the concrete-floored room to the door, and opened it. It was Leonid Popovich, the Lieutenant Colonel in charge of all security on the base. Petkov immediately assumed he had somehow missed his watch. He was about to begin a profuse apology when he noticed another man with Popovich.

"I want to introduce you to someone," Popovich said in his distinctively raspy voice as he stepped through the door into Petkov's room. The second man followed closely behind. He quickly surveyed the room with the expertise of someone who always watched his back.

Petkov noticed that the visitor was wearing a Russian hat against the cold, but not the hat of the Russian Air Force, or even the Army. He was a civilian, and his hat was made of seal fur. Beautiful, dense, black seal fur. Very expensive and hard to find. The man himself was short and ugly and had mean eyes.

"Sergei Alexei Gorgov, this is Major Vladimir Petkov, the one I told you about."

Gorgov looked up at Petkov with his mouth open. "Ah," he said slowly, with a deep, penetrating voice, "you're the drunk."

Petkov tried not to show the impact the comment had on him. He chose not to respond.

Popovich closed the door. "He works for me now," he said to Gorgov.

"So," Gorgov said, removing his gloves, "what do you want?"

Petkov was confused. "I don't understand."

"What do you want?" Gorgov repeated. "What do you want from life now that you have pissed it away?"

Petkov wanted to yell at the man, to strike him. "Just to do my job."

Gorgov smiled, revealing his yellow, uneven teeth. "Your job," he laughed. "Your job." He shook his head. "From what I hear, you were one of the best pilots in the wing. Part of your job, then, was to not become a drunk, and you couldn't do that, could you?"

Petkov said nothing.

"You want to do your job? What job?" He looked around at Petkov's small room. "That's all you want? To do your job? And then what? Become an old man and retire somewhere to sit alone and hold your dick?"

"What do you want?" Petkov said angrily. "Why are you here?"

"Colonel Popovich and I have been working together for some time now. He told me you were interested in a similar arrangement."

Petkov's eyes darted to Popovich, who was staring back at him, warning him. They had never had any such conversation, and Popovich knew it. "I don't know what you mean."

"An arrangement of mutual convenience. You have many skills. You can be of great value to me and my friends."

It suddenly hit Petkov where he'd seen the black seal hat before. Riding in the back of a black Mercedes, with the tinted window down just enough for him to see the hat on a short man sitting in the backseat of the car, the sign of a member of the Russian Mafia. "In what way?"

"In your current position, by doing nothing. Or, I should say, at least doing nothing at the right time. The Air Force does not fully appreciate your skills. You, like most others, are underpaid. I can provide you the pay you deserve. You can own a car, you can own a *dacha*. I can get you all the women you want. You can live the life you're entitled to live." He studied Petkov's face. "To get drunk every day, if that is what you want."

"I will *never* get drunk again—"

"Major, please," Gorgov said slowly. "Please." He paused. "Have you ever said that before?"

"It is hard."

Gorgov nodded, then paused, waiting for Petkov's attention. "When I say so, you make sure your security watch does not interfere with my friends." His mean eyes were locked on to Petkov's. "Understand?"

"I'm not *interested,*" Petkov replied angrily.

Gorgov looked at Popovich, then back at Petkov. "I don't think you understand. It has already been decided. Tonight will be the first time. At three in the morning, my friends will be coming onto the base to complete one small transaction. You will make sure they are not bothered. Do you understand?"

"I won't—"

"He understands perfectly," Popovich said, glaring at Petkov.

Gorgov smiled his yellow smile and put his gloves back on. "Excellent. I knew you were a man of integrity." He opened the door and turned back to Petkov. "If you do these things well, I have much bigger plans in mind for you." He could feel Petkov's resistance and knew where his temptations lay. "It will be very lucrative for you. I can get you out of this shithole. Perhaps even to the West." Popovich held the door as they headed out. "If you do your job. Your *new* job. For me." Gorgov walked to his Mercedes without looking back.

Petkov took a deep breath as he closed the door behind the two men. He felt as though he were suffocating. When dealing with the Mafia, you did what they asked or you ended up dead. He couldn't see a way out of the downward spiral his life had become.

6

Luke looked down through his visor at the green, tree-filled terrain of central Ohio around Wright-Patterson Air Force Base. They had slapped tanks on their planes and flown cross-country from Fallon to Wright-Patterson. The Operations officer who had approved the cross-country flight felt that he owed Luke one last good deal. Everyone knew he was getting out. They all felt sorry for him.

"TOPGUN 23 cleared to break."

"Roger," Luke replied. He checked the downwind leg for any other traffic he hadn't already seen. He looked over at Thud flying tightly on his wing and started nodding slowly. He was counting, as he always did. Then he put his left hand up to his oxygen mask and kissed Thud off.

He pushed the stick slowly but steadily to the left, putting the F/A-18 into a slow left roll until it reached a ninety-degree angle of bank. He pulled back hard, and the Hornet bit into the air and turned sharply from the runway below him as he reduced throttle to slow down his jet. Thud counted to four, then put his own Hornet into an identical five-G turn behind Luke.

As Luke leveled out downwind, he lowered his flaps and landing gear. He waited until he was parallel to the runway and at its end. *"Tower, TOPGUN 23 at the 180, three down and locked."*

"Roger, TOPGUN 23 cleared to land Runway 6. Winds 070 for four."

"Roger," Luke answered as he continued his turn and steep descent. He landed perfectly on the runway. He turned off at the end of the runway and looked for the truck to guide him to the transient line, where he could park his jet and the Air Force would refuel it for him.

Luke and Thud taxied together and followed the directions of the ground crew who were waiting for them. They held their brakes while the Air Force men put wooden chocks by their wheels. They were finally in place, and they were given the signal to shut down.

Luke pulled his throttles around the stop to the off position and had a quick idea. As his engines wound down, he glanced at Thud, who was watching him, knowing he was going to think of it. Luke brought his head back slowly, then quickly forward. When he did, both he and Thud pulled the canopy lever back, and their two canopies opened as if linked together, a perfect precision canopy-opening exercise. It was what all Navy squadrons did after a fly-off, when they'd been on a cruise for six months, and they had flown back off the carrier to their home base as a squadron. Their families waited expectantly, and the pilots, with their stomachs fluttering and yearning to hold their spouses again, would all leave their radios on, and the skipper would signal for everyone to shut down their engines and open their canopies at the exact same time.

They climbed down from their planes and walked to the line shack together.

"My butt is killing me," Thud commented.

"Long flight."

They paused at the maintenance counter and put their helmets on it. A senior Air Force enlisted woman approached them. "Do you have your gas card, sir?" she asked.

Luke removed a credit card from the small pocket on the left shoulder of his flight suit.

"Your jets okay, sir? Need any maintenance?"

"No, they're fine, thanks."

"When do you expect to depart, sir?" she asked, writing.

"Tomorrow at 0600."

"Yes, sir, the tower should be open. You might give them a few minutes to have their coffee so they don't taxi you into a C-17."

"Good point. Make it 0630."

"Will do, sir," she said, smiiing as she glanced over his shoulder, apparently at someone approaching them from behind. Her face expressed sufficient concern for Luke to turn around and see a man walking toward them from two cheap black couches that formed the transient pilot waiting area. He was wearing polyester pants that might have fit once but certainly didn't now and a short-sleeved plaid shirt that might sell for ten dollars at Kmart. The man was staring at Luke as he walked directly at him. He was unshaven. His hair was black and unkempt. He had clearly slept on his hair and hadn't seen a mirror since.

Luke's concern grew as the man approached him.

The man spoke with an accent. "Navy Lieutenant?"

"Who are you?" Luke asked, not really wanting to know.

"Are you Navy Lieutenant? From TOPGUN?" he asked, putting the emphasis on "gun." He looked out the window at the two desert-camouflage F/A-18s with the distinctive circular TOPGUN logo and the lightning bolt.

Oh, great, Luke thought. A wannabe who's been obsessing his whole life in a basement somewhere about flying at TOPGUN. They were everywhere. Every air show, every port of call, every tour of a carrier, everywhere. Guys—almost always men—who knew more about the airplanes than the pilots who flew them did. They knew the manufacturing specs for the canopy and the number of landings the tires could take before they had to be changed. They were information sponges and generally not very much fun to be with. They almost certainly had never actually flown an airplane—or had a normal human relationship. "Yeah, that's us," Luke admitted reluctantly as he turned back to the female Sergeant.

"We must talk," the man insisted.

Luke listened carefully to his accent. He'd heard it before but couldn't place it. "What?" he said over his shoulder as he and Thud examined the paperwork that had been handed to them.

"We must *talk*," the man said again, touching Luke on his elbow.

That was too much. Luke put down the papers and turned to the man, looking at him more carefully, to see if he was a threat. "Do I know you?"

"I'm sorry, sir," the Sergeant apologized, growing concerned. "He said he was a friend of yours. He was supposed to meet you here."

Luke looked at the man again, waiting for an explanation.

"I am Vlad, from MAPS," the man said quietly, with authority.

Luke hesitated. "Vlad? Have we spoken?"

"Yes, but I'm sure you have forgotten. I am very new at MAPS, and they have just assigned me to the idea you have sent them about this new TOPGUN School."

Luke quickly looked at the Sergeant to see if she was listening. She wasn't. Luke headed away from the counter. "What are you doing here?"

Vlad smiled and shook Luke's hand with enthusiasm. "I didn't warn you that I was coming. I for this apologize," he said in his heavy Russian accent. "It was on the moment of a spur. They said you had told them you planned to inspect the MiGs this weekend and would try to get them the serial numbers. I offered to come help, and they told me to come."

"This is Thud," Luke said, indicating Quentin.

Vlad shook Thud's hand with equal vigor. "I have heard of you. You are part of this, too. Yes?"

"Yes," Thud said, smiling as he evaluated the man on whom so much might depend.

Luke said, "But I'm not sure they'll let you come with us."

"They must," Vlad said with confidence. "First you check into VOQ," he said, putting the emphasis on the O of the acronym for the Visiting Officer's Quarters. "I will drive you there. Then we go to find MiGs."

Luke looked at Thud, who said, "Forget the VOQ. Let's see the MiGs. It's already almost 1400."

Luke and Thud followed Vlad out of the small building to the parking lot by the operations building. "What is your last name?" Luke asked.

Vlad fished in the pocket of his tight polyester pants for the rental-car keys. "Petkov," he replied in such a way that the name sounded like an explosion.

"Nice to meet you," Luke said. "Where'd you get this . . . car?" he asked, suddenly concerned.

"Cheapest rental car place I could find. Nineteen and ninety-five per every day."

"I'll drive. I've been on this base before—" Luke said.

"I know base. I got here before you. I was driving around, until I saw Navy pilots do snappy break in F-18s, not pull up rolling break like Air Force. Then I just watched where you go."

"You're very clever."

"Yes, very clever. I can do anything," he said, stating a simple fact as he saw it.

"Keys," Luke said, holding out his hand.

Vlad looked at Luke and immediately saw that this was nonnegotiable.

Luke opened the driver's door, unlocked the other doors, and pushed the button that released the trunk. They tossed their bags into the back and climbed in, with Vlad in the backseat. Luke and Thud glanced at each other as the body odor that was following Vlad around settled inside the car.

They made quick faces of horror at each other but said nothing.

"You could trust my driving. I was MiG pilot before maintenance," Vlad said.

Luke was surprised. "What kind?"

"MiG-29. NATO calls Fulcrum. The ones we are now going to see."

"Then you stopped being a pilot?"

"Yes," he said bitterly.

"Why?" Luke asked, watching him through the rearview mirror.

Vlad turned his head to look out the window at the passing buildings. He was surprised at the beauty of the base, the officers' brick homes, the lush trees, the groomed golf course, and the pond. It was somehow comforting. "Disagreement with my commanding officer. It was unwise on my part."

"So what happened?"

"So I left Air Force and went to work with MAPS. Much easier. Plus we get paid."

"You live in Germany?" Thud asked.

"Yes, but . . ." he said loudly and then paused. "When you—Turn here—" he yelled at Luke, who had almost missed the turn. "When you two start your own TOPGUN school in Nevada, I hope to be there to help you with MiGs. As chief maintenance officer."

"That would be great," Luke responded with a tone of caution.

"And then maybe you will help *me* get to be American citizen."

Luke glanced at Thud, then at his watch. "We're supposed to meet a PAO at the operations building at 1400," he said.

"Yes, it is right over there," Vlad said, pointing from the backseat.

Luke drove right to it. They climbed out and walked

stiffly into the lobby. Luke saw a female officer standing there, obviously waiting. She looked at his flight suit and quickly examined his patches—his NSAWC patch, the round TOPGUN patch on his right shoulder—and the brown leather nametag that had Navy gold wings, TOPGUN, and STICK on it. "Good afternoon, sirs," she said. "Welcome to Wright-Patterson Air Force Base. I'm Captain Lisa Gannon." She wasn't sure exactly whom to talk to, who was in charge. "It's my understanding you wanted to see the MiG-29s," she said.

"We're here from TOPGUN," Luke said. "We're preparing a presentation to the DOD, a part of which will be about these MiGs," he said seriously, implying much more than was there.

"Yes, sir, which is what confused me a little. That sounds like something that is official and should have come through Colonel Robinson, as the MiGs really come under his—"

"It really isn't official." Luke looked at her sympathetically. "We just need to see them, and whatever help you can give us would be appreciated."

"Yes, sir, I just thought you might get more information from Colonel—"

"Thanks, we just want to see the planes. I'm sure this will be fine," Luke said. "Can we walk there?"

"No, sir, they're over at the other side of the base. There really isn't anyone over there except security."

"Excellent. We'll follow you."

Captain Gannon hesitated. This wasn't the way the Air Force operated. They didn't do unofficial visits. "Very well," she said finally. She walked out of the hangar, climbed into a dark blue Air Force van, and drove out of the parking lot. Luke got behind the wheel of the dented Taurus, and they followed her all the way around the base to the remote, lonely spot where the MiGs were parked, next to a small white building that seemed to be there only to support the MiGs.

Luke, Thud, and Vlad got out of the car and walked around the building. Soon they stopped dead in their tracks. There were twenty-one MiG-29s, lined up in two rows just like an operating squadron, waiting for the pilots to walk out and start them up. Luke felt his heart beating faster. He had never seen a MiG-29 in his life. He'd seen photos, videotapes, and three-dimensional simulations. But he'd never seen one of the planes that he had spent the last few years studying and thinking about and fighting every day in his mind.

His enthusiasm was dampened, though, by the appearance of the MiGs. They looked beat up. Their paint was blotchy, some of the fasteners appeared to be coming loose, and they looked sad from the reflective covering that had been placed over the canopies, as if they'd been blindfolded. "What do you think, Thud?" Luke asked.

"Let's take a look."

Their eyes pored over the MiGs; Vlad was particularly attentive. Each airplane had its own story and its own foibles. They knew there would be one or two that would be hard to fly in trim, that would want to fly slightly sideways all the time. They knew that one would have electronic gremlins and that systems would fail for no apparent reason, and that others would be the iron horses that never broke down. It was like having a family.

There were two security officers watching them approach the planes. Captain Gannon nodded at them.

They went over to the first airplane and stood near its nose. The white circle with multipointed red-and-gold star on the tail was a tail marking Luke had to admit never having seen before. In fact, before he read the interview in the newspaper with the Secretary of Defense explaining why the

United States had acquired twenty-one MiG-29s from Moldova, Luke wasn't even sure where Moldova was.

Vlad spread his arms in joy as he walked toward the MiG. "The most beautiful airplane in the entire world!"

"What's up with the puke-green paint job?" Thud asked, distressed.

Vlad answered, "Just the Moldovan camouflage. Not a very good job, true, but look," he said, hurrying forward to the nearest MiG. "This is C model. Look at dorsal spine," he said, pointing to the area behind the canopy. "Larger than the A model." He smiled. "It," he said, pronouncing the word as "eat," "has active radar jammer there. Here is radar warning receiver. Very good one." He gazed at the intake, which was closed by the movable doors. "Big engines." He smiled again, looking over his shoulder at Luke and Thud, who were watching him with amusement. "Eight thousand three hundred kilograms of thrust."

"Eighteen thousand three hundred pounds each," Luke replied.

"You know this?"

"Sure." Luke grinned. "This is my number one most likely enemy. My biggest threat."

"That is more thrust than your F-18, yes?"

"Yep. But the F/A-18 is lighter."

Vlad stood up straight and turned around. "No, my friend. Maximum takeoff weight for the F-18 is twenty-three thousand kilograms. Yes?"

Luke quickly multiplied the number by 2.23 in his head. "About."

"Maximum takeoff weight for the MiG-29 is eighteen thousand five hundred kilograms."

"That just means the F-18 can carry more."

"Ha!" Vlad exclaimed. "Ha!" He walked around to the front of the airplane with Luke and Thud in tow. "These airplanes have 1:1 thrust-to-weight ratio at maximum takeoff weight! F-18 is not close to that."

"What kind of shape do you think they're in?" Luke asked, trying to change the subject.

"Fine shape," Vlad said. "Look here," he said, crouching at the side of the nosewheel. "See this?" He pointed to a small fender on the wheel. Not waiting for them to answer, his accent becoming stronger with his excitement as he tried to talk faster; he continued, "This is to clean mud and dirt off wheel before it is pulled up into plane on takeoff. You know why?"

"Unimproved runways."

"Ha! Not just unimproved, but dirt! Or grass! What other jet fighter in world can take off from dirt strip? Wheel stays clean, and engine intakes stay closed until takeoff. Did you know that?"

Luke and Thud nodded.

"You know about louvers on top of wings for air during start and takeoff?"

Again they nodded.

The Air Force Captain was watching them with growing skepticism. The loud, smelly Russian made her uneasy. She understood that the Russians were now our friends, but she also understood that Americans still got arrested now and then for "spying" in Russia. But these were Russian airplanes. There wasn't anything particularly secret about them. Their purchase from Moldova had been announced at a press conference by the Secretary of Defense. And if there was anything secret about the planes, they were Russian secrets, not American. She just stood with her arms folded and watched them.

"Let's look inside," Vlad said. He looked around for the standard yellow ladder and found one lying beside the MiG two places down. He jogged to it and lifted the ladder upright, expertly placing it against the side of the jet.

The Captain didn't want them opening the planes at all. She unfolded her arms and began walking quickly toward Vlad.

Suddenly there was an electrical noise as the canopy opened. The Captain saw Vlad grinning as the canopy on the second MiG started up toward the sky.

Before she could say anything, Vlad had scrambled up the side of the MiG with Luke right behind him.

"Run interference for us, Thud," Luke said.

Thud intercepted the Captain with his hands up. "They just want to take a look," he said.

She hadn't been prepared for this at all and wasn't sure if it was even allowed. She wanted this visit to be as uneventful as possible, a "nonevent," as she wanted to describe it to her boss. But now it was an event.

Vlad didn't even hesitate. He climbed into the cockpit with a knowing, fluid motion that Luke knew could come only from hundreds of repetitions. His hands quickly dashed around the dusty cockpit, reveling in the familiar sensations and appearance.

Luke followed him up the ladder and looked over his shoulder. "What do you think?" he asked, full of hope and expectation.

Vlad smiled. "Compared to your multifunction displays, not fancy. But it will work. They have all their instruments—radar, weapons wiring, everything. And look here," he said, pointing to the weapons panel.

"What?" Luke asked.

"Nuclear capable. These C models are wired to carry nuclear weapons."

"Holy shit," Luke said, looking down at the nervous Captain, who was deep in conversation with Thud and glancing their way. "Do you think that will make it harder?"

"No, it makes no difference," Vlad said, running his hands

over the stick, the throttle, and the innumerable switches throughout the cockpit. He looked at Luke. "Unless you have some nuclear weapons."

"Not yet," Luke said, smiling.

Luke's eyes raced from one instrument to the next. He'd seen pictures of MiG-29 cockpits before, but had never studied them to learn specific instrument locations. The Cyrillic notations on the glass gauges threw him. He thought he could probably guess what each instrument was—which was the airspeed indicator, which was the engine temperature, the fuel flow, the accelerometer. But he wasn't sure. He wouldn't want to climb into the plane right now and try to fly it. He realized that getting accustomed to this plane would be a longer process than he had anticipated.

"Will it fly?" Luke asked.

"Don't know," Vlad answered. "Depends more on the engines." Vlad started to get out of the cockpit, and Luke backed down the ladder to the tarmac. Vlad made straight for the nosewheel well, stood up inside it, and took out a small notebook and pencil. He wrote down the airplane's identification number and ducked out of the wheel well. Luke watched Vlad head for the engine intake. Luke climbed back up and sat in the cockpit. He held the stick and studied the buttons all over it. He put his left hand on the throttles of the two powerful but cold engines. He found the lever to allow him to adjust the location of the rudder pedals and moved them back until they were at a comfortable distance. He looked at Vlad's Taurus through combining glass HUD—the Heads-Up Display—and smiled. He felt more comfortable in the cockpit of a fighter than anywhere else in the world. It was where most of what he thought and cared about came together.

"Sir," the Captain cried up to him with a hint of distress.

"Yeah?" Luke replied.

"I really don't think we're supposed to be in the cockpits . . ."

"I'll be right down," he said as he tried to memorize the cockpit and its instruments. He waited as long as he could and still be responsive to her. He climbed out and removed the ladder. Vlad closed the canopy.

"What do you think?" Thud asked.

"I think they'll work," Luke said enthusiastically.

"For what?" the Captain asked, deeply confused and a little concerned.

"Sorry, that's classified," Thud said in dead earnest, before Luke could say anything.

"Oh," she said, disappointed. "Have you seen enough?"

"We'd like to see all of them," Luke answered.

"I can't let you open the cockpits," she said.

"That's fine," he replied. He smiled as he saw Vlad behind her. He'd taken a special tool out of his pocket, opened the engine-access compartments, and was copying down serial numbers from the engines.

They spent the next hour examining the entire group of MiGs, with Vlad writing down all the identifying information he could find.

"You get enough?" Luke asked.

"Never," Vlad answered as he climbed into the backseat of the Taurus and put his small notebook down next to him. "Can't get into rest of cockpits? Why not? She should be Russian officer. Stupid rules for no reason. That is what I'm trying to get away from."

"I like your spunk," Luke said as he glanced at Vlad in the mirror.

"What is spunk?"

"Determination, sort of, but with a confident . . . I don't know . . . independence, I guess."

Vlad was silent as he considered whether he understood

the word or how someone might consider him independent. "Coffee," he suddenly said. "I need strong, thick coffee, and we will talk about the airplanes."

"You got it," Luke said as he watched for a place to stop. He saw a McDonald's ahead and pulled into the parking lot.

They sat in a booth. Vlad took a sip of McDonald's coffee and frowned. "This is coffee?"

"Sort of. How long you been with MAPS?"

"Not long. I retired from Russian Air Force just three weeks ago. I got this job with MAPS right away and moved to Germany. Very lucky. Very hard job to get. I have many hours and much maintenance experience. When I got there, they told me about this. I was very interested. They told me to do work on it."

"What do you think?" Luke asked.

"About coffee? Is terrible."

"No, the MiGs."

"I need to see maintenance records. I need to see how much hours are on the engines. They don't last that long. Russian engines run very hot. But if engines work good, I think they will do."

"Did you get the numbers?"

"Yes. We will be able to reconstruct the entire history of the airplanes. We keep track of all MiG-29s in the world. We keep duplicate maintenance records for all planes so we can track failures and times. No question," he said, downing another deep gulp of the hot coffee. He looked at the serial numbers. "I am afraid of many of the engines. They are old numbers and may not have too much hours left on them. You make sure in planning you have money for many engines. They only fly four hundred hours before need overhauls."

Luke frowned. "When the U.S. bought these planes from Moldova, they bought the spare parts, too. I hope there are also some spare engines."

"Yes, there are. But you will need more."

"Where are we going to get extra engines?"

"*I* get them. You pay for them, but we can get you anything. You forget that MAPS is half Russian. Owned by company that makes MiGs. They want to sell lots of parts. They make them, so we can buy them. You just have to be *able* to buy them."

"I need you to do some things for me."

Vlad looked across at him. He glanced down at his grubby little notebook with Russian writing and numbers in it. "Anything."

"I need an estimate of the costs of refurbishing the MiGs, bringing them up to NATO specs, and the expected cost of maintenance for five years on an annual basis."

"Yes, yes," Vlad said as he wrote in his notebook with a stubby pencil, the kind one might find at a golf course.

"And then, if you can, I need an estimate for MAPS to train Thud and me to fly the MiG-29, in Germany or Russia or wherever."

"Germany. Much easier."

"Okay. How long it would take—"

"For TOPGUN instructor? Ha! You could fly now. No question. I could tell you in five minutes things you need to know. Fighting in air combat would take longer, and learning weapons. But flying? Easy. Very forgiving airplane. And no fly by wire. No computer tricks. What you ask for from the stick is what you get."

"Still, for a syllabus—the kind the German Air Force went through when they got the MiG-29s from the East German Air Force."

"Sure. MAPS would do that for free, if we do business."

"Would MAPS actually be able to contract to do the maintenance for us? Here? In Nevada?"

Vlad's already red eyes grew more intense and cloudy. "Yes," he said, but with some reservation, Luke could see. "I want to do it. I want to come to Nevada to do the maintenance, train your own people, take care of everything for you." Vlad reached down to his beat-up brown leather briefcase and pulled it onto the small table in front of them, nearly knocking over his half-full coffee cup. "I have something for you." He pulled out two thick manuals and handed them to Luke and Thud.

"What is this?" Luke asked.

"Pilot manual for MiG-29."

Luke stared at the manual. He was skeptical. He opened it to an arbitrary page and began reading. The English was excellent, and it had all the diagrams and charts in the right place. He was shocked. "Outstanding," he said.

"Good. So do we do business?"

"I don't know yet. I have to get the U.S. government to approve all this. They own the MiGs and have to agree to lease them to us."

"You have money?"

"I think so. We've had interest from investors."

"You have a lot of money?"

"What do you mean by a lot?" Thud asked.

"Many millions. You won't be able to maintain these airplanes for less than many million dollars a year."

"We think we have enough. If you get us the estimates, we'll have a better idea."

"I will do it." Vlad looked down and was clearly considering whether to say what he had in mind.

Luke and Thud could both sense what was happening.

"What?" Thud asked. "What's eating you? You don't think this will work?"

"Oh, no, it will work. Your idea is brilliant. And good for my company."

"What then?" Luke asked.

"I have two dreams," Vlad said. He studied their faces. "Two things I want in life. I have no wife. No children.

Maybe one day . . . but I want to fly again. It was taken from me. I am good pilot. Maybe you could think of having me as your instructor pilot for other pilots, when you start your company. You should get eight C models and the one two-seat UB. I will do training for you. I trained many to fly MiG-29. I could do it."

Luke was leery. "What else?" he asked noncommittally.

"I want to live in United States. I want to work with green card."

"How do you expect us to help?"

"You could employ me. Could ask INS for green card. I will take care of you. You can be sure I'll take care of everything. But I want you to help me."

"I don't know, Vlad. Those are pretty tough—"

"You need to have special skill. I have that. There is not another MiG-29 flight instructor in the country. I am sure." He looked at their eyes, watching him. "You don't know if you can believe me. I understand. I have copied my Russian flight records and had them translated for you. You can have them translated again. I have one thousand hours in MiG-29. I can teach your people. Give me chance."

"We'll think about it," Luke said, not giving him any tone of encouragement at all. "Have you talked to MAPS about it? Would they let you?"

"They have given me permission."

"You want us to keep those?" Luke asked, indicating his translated flight records.

"Sure," Vlad said, his optimism renewed. "You keep and look at these."

"Great," Luke said, taking them and putting them on the pile of MiG manuals. "Why don't you let me have the copies in Russian, too."

Vlad understood immediately. "Of course," he said, handing them across the table. "What is next?"

"I need to get those maintenance-cost estimates from you. In writing. Numbers that MAPS can commit to. Then it's up to me to sell it."

"You will have it."

"We'll need it right away. We've got a meeting with the government this week."

"Yes, of course. What is name of person?" Vlad asked.

Luke glanced at Thud, his mind drawing a blank.

Thud tried to remember. "He's an Undersecretary of Defense. Merewether, or something."

7

Luke walked down the passageway of TOPGUN toward the glass doors to the parking lot. He had just left Commander Beebe's office. The letter of reprimand, the copy of which Gun had given him with no explanation or ceremony, no softening apology, was smoldering in the pocket of his flight suit. Gun had given it to him as if it were next month's watch bill.

Gun had finally shown some surprise, though, when Luke handed him his letter of resignation in return, without even looking at the letter of reprimand. He'd said he understood. Would have done the same thing, he'd said. Right, Luke had thought. Gun had said he would approve Luke's request and forward it up the chain of command. "Great," Luke had said, not even attaching a "sir" to the end of his sentence. He couldn't possibly. He had no more respect for Beebe.

As he headed out the door to his car in the hot parking lot in front of the building, he saw Brian Hayes, almost completely masking his ongoing fight with MS. "Hey, Spy Man," Luke hailed. "What's up?" Luke could see that Hayes had been standing by the door of his car without moving for some seconds. Hayes's face was filled with emotion. "What's the matter?" Luke asked as he walked over to him.

Hayes's eyes were swollen and pink. "They're giving me a medical discharge."

Luke knew that would be the result. The Navy wasn't about to keep someone with MS on active duty. "I'm really sorry, Brian."

Hayes spoke quietly. "This is all I've ever wanted to do, Stick. This is where I belong. I'm good at this."

Luke nodded. "The best."

"What are you up to?"

"Just submitted my letter of resignation."

"From what?"

"The Navy."

Hayes looked over his shoulder to make sure no one else had heard the heresy. "Are you crazy?"

"I can't stay in with a letter in my jacket. You know that."

"I figured you'd appeal it or something. Everybody in the Navy loves you, Stick! They can't let you get out."

"Apparently not everyone."

Hayes let the truth of that sink in. "Now what? Airlines?"

"I'd rather die."

"So what'll it be?"

"I'm going to start my own TOPGUN school."

Hayes frowned. "You serious?"

"Serious as a heart attack."

"How?"

"Lease some MiGs and an airfield from the government and hire former TOPGUN instructors as pilots."

"You're not kidding. How you going to finance that?"

"I've got an appointment with Thud's dad—"

"The billionaire?"

"The same, on Saturday, and if he's interested, I've got an appointment with the Undersecretary of Defense on Thursday to explain it to him. Thud and I just got back from checking out the MiGs."

"Unbelievable."

"You want to come work with us?"

Brian didn't want to look desperate. "Seriously?"

"Sure. We'll need an intel officer to do the same stuff you do here."

"Classified?"

"Don't know yet. Could do it a bunch of ways. May be classified, may not be. You could be the admin officer, too, setting up the classes and all kinds of stuff. You interested?"

"I don't know really, how long . . ."

"Do it as long as you want." Luke smiled. "I'll keep you posted. Keep your fingers crossed for us with Thud's dad and the DOD."

"Does Thud know you're going to ask his father?"

"He's going with me."

"I didn't think they were on speaking terms."

"They're not."

"Is he going to get out, too?"

"Gun doesn't know it yet, but if I get the money and the DOD approval, Thud is going to put in his letter."

"The skipper will go completely postal!" Hayes laughed.

"Yeah. That would really rip me up," Luke said as he headed toward his Corvette. "I'll call you."

ONE week later Luke stood at the pay phone in the cafeteria at the Pentagon. He finally pressed his home number into the pad, then his credit card number, and listened to the phone ring at his house. Thud stood behind him and listened in on the conversation.

Katherine picked it up after one ring. "Hello?"

"It's me."

"How did it go?" Katherine asked.

"I don't know what happened," he said, trying not to sound as discouraged as he felt.

"Did your computer crash?"

"The Undersecretary's a train wreck. All disheveled. I didn't even get to do my whole presentation. He didn't want to have anything to do with it."

"He didn't want to hear it?"

"Completely uninterested. He had the time set aside, and we had a conference room, and his staff was there. Everybody seemed enthusiastic except him. He's just a bitter guy."

"What did he say?"

"He said it wasn't happening on his watch. Said it sounded like a waste of U.S. assets."

"Are you serious?"

"Yeah. We're finished."

"But it's a *fabulous* idea. Especially since Thud's dad signed on!" Katherine knew what it would do to Luke if he could never fly fighters again.

"I think the Undersecretary is one of those guys that hates it when other people succeed. It makes him feel better about himself to bring down other people."

Katherine sighed. "I guess we'll just have to regroup, find other airplanes and a different airfield. They can't really stop you from doing this."

"Yes they *can,* Katherine. This is the guy who would approve the contracts to use our school at all. If he doesn't want us out there competing with TOPGUN and Red Flag, he'll just make sure we don't get the contracts. He can sink us!"

She didn't know what to say. "I'm sorry, Luke."

"I guess it'll have to be the airlines," he said bitterly. "Our flight leaves from Reagan in about three hours. I'll see you tonight."

"Okay," Katherine replied. "I love you. And it doesn't matter how these things go. I always will."

"Yeah, I know. See ya." He leaned back against the pay phone and closed his eyes. All he could think of was sitting in the cockpit of an airliner, trying to sound cool as he made an announcement to the passengers about how they were going to try a different flight level because it would be smoother . . . He didn't *want* smooth air. He wanted to *scream* through the sky and across the desert floor, and pull on the stick of a jet until vapor trails ripped off the wings, and zoom straight up into the sky so the only way he could see the earth was through his rearview mirror, and get his radar to lock up another airplane, and hear the growl of a Sidewinder missile in his headset, and watch the sun set— upside down—and look at shooting stars in the night sky through his bubble canopy, and head to the O' Club full of the piss and vinegar and exhilaration of a day of air combat maneuvering. He couldn't imagine life without it.

THE Undersecretary wrestled with the lock on his apartment. The key didn't fit perfectly, and unless he jiggled it just so, the door wouldn't open. It was the perfect end to a very aggravating day. Now he was prevented from even getting into his pathetic apartment. The apartment he hated. He became so annoyed that he put too much force into the key, and it started bending inside the lock. He took his hand off and backed away and began breathing heavily. He wanted to kick the door open and rip it completely off its frame. He closed his eyes, continued to breathe, then tried the door again. He forced himself to grab the key lightly and turn the lock gently. It finally opened, and he stepped through the door. He threw his raincoat onto the wooden dining room chair and dropped his briefcase on the floor. It was full of memos and papers from work that he knew he wouldn't touch all night. He just took them home so the others in his office would think he was being diligent.

He had only two things to look forward to that evening— a basketball game on television and a refrigerator full of beer. He could lose himself in the game. Merewether walked into the living room to switch on the television and noticed for the first time that something was amiss.

"Good evening, Mr. Undersecretary."

Merewether felt the chill of pure panic race through him. He spun to his left and saw Yushaf. "What the hell are you doing here? About gave me a heart attack! How did you get in?"

"It was open."

"No, it wasn't. I just used my key!"

"You just used your key to lock it, and then you got frustrated and unlocked it."

"*What* are you doing in my apartment?"

"I need to talk to you."

"Why couldn't you talk to me at the office? Or set up another one of those lunches at one of those fancy stupid restaurants?"

"I could have. But I wanted to talk to you tonight. I drove over to your house to see you, forgetting that you didn't live there anymore. I saw your wife. It's a very nice Lexus that she has. And that house is so beautiful. It's too bad you had to give all that up." Yushaf stood. "Would you mind if I got myself a glass of water?"

"No. That's fine." Merewether's mind was immediately fixated on his huge brick colonial house in northern Virginia, where he'd lived with his wife and their one daughter. The Lexus was the car he'd bought for himself last year. He'd been successful in financial matters, and had invested everything they owned in the stock market during the nineties, the greatest bull market in history. In 1999, when it seemed to peak, he'd pulled out his money, invested in treasury bonds, and bought himself a new car. And then he'd lost it all in the divorce, the cause of which was his own juvenile, sexually driven behavior. One of the young secretaries at the Pentagon was far too willing to play around for him to resist a temptation that he had not faced before. Throughout his life women simply hadn't looked his way. It was what he was accustomed to. When this one had, it had been too much for him to handle.

He thought of the fireplace that almost certainly had a fire in it, as his wife, also a basketball fan, settled in to watch the basketball game with his daughter. Without him. And it was all his fault. And he knew it. He hated himself for it.

The Pakistani came back into the living room and found Merewether sitting on the couch with his head back. He was sprawled out, his soft belly pressing his shirt over his belt. "Are you all right?"

Merewether sat up. "Yeah," he said gruffly. "Don't come in here without permission again. I'll call the police."

"I'm sorry. Perhaps I should have waited in the hallway, but I cannot stand long. My legs began—"

"Yeah, yeah. Fine. Whatever." Merewether looked at Yushaf and his thousand-dollar Italian suit. "What do you want?"

"Yes, right to business." Yushaf sat down in the threadbare chair across the coffee table from Merewether. "I understand you had a meeting recently. About starting a new TOPGUN school. It would be called the Nevada Fighter Weapons School and would use the U.S. MiG-29s from Wright-Patterson Air Force Base. They would fly out of Tonopah airfield in Nevada."

Merewether's eyes narrowed. "How the hell do you know *that*?"

"A friend told me," he said innocently. "It is my understanding, in fact, that the two naval officers are planning on resigning their commissions for the sole purpose of starting the school. I didn't know it was secret."

"It's not secret. But it just happened last week. I'm surprised you heard about it." Merewether studied him. "How *exactly* did you hear about it?"

"Let's just say that you are not my only friend in Washington."

Merewether was annoyed. "What's your point?"

"It is my understanding that you turned them down and told them it would never work."

"It's impractical. They haven't even thought it through well enough yet."

"I must differ," the Pakistani said. "It sounds brilliant to me, and it would alleviate the pressure that currently exists on TOPGUN and Red Flag to get more people through the school."

"Why does it matter to you?" Merewether demanded.

Yushaf shrugged, then paused. "I simply want you to make the best decisions you can," he replied. "But of course I do have an interest of my own," he continued, "and perhaps, one day, it could all work out. As you know, I want to get some of my pilots through your schools. It is not asking much. It is asking only what you have already promised, but so far . . ."

"You continue to remind me."

"So maybe this could be the solution we both need. Let my pilots come through this new school instead of TOPGUN."

"How do you figure I need this?"

"It could solve some of your problems, with people like me. And if you help *me,* your good friend . . . who knows? Perhaps I could help you, too." His hand went up as if in sudden recollection. "In fact, you've mentioned to me that you dislike this apartment." He looked around and nodded with understanding. "I'm sympathetic to that. A man of your stature should have a residence worthy of his position. Sadly, that was taken from you in a way that was outside your control. One of our embassy staff has been called back to Pakistan. Unfortunately, he just entered into a very long-term lease on a beautiful American house. He is no longer there, and the house sits empty." He looked at Merewether to evaluate his next sentence. "Who knows? Perhaps you could house-sit it until he comes back. And who knows when that will be? It could be a couple of years."

"Do you think I'm *stupid*?" Merewether asked.

Yushaf realized he had miscalculated. "Of course not. Why would you ask me that?"

"Lunches are one thing. A loaner car is one thing. But the

use of a house for two years? That's worth thousands of dollars!"

"It is yours if you are interested. I certainly do not want you to feel obligated. I know that house-sitting can be a burden when the house is furnished with Persian rugs and a state-of-the-art home theater system and the like. You'd have to take care of all of that. I understand it might be asking too much."

"Cut the bullshit. You're trying to influence my decision."

Yushaf smiled. "Of course I am. That is my *job* with the Pakistani embassy, to influence America to be a closer friend than it already is. What is wrong with that?"

"Nothing, until you start offering me things." Merewether was angry and tempted.

"Consider all that I have said withdrawn. I do not understand the American culture as well as I should. I did not intend to offer anything, simply to exchange conveniences."

"This private TOPGUN school would be nothing but a headache for me. A bunch of contracts, new applications for quotas by Navy and Air Force pilots. I'm sure it would cost the government money."

"I thought they would be paying the U.S. government leases on the airplanes and airfield."

"Yes, but they'll be charging for each American student that goes through."

Yushaf smelled an opening. He sat forward on the chair edge. He gestured enthusiastically with his hands. "But if those numbers are equal, it will cost the government *nothing*."

"What?"

"If you charge them enough to lease the airplanes and the airfield to put the military officers through the school, the net cost to the government would be zero. And then charge double—or *triple*—for the foreign students. Make up the difference and then some. You could lease the airfield and the airplanes to the school in exchange for a certain number of American pilots to go through. Even even. Then have foreign aircrew come through and charge them two or three times what the equivalent rate was for Americans. They would understand that. They would be willing to pay. The school would be profitable as a going concern, and the United States would be putting out no money at all."

Merewether looked at him unenthusiastically. "It would still be a pain in the ass."

"I don't think so. You could delegate to the right person, who could handle most of the details. You might look like a hero for finding a way to relieve all the pressure to get more aircrew trained. Everybody wants to go through the school, but very few ever get to. Open it up a little bit."

Merewether shook his head vaguely. "How would your pilots even get there? Would they fly all the way from Pakistan?"

"No. I have been in touch with several states about leasing four of their F-16Cs from their Air National Guard units for our pilots to fly. They were more than willing."

"Which states?" Merewether asked, stunned.

"California has already agreed."

"Before *we* have even agreed?"

"I have to make many plans."

"Whatever," Merewether said, losing interest.

The Pakistani decided to fire his last arrow. "It might also alleviate another looming problem for you."

"Like what?"

Yushaf stood up and walked around his chair as if he were about to leave. "I have heard that ever since those MiGs were bought, the United States has been anxious to test the missiles."

Merewether was startled. "What missiles?"

"The *five hundred* Russian-made air-to-air missiles that were bought from Moldova with the MiG-29s—"

"How did you know *that*?"

"And when the MiGs were purchased, there was a guarantee issued that those missiles would be test-fired, and the Navy and Air Force would know, from the telemetry, every last thing there was to know about them." The Pakistani spoke slowly, as if quoting a document that he had seen.

"How in the hell did you get that?"

"As I said, you are not my only friend."

Merewether was dumbfounded.

"Don't you see?" the Pakistani said encouragingly. "The reason the missiles have not been test-fired is that there are no airplanes in the United States that can fire them as they were designed to be fired. It takes the MiG radars as well. No one has flown the MiGs since they have been purchased.

"If you allow these Navy Lieutenants and their new TOP-GUN school to be your test facility, to keep the radars up, to load the missiles and test-fire them for you—you could even pay them for that—you would be a hero in the intelligence world, and everyone would then have access to the telemetry, and the Russian missiles would be known by United States military."

Merewether frowned. "Those Navy Lieutenants said they would disarm the MiGs. This would mean that they would have to keep them as legitimate fighters, capable of firing missiles."

"What is wrong with that? You can guard the missiles at all times. It should be without risk."

Merewether's mind spun through the possibilities. It actually might solve several problems. "You have any other cards? Anything else you got hiding out there that you want?"

The Pakistani smiled knowingly. "There is always something, isn't there?"

The Undersecretary nodded.

"We want the results of the missile tests."

"Is that it?"

"We are your strongest ally in South Asia, and you know it," he said with too much emphasis. "We *need* that information, because India flies the MiG-29 and has those same Russian missiles. We need to know it for the safety of our pilots." Yushaf lowered his voice. "And we need four of our pilots to be in the first class at that school."

"I think that's enough for me to think about tonight," Merewether said, standing. "Now, if you'll excuse me."

"No, I need to know, I'm sorry," Yushaf said, seeing the anger on Merewether's face. "I would like your commitment tonight. I am getting pressure from my home office. They don't believe I can produce results. If I don't, I will be recalled . . . I—"

"So what?"

"Thomas," Yushaf said, trying to keep the desperation out of his voice, "your country *owes* this to my country."

"How the hell do you figure that?"

"Do you not remember the largest battle the Americans have been involved in since Vietnam?"

"What?"

"Eighteen American Rangers and Delta Team members killed, five hundred to a thousand enemy killed, with thousands more wounded . . ."

"What?"

"Mogadishu. Somalia. You Americans were pinned down. Three of your Blackhawk helicopters were shot down. You were completely surrounded. The city was teeming with armed people who hate Americans. And who came to your rescue? Who charged into that city and pulled the Rangers and other Army men out?"

"Who?"

"Pakistani armor led the column back into Mogadishu and into the fight to rescue the Americans." He paused. "Can you not allow a few of our pilots to train here? Is that too much to ask?"

"I don't know much about Mogadishu . . ."

"You can look into it. I am not making it up."

"When was that?"

"1993."

"Well, I don't know . . ."

Yushaf was in deep trouble. There was only one acceptable answer. He couldn't leave any cards unplayed. "I have been listening to you over the past few weeks. I detect that you are in some financial trouble. Perhaps I could arrange a loan . . ." He watched Merewether's face for any offense. There was none. "It would allow you to take care of all your problems."

"Yushaf, I can't pay back a damned loan. Every cent I make goes to my wife and her house and her car—"

"It would need to be paid back only when you were able to pay it back at one time, in one lump sum, in cash. Until then no problem, no interest."

Merewether thought of what he could do with money. It would solve everything. He could quit his job and finally go do whatever he wanted to do. "How much of a loan did you have in mind?"

"Without knowing your needs, I could only estimate, but I thought something around two hundred fifty thousand dollars might help."

Merewether tried not to gasp audibly. It was ten times his current net worth. He looked at Yushaf and noticed that he was sweating. "How soon could you get the . . . loan to me?"

"Tomorrow."

"If I have it tomorrow, I'll approve the school and get you your quotas. How many?"

Yushaf took a breath. It felt like the first one he'd taken in days. "Four."

"I'll see you tomorrow."

8

Luke opened the front door and walked out in his flight suit and boots to retrieve the morning newspaper. He had an early brief, but he lacked his usual enthusiasm. It had started to feel pointless. He knew that his time was limited. It was hard to hurry to work, excited to get every day under way as he had since reporting to TOPGUN. He'd begun to feel like an outsider.

He glanced up at the sky the way he always did. It was cool and clear. The stars were fading. He bent over and picked up the newspaper on the long dirt driveway and noticed a black sedan parked in the mouth of the driveway just off the state road. It startled him. He was annoyed he hadn't seen it before. There was never any traffic on the country road in front of their house, and no one ever turned down his driveway by mistake. This sedan had turned down and stopped. Luke felt exposed and vulnerable. He looked at the car again. There was no frost on the windshield and no dew on the hood.

The hell with this, he thought. He walked straight at the car, armed with only his newspaper. He approached the driver's side. His muscles tensed as he approached. He noticed that the windows were tinted just dark enough to keep him from seeing inside. He could see a man's hand on the steering wheel and slowed as he got nearer to the car. He wanted to go back the other way. The hair was beginning to tingle on the back of his neck.

The driver's door suddenly opened, and a tall man in his twenties climbed out. "Lieutenant Henry," he said quietly as he walked toward Luke. "We've been waiting for you."

"Who are you?" Luke said as he started backing up, shocked to hear his name from someone he'd never seen before in his life.

"I'm Jason Townes. You have a minute?"

Luke put his hands on his hips and tried to control his breathing as he examined the young man, who was about his size and very intense-looking. "What are you doing sitting in front of my house at six in the morning?"

"We need to talk to you."

"*We* who?" Luke asked, his annoyance growing.

The young man glanced at the sedan, and the back door opened. Merewether got out, closed the door, and adjusted the coat on his blue pin-striped suit. "Good morning, Lieutenant."

Luke was speechless. He couldn't imagine what the Undersecretary of Defense was doing in front of his house on a Tuesday morning at six o'clock. It was disturbing. "Mr. Undersecretary," Luke said. "I'm surprised to see you here, obviously."

Merewether nodded sympathetically. "I wanted to catch you before you went to work, but I didn't want to call and wake your pregnant wife."

Luke's eyes narrowed. "How did you know she was pregnant?"

"You told me in Washington."

Luke didn't remember even mentioning his wife. "Thank you. That was considerate. But why didn't you write or send me an e-mail? You left me with the impression in D.C. that you didn't have any interest in me at all."

"I'm afraid we didn't treat you as we should have, and frankly, I didn't give your proposal the consideration it deserved. But since you left, I have." The Undersecretary looked around, pleased with the surprise he had occasioned and the image he had pulled off. It was the kind of thing he loved to do—show up when not expected and imitate a government official who actually knew what the hell he was doing. "Is there somewhere we can talk?"

"This is fine right here," Luke replied. "I don't want to wake my pregnant wife."

"Right," Merewether replied. He stood awkwardly in the middle of the drive. "We looked at the PowerPoint presentation you left for us in hard copy, and the written report you did. I would like to discuss it with you further."

Luke's heart jumped, then quickly returned to normal as reality reasserted itself. "Go ahead."

"I think the idea of starting a new, civilian-run TOPGUN school is frankly rather brilliant. It would give the United States government several options and outlets, as well as employ the assets we've purchased that are currently sitting idle, in addition to keeping Tonopah active, which is to the benefit of the airfield. Airfields are meant to be used, not sit and gather dust."

"What do you have in mind?" Luke asked cautiously.

"The United States government would like to accept your proposal."

Luke's eyes widened. It couldn't be.

"On two conditions."

"What?"

"First, that you allow the United States to send through your school certain . . . foreign students who have been clamoring to get into our TOPGUN or Red Flag for a long time. This would be a means for us to encourage and . . . um, reward our allies who do not have the same training opportunities that U.S. pilots have. Sort of a diplomatic plum."

"What foreign students?" Luke asked, searching for future problems.

"I don't really have any in mind right now. It could be any

number of them with whom we currently have defense treaties or to whom we sell arms; but they would have to be capable of accomplishing the rigorous training conducted at the school."

"Who would decide who comes?"

The Undersecretary looked into Luke's eyes. "I would."

"What about clearances?"

"That would all be in my area of responsibility. They would all be preapproved. You would simply need to give me the quotas I request, and I would then tell you who would be coming. The countries would pay you directly, and you could charge whatever you want. Perhaps an amount substantially over your actual cost, so that you can make a profit. The U.S. students could be charged at cost, which would include your amortized expenses of the airplane leases, the airfield, and the like. In fact, we could even reserve certain quotas for American students that would equal the amount attributable to the lease value of the MiGs and the air base. You could charge the foreign students whatever you want and get whatever you can from them. That's where you would get your profit."

Luke was amazed. "You've actually thought this through. I'd never even thought of that approach."

"There are many possible scenarios."

Luke looked around to see if anyone was nearby. The road was silent, and the sky was growing lighter by the minute. "You said there were two conditions."

"Yes. The second will be acceptable to you. I promise."

"What is it?"

Merewether took a long time to remove a cigarette from a pack and light it with a gold lighter that looked very expensive. He inhaled deeply and looked at Luke again as he slipped the lighter into his coat pocket. "As you probably know, when we purchased the MiG-29s from Moldova, we also purchased five hundred Russian air-to-air missiles."

Luke nodded.

"It has long been our intention to conduct actual air-to-air test firings of those missiles with telemetry, so we can get the most accurate information possible on their performance. It has never been done because we don't have airplanes capable of firing them. The MiGs are capable. So part of this deal is that you would agree to test the Russian missiles from the MiG-29s within the first twelve months of the school's being open. That way we can get the telemetry we need."

"Seriously? You want us to actually fire them?"

The Undersecretary smiled. "I thought you might be agreeable to that condition."

"We'd get *paid* for that work?"

"Aha, the businessman wakes. Yes. Of course. You would be paid handsomely through a government contract for your work."

"Why did you need to come here to tell me that? Why not call?"

"I'm not actually here to see you. I'm on my way to Tonopah to see how much needs to be done to get the air base ready. I flew into Reno, and you were nearby. I thought I'd stop and tell you myself."

"So what do I do now?" Luke asked.

Merewether grinned in a way that made Luke uneasy. "Someone from my office will be in touch. Your letter of resignation has been accepted, as well as that of your friend, Lieutenant Thurmond. You'll both be out of the Navy in sixty days." Merewether extended his hand.

Luke smiled as he shook Merewether's hand and tried to control his excitement. He couldn't wait to tell Katherine. "I look forward to it," he said, as Merewether returned to his car and it began backing out of his long driveway. Watching it go, all he could think of though was what Thud's father had said in their meeting: "Don't trust the government, don't trust the government." But then Thud's father was paranoid.

* * *

BILL Morrissey wasn't accustomed to getting interesting data that didn't fit with other things he knew. He was used to getting no data, or bad data. But having good, hard intelligence that he couldn't explain drove him crazy. And now there was more. He looked at Cindy Frohm who had asked to see him right away. She had new information that had just come across her desk. "Talk to me," he said.

"The armory was attacked in the middle of the night. Pakistan isn't telling anyone about it. Not even us, officially. We got this through our Air Force attaché in Islamabad. We've had it confirmed. Ten or more men attacked the armory, killed the gate guard and three guards at the armory itself. No shots fired by the guards at all. Two of them were found miles away and two at the armory."

"And this was on a Pakistani Air Force base."

"Yes."

"How the hell do you break into an armory on an Air Force base? You just walk in?"

"Hard to say. Pakistan isn't sharing any of this with us."

"What was taken?"

"They're not sure."

Morrissey rolled his eyes. "How can they not be sure?"

"Whoever took the weapons destroyed the records."

"Isn't that where we think they kept some of their nukes?"

"Right, but not the warheads. Just the bombs that were to carry the nuclear warheads."

"So were those taken?"

"Nope. We're sure their nuclear program is unaffected. And their nuclear warheads are known to be stored elsewhere."

Morrissey was puzzled. Especially when he tried to match it to the border incident. Warhead-grade plutonium and nuclear-warhead-carrying bomb casing. That was what was common. Except they didn't get the plutonium at the border, and they didn't take the bombs from the armory. "Why destroy the records?" he asked.

"Only reason would be because they didn't want anyone to know what they took."

"But why? What's so unique or valuable that they wouldn't want anyone to know?"

"Only the nuclear-capable bombs, but those are all accounted for."

Morrissey closed his eyes and rested his chin on his hand. "I don't get it. You?"

Frohm was equally confused. "No, sir. I don't."

"See anything about this that makes it look like it has anything to do with the U.S.?"

"No, sir. I don't."

"Me neither. But I sure don't like what's going on over there. Keep working it," he said as he walked out of her office.

AFTER the Undersecretary's strange early-morning visit to Luke, it was as if someone had said "Open sesame." All resistance seemed to fall away. Tonopah Air Base was his, subject only to getting those who had been working there on active duty off the base. The contracts that would be required appeared in a few short days, and even Katherine's skeptical eye as the new general counsel of the Nevada Fighter Weapons School, Inc., couldn't find anything to complain about.

The former TOPGUN instructors whom Luke and Thud called to ask to join them were falling all over themselves to make sure they got picked to work for this new school. It didn't seem to matter what they were doing; they all offered to quit the next day if Luke wanted them to.

Once Thud had gotten up the nerve to actually submit his letter of resignation to Gun, he'd jumped in with both feet.

And Thud's father had transferred the initial money to the corporation. Thud had seen it as his opportunity to mend fences with his father. Not only would he be doing what he wanted—flying fighters—but he'd be doing what his father had wanted him to do—run a business. Thud's father had finally dropped the other shoe, though. He told them that his financial support was contingent on his getting to fly the MiG-29. Luke had initially balked, but when he remembered that Dr. Thurmond had a couple thousand hours in the F-105 in Vietnam, Luke figured he might actually be able to fly the MiG. They'd start him in the two-seater and see how he did.

Luke and Thud had just gotten back from Germany and had fallen in love with the MiG-29 even more than they'd expected to. It was a rocket. A fast, maneuverable, predictable, and deadly fighter. Vlad had been an amazing instructor, teaching them not only how to fly the Fulcrum but also how to employ its weapons. Luke and Thud were glad to have him.

Luke stepped over a ladder that had been left in the passageway and walked up the stairs to the second deck of the hangar that was going to be the headquarters of the Nevada Fighter Weapons School at Tonopah.

Vlad and the others who'd come over with MAPS had already arrived and spread out in the hangar, taking over spaces Luke hadn't even thought about yet. The base was vast and full of opportunity but could easily become disorganized.

MAPS had opened the dormitories and set up residence. Vlad was clearly in charge and had organized it in a military fashion, with "officers" in the fancier, slightly plusher facility and "enlisted" in another.

Luke had also decided that they would wear uniforms, specifically flight suits. He wanted to wear military insignia, but not American insignia. That would be improper, and probably illegal. With Vlad's help he decided that they would wear the insignia of the Russian Air Force, since they would be generally imitating Russian tactics.

Thud walked into Luke's office carrying rolled-up diagrams the size of blueprints. "You been down to the hangar?"

"Not today," Luke replied.

"You should see all those Russian mechanics. They look like a MASH unit waiting for patients. They got everything lined up by bureau number."

"Are those the drawings for the tail design?"

Thud nodded vigorously. "Check it out." He put the two pieces of paper flat on Luke's desk next to each other. One was a drawing of a MiG-29 with a desert camouflage paint scheme, the other a close-up of the MiG-29's tail with the new tail design.

Luke studied the paint scheme first. "Not bad," he said quickly. "But I'm thinking maybe we go with a little different desert camouflage. I was thinking something a bit more angular. More straight lines. We might even use water-based paint and change it every few days just to keep our students on their toes. Blue-sky camouflage one day, desert camouflage the next, flat gray the next. Always keep 'em thinking." He pushed the camouflaged MiG-29 aside and studied the other picture. It was a silver circle with a black star in the middle of it. "I love this. It looks sort of sinister."

Thud laughed. "My thought *exactly*. Go with it?"

"Do it," Luke said, handing it back to him. "On all the tails and wings. And get the patches and stickers under way."

Thud looked at his watch. "The first C-17s are supposed to touch down in five minutes."

Luke jumped up. "Let's go watch."

The mechanics waited anxiously in their spotless dark blue coveralls for their beloved MiG-29s so they could go to work. Each had memorized what needed to be done with his airplane. Vlad had assigned a team of mechanics to each plane, with those highly skilled in a particular area assigned to the aircraft with the greatest needs in that area. There weren't enough mechanics for each airplane to have its own complete team, but there was one person assigned to be the maintenance chief for each MiG, with others to help. They would share and assist each other as necessary, but Vlad wanted to make it perfectly clear that one person would be responsible for the maintenance condition of each individual MiG.

Luke looked for Vlad and saw him at the far end of the hangar. "Vlad," Luke called.

"Yes," he replied, instantly breaking off his other conversation in Russian.

"The transports are on final approach."

Vlad's face lit up. "That is very good news. I will tell everyone. We are ready for them, Colonel."

"It's 'Commander.' "

"Your insignia is of a Russian Lieutenant Colonel."

"We're going to call ourselves by Navy rank."

"If you insist," Vlad said, confused. "Even though it's the end of the day, I'd like the mechanics to begin working on the airplanes tonight. I want them to get in and identify any problems so we can be sure where we stand. If we don't have big problems that we do not know about now, we will be ready in time."

"Sure," Luke said, feeling particularly responsible and in charge. "I want every single jet to be in perfect condition and ready to fly within thirty days. You think we can do that?"

Vlad replied, "Yes. Of course."

"I want the two-seater ready to fly in a week. What do you think?"

Vlad considered for a moment. "Unless we find something we do not anticipate, we should be able to do that, too."

Luke smiled. "What would we do without you?"

Vlad laughed. "You would have many broken airplanes!"

The enormous Air Force C-17 cargo plane was on final approach to Tonopah. Luke glanced up at the tower and saw the controllers working efficiently at their jobs. The C-17 was so big it appeared to move at the speed of a walk. Each of the cargo jets carried two MiG-29s inside with the wings and tails removed.

The lead C-17 flared gently, touched down at the end of the runway, and rolled to a stop. It taxied to the flight line directly in front of Luke and Thud. Two men quickly put chocks behind its wheels and told the pilot to shut down his engines. As he did, the second C-17 touched down on the runway with a third on long final. The cargo plane's large ramp moved down slowly and touched the tarmac. Two Air Force Sergeants wearing ear protectors came down the ramp and looked for someone in authority. Luke raised his hand, and the men crossed over to him.

The older Sergeant looked at Luke's flight suit and the unfamiliar insignia and hesitated. He wasn't sure how to conduct himself. Finally he saluted Luke and said loudly, "Good morning, sir."

"Good morning, Sergeant," Luke replied.

"These your MiGs, sir?"

"They are for now," Luke said, realizing the implications of what he was saying.

"Where do you want them?"

"What number is this one?"

The Sergeant took a piece of paper out of his pocket and looked at it. "First out is 109904, then 110433."

Vlad pointed down the tarmac. "The first is the two-seater. It goes down there. The other is in bay three."

The Sergeant looked at Vlad, whom he had not asked anything, and quickly correlated the insignia he wore with his heavy accent. He suddenly didn't like his mission, taking direction and giving a Russian MiG to a Russian pilot on American soil. Something was out of balance, but he couldn't quite figure out what he was dealing with well enough to form any hard opinions. "Yes, sir," the Sergeant said brusquely as he turned and began indicating to the other Sergeant to pull the MiG-29 out of the C-17.

The second C-17 taxied toward them as the third touched down. Two more were lined up in the pattern to land at Tonopah and discharge their cargo of Russian MiG fighters.

Vlad had walked down to alert the mechanics that their jets would be first out. One after another, the C-17s taxied loudly to the hangar and the Sergeants in charge of the cargo supervised the rolling-off of the blotchy, dismembered MiGs. Each MiG was rolled to its place in front of the hangar ready to undergo either major surgery or simple reassembly. MAPS had it planned to the last bolt, parts waiting.

Luke looked at Thud standing next to him, a big grin on his face. "I think we ought to let Vlad fly with us."

Thud tore his eyes away from the last MiG being unloaded. "Just like that?"

Luke nodded. "When I was in Germany, I was impressed. He took me through every maneuver you could imagine. I felt like he made me competent in the airplane in ten hours." He looked at Thud. "He's a good instructor."

Thud watched Vlad scramble around the two-seat MiG with unfettered enthusiasm and energy. He looked back at Luke and shrugged, then nodded. "You're the boss."

KARACHI was famous throughout the world as a place where you could buy or sell anything. The port served not only Pakistan, but all of the upper region of Central Asia: Afghanistan, Kazakhstan, and Uzbekistan—anywhere roads or railroads could reach. While not the capital of Pakistan, it was the largest city in the region. It was also famous for its corruption and crime.

Ships were loaded and offloaded continuously. Some arrived at night just so their unloading or loading could be done before fewer eyes.

Riaz Khan stood back from the window to avoid being seen. He watched the ordinary-looking cargo ship of Liberian registry. It carried bulk cargo and containers, but preferred bulk. The ship had its name painted in rusty white letters on the stern: EIGHT SEAS. It had large cranes for loading the few shipping containers it carried on deck and open hatches for the bulk cargo. The cranes lifted large pallets of wool and lowered them into the hold. The men supervising the loading looked bored. They also cursed the crane operators or anyone else nearby for their having to load the ship at two o'clock in the morning. The Filipino ship's crew supervised the loading of the hold and told the dockworkers when it was full. The last pallet was placed on deck, and a tarp was placed over the wool. The cranes swung over for the two containers to be loaded aboard and lifted them effortlessly. The containers swung to the deck of the ship and were carefully lowered to their spots on the deck.

When the containers were secure, the loading lights cast large shadows behind them. The Pakistani dockworkers were done. The loading had gone flawlessly, in spite of the tension they'd felt. They knew that their load was important to someone but weren't sure who or why. They didn't really care. As long as they got paid and the ship sailed on time, they were content. They walked away to the next ship in an endless stream of ships, their bodies showing their fatigue even in the low light.

The ship's crew prepared to get under way immediately. They all knew that their orders were to sail the instant the containers were secured to the deck. They scurried to their places. The captain yelled to the men on the pier to release the lines for the *Eight Seas*. As soon as the massive, frayed lines were free, the two tugs on the port side pulled slowly, and the rusty ship inched away from the pier. The *Eight Seas* sat low in the inky water and pointed out to the Indian Ocean.

Riaz turned from the window as the ship got under way. He didn't trust anyone to do anything right. Not anymore. He would personally supervise everything himself if that was what it took. A dark, unremarkable car was waiting for Riaz when he came out of the building onto the street. The back door opened as he approached. He looked straight ahead and made sure his face stayed in the shadows. He slipped quickly into the backseat, and the car pulled away. They drove down the waterfront, past rows of cranes, ships, and men, to another pier where another ship was just loading its containers.

Riaz touched the shoulder of the driver, who slowed the car as they all watched a Pakistani customs official approach the ship and call for the loading supervisor. Riaz didn't like what he was seeing at all. The official pointed up into the spotlights to the container that was being swung onto the ship. The loading supervisor looked angry as he replied. Riaz stared through the tinted window.

The customs officer gestured quickly, with authority. The supervisor shook his head in frustration. The crane stopped, and the container, the size of a semi, hovered thirty feet off the pier and began to turn slowly.

"Call," Riaz said quickly.

The man next to him in the back put the handheld radio to his mouth and quickly transmitted in Urdu. He received a click as an acknowledgment. The men in the car waited as the customs officer continued to argue with the loading supervisor. The customs man was suddenly interrupted and reached for the radio on his belt. He pulled it out and began talking into it. He looked at the container and went on talking back to the radio while waving his arm. He was confused and put out. He argued into his radio, then finally capitulated. He spoke to the supervisor, who nodded his approval.

The container began its slow trip to the ship again and was finally lowered to the deck.

Riaz nodded, and the car pulled out of the shadow of a building and onto the Karachi street.

9

"**C**rumb!" Luke bounded across the room and extended his hand to Delbert Crummey, one of his favorite Navy pilots and the one with the funniest name, a name that gave rise to absolutely endless jokes. His enthusiasm was legendary. "How you been?"

"Stick!" Crumb said. He'd left quite a mark as an instructor at TOPGUN, until he, like so many others, decided not to go back to sea. He got out of the Navy and took a job flying Falcon jets for a large company. As far as civilian flying went, it wasn't bad. There wasn't any high-G inverted flying, but Falcons were good performing jets, and once he got over having passengers, he'd grown not to hate it. But as soon as Luke had called, he offered to quit his job that day. He'd said he missed the flying, but he missed the camaraderie even more. "Where's Thud?"

"Next door. Let's go see him." They walked from Luke's office to Thud's. "Thud! Crumb's here!"

Thud shook his hand vigorously. "Welcome aboard! It's great to have you."

"You're the *XO*?" Crumb asked, surprised.

"Yeah. Benefits of partial ownership. We get to appoint ourselves as the bosses."

"Who writes your fitness report?"

"Nobody, except maybe Luke."

"And who writes *your* fitness report?" Crumb asked Luke.

"Nobody. That's the beauty of it. How do you like the setup?"

"This is unbelievable," Crumb said, looking around. "This is like the greatest job in the history of the world. Thanks a lot for calling."

"Did you see the MiGs?"

"Yeah. I hadn't ever seen one in person." He glowed. "That's a beautiful airplane—or at least somewhere there are beautiful MiG-29s, but yours look like *shit* right now. They need a lot of work. The one I saw looks like a jalopy you'd find in a barn that you try to turn into a hot rod."

"Don't let the paint fool you. They're in good shape. Did you see the two-seater?"

"Yeah. That's a good thing, so we don't prang ourselves on our first flight."

"It's supposed to be ready to go Monday."

"When is everyone else due to get here?"

"Monday except for Lips, who won't be here until next month, and Stamp, who has a bunch of air shows to fly."

"So what's the plan?"

"Vlad has set up a ground school and a flight instruction plan. Believe it or not, this guy who's the head of the MAPS group for maintenance is a former Russian instructor pilot in the MiG-29. He's going to do a lot of the instruction for us and run the ground school."

"A Russian?" Crumb's eyes narrowed, and he grew serious. "You're going to let a Russian fly as an instructor?"

"Sure. Why not?"

"How do you know he's not a Russian spy?"

"What the hell would Russia get out of spying on *us*? Maybe learn all about the MiG-29?"

"No, the syllabus. The whole way of running a TOPGUN school. I don't know. Doesn't it bother you? We've all flown as instructors. We're probably going to do it exactly the same way. Russia could never get inside the real TOPGUN. So maybe they sent him here to get it from us."

"Hell, Crumb. We're going to be giving instruction to foreigners. This is no big secret deal. We might even do it on an unclass level. It might be secret level, but certainly not anything higher than that. I'm not worried about it. But if you see something that bugs you, tell Hayes. He's the resident spook."

Crumb knew the whole story about Hayes. "I will. Too bad about his discharge."

"Yeah."

"How will I know which one is Vlad?"

Thud smirked. "Just follow your nose. He's down with the jets. Speaking of which, let's go down there and get a sandwich."

They walked downstairs into the main hangar area, to a small deli that some of the employees had carved out of a space at the back. They'd scrounged an old refrigerator, and on the counter next to it were mayonnaise, bread, mustard, and some meat and cheese that had come together as something of a center of gravity where people could fix lunch sandwiches. Luke asked Thud, "How's the Officers' Club?"

"Almost done. I've got a new name: 94th Aero Squadron."

"What's that?"

"The only Navy ace of World War I flew for them."

"Perfect. Who's going to head it up?"

"I'm not sure yet," he said, glancing at Crumb. "But Crumb here would be a good candidate."

"Thanks for volunteering, Crumb," Luke said, his voice full of feigned appreciation. "Thud'll tell you all about it."

Crumb frowned and smiled at the same time. "So . . . it really is just like the Navy? You check in and they start dumping all the shitty little jobs on you right away? It's like I never left! What just happened? Am I now the coffee mess officer?"

"You're the O' Club officer. In charge of all the petty little details," Thud said. He turned to Luke. "That reminds me; the guy from my father's company is here to interview. He's waiting topside."

Luke was unenthusiastic. "Remind me why we need to hire this guy."

"He just heard about the company and asked my father if he could come interview with us."

"Right. But what exactly does he bring to it? What's his area?"

"Said he'd do anything."

"What does he do for your father?" Luke asked.

"Security guard."

Luke finished putting his sandwich together and glanced over his shoulder at Thud with a "you've got to be kidding me" look. "We're set for security. Remember? It's part of our contract. We can't just hire some minimum-wage flunky to join them. Why are we doing this?"

"I told my father we'd interview him. My father likes him."

"Here we go," Luke said, with a tone of having been offended in a way that was anticipated, "We do things just because your father hints at it?"

"Hey, the way I see it, if my father asks us to do something that isn't *illegal,* we *do* it. If he *tells* us to hire somebody, we will."

"Fine, you interview him. Hire him. I've got too many things going on."

"Nope. We're going to interview him together."

"Says who?" Luke asked, annoyed.

"Says me."

"What is this, a mutiny?"

"No, just some friendly advice."

Luke slapped his sandwich onto a paper plate and headed to his office. Before he could take one bite, Thud walked back in with a middle-aged man whose gut was hanging so far over his belt that Luke couldn't even tell what his huge brass buckle said. He was wearing a black baseball cap that had "51" on the front in numbers so large they could be read a hundred yards away. It was the kind of baseball cap you would see at a tractor pull. It sat on top of his small head like a dunce cap. It appeared to be made out of Styrofoam, or the cheapest polyester possible. It puckered in the front and had mesh around the sides to the back. He showed absolutely no inclination to remove it as he walked into Luke's office.

The man was about five feet ten and weighed at least two hundred fifty pounds. He had a swollen, serious look on his face and watery eyes behind silver-framed glasses. Luke stood up. "Hi. My name is Luke Henry."

"Raymond Westover, sir," the man replied in a low, confident voice. He took Luke's hand with his own small, pudgy one.

"Sit down, please," Luke said, pointing to the chair in front of his desk. He rubbed his hand on his flight suit to remove the man's sweat. Thud sat next to Westover across from Luke. "So. You want to come to work for the Nevada Fighter Weapons School."

"Yes."

"Why?"

"Because you're here."

Luke smiled. "Like why men climb mountains—because they're there." He looked at Thud. "Who said that? Was it Sir Edmund Hillary? Or . . . that guy whose body they found frozen like an Otter Pop on Mount Everest a couple of years ago? What the hell was his name?"

"Mallory, I think."

"Yeah." Luke returned his gaze to Raymond. There was no recognition in his eyes. "What do you mean, because we're here?"

Raymond looked around, pointed to the floor, and said enthusiastically, "Because you're *here*. Here, meaning . . . *here*."

"Tonopah?"

"Exactly. Tonopah."

"What's so special about Tonopah?"

Raymond's eyes narrowed. "You don't know?"

"Sure. A perfect airfield," Luke said, knowing it wasn't what Raymond had in mind.

"Sir, I understand why you guys want to be here," Raymond said, looking back and forth at the two principals. "I'd just be excited to work out here in the desert."

Luke decided to do it a different way. "What kind of work did you have in mind?"

"Security. I've been a security guard for over thirty years now, sir. Never had an incident on my watch."

Luke nodded understandingly. "Unfortunately, our security is being handled by a private company. The DOD had to sign off on them. They have lots of experience in this sort of thing. They do their own hiring."

Raymond was visibly disappointed. "I can do anything. I'm pretty handy. I can fix toilets, replace electrical outlets, things like that."

Luke nodded again. "Well, we don't really have a handyman. I'm not sure—"

Thud jumped in. "How about a deli?"

"What about a deli?" Raymond asked.

"Would you be willing to build and maintain a deli for the aircrew and maintenance people to eat at during the week?"

"I don't know much about that," Raymond said, thinking it over. "I've never been much of a cook. Glenda always fixes my lunch."

"Who's Glenda?"

"The little lady. Thirty-one years."

"Bring her. She can make the food, and you can take care of the deli and other things. You can do it as a team. Do you think she'd be interested?"

Raymond considered it. "She may very well be. She's kind of just knocking around the house right now. Sort of looking for something to do, now that the kids are gone and all."

"Can she cook?"

Raymond nodded vigorously enough for the jowls on his cheeks to move. "Yes. She can cook very well."

Luke couldn't resist. "So, Raymond," he said, "what's up with the hat?"

Raymond looked at Luke intently. "*Area* 51."

"What?"

"Area 51. It's out here. It's *all* here."

"UFOs," Luke said, finally understanding. He glanced at Thud, who was trying not to snicker. "You follow UFO sightings?"

"Yes, sir. I've even written articles for *UFO Today*."

"*That's* what you meant by 'here.' "

"This is one of the places that the UFOs have landed. It's well documented. I'm thinking maybe I'll see some."

Thud turned in his chair and looked hard at Raymond. "Can you and Glenda do the work on the deli without that interfering?"

"Yes, sir. Extraterrestrial Highway is driving distance from here, but I won't have to go there all that much. I think you can see more from here, frankly," he said in a tone of secrecy. "I think more happens up here than over at that Groom Lake. That's been picked clean. They know people are expecting things over there. I think I'll be more likely to see something—"

"Thanks for coming," Thud said, standing up. He shook Raymond's hand.

Luke also stood and shook Raymond's hand. "We'll give you a call as soon as we decide," Luke said.

"Look forward to it." Raymond's mind had started to work. "How big a deli you anticipate?"

"We hadn't really thought about it," Luke answered. "But

the more I do, I think something with tables and chairs, maybe even an outdoor patio."

"Maybe even a jukebox," Thud said.

"That would be great." Raymond nodded. "I can build anything, you know. I'd like to get right on it if you guys are ready. Just give me a call." Raymond waited for one of them to say something, then realized they weren't going to. He turned and walked out of the room.

When his footsteps died away, Thud turned to Luke. "Sorry. I had no idea he was off."

Luke smiled. "He'll be fun to have around. The students will love the whole UFO thing. We'll have to make sure he keeps copies of *UFO Today* around the deli. Think he can handle it?"

Thud nodded. "My dad said he was a steady employee. He just has some weird ideas."

"Put him to work. Sure hope Glenda can cook—"

Just then Hayes came into the office, breathless. "I'm going to forward a call. It's important," he said.

The phone rang, and Luke glanced at his untouched sandwich and picked up the phone. He was annoyed that he hadn't had more warning of whatever it was that was so important. "Yes, sir," he replied as Hayes and Thud looked on. He nodded, listening. "Where? Why there? Yes, sir. No, not a problem. Yes, I am, sir. Very much, sir. Thank you. Yes. Good-bye."

Luke put down the phone and smiled. "We've got our first students," he said. "That was the Undersecretary's office. We have four students for the first class, four foreign students."

"Where from?" Thud asked.

"Pakistan."

Hayes frowned. "Pakistan? Why?"

"What's the matter with that? They fly American airplanes. They face India on the other side of the border.

They've had two wars with India, and they still kill each other over Kashmir about every day. And the kicker, probably the reason that we got the deal, is . . . what's the front-line fighter for India?"

Hayes nodded. "MiG-29."

"Exactly. So if you were Pakistan, where would you go for training?" Luke stood. "Now we just have to get the other twelve students lined up."

Hayes wanted more information. "What were you writing? You wrote something down when you were talking on the phone."

Luke turned around quickly, recalling just that. "Oh, yeah. He gave me the name of their OIC. Head pilot. A Major"—he looked at the piece of paper and tried to read his own writing—"Riaz Khan, of the Pakistani Air Force."

"Khan?" Hayes said, frowning. "I hope he isn't any relationship to the Khan who's the head of the ISI."

"What's that?" Luke asked.

"Internal security division for Pakistan. Sort of their FBI and CIA rolled into one. They're mean and nasty. And they're deeply involved with the Taliban in Afghanistan."

Thud was lost. "Who?"

"The Islamic ruling party of Afghanistan. They're very dangerous. Plus, I don't need to remind you, it's the Taliban that hid and defended Osama bin Laden for so long."

The humor had drained out of Luke's face. "You think we ought to be worried about this?"

Hayes considered. The last thing he wanted to do was jeopardize the first class. "The Undersecretary is responsible for their security clearances. It's not really our problem. But I sure as hell would have picked some other students if it had been up to me."

"Does this go on your to-do list?" Luke asked.

Hayes nodded. "I got a real uneasy feeling when I heard

Pakistan. Khan's a common name in Pakistan. Chances of him being related to the head of the ISI are pretty low. But still, I don't know. I'll give it some thought. Next time I talk to the Undersecretary's office, I'll remind him that we'll need copies—*written* copies—of the clearances for all the students, including the Pakistanis."

"Fair enough," Luke said. "Guess what they're going to do for jets?"

"Fly their F-16s from Pakistan?"

"Nope. They're going to lease four F-16s from the California Air National Guard. How clever is that? Let's put that on the agenda for the next department heads meeting. Maybe we can set up some kind of a pipeline so other foreign students can do that. Why don't you get on the horn with the air national guard units west of the Mississippi to see if they'd be up for that. We can have a list."

"You got it," Hayes said. He was about to leave, then turned toward Luke. "You wouldn't mind if I just did a little checking into this guy, would you?"

"How?"

"My brother."

Luke nodded. "Good idea. Can't have too much knowledge."

LUKE stood in front of the energy-charged room in his khaki flight suit. Russian pilot wings were embroidered on his nametag, with NFWS and STICK embroidered underneath the wings. He wore the newly designed NFWS patch on his right shoulder, with a black background and a gray F/A-18 in the foreground. Superimposed over the F/A-18 was a MiG gunsight. It was an F/A-18 caught in a MiG gunsight, a reversal of the TOPGUN patch, which has a MiG-21 caught in an American gunsight. Luke's round patch read around the outside, NEVADA FIGHTER WEAPONS SCHOOL. It was the same patch that would be handed out to graduates of his school. One patch for each graduate. It was Luke's hope that this patch would be worn as proudly as the TOPGUN patch was worn by the few who earned it.

The newly completed ready room was on the second deck of the hangar. It still smelled of fresh paint. All except one of the newly hired instructors were there. They were all wearing their NFWS flight suits with Russian insignia. Each had completed the ground school and at least his introductory flight in the MiG-29. Several had completed the syllabus. For the first time the squadron was intact. All but one of the pilots were aboard, and all the administrative and maintenance people were in place.

The ready room itself was a study in aviation decor. On one wall it had silhouettes of every major fighter airplane in the world, in the same scale. Hanging underneath the silhouettes at the end of twelve-inch dowel rods were models of each fighter, built to perfection, all in the same scale.

Luke stood at the lectern, his hands on its sides, and got everyone's attention. "Good morning," he said.

They all smiled. "Good morning, Skipper," one said loudly.

"Do we have to call you 'Skipper'?" another asked.

"Absolutely. As each of you knows, this company will be run exactly as a Navy fighter squadron is run. We will have pilot duties, instructor duties, collateral duties, a chain of command, and thirty days of vacation a year. One big difference, though, is we will pay you exactly *twice* what your counterparts in the Navy are paid. Your pay is based on twice the published Navy pilot's scale for the same rank. That makes it very easy to track. It should also make you want to write your congressmen to convince them that Navy pilots are underpaid. Feel free." He smiled.

"Are we all here?"

"Everybody except Stamp and Lips," Luke replied.

"Stamp's coming?"

"Yep. And get this: Who knows what Stamp's doing right now?"

"Some air show thing?" Pug asked.

"Yep. He's flying a plane that has SMIRNOFF VODKA painted on the side. Anybody know what kind of plane?"

"Seventeen."

"Yep. A MiG-17. He and his partner own *two* of them. They fly them in air shows. Hot deal, but not quite like flying as a TOPGUN instructor in MiG-29s. He'll be here next week."

"Is he quitting the MiG-17 thing?"

"Nope. He's going to do that on the weekends. He's going to live in San Jose, where he's based, and commute here in his MiG."

"What?" Sluf asked.

"As I told most of you when you checked in, including Sluf, if you want, you can commute to work here in your own airplane. We have plenty of ramp space, and it means you can live anywhere nearby that you want to," Luke said. "You can commute here every day if you want, in your own biplane or Learjet. Whatever you want." He watched them nod. "So now let me get going. Welcome! Thanks for agreeing to be part of this new school. I can't tell you how excited I am about it, and after talking to each of you, I know you are as well. It is one of the most exciting developments in fighter aviation in twenty years.

"We have six weeks to get ready for the first class. The demand from international Navies and Air Forces is enormous. We've received calls, letters, e-mails, faxes from all over the world asking for space in a class. Brian Hayes, our intel officer, whom many of you know . . ." He pointed. Hayes was sitting at the duty officer's desk, and raised his hand. "Brian is also our acting admin officer. He's the one in charge of school quotas, student enrollment, clearances, and the like. Ever since the Nevada Fighter Weapons School Web site went active, he's been getting *thousands* of hits a day. Word is out.

"Another thing that has surprised me is the demand within U.S. forces. TOPGUN's tough to get into. But an awful lot of pilots want to go, and an awful lot of squadron commanders want their pilots to go. We all know that. And since they changed the setup at TOPGUN, where squadrons don't send their pilots through until they've completed their squadron tour, the squadrons don't get any immediate benefit from sending anyone through the school. Well, here we're going back to the old model, where squadrons send a pilot or two in a given year, and they return to their squadrons to teach the other pilots what they've learned. What I *didn't* anticipate, at least not at the demand we're seeing, was that the DOD would spring for the money to send them."

He went to a slide in his PowerPoint presentation. It was a picture of their MiG-29s sitting outside the hangar with their new angular, choppy desert camouflage and the black star markings. "One thing driving the demand, frankly, is the fact that we fly MiG-29s. Everyone wants to fly against a MiG-29. Some of you may recall back in 1999 when the German Air Force brought six MiG-29s over to Red Flag, at Nellis. They were the prettiest girls at the dance. Everybody wanted to know everything they did, how they did it, their specifications, their maneuvering diagrams—everything. Demand has, if anything, increased since 1999. In six weeks we start meeting that demand."

"You think we can actually be ready in six weeks?" Sluf asked. Sluf had joined them from the Forest Service. After his tour as a TOPGUN instructor, instead of flying for the airlines he'd gotten a job flying tanker planes to fight forest fires.

"Sluf, I really appreciate your participation in this meeting. As a reward"—Luke smiled—"I'd like you to be in charge of facilities. Hangars, foreign object damage walk-downs, roads—all that good stuff."

Sluf put his head back and rolled his eyes. His black hair reflected the light because of the hair gel he always wore. He laughed. "I get it. The first dissent is met with the assignment of a shitty little job?"

"Welcome to the Navy," Luke replied.

"This isn't supposed to be the Navy!" Sluf protested.

"No, seriously, I really appreciate you volunteering for that difficult job. As to your question, we *will* be ready. We're going to have to work eighteen-hour days six days a week. We'll take Sundays off because I think it's smart to rest. When September first comes around, we'll have sixteen fully trained instructors, a syllabus in place, the airspace reserved, and we'll be ready to go.

"We'll take two weeks off before the second class, which, I am proud to report, is also full. We expect to fill up every class for the whole year before January one."

Pug, one of the instructors who'd been flying 767s for Delta three weeks before, was troubled. "This whole thing turns on keeping these MiGs flying. What do you know about MAPS? Can they pull this off?"

Luke looked at Vlad, who was sitting in the back listening to every word. "Vlad, why don't you talk about maintenance for a minute? Most of you have met him, but this is Vladimir Petkov, a former Russian MiG-29 instructor who now works for MAPS."

"What's his call sign?" Sluf asked.

Ted Bradley—Rain—jumped on that idea. "How about Commie?" He laughed.

Vlad did *not* laugh. He was angry. "I was not Communist. I was against Communist. To be called that would be insulting."

"All the more reason," Rain replied, looking around for support.

Luke was uncomfortable. He didn't want a rift. "We may follow a lot of Navy traditions here, but call signs that insult people will not be one of them," he said to Rain, who looked chastised. "How about we call him Vlad? That okay with you?" he asked.

"Vlad is good."

"Good. Come up here and talk about the maintenance."

"Good morning," Vlad said awkwardly. His hair was plastered to his head, and those in the two front rows could smell him. They curled up their noses and looked at each other, wondering how someone who was such a hygienic wreck could know much about anything. "I'm Vladimir Petkov. We have six of the MiGs ready to go now. The other two will be finished within two weeks, and of course the two-seater has been ready. The ones that are flying are holding up good. The desert air is good for them, and everything is on schedule. They are durable airplanes, but we will certainly have failures. We expect eighty-five percent flying at any given time, and enough spare parts to have a twenty-four- to forty-eight-hour turnaround for any airplane the breaks down. I do not think we will have a problem."

"Thanks," Luke said as Vlad returned to his seat. "I have given each of you two notebooks. The first is the instructor's manual with a syllabus. That's what we will be doing between now and the first day of class. Some of you have been here and have completed a good part of that syllabus. The rest of you need to catch up and make sure that you finish it before classes start. The pilots who finish the syllabus first will act as instructors for the remainder of the syllabus for the others. It will be a large team effort, but I'm sure we can do it.

"We will be going from basic familiarization of the MiG-29 to NATOPS sign-off—which of course stands for Nevada Air Training and Operating Procedures Standardization." He smiled, referring to the Navy NATOPS that everyone knew about, the Naval Air Training and Operating Procedures Standardization. "The reason we're doing things the old Navy way is, even though we hated some of the Navy ways, we're all familiar with them and we know what works.

"The second book that you have is the proposed student syllabus for our first class through the Nevada Fighter Weapons School. It is, as you can see, based on the TOP-GUN syllabus. We've made some modifications. There isn't much air-to-ground work. Our objective here is to teach not strike warfare but air-to-air combat. We will do a little air-to-ground, but that's not our focus."

Luke looked around at the excited faces. "A couple of other things. As the squadron progresses, we expect to be able to do some road shows. If MAPS can support us, we'll be prepared to take our MiGs overseas. It's something that very few others have been able to do, but if we can arrange for the appropriate tanking—which will also require us to modify our airplanes—we can work anywhere in the world."

"We can start our own war!" Sluf said. "Shit hot!"

"Good old Sluf. You know, you should have stayed with the forest service. At least that way all you're going to kill are a few trees. Always there with a good idea." Luke continued, "We've got a lot to do, a lot to talk about, and we're going to be doing most of it for the first time. There will be some bumps in the road, I guarantee you. But give me some room to maneuver and we'll figure out whatever needs to be figured out. Let's get this school under way."

10

The intense bearded man walked quietly off the Qantas flight from Sydney into the terminal at San Francisco International Airport. To someone watching him closely, he looked uncomfortable in his Western clothes. He was careful not to look around for law enforcement people or immigration officials who might examine his passport and other documents too carefully. He had nothing to hide. No contraband, no weapons, nothing that would give him away. Just false documents. Once through immigration, he would have no problems. He knew that the others with him were in the same position. They were all on different flights from different countries with passports from different origins. They would all arrive within four hours of each other.

He gathered his suitcases, full of secondhand clothes he had never seen before yesterday, and put them on the rolling SmarteCarte to stand in line for the customs and immigration stations.

He walked to the "Nothing to Declare" line and was waved through without comment. He maneuvered his SmarteCarte to the INS station and stood behind the yellow line in the "Non–U.S. Citizen" line. Finally the person in front of him was done, and the INS agent looked at him as he approached. The agent extended his hand. "Passport," he demanded.

The bearded man, perhaps thirty years old, handed it to him, trying to look completely unconcerned.

"Final destination?"

"Mountain View," the man replied.

"Business or pleasure?"

"Family. My sister lives there."

The INS agent ran the Bangladeshi passport through a scanner and looked carefully at the photograph and the paper. There was something about the man's eyes that bothered him. "What's her name?"

He hesitated. He hadn't expected that question. "We call her Shiri."

"Is she a permanent resident of the United States?"

"Yes."

"Is she employed?"

"Yes. She is a computer programmer."

"What do you do?"

"I am a mathematician."

"How long do you plan on staying?"

"Four days."

"Do you have a return ticket?"

"Yes."

The agent held out his hand for it.

The man pulled the ticket out of his shoulder bag and handed it to the agent.

The agent examined it carefully, looked at the man again, hesitated, and stamped his passport. "Welcome to the United States," he said, smiling as he handed the man his passport.

THE ice blue MiG-17 flew gracefully over the runway at Tonopah and snapped into a left-hand break. Luke and the other pilots standing on the flight line watched carefully, noting whether the MiG pilot was losing altitude, whether he was maintaining a constant angle of bank, and whether he had to correct his turn before rolling level on his downwind leg. He made no corrections. He leveled his wings in a perfect downwind position and lowered his landing gear. The blue jet was being flown with tremendous precision.

It was a beautiful airplane. It most closely resembled the American F-86 Super Sabre from the Korean War. It had made quite a name for itself flying against Americans in Vietnam. It had a T-tail and swept wings with the single jet intake in the mouth of the airplane giving it a sports car look, with a bubble canopy sitting on top of the sleek, clean exterior.

Everyone on the ground immediately wanted to fly it. The MAPS mechanics, half of whom were Russian, looked on with unfettered joy at one of their favorite airplanes.

The MiG-17—the Farmer, as it had been called by NATO for the last forty years—landed perfectly and turned off the runway. It taxied quickly to the flight line.

Paul Stamper had checked in to the school a week before and had finally brought his own MiG. Stamp opened the canopy and scrambled down the ladder that one of the MAPS mechanics put next to his jet. He was wearing a custom-made blue flight suit and a metallic blue helmet. It was his MiG, his own fighter, and he was prouder of it than of anything he'd ever owned. The pilots walked over, gathered around the jet, and studied it as he walked toward them. Stamp called out, "Greetings, earthlings. I have come in peace."

"Blow me," Thud said, eyeing the MiG enviously. "Stamp, how the hell'd you get this ride?"

"Bought it."

Vlad stared at the MiG with the look of someone who knew more about it than every other pilot there, including Stamp. He was almost speechless. He spoke with astonishment, "You can *own* MiG planes in U.S.? Anybody?"

Stamp nodded. "If it's defanged. Can't have guns and shit."

"But *we* could put those back on with ease," Vlad said,

smiling, looking around at the Russian mechanics who were studying the plane with a glazed look.

"Yeah." Stamp laughed. "Second Amendment! The right to bear arms! I need my damned airborne thirty-millimeter gun in my MiG for home defense! Shit, Vlad! Why didn't I think of that?" He laughed again. "Actually, Vlad," Stamp said, "I was thinking of asking you guys if you could take over the maintenance. The guys I have doing it in San Jose are good, but if you can do it cheaper or better . . ."

"Could I fly it?" Vlad asked, his voice full of hope.

"Got any hours?"

"Five hundred. All my early time was in MiG-17s, as you call them."

"Maybe. I'll think about it."

Vlad was amazed at the life this pilot had carved out for himself. "We can make deal. I will put together proposal. MAPS can get all the parts for MiG-17. We can keep it in top condition. And I will take part payment in flight hours for me. I would like that. Maybe I can show you some things."

"So, Stamp, what do you do with this thing?" Sluf asked.

"Flight of two MiGs, formation go, high-speed passes, Cuban eights—all kinds of cool stuff the crowds like, but mostly it's just the uniqueness of seeing two MiGs streaking through the sky, burners going. There's something forbidden about it." Stamp took off his gloves and put them inside his helmet.

"What's up with the vodka?" Thud asked, pointing to SMIRNOFF written in large script on the side of the airplane.

"They're the ones who make all this possible. They pay for the whole show, plus whatever fees we get out of it. But with my *new* job, here at the greatest place to fly in the entire free world, I can use the profits of the air show gig to commute in my MiG and live off my new salary. And Captain Luke here," he said, pointing to Luke, "says I'm okay to do the air show thing on the weekends."

"Got any room for a third?" Thud asked. "I want *my* own MiG-17. How much does it cost to get one?"

"You wouldn't believe it if I told you. Ninety-five thou. But it's getting the thing completely up and flying and keeping it there that will cost you."

"Can you get a MiG-21?"

"Sure. I know where you can get a couple of those right now."

"Truly?" Vlad asked. He looked at Luke. "Maybe you should get some 21s and 17s for your school. It would give your students a different look. They wouldn't ever know what was coming. And the MiG-17's slow-flight performance is better even than the MiG-29."

Luke thought about it. He'd never even considered it. It was a fabulous idea. "Maybe one day. Right now we've got a big enough sandwich to chew. One thing at a time."

Luke thought about Vlad's comment as he watched the pilots walk around the MiG-17. Stamp stood next to him and smiled as he watched the insatiable interest over his airplane. "So, Stamp . . ."

"Yeah?"

"What if we had you plan on flying your hot little MiG for a couple of guest appearances as the mystery fighter in our syllabus?"

Stamp glanced at him. "Seriously?"

"Seriously."

"You mean," Stamp said to those around him, "my big issue when I get up every day will be whether to fly my *own* MiG-17 or *your* MiG-29 in aerial combat?"

Luke grinned. "That about sums it up."

Stamp laughed. "*Hurt* me."

HAYES grabbed Luke as he walked down the passageway on the second deck of the Nevada Fighter Weapons School. "Luke. When do our foreign students arrive?"

"Canadians arrived yesterday. You met them. The F-18s are right out there," he said with a mischievous smile.

Hayes did not return the smile. "You know who I mean."

"They've checked in with approach and should be entering the break in a few minutes. We're going to go down and greet them on the flight line when they taxi up. You should come."

"I wouldn't miss it."

"You worried about them?"

"I just wanted to meet them."

"You still doing research on this guy?"

"Not as much as I'd like. I've been busy."

"I'll say. You've got us sold out through February."

"That didn't take any skill on my part. Once word got out to the fighter squadrons, it was all over. It'll be a pipeline. If we do a good job with the first classes through, it'll take care of itself."

"That's the idea."

"How's Katherine?"

"Morning sickness is gone, thankfully. She's doing great. I think she likes the idea of working for herself. If I could only teach her how to drive the bulldozer, I'd get my airstrip finished faster."

"Airstrip?"

"Sure. That's why I bought fifty acres. I want my own airstrip where I can fly my own biplane from home and do aero over my house and run out of gas and dead-stick down for dinner."

Hayes smiled. He could only imagine the joy of owning his own airstrip, his own airplane, and commuting to work to his own private TOPGUN. "I'll see you down at the flight line. Thirty minutes?"

Luke glanced at his watch. "Maybe sooner than that. They'll probably be coming into the break in about fifteen minutes."

"I'll be there."

Hayes was not the only one who wanted to see the last four Nevada Fighter Weapons School students of the first-ever class. All the other students were there. All the instructors were there. All the maintenance operators from MAPS and the enlisted sailors and Marines who had come with the fleet airplanes to work on those airplanes during the school month were there.

The men stood around in small groups waiting. Luke had had speakers rigged all along the front of the hangar so that those on the flight line and inside the hangar could hear the radio communications with the tower at Tonopah. They could monitor the comings and goings of all the airplanes. The loudspeaker crackled to life with a voice that was deep and heavily accented: *"Tonopah tower, this is Gulf Echo 334, a flight of four for the break."*

A calm, highly experienced voice replied, *"Roger, 334. You're cleared for a left-hand break at the numbers."*

All eyes were over the airfield as the four F-16s came over the runway in tight formation. The beautiful silhouettes with the aggressive air intakes under the noses of the small airplanes were beautiful against the crisp blue sky. They were painted a light gray with large block-lettered CANG on the tail, for the California Air National Guard. The lead F-16 rolled into a gentle left-hand turn, followed by his wingman, then number three and number four. They all rolled gently in an arc and followed their lead onto the downwind leg, beautifully spaced. The pilots on the ground watched with a critical eye for any signs of incompetence or impressive precision. So far they were impressed. Most of the students—and, if the truth were known, all the instructors—expected the Pakistanis to be hacks, pilots with few hours in the aircraft and virtually incompetent.

The lead Pakistani F-16 turned onto the base leg of his approach and rolled into the groove precisely. His rate of descent was steady, and there was virtually no correction in the approach. Just before hitting the runway, the F-16 flared and touched down quietly. The pilot reduced throttle, and the F-16 coasted. The radio came alive again: *"Gulf Echo 334, turn off at the next taxiway."*

"Roger, 334 off at the five board."

The next Pakistani F-16 executed an equally beautiful approach and landing and turned off on the same taxiway. A small truck with flags and a large white sign on the back that said FOLLOW ME pulled in front of the lead Pakistani F-16 and began driving down the taxiway, leading him to the NFWS hangar. The four F-16s taxied in line, trying to maintain an interval to look sharp all the way to their designated parking spots. NFWS linemen waited in front of their parking spaces to the left of the hangar. They were the last student spaces available. The planes reached the tarmac as everyone waited. They turned in sequence and put their nosewheels directly on the yellow spots designated for them. The pilots shut down their airplanes and hustled down the ladders that had been provided. Luke walked out of the group toward the Pakistanis.

The Pakistani Major recognized the Russian Colonel's insignia on Luke's shoulder and saluted him. Luke was somewhat embarrassed but returned the salute. "Good morning. You must be Major Khan."

"Major Riaz Khan, Pakistani Air Force." The two men shook hands, and the other Pakistanis joined them, each saluting Luke in turn. They were extremely formal.

Thud, Stamp, and Hayes joined them in a small circle, and salutes were exchanged all around.

"Welcome to Tonopah, and to the United States."

"Thank you," Khan said as he removed his Nomex gloves and his helmet.

Luke noticed that Khan was much shorter than he was,

with an amazingly thick neck, dark coarse hair with a matching mustache, and dark, mean eyes. Luke formed an instant dislike for him, about which he immediately felt guilty.

Khan asked, "Where shall we go?"

"This way. In the hangar," Luke said.

Khan spoke as they walked, "My maintenance men were delayed. I believe they will arrive tomorrow."

"Yes. We received word. Tomorrow morning."

"Excellent. My pilots are looking forward to this new TOPGUN school," Khan said.

"We've been looking forward to having you as our first foreign students, you and two Canadian F/A-18s."

"All the rest are Americans?" Khan asked.

"Yes. Marines, Navy, a couple of Air Force planes."

They walked into the hangar. Stamp spoke up, asserting himself in his new job as operations officer. "We start first thing in the morning. Will you be rested enough?"

"We are rested now," Khan snapped.

The instructors exchanged glances. "I'll show you the paraloft and the locker room," Thud volunteered, shifting a wad of gum to the back of his cheek as they walked to the far end of the hangar. Khan and the others followed him to both. They reconvened in the ready room.

"So this is where your officers gather," Khan commented, surveying the room.

"We have meetings in here, some instruction, some briefs, and this is also where the duty officer has the radio if you need to talk to us while you're in the air."

"Very well organized. I commend you," Khan said.

"It's pretty much like any other Navy squadron," Stamp replied. "You speak English very well. You study abroad?"

"No. Only in Pakistan," Khan answered. "It is the language of much business and is spoken by government officials often. Most also speak Urdu, of course." Khan nodded to Hayes, then turned to Luke. "We have much to discuss. I'm disappointed in the syllabus, and I would like to talk about it."

"Um, sure," Luke replied, trying to ignore Khan's tone. "Anytime. We need to start tomorrow at 0730. You think you can be ready to go by then?"

"As I *said,* we're ready now. We will be here at 0730 tomorrow to start our class. I will be here at 0600 to discuss the syllabus with you."

"No need to be here that early."

"You said anytime." Khan's eyes were dark and menacing. "So 0600. We won't be disturbed."

Luke stared back at Khan. "Sure. See you then."

Khan nodded and headed out of the room. Luke watched him go, and without taking his eyes off Khan said to the other instructors in the squadron, "I want you all here way before 0600."

They exchanged knowing looks of dread.

"What an asshole," Crumb muttered. "He's going to be trouble. You heard it here first. He's trouble."

THE salesman was wearing a tie. He was the only salesman who did, and he was sure it gave him an advantage. Customers liked dealing with someone who appeared organized and together. Someone who took care of himself. That was one of the reasons he'd received salesman of the month once last year.

He eagerly approached the dark, bearded man looking at commercial trucks. "Good morning!" he said. "Can I help you?"

The bearded man didn't even look at him. "How much will this truck hold?"

"Well, now that there is the 650 commercial truck. It holds a hell of a lot. But what were you planning on carrying?" he asked, wondering whether this foreigner was a serious buyer. It was common to get walk-up traffic for the light trucks, the F-150s or F-250s, but not for commercial trucks. Foreigners thought differently, though, and he was accustomed to dealing with foreigners. The entire Bay Area was like the UN, and the South Bay was crowded with companies where there wasn't one native English-speaking person. "Where are you from?" he asked, curious.

"Here. I live in Sunnyvale. I am a programmer," he replied.

"No, I meant originally. Sounds like you're kind of new here. Where'd you come here from?"

"Khartoum," the foreigner lied, knowing there was no chance the salesman knew where that was.

"Wow," the salesman said, having no idea where that was. "Sounds far."

The foreigner was inspecting the back of the truck. "How much is the truck?"

The salesman looked at him, wondering if he was actually considering a purchase. "Well, this here is the XLT, one-hundred-ninety-four-inch wheelbase. We can talk about it, but the sticker is forty-three thousand dollars and change."

"How much can it carry?"

"About nineteen thousand pounds. What you planning on hauling?"

"I will give you forty thousand dollars, cash."

The salesman had seen a cash purchase before. In fact, several times. But never for a commercial truck. "Um, let me check with my manager on the price. Cash, you say?"

"Yes."

"We have to fill out a form for a cash transaction over ten thousand dollars, you know."

The man was unmoved. He said nothing.

"Okay. I'll be right back. Um, can I see your driver's license?"

The man showed him a current California driver's license.

"You do software, did you say?"

"Yes."

"Great. I'll be right back."

11

Luke was tired from so many early mornings in a row, but because it was the first day he bounded up the ladder to the second deck of the hangar to meet with the others. It was 0530. Hayes and Stamp were in the back of the ready room trying to coax cups of coffee out of the coffeepot while it dripped. Thud sat in one of the ready-room chairs rubbing his eyes. "Morning," Luke said as he walked in. "How is everybody on this fine morning of the first-ever class at the Nevada Fighter Weapons School?"

"Fine," Stamp said dourly.

"So why isn't everyone happy?" Luke asked, truly perplexed by their expressions.

"Two reasons," Thud replied. "We don't want to be here at five-thirty in the morning, and this Pakistani guy is already a pain in the ass."

"Cultural differences," Luke said, not believing it for a second.

Thud and Hayes exchanged a glance. "Maybe," Hayes said.

"He said he had a concern about the syllabus. I have no idea what his problem with it is, though, but my real question, and the reason I wanted to talk to you guys, is to see whether we should discuss it with him at all."

Stamp took a sip from his coffee. "If we start opening up the syllabus, then every student or squadron that comes through will want to customize it. I'm not sure we want to get into that."

Luke said, "It might make sense. It would be a good marketing tool. There are a lot of things we could spend more time on."

Thud frowned.

Hayes stood up and moved toward the coffeepot, waiting for the last bit to drip. He pulled it out, filled his cup, and spoke to Luke. "I'm not too worried about his syllabus problems. I'm more worried about him."

Luke was surprised by Hayes's position. "You don't even know him." Then he remembered that Hayes had recognized the name as the same as some Pakistani intelligence official's. "Did you tie him to that intelligence group?"

Hayes shook his head. "No. I'm worried about the way this whole thing has come together. We don't know this guy from Adam. We have no idea who these pilots are, other than that they're Pakistani," Hayes said. "I pulled their clearance documents this morning and looked at them again. They have everything they should have, and they've been reviewed and approved by the Undersecretary *himself.*" He looked at the other three officers waiting for a response. There wasn't any. "Don't you guys think it's a little unusual that the Undersecretary of Defense signs off on a foreign pilot's clearance? You think he actually checked out these guys himself? I'm sure he took whatever Pakistan gave him as the final word."

"He's not going to just let anybody come here. Look, Brian, I appreciate your thoughts, but we're not really here to start second-guessing the Undersecretary. He has that on his shoulders."

"But it's our skins that are at risk."

Stamp didn't get it. "How? Did you call your brother yet? He tell you something we should know?"

"No. I didn't want to sound stupid. But that's what haunts

me. I can't imagine what these guys are up to—*if* they're up to something."

Luke shook his head. "Up to something? Like what? Overpaying us? I just know we have to get this class under way."

Hayes sensed the coolness of the others. "Have you guys just completely forgotten our history with Pakistan?"

"What history?" Stamp demanded, wishing Hayes would just drop it.

"We gave hundreds of millions of dollars to Pakistan when they were helping us support the Mujahedeen in Afghanistan against the Soviet Union," Hayes said. "Pakistan was our best friend," Hayes said. "They kept the pipeline open and got the money and weapons to the right places. Worked like a champ. We increased our support of the Pakistani military, too, selling them first-rate weapons systems and making them into our big-time South Asia ally. Then, when the Soviet Union pulled out of Afghanistan, we stopped supporting Pakistan, and the money and weapons dried up. But you see, their threat wasn't the Soviets. Never was. Their threat has always been India. And that threat wasn't going away. So we get them hooked on American aid and weapons, then cut them off.

"Then in '96 this Pakistani guy walks into an intersection just outside of CIA headquarters at Langley. Whole bunch of CIA commuters. Pulls out an AK-47 and starts shooting people. He killed three or four CIA people. It was an incredible move. And he actually escaped! But the CIA wasn't just going to let *that* happen. They tracked him down in Pakistan two years later and pulled him out of his bed in some fleabag motel. They brought him back to the United States, where he was convicted of murder."

"I remember that," Thud said, nodding.

Hayes went on, "So right after he's convicted, some unidentified men attacked a bunch of American businessmen in Karachi. Murdered them in their car on the way to work in broad daylight, right in the middle of a busy street. Just machine-gunned them to death. Oil workers from Texas. The Pakistani government said they were really sorry, but of course they had nothing to do with it. They promised to work real hard to find out who did. And nothing ever came of it. The people were never captured, and no one was ever put on trial, and the Americans are still dead.

"Then India tested a bunch of nuclear bombs in 1998. Something like three or four underground explosions. Pakistan said, 'Oh, yeah? Watch this,' and tested something like eight of them underground. So the United States jumps up and starts condemning people left and right. Remember?"

Luke half shrugged, indicating he didn't have much other than some vague memory.

"The United States condemned Pakistan. Said they were renegades and were in violation of the nonproliferation agreement. We sanctioned them both. We turned on them at the most critical time of their military development. And Pakistan has supported the Taliban militia in Afghanistan— which we condemn for hiding Osama bin Laden. Lots of people in Pakistan probably think we're dogshit.

"So that's the background. Now all of a sudden, out of nowhere, out of *all* the countries in the world that could come here as foreign students, Pakistan shows up. And it was greased by the Undersecretary of Defense. I don't know," he said, sitting on the counter by the coffeepot. "It just makes my hair stand up. But that's my job." He smiled.

Stamp didn't like what he'd heard at all. "Well, shit, Hayes. Now you're making *my* hair stand up. We'll have to keep our eye on these peckers."

"And what exactly does *that* mean?" Thud asked. "How do we keep our eye on them any better than we keep it on the other students?"

"That's what we're going to have to—" Hayes said, but he stopped in midsentence as he had the inescapable feeling of being watched. He turned his eyes toward the door and saw Khan, who had obviously been standing there listening.

The others turned toward the door, following Hayes's gaze. "How long have you been standing there?" Hayes asked.

"Long enough," Khan answered loudly as he stepped slowly into the ready-room door, blocking it.

"Were you listening to our conversation?" Hayes asked.

"I could not help but hear," Khan answered. The other three Pakistani pilots appeared behind him in the hallway and peered into the door that Khan was blocking. "You were talking about us, although I'm not sure what a 'pecker' is or how that might relate."

Luke started to respond, but Hayes cut him off. "We thought it was kind of extraordinary for foreign students to land, introduce themselves, and demand a change in the curriculum. We were trying to imagine what it was that would cause someone to do that."

"It is simple." Khan crossed to the other officers. "We have some concerns with the syllabus."

Luke tried to stay cordial in spite of the elevating tensions. "Well, that's why we're here. So come in, tell us what your concerns are, and we'll tell you what we think."

Khan nodded, as if he knew what Luke was going to say before he said it. He then looked each of the four Americans in the eye before he began to speak. "First of all, as you know, our sworn enemy is India—"

"Potential enemy," Luke corrected.

Khan stared him down. "Our *sworn enemy* is India." He paused, then went on. "They fly the MiG-29. It is why we're here. To see that airplane in action. But better than seeing it is flying it. Since you have a two-seat version, I would like each of my pilots to get enough time in the MiG-29 to know how it flies, how it operates, where the visibility problems are—everything."

"Major, I understand," Luke said. "That is something that would make sense. We will try to accommodate that request. I don't know about hours, but we'll get each of you into the airplane to see how it flies."

Khan nodded. "The other thing is that we were told when we first agreed to send officers to the Navy TOPGUN school in Fallon, Nevada, that a good deal of the syllabus was air-to-ground. It is an area that interests us greatly, as we feel our training in Pakistan is weak—"

"Look," Luke cut in, "I don't know who told you you were going to get to go to TOPGUN. They don't let foreign students in there at all. It is strictly for Navy and Marine Corps. I was an instructor there six months ago. We never had foreign—"

"We were promised."

"You may have been promised, but I'm telling you that whoever told you that doesn't know what he's talking about."

Khan ignored him. "We were pleased when we learned of this new TOPGUN school with equivalent instructors and even MiG-29s, the premier fighter of our enemy. But then"—he glanced at his other pilots—"we received your syllabus by e-mail and noted that there was very little air-to-ground training in it. We were concerned at the time, but it would not keep us from coming to the school. We are here. I do not now demand a change in the syllabus; I came simply to ask you if you could modify it or supplement it for us," he said, looking at the faces of the instructors for reactions. "We want to get to your level of skill in air-to-ground. That is all. Nothing that would require you to have a meeting early this morning in anticipation."

"Nobody said anything accusatory, Major," Thud responded, annoyed at Khan's entire delivery.

"Really." Khan stared at Thud. "So what is the answer?"

Luke shook his head slightly. "We really are not inclined to change the syllabus. We haven't even gone through the first class yet. We want to keep it all uniform, and we want to do the best job we can. So I think the short answer is no. But I will say this: If we have the time and the jets stay up, then we will give you two or three extra air-to-ground sorties. How does that sound?"

Stamp looked at Luke. He didn't know how Luke was going to fit that into the syllabus. Every day was accounted for. They might be able to do some flights on a weekend, but it would put a strain on the pilots and the maintenance personnel. "Luke, I'm not sure—"

Luke interrupted, "Like I said, assuming availability of pilots and airplanes—and availability means proper crew rest and everything else—assuming all that, we'll see what we can do."

Khan nodded, understanding Luke's position. He slowly scratched his closely shaven face. "I understand. But that is not good enough." His eyes bored into Luke's. "We're paying you an amazing amount of money. Probably too much. We made arrangements on our own for airplanes, our own maintenance personnel, our own transportation, our own logistics. All you are providing us is the instruction. I had hoped that you would be more responsive." He paused, clearly for effect. "I do not accept your answer. It was apparently arrived at in some haste based on a meeting this morning that was, from what I could tell, unfinished. Why don't you meet again with your fellow officers in charge of this new school and reconsider that idea? Perhaps we can talk about it again on Friday, at the end of this week."

Luke was growing angry. He replied, "We don't need to

reconsider. We *have* considered. Talking again on Friday would be fine, but right now we have to get this school going." He glanced at the clock on the bulkhead in the back of the ready room. "The welcome-aboard meeting is in this room. I need to do some final preparation. If there are any other things you need to do before then, I suggest you do them now. Otherwise, we'll see you at the meeting. Good morning," Luke said as he walked briskly out of the ready room.

The other instructors knew that Luke had made an exit to leave an impression, but it left them without an excuse to make their own equally dramatic exits. "I have some other work to do. I'll see you back here," Hayes said as he walked out quickly.

The Pakistanis watched him curiously as he dragged his right foot slightly.

"Me, too," Thud said.

Stamp stayed and waited until the others were gone. He faced Khan and spoke in a direct, subdued voice. "I wouldn't cross Commander Henry," Stamp advised. "Not only is he one of the best pilots in the country and one of the best TOPGUN instructors ever to hold the position, but he owns this company, this school. He *owns* it. He can ask you to leave anytime. He doesn't have to answer to any government. Nobody can tell him what to do. I think you should bear that in mind."

Khan was completely unaffected. "I know exactly who *Lieutenant* Henry is, Mr. Stamp. I know it is the highest military rank he ever actually achieved, and I know that he owns this company because Lieutenant Thurmond's father is a rich man who wants to relive his failed Vietnam fantasies. I know he left the Navy in disgrace after being involved in a midair collision and receiving a reprimand. Your Mr. Henry has taken to calling himself 'Commander' and wearing the insignia of a Russian Colonel. I know what his position is, and I know that he can ask us to leave. But I also know that the amount being paid by my government is more than that paid by all the other students *together*. Without us, this school will *fail*. So please don't patronize me with talk about how powerful Lieutenant Luke Henry is. We have power of our own. As to whether he answers to someone else, I assure you that he does. Who *owns* the MiGs and this airfield? Not Lieutenant Henry. Please don't insult me again with your very poor advice and your very veiled threats of what will happen to me if I should 'cross' Lieutenant Henry. I will cross him when I need to and when I choose to."

Stamp glowered at Khan. "Just watch yourself, that's all I'm saying. Show Mr. Henry some respect. But what you do isn't up to me."

"I never thought it was, Mr. Stamp."

COLONEL Stoyanovich never went to see anyone. It was beneath him. He hadn't spent his entire life climbing the ladder in the Soviet—now Russian, he lamented—Air Force so he would have to go seek the approval, or the ear, of a subordinate. But Popovich was a different question. Since winning his position as the commander of the fighter wing and being assigned to this base—a base where he had never before been stationed—he'd heard Popovich spoken of in whispers and with deference.

Personally, he hated Popovich. He was a pompous nobody who'd never held a real military job as far as Stoyanovich could tell. He always had a smirk on his face, as if he were privileged to have all the secrets and wasn't about to share them with anyone except his closest friends—and then only if they paid him handsomely.

Stoyanovich had learned that when the issue went through Popovich, *you* went to see *him*. It didn't matter who you were. Even the base commander went to see Popovich, the head of security, because Popovich was connected. Connected to those who drove black Mercedes-Benz automobiles and wore tailored Italian clothes. Whatever Popovich wanted to happen seemed to happen.

Stoyanovich walked into the office and took off his officer's hat. He placed it under his arm, keeping his long coat on, in spite of the overheated room, with steam hissing out of a radiator behind him. "Colonel Stoyanovich to see Lieutenant Colonel Popovich," he said to the young airman at the desk.

The airman stood up quickly, assumed a pose of forced attention, and nodded. "Yes, Colonel. I will tell him that you are here. Is he expecting you?"

"I don't believe so. I simply need to discuss one thing with him."

The young man disappeared, and Stoyanovich unbuttoned his coat.

"He will see you, sir," the young man said, returning to the outer room.

Stoyanovich nodded. He had better see me, he thought. He walked quickly into Popovich's office. "Good afternoon," he said.

Popovich stood up and gave a slight bow. "It is an honor to see you, Colonel Stoyanovich. An honor." He said it with just enough respect to be too much, just enough for Stoyanovich to know he didn't mean it at all. "What can I do for you?"

Stoyanovich towered over Popovich but could see he wasn't intimidated at all. "Major Vladimir Petkov," he said.

"What of him?" Popovich asked.

Stoyanovich stared at him. "What of him?" Stoyanovich asked incredulously. "Where is he?"

"He has resigned," Popovich said. He fought back a smile as he lit a Camel cigarette and slipped the lighter back into the pocket of his uniform.

"Resigned? That is impossible," Stoyanovich sputtered,

knowing it was exactly as Popovich had said. "He could not *possibly* have resigned. That would have to be approved by me. You must be mistaken."

"No. I am sure."

"I sent him to you for temporary security duty, not retirement! How can this be? I am his Wing Commander!"

"You *were* his Wing Commander. No longer. He is no longer in the Russian Air Force, defending our crumbling country from all its enemies."

"But the paperwork must come through me for any resignations! This is impossible."

"You are ignorant," Popovich said, as if slapping Stoyanovich in the face. "If certain people want an officer out of the Air Force, it simply happens. No Colonel is going to stop that. There is no need for your signature on a silly piece of paper if the right people don't feel it is necessary."

"What 'right people'?"

"That is none of your concern. It has been taken care of."

"But why? He was going to be returned to flying."

"You told him he was grounded for the rest of his career."

"Only so he would take his problem seriously. You knew that. I was going to transfer him back in six months."

"No longer."

Stoyanovich heard the contempt in Popovich's voice. "Where is he?"

"He has moved."

"Do you know where he is?"

Popovich sat down. "Of course."

"Where?"

"He is no longer any of your concern."

"But he is still *your* concern? You, who run security on this godforsaken base, still need to know where a retired pilot is who has moved away?" Stoyanovich asked, his voice growing louder.

"Yes. He is still my concern."

"Why?"

Popovich leaned forward and said with a leering, biting tone, "You still don't understand, do you? You still believe one day you'll open your eyes and everything will be like it was, a red flag with hammer and sickle and the world respecting us again. Well, that isn't going to happen. You should let go of your fantasy world and retire yourself. You are just in the way."

Stoyanovich yearned to respond in kind, to show Popovich where the real power lay in Russia. But he was determined to find out what he'd come to learn. His deep voice boomed around the room as he yelled at Popovich, "Where is he?"

Popovich thought of how troublesome this fat Colonel could be. Although Stoyanovich didn't have the power he thought he had, he was not without resources. Popovich answered reluctantly, his confidence receding slightly, "He has taken a job with a civilian company."

"*What* company?"

"MAPS."

"How? Those jobs are impossible to get. With his record, he would not be able to do it, not without my help. He should have come to me . . ."

"He didn't need your help. He had friends that got him the job."

Stoyanovich paused. "What friends?"

"New friends."

"The same criminals *you* call friends? Those friends?"

"Such words. You do not need to speak like that."

Stoyanovich took his hat out from under his arm. "Gorgov?" he asked.

"What better friend could one have?"

Stoyanovich stormed out of Popovich's office. The decay was all around him, closer than it had ever been.

12

Luke stood in the back of the ready room and made sure all the students from the first class were in their seats. They talked nervously. The minute hand on the clock in the back of the ready room clicked audibly to the 0730 position. Luke nodded to Hayes, who turned off the lights, throwing the windowless room into total darkness. Suddenly the loud sounds of an alternative rock group blared from the Bose sound system hidden in the overhead of the high-tech room. It was a pounding, rhythmic acoustic guitar that sent chills up the spine of every officer in the room. The music was far too loud to permit conversation.

Luke wanted to make Tonopah the true Fightertown, the place where all fighter pilots in the country would want to hang out, leave stickers and plaques on the wall, and build tradition and camaraderie. Ever since Miramar had reverted to a Marine Corps Air Station and TOPGUN had moved to Fallon, there hadn't been that one place that lived in the mind of Navy pilots as the place where they all wanted to be, where they would spend every waking hour if they could. Fallon was trying, but it wasn't there yet. Oceana in Virginia Beach was trying, but it lacked a certain something, a certain exotic feel, remoteness, or color.

Flying fighters was as much about morale and pride as it was about any one other thing. Airplanes, training, tactics, courage, opportunity—they all mattered. But without a certain belief in one's abilities and skills, without pride, these students would almost certainly fail. Everything about the new school, including the first morning, was calculated to build excitement and enthusiasm about what they were doing.

As the music pounded, the screen in the front of the room sprang to life with video images of the MiG-29. The color footage was vivid and impressive. It was an air show routine being flown by Anatoly Kvotchur, a professional Russian Fulcrum pilot. It was probably the most famous flight demonstration ever given by a MiG-29.

The class watched in total absorption as the pilot wrapped the airplane into a tight turn in front of the throngs of people at the Paris Air Show. The airplane twisted and turned beautifully in the blue sky above Paris. The noise of the air show was barely audible over the music. The thirteen members of the new NFWS class sat enthralled by the images and the excitement. They all loved jets. They loved flying fast. They loved the concept of air combat and having the ability to beat somebody in the air. The image was clear as the MiG-29 came across the runway at Le Bourget airport and pulled up into a Cobra maneuver, in which the airplane transferred its forward airspeed into an immediate nose-up pitching maneuver intended to cause a less agile airplane following closely to streak by. The crowd was obviously amazed. But then something happened. A flame shot out of the right engine, and the airplane departed, rolling right. It pitched toward the ground in a steep dive. Everyone watching the film knew that there was no way that airplane could pull out at that attitude. The pilots in the room had all heard of the '89 air show, but none had ever seen it. They held their breath as they watched. With the MiG-29 barely above the ground, an explosion threw off the canopy, and the pilot's ejection seat came rocketing out of the airplane. Just as the ejection seat cleared the airplane, the MiG-29 plunged into the grass next to the runway in a ball of flames right in front of the air show crowd.

"The Zvedza K-32D ejection seat," Luke said into his wireless microphone. "Best ejection seat in the world. He got out when he was sixty feet off the ground, his airplane headed straight down, with one engine dead and the other in full afterburner. He was outside the envelope of every Western ejection seat. Yet in his Russian seat he survived this incident uninjured." The camera lingered on the burning wreckage as the pilot floated down next to his dead airplane.

The screen faded and the lights came up slightly, showing Luke standing at the lectern in front of the room. He turned down the music. "Good morning. My name is Luke Henry. My call sign is Stick. You may hear that it's because I'm skinny. That, of course, is false," he said, as they all snickered, examining his lean frame under his flight suit. "The truth is, I was the best stick at TOPGUN, and my call sign is simply an acknowledgment of that fact by the other pilots." They laughed.

"That's my story and I'm sticking to it. What you have been watching is a videotape of the MiG-29, one of the best fighters in the world. It is the jet you are most likely to face if the balloon goes up.

"The reason you're here—the reason we're all here—is that airplane. We have them, we know how to fly them, and we want to teach you how to fight them and fight them effectively. In the course of learning to fight the MiG-29 you will learn fighter maneuvers that will put you in good shape to fight any other fighter you might encounter, because the MiG-29 is about the best fighter out there. It has been the leading export fighter from Russia since 1985.

"Let me welcome you to the Nevada Fighter Weapons School. It is an honor to have you here." Luke looked at all their eager faces. He glanced around the spotless, fresh ready room. The NFWS colors of desert camouflage and black and silver dominated the entire room. The ready-room chairs were the same chairs one could find in a squadron ready room ashore or at sea. They were the Navy standard-issue one-hundred-pound steel chairs with leather seats and high backs that reached up above one's head. Glenda, Raymond's wife and the co-proprietor of the Area 51 Café—as they'd insisted it be called—had stitched head covers for each ready-room chair out of black leather embedded with the squadron's logo.

"All the instructors have had at least one tour as an instructor at TOPGUN. This is probably the best accumulation of pilots anywhere in the world. That's the good news for you, because they are *really* good instructors and they really understand flying fighters. It's also bad news for you, because you're going to have to fight for your life every day against those pilots in Russia's best fighter and the number one threat you will ever face. Let me introduce them to you." All the instructors stood and were introduced in turn, after which Luke ran through his PowerPoint presentation of the class syllabus.

"We want to get you flying right away. After a couple of lectures we'll start with basic fighter tactics. 1 v. 1 maneuvering. We will show you how to maintain your lookout, how to make your opponent's lookout more difficult. We will teach you energy maintenance and various nuances of air combat. Some of you may know most of the things we'll teach you, in which case we'll just refine your skills. The first lecture will be given by Stamp—Lieutenant Commander Paul Stamper, the operations officer. That class will commence in"—Luke glanced at the clock on the back bulkhead—"forty-five minutes, at 0830. Other lectures will follow during the morning, including the AIM-9 missile. I will be giving that lecture at 1000. Then we will break for lunch. In the afternoon each of you will have your first 1 v. 1 hop against an instructor.

"By the way, unlike in the movie, neither the real TOP-

GUN nor this school will rank you. There is no TOPGUN trophy, and there will be no NFWS trophy. But we will know. And you will know. The best will percolate to the top. We expect you to be at your best. Any questions?"

Major Khan had been staring coldly at Luke throughout the lecture. He raised his hand, and Luke recognized him reluctantly. "Are you willing to consider changes to the syllabus to better fit your students' needs?"

Luke smiled. "Major Khan." He looked at the other students and spoke to the group before responding to Khan. "These are the pilots from Pakistan. Their lead pilot is Major Riaz Khan. Let me introduce him."

The other students murmured their hellos. Khan continued to stare at Luke. Luke kept a friendly tone in his voice, but the words had very sharp edges. "Major Khan, as I told you this morning at the special meeting we set up to discuss that very topic, we're not going to be changing the syllabus. We told you that we would be willing to accommodate you with two or three additional hops so you could get the additional air-to-ground training you yearn for. You told me that was not good enough." He paused. "I understood you when you said that. I would really prefer that you and I discuss this at a later time. Clear?" Luke stared back. Khan didn't respond at all.

"After your flights at the end of the day, I'd like to invite you to our first social event at the Officers' Club—the 94th Aero Squadron, as it is called—which is the next building over. It is the old Officers' Club from when Tonopah was an Air Force base, but we've added our own touch. We call it the 94th Aero Squadron because that was the squadron in which the first Navy ace flew, in World War I. He was nineteen years old when he got his fifth kill."

Luke paused. "We're here to give you the tools to be an ace if you ever find yourself in combat. But what makes an ace? What makes one man seize history by the balls and shoot down dozens of enemy airplanes while his squadron mate, with the *same* airplane and the same opportunities, gets maybe one kill over the course of the same war, or two, or none, and has a lot of mechanical problems that 'make him' go back to the base before the real fighting starts?" He scanned their faces. "What is it that makes the difference? If you talk to aces, they'll tell you that in their squadrons they were able to predict who was going to get the kills before the shooting even started. Some never seemed to see the enemy. Some would engage but never get a shot off." He paused again.

"There are a lot of ingredients that go into it. Courage. Tenacity. Eyesight. Or is it all just 'luck'? I don't believe in luck; I believe in physics. But there are other factors. Training, maybe. Skill—being a great pilot—that also comes into play. But there is an intangible.

"There aren't that many aces around anymore. There was only one Navy ace in Vietnam, Duke Cunningham, and one Air Force ace, Steve Ritchie. Think about this," he said intensely. "The youngest American ace is over *sixty.*

"We're going to see if we can help you find your intangibles. The things that will make you stand up and be counted when it really matters.

"So tonight, after your first flights, come over to the O' Club. I think you'll like the World War I decor. There is a Nieuport and a Fokker triplane parked out front. You can't miss it. And on the inside are sandbags and our Wall of Fame—the wall in the dining room where every ace in American history is mentioned. We'll convene there about 1900, after you've had a chance to have some dinner. We'll grab a beer and debrief and—"

"We do not allow alcohol," Khan blurted.

"Feel free to have iced tea, or lemonade, or a Coke, or . . . water. Whatever you want," Luke replied, ignoring Khan's smoldering stare. "We will adhere to the standard Navy policy of twelve hours from bottle to brief." He stopped. "Any questions?" There weren't any. "All right. Let's get this class under way."

BRIAN Hayes stared at the new digital telephone on his desk. He picked up a pencil and began doodling on the notepad in front of him. He felt like someone who was leaving on a trip and was forgetting something critical, that jarring, "damn it!" feeling. It was with him all the time, as if something right in front of him were about to explode. Whenever he tried to trace the feeling, it always came back to Khan. He didn't know why exactly, just that in the back of his mind it was always about Khan.

He dialed the number from memory. It rang several times and was about to kick over into voice mail. Suddenly the receiver was picked up at the other end. "Yeah."

"Hey, bro," Brian said, glad to hear the voice.

"Brian, what's up?" Kevin Hayes was Brian's older brother by eleven months and one day. Irish twins. "You okay?" he asked, his mind immediately drawn to Brian's condition.

"Yeah. Fine."

"You getting along all right?"

"Fine. It bothers me, but I'm doing okay."

"You actually getting better?"

"It doesn't work that way. But it's not getting worse as fast as I thought . . ."

"How's your new job?"

"Great. Incredible," Brian said. "Secret level, which isn't very sexy, but it's fun. First class started today. We've got sixteen instructors, and all the MiGs are FMC."

"FMC?"

"Fully mission-capable. Ready to go."

"I can't believe you got those MiGs flying. I heard they were at the end of their useful life."

"That's what the DOD said for public consumption. They only had a couple hundred hours on them. I think they had other things in mind for them but never got around to it. Probably a budget issue. And Luke found this company that's joint German and Russian. They're doing the maintenance. They can take any Russian airplane down to its serial number and build it back up. Some of the airplanes needed a lot of work, even new engines, and others didn't. But if you've got the money, they can make them fly."

"Unbelievable. What a great deal. So what's up? You don't sound like you called just to talk."

Brian hesitated. "I need your help."

"What kind?"

"It's one of our students. I was wondering if . . . if you could have somebody check into him."

Kevin was cool. "We don't operate inside the U.S. You know that. That's FBI."

"CIA looks at foreign issues. Right?"

"Go on."

"The student, the foreigner—"

"Where are you calling me from?"

"The school."

"You have access to a STU-III?"

"No. We don't have any secure communications."

Kevin Hayes paused. "Don't say anything you don't want to read in the newspaper. What's going on?"

"We have four foreign students—six actually, but four of them are from Pakistan. Ever since I heard about these guys, the hair has been standing up on the back of my neck. The way the school got going, the way they show up as the first foreign students with the path completely greased for them. The way their head guy shows up with this attitude, a total *asshole,* like he's completely in control, gives our CO a faceful of crap, but there's more to it. I don't know. That's why I hesitated to call. There's nothing I can really point to. I just wanted—"

"Look, Brian," Kevin said sympathetically, "I trust your instincts, but you don't crank up the big bad Agency to investigate some random suspicions. Assholes are not on our list of things to look into."

"He has the same name as the Pakistani director of ISI."

"Internal Security? Shit, Brian, those are some serious people. You think he's related?"

"I don't know."

"But where does that get you? Some foreign country's going to be investigating the son of the Director of the CIA if he shows up for some exchange program?"

"Yeah. I don't think it gets us anywhere. It's just the only thing I can point to. I don't trust the guy. Can you have somebody look into him?"

"You know how hard it is to get the CIA to 'look into' anything?"

"I thought you worked there. You can get them to do whatever you want."

"Yeah, right."

"Sorry. I shouldn't—"

"I didn't say I wouldn't *do* anything. I just want you to appreciate how hard it is. Especially when you have nothing to go on."

"Well, if you can—"

"Pakistani, you say."

"Right."

"You got anything you can show me?"

Brian picked up the brown envelope lying on his desk. He opened it and pulled out the documents. "I've got the information they forwarded to us to verify their security clearances."

"Fax it to me. I know somebody in Pakistan. Let me make a couple of calls."

"Thanks. I owe you one."

"Counting this one, I think you owe me about a thousand."

"No doubt."

"YOU'RE working yourself into the ground," Katherine said as she walked outside behind Luke.

He had changed into his jeans and his usual gray fleece pullover. "No harder than you used to work in your law firm."

She couldn't argue with that. "And I was working myself into the ground . . ."

They walked across the sandy area that passed for a back-yard behind their sprawling ranch house toward the well-used Bobcat. Luke climbed up into the cab and sat on the cushioned seat. "I can't take three months to build the runway. I only rented this Bobcat for two weeks. I've got to get it done."

"Do you think maybe you're thinking about too many things at once?"

There weren't many hours of daylight left. Luke had his hand on the starter lever but resisted the temptation to start the engine. "Like what?"

"Think about what you're doing—starting a new company, leasing a fleet of fighters and one of the world's best airfields, borrowing a hundred million dollars . . ."

"He *invested*. I didn't borrow anything."

"You know what I mean. Plus buying a new house, building your own private airfield, trying to buy an airplane. Don't you think you're taking a little too much on your shoulders? Oh, and starting a family."

"I feel more in control of my life than ever. Nobody's going to tell me to leave my family to go to sea. Nobody's going to move me across the country for the needs of the Navy. We're finally where we can decide exactly what we want to do. And I happen to have the best job in the world. It's going to take a lot of work to get through the first year. We both know that. But it's worth it to me. The runway," he said, looking at his half-done strip for his nonexistent airplane, "is a dream. You know me. I've always got some project going. Keeps me from watching television."

"How is that Pakistani student?"

"Khan?"

"Yeah. You had a lot of questions about him after the first two days."

Luke got quiet. "I still do."

"Serious questions?"

"I don't trust him at all. I don't know what the hell he's up to, but his goal in life sure isn't trying to be the best student in the school. He's got something else in mind."

"Need me to do anything?"

"Brian is working the problem. He *really* doesn't trust the guy. And he's got his brother at the CIA looking into it."

"The CIA?" She thought about the implications. "Should we call the Undersecretary and ask him about Khan?"

"He's the one who sent him here. I don't think that would do much good." Luke pushed the starter. The Bobcat's diesel engine rumbled to life. "I've got to get working before the sun sets."

"I still say you're taking on too much."

He put the Bobcat into gear. "You have any problem with me buying an airplane?"

"With whose money?"

"Ours."

"We don't have any."

"I could get a loan."

"I quit my job to move here, Luke. We don't have enough money to buy an airplane."

"Sluf just bought an airplane. He moved to Vegas. He's going to start commuting from there every day."

She frowned. "What did he buy?"

"Just a little Cessna. Used. Paid about thirty K for it." He paused. "What if the company bought it?"

Katherine pulled her hair off her face, where the wind had blown it. She glanced at the sun heading for the western mountains. "Are you asking me as the general counsel or as your wife?"

"Both."

"You can't use company money to satisfy your personal hobby desires. The company certainly does *not* need an acrobatic biplane. The company has lots of airplanes. I don't see a biplane fitting into the mix."

"Then maybe I'll buy a MiG-17, like Stamp."

"I don't think so. And you're sure not landing a jet here and starting it at six in the morning with a cup holder for your commuter mug."

He smiled at the image. "Maybe I can find a fixer-upper."

"Now, *that's* comforting."

"Just kidding. I'll save, I'll scrimp, I'll borrow, I'll do it all. But I *will* have my Pitts Special before the year's out."

"We shall see."

Luke looked at the sky. "I need to get working."

Katherine stood back and gestured to his beloved runway.

KEVIN Hayes pulled the sandwich out of the bag sitting on his desk in his cubicle. He studied the bacon sitting on top of the turkey and wondered how long ago it had been cooked and whether trichinosis can resurrect itself in cooked bacon if it sits in a cold pan for long enough. The dark red, almost black meat was entirely limp and now held tomato seeds in its valleys. He decided to pull the tomatoes and microwave it. He pushed his chair back and stood up when Theresa Crane walked around the side of the cubicle and stood looking at him. He rose and faced her, trying to hide the concern he felt. She'd *never* been to his cubicle, even though he'd worked for her for two years. "Hello," he said casually.

"What section are you in?" she asked.

He looked at her with a puzzled expression. "Excuse me?"

She folded her arms. "What section are you in?"

Hayes was really confused. "*Your* section. Africa."

"That's what I *thought*," she said sarcastically.

"What am I missing?" he asked, putting the sandwich back in the bag, ready to carry it to the lunchroom.

"You want to explain to me what you're doing making inquiries in Pakistan?"

Here we go, he thought. "Checking on Major Riaz Khan of the Pakistani Air Force. He's attending a school in Nevada. The Nevada Fighter Weapons School, where he's flying F-16s against American adversary pilots."

Crane looked at him suspiciously. "Is Pakistan in Africa?"

He was able to hold his tongue, but not his sarcastic tone. "Uh, no."

"Is Nevada?"

He sighed. "No."

Her eyes narrowed.

He answered her unasked question. "Some people have some . . . concerns."

"What people?" she asked as she continued to stare. Her mind was spinning quickly. Finally her face showed recognition. "Your brother."

He nodded slowly, knowing what was coming.

Now she was truly angry. "You're doing private intelligence consulting on the side? Using United States government *assets*?"

"Where'd you hear about this?"

"That doesn't matter. You've got no business working for your brother. Not from here."

"I'm not working for my *brother*. I'm working for the

United States. Our job is to protect the United States. I admit it's a little unorthodox. I figured if somebody needed to follow up, I'd pass it on."

"No. You're not passing on anything. You do the work I've given you. If you have extra *time* on your hands, you let me know."

Hayes didn't respond. Nothing like a lecture from a parasite bureaucrat who'd violated the Peter Principle three jobs ago.

She looked at him, waiting for a response, then realized he wasn't going to respond. "I'm serious."

"Why do you care?" Hayes replied. "You ever make calls from work that may benefit the country that aren't *directly* related to work on Africa?"

"No. And you shouldn't either."

"Whatever."

"Don't start that tone with me, Kevin. I won't put up with it."

"Yes ma'am."

She waited for him to say one more thing, something that she could really jump on. He didn't. She walked quickly out of his corner cubicle.

"Bitch," he said to her back after she left.

SLUF closed the door on his Cessna and leaned down to walk out from under the wing. He stood straight up and looked at the sun just rising in the east. He smiled. He had never been more content in his life. He'd found a new condo in Las Vegas near both the Strip and the airport where he kept his "new" Cessna. He commuted every day from Las Vegas to Tonopah, arriving early and leaving early.

He checked his watch. It was an hour before he had to be at his first brief. He saw the auxiliary hangar out of the corner of his eye and immediately felt guilty. Luke had been serious about his being the "facilities officer." He was supposed to check out the entire air base and make sure nothing was about to blow up or burn down or fall in on someone. He was to see what needed to be painted and when. He sighed. He hadn't done one thing since Luke had asked him.

He glanced at the Area 51 Café and felt the pull of his first cup of coffee. He had it there every morning. It could wait. He walked to the auxiliary hangar, a good eight hundred yards from his airplane, away from the activity of the base. The hangar wasn't being used for anything. He figured it would take him thirteen seconds to make sure it wasn't going to collapse, and then he could get his coffee.

He walked quickly to the hangar and looked for the entrance. He saw a door on the side and decided to try it. It was solid steel and rusted at the corners. There was no lock, and the door was slightly ajar. He pulled on the edge of the door, and it swung open easily. Great, he thought. Perfect place for a bunch of coyotes and snakes to be lurking. He stepped through the door, and it swung closed behind him. It was nearly dark in the hangar. There were windows in the back of the building, opposite the huge sliding doors, but not enough to cast anything but the dimmest light onto the floor. He shuffled his feet forward carefully, waiting for his eyes to adjust to the darkness.

He frowned as he heard the faint sound of metal on metal. He squinted to see where the sound had come from—somewhere in the back corner of the cavernous hangar, to his left. He moved slowly toward it. It suddenly stopped.

He stopped. His breath came more quickly. He listened carefully but heard nothing. The far walls were now coming into focus, and the hazy windows to his left, high off the concrete, grew brighter in the morning light.

He walked farther and was thirty feet into the hangar when he suddenly realized he wasn't alone. He saw someone in the far corner. He squinted. Whoever it was wasn't moving; he was standing there, staring at Sluf.

Sluf began walking more quickly toward the person. He could now make him out fairly clearly but then was startled to realize that the man wasn't alone. There were at least eight others with him. Sluf stopped dead in his tracks. He recognized the man just before he spoke.

"Mr. Sluf," Khan said.

Sluf was too shocked to say anything. They were all Pakistanis, all four pilots and several maintenance men, gathered around a small crane and a bomb dolly, with charts and diagrams all over the floor. Sluf looked around the rest of the hangar but didn't see anything out of the ordinary. "What the hell are you doing in here?" he finally asked.

Khan and the others began walking toward him. "I could ask you the same thing," he replied.

"Except that I have a reason to be here and you don't."

"Of course we do. We are doing training."

"With a crane and a bomb dolly?" Sluf said skeptically.

"Yes. It is part of what we do. We must always train. We needed a quiet place away from the rest of the people."

"You never got permission."

"On the contrary. Mr. Luke gave us permission to use this hangar whenever we wanted."

"That's bullshit, Khan. He put me in charge of facilities. No one is to use this hangar. It isn't available. And you sure as hell never told us you were going to practice bomb loading. Where the hell did you get that crane anyway?"

"We brought it with us," Khan said as he reached Sluf and stood directly in front of him.

Sluf shifted uneasily as two of the Pakistanis moved around to either side of him. "Why would you bring a crane with you?"

"For these practices. All of our men must practice all the time. We must always be ready for war with India."

Sluf wasn't buying it. "At six in the morning?"

"Yes. Before our other obligations begin." Khan studied

Sluf's face. He glanced at the two men flanking Sluf and nodded very subtly.

"I want you guys out of here. Just leave the crane, and we'll see about getting you some space to—"

Sluf stopped as the man to his right suddenly gasped and bent over in pain. Sluf was completely confused by what might have happened to the man but realized too late it was just to cause him to turn his head. The Pakistani now directly behind Sluf grabbed him in a choke hold and pulled back hard on his neck with his forearm.

Sluf fell backward into the man as he fought the pressure on his throat. He pulled on the man's arm and tried to scream out. He had no air. He knew he had only seconds to get out of the hold or he would be dead. He tried to get his feet under him so he could lift up against the shorter man, but the man kept shifting to keep Sluf off balance.

Khan stepped forward with lightning speed and drove his fist into Sluf's solar plexus, driving out the remaining air in his lungs. Sluf began to see stars. He flailed at the man behind him with his fists but couldn't land a punch. He tried to kick but realized his kicks were going in directions he couldn't control.

Then his vision started to go, as if he were pulling too many Gs. Sluf's gelled hair fell into his face as he expired in the arms of the Pakistani, who waited until there was no movement. He lowered Sluf slowly to the hangar floor.

Khan knelt down and felt for a pulse in Sluf's throat. There was none. "He is finished." He stood and looked around, then at the man who had killed Sluf. "Put him in that tool locker. Tonight you will go to Reno to buy those GPS receivers we have told them we need. On the way you will find a bridge or a cave and take care of this," he said, looking at Sluf. "They will never find him in time to stop us now."

13

"**M**orning," Luke said to Glenda as she stood behind the counter.

"Well, the big boss. I'm surprised to see you here. I don't think you've had breakfast here before," Glenda replied, smiling. She was a kind-faced woman in her mid-fifties who exuded humility.

Luke looked around, surprised, at the crowd. There were ten students eating breakfast and five instructors. Other staff members were spread throughout the café, and Stamp sat at a table by the door. He had arrived early in his MiG-17 and walked straight to the Area 51 Café.

"Did you agree to call this the Area 51 Café?" Luke asked Glenda.

"You know how he is. If I didn't let him, then we'd have to explain him wearing that hat all the time, wouldn't we? Now those who don't know just figure he's wearing a hat after the name of the café."

Luke laughed out loud. Just then Raymond walked in from the back of the café. Luke and Glenda exchanged a glance without saying anything. "Three eggs scrambled with some bacon, and an English muffin."

Glenda nodded.

Luke stood by the counter and watched Glenda put the eggs on the grill. He watched her husband fill the refrigerator with gallons of milk from the back. Luke addressed

Glenda again: "Have you decided whether to let Vlad use your voice?"

Glenda shook her head. "I just don't know about that, Mr. Henry. I don't think I even understand."

"Simple. A lot of the warnings in the MiG-29 are voice recorded. They say things like 'Raise your landing gear,' " he said in a quiet voice, like HAL, the computer in *2001*. "Or 'Your left engine is on fire.' That sort of stuff. The MiGs came with Russian warnings, which of course are not a lot of help to those of us who don't speak Russian. Vlad—probably his company, actually—had some *German* woman record the warnings for us, but in English. They sound hilarious. Nobody can understand her—'You haff ze left enchine on fi-ah!' He must have paid her about five bucks. She is as far from fluent as you can get. We're all running around saying, 'Achtung! Race ze lahnding gee-ah?' We're starting to talk in German accents. Vlad's tired of taking shit all the time, so he decided to ask you. I think you'd be perfect. It'd be like our mothers warning us that we were about to fall out of the car or something. I *guarantee* you your voice would get our attention." He spoke quietly and gently, " 'Low fuel!' "

"I don't know, I'm afraid I would do something wrong," she said, smiling warmly.

Luke grabbed a porcelain cup off the stack next to the Bunn coffeemaker and poured himself a cup. "There's nothing *to* go wrong. If it gets screwed up, we'll just redo it. We can record it here. Why don't you? It'll make you famous."

"Oh, all right."

Luke spied Raymond again. "Hey, Raymond. How are you doing?"

He replied in his humorless way, "Fine, Mr. Henry. How do you like the café?"

"Great. Don't know about the name, though." Luke didn't

realize that Vlad had come into the café and was standing right behind him. "You seen Sluf? His airplane is already here."

Glenda answered. "Not yet, but he always comes here first thing. He's so nice."

"Don't be too charmed," Luke warned. "He's a ladies' man. They all like him, and he just uses them."

"Good morning, Vladimir," Glenda said over Luke's shoulder. "I've got your bread ready."

"What bread?" Luke asked.

"Black Russian bread. Good for butter and jam. Filling," Vlad said enthusiastically.

Luke turned and looked at Vlad, whose hair was a wreck. "Hard night?"

Vlad frowned. "What you mean?"

"You look like something the cat dragged in."

"What does this mean, cat dragging?"

"I finally got my cell phone working, Mr. Henry," Raymond said, proudly taking his phone off his belt clip.

Luke glanced at him. "That's great."

"I need your home phone number."

Luke was surprised. "What for?"

"I always keep the home phone number of my boss in the cell phone, in case of emergency. I mean, around here *anything* can happen. Right?"

Luke looked at Raymond's hat again. "Right." He gave him his home phone number. "Don't be giving that out to any intergalactic salesmen."

Raymond frowned. "Like who?"

"Any of them. And make sure you get Vlad's number at the BOQ, too. Wake him up first if there's an emergency. He's much more likely to actually be able to do something about it."

He nodded. "Your number's safe with me."

Glenda handed Luke his plate. "Several of the others are outside, if you want to join them."

Luke nodded and went outside. Thud, Crumb, and Stamp were chuckling at one of the tables under an umbrella. They had finished their breakfasts and were leaning back in their chairs.

"Morning," Luke said. He sat down at the table.

"Hey, boss," Crumb said. The others greeted him quietly.

"What did you think of that mission-planning session with Khan and his boys yesterday?" Luke asked as he sat down.

Thud shook his head. "Bizarre. It was like we were planning an actual mission for him. I mean, hardened concrete targets, laser-guided bombs, no SAMS, some possible fighter defense? It sounded like an actual event to me. It was spooky."

"I saw you give Stick that 'dial it down' signal, Thud," Stamp commented.

"Absolutely. I'm giving this guy only C-plus or B-minus information. He'll never learn all I know about fighters—"

Crumb laughed. "Shit, Thud. You don't *know* anything about fighters! I could kick your ass with my visor taped over!"

"Except for Crumb," Thud continued, "who is unbeatable and therefore would gain nothing from whatever I know, others, like Khan, I wouldn't tell left from right. We just need to get him through the class and get him out of here."

Luke nodded. "You know what I noticed?"

"What?" Crumb asked.

"One of his guys was writing down every word and copying our rough drawings of flight paths we did on the board."

"I just don't get it," Thud said. "Hayes may be right. He get anything from his brother yet?"

"Nope."

"You know, maybe we should take it up a notch. Maybe we should formally ask the CIA to look into them for us."

Luke frowned. "And what would we tell the Undersecretary?"

"I don't know."

"Me neither."

"More coffee?" Raymond asked as he brought the carafe to the table. He left the coffee and was about to turn and walk back inside when Crumb stopped him. "Hey, Raymond," he said. Raymond looked at him. "I hear you been watching for aliens."

Raymond frowned at Crumb. He was growing tired of constantly being belittled for his interest in UFOs. "Who told you that?"

"Word is you go out in the middle of the night and sit on the hills." Crumb watched his face. "Is that true?"

"What if I do? Something wrong with that?"

"Depends."

"Leave the poor man alone," Thud said, taking a bite of his omelet. He felt responsible for Raymond and Glenda's being there. Anything Raymond did that was odd reflected on him, he thought.

Crumb pressed right on. "And you use these *huge* binoculars."

"Something illegal about that?"

"No," Crumb said, controlling his mirth. "I'm just wondering if you've seen anything. Had any close encounters?"

Raymond assumed a tone of authority. "I've seen some curious things, but nothing I'm prepared to report on to you."

"Well, shit, Raymond, how are we going to know all this good stuff if you won't tell us?"

"Because you don't believe anything I say about it. You think it's a big joke."

"Where did you hear that?"

"I can tell," Raymond said, putting his hands on his hips. "Everybody thinks it's all real funny."

"Just tell me something that will convince me there are UFOs out there. Just one thing," Crumb said.

Raymond thought about it. There were so many things he could tell. Finally he said, "All right. This here Area 51 that's nearby. What goes on there?"

"Groom Lake? Beats the hell out of me. It's run by the Air Force." Crumb glanced at Luke. "You know?"

"No idea."

"Well, Mr. Crummey," Raymond said, "it's where they keep all the *evidence* of aliens. They claim it's related to the Air Force and keep it in 'black programs' and don't tell anybody about it. And how about this, what about John Denver?"

"What about him?" Crumb asked, looking at Luke, who was equally perplexed about how John Denver might be related to black programs.

"You've heard of Roswell, New Mexico? The Roswell incident?"

"Sure. I saw *Independence Day*. Everybody knows about Roswell."

"Yeah, well, John Denver wasn't his real name. You know that?"

"What was his real name?"

"Schickelgruber."

"No it wasn't." Crumb guffawed. "That was Hitler's name!"

"Well, it was something like that. It wasn't Denver."

"It was Deutschendorf. So what?"

"So he was living his life in disguise. Then he suddenly has an airplane accident in the middle of the ocean and disappears."

"And?" Stamp asked.

"Know where he was born?"

"No idea."

"Roswell, New Mexico." He beamed. "*And,* his father was in the Air Force."

Luke fought back a laugh. "Well, there it is."

Crumb just stared at Raymond. "Raymond, I had no damned idea."

Raymond gained a look of vindication as he stood a little taller and adjusted his hat. "So I'm always on the lookout. And if I see anything, I *will* let you know."

"Thanks a lot," Crumb said, his sarcasm ringing in Raymond's ears.

Raymond started to leave, then turned back after Crumb's tone began to sink in. "You think you know so much." He put the tray down on the table next to their plates and sat quickly in an empty chair, uninvited. He pulled a thick stack of folded papers out of his back pocket. "You have any idea how much money is spent on black programs?"

"What do black programs have to do with UFOs?" Luke asked.

"They're called Special Access Programs. SAPS. Government won't even tell you that they exist. There are over a hundred fifty of 'em. That includes the CIA, the Department of Energy, and the Department of Defense. Most people think they have to report to Congress at least. *Not true.*" Raymond grew more intense, speaking slowly. "The Secretary of Defense can waive the reporting requirement completely." Raymond unfolded a piece of paper. "Listen to this. I want you to *listen* to this." He read from the paper. " 'Some classified programs are carried out at Edwards North base, but the most secure and sensitive programs are the responsibility of an Air Force Flight Test Center detachment based at the secret flight test base on the edge of the Dry Groom Lake, Nevada, and known as Area 51.' Listen to this here: 'The USAF still refuses to identify the Area 51 base, referring to it only as an operating location near

Groom Lake. It is protected from any further disclosure by an *annually renewed presidential order.*' " He looked up and whispered, "This goes as high as the *President* of the United States."

"Shit, Raymond, you're jumping to conclusions. Just 'cause the government won't tell you what's going on at Area 51, it must be UFOs? How do you figure that? Why not assume they're building some superhypersonic fighter that hovers one foot off the ground, weighs fifty pounds, and carries the fastest missiles ever designed? Why assume it's a bunch of green aliens?"

"We can't believe a thing they say. Listen." Raymond read on: " 'Area 51's linkage to Edwards Air Force Base is a form of cover, and statements which are intended to conceal the existence of a black program by creating a false impression in public are routine.' You hear that? The U.S. government is deceiving the public intentionally! We're talking billions and billions of dollars that are unaccounted for!"

Luke stared at Raymond. He couldn't decide whether to ask him to shut up or to laugh it off. "Maybe it's just where the United States government does secret airplane testing, and they don't want you to know about it. Why can't you let the government have some secrets?"

"It's not secret airplane tests I'm worried about. It's UFOs, and they're there. I *promise* you."

Luke looked at Stamp and rolled his eyes as he sat back in his chair.

Raymond could read their body language. He'd had enough. He folded up his papers, tattered from months of being carried around in the pocket of his jeans. He jammed the papers in his pocket and headed back into the café. "You'll see," he said over his shoulder, more in the nature of a mutter than a farewell, "you'll see."

"There goes one of our crack employees," Stamp said. "Completely off his rocker."

"He's harmless. They're doing a good job running the café," Thud said.

"He's gonna scare off the students if he starts telling them those stories about how John Denver got called home by the big UFO." Crumb laughed.

"I don't think too many people ask him about it, and I don't think he feels free to share that kind of . . . insight with just anyone. I think he's pretty touchy about it."

"I sure as hell hope so."

KEVIN waited as the phone rang. It was late on the East Coast, and almost late in Nevada.

Brian picked up on the third ring. "Hello?"

"Hey," Kevin said.

"Hey! What's up?"

"I talked to my friend in Pakistan."

"What'd you find?"

Kevin could hear the anticipation in Brian's voice. He hated to disappoint him. "Really interesting. Nothing very specific, but one thing surprised me. They ran it by the Air Force attaché in Islamabad. He had actually heard of your guy."

"Why would an attaché know about a Major?"

"A lot of people know his name. It's one of those names that gets everybody to clam up and look over their shoulder. He's spooked a bunch of people, but no one seems to know exactly why. Or how. The thing everybody says about him is he came out of nowhere. He wasn't known in the Air Force at all, until recently. The attaché knows about all the movers, all the hot officers. He'd never heard of this guy before six months ago. Now everybody knows about him."

"So do we need to worry about him?"

"There's nothing anybody could put their finger on. Best we can tell right now is that he's a regular Air Force Major who seems to be well connected."

"That isn't much. Keep looking," Brian said hopefully.

"I can't, really."

"Why not?"

"I got busted. My division head jumped on my ass for calling Pakistan."

Brian asked, "How did she even know about it?"

"No idea. It's kind of spooky."

"You think she had your phone monitored?"

"I'm sure she does. They're all monitored. But what would make her listen to it? What would make her think that she even had to worry about listening in on my phone? That's what I can't figure out."

"That's just weird."

"I agree, but, dude, I ought to lay off for a while."

"I don't know," Brian wondered. "Is she really worried about you wasting time, or is she trying to protect somebody?"

"Don't go paranoid on me. Who would she be trying to protect?"

"How the hell would I know? You're the intelligence puke."

"So are you. Do you sniff anything? Anything else about the government? Any side shows going on I ought to know about?"

"Just the Pakistani guys. I'm probably chasing smoke. The other day, though, when the Major found out we're going to be test-firing some live missiles, he about came unglued. It was like news he hadn't anticipated, that *really mattered* a lot, for reasons we can't figure out. It's probably some sort of bias on my part. I don't know. Maybe you should just forget about it."

"I trust your judgment, Brian. I trust your instincts. If you want me to keep pushing, I will. I'll be hanging my ass out, but if it's *really* important to you . . ."

"What could you do?"

"I'll get my person in Islamabad to do some active questioning. She has some sources. She wouldn't tell me about them, but I know she has some."

"It'll get you fired."

"I'm sick of this shit anyway. Sitting in a cubicle all day trying to patch little pieces of information together about a continent so screwed up I don't even know where to start."

"I can't be responsible for you getting canned."

"You probably need an assistant intelligence guy at the Fighter Weapons School anyway. Don't you?"

"I'll split my salary with you."

"There it is. I'll live on scorpions and rattlesnake meat."

"It tastes like chicken."

Kevin laughed. "Everything tastes like chicken."

Brian laughed, too. "Rattlesnake really *does* taste like chicken."

"You're so full of it. How would you know?"

"SERE school, bro. Navy survival and POW training."

Kevin laughed at the image of his little brother chasing snakes in the desert and eating them. "I'll let you know what I find out."

"Don't do anything stupid."

"Don't worry about it. I've got it for action." Kevin hung up and looked over his shoulder. No time like the present. The Wicked Witch had gone home for the night, but not until she'd checked on Kevin and all the others who worked for her, to make sure they weren't playing solitaire on their computers. He went into the conference room and closed the door silently behind him. He was breathing more heavily than he would like. He turned on the lights and went to the secure encrypted phone. He opened up his PalmPilot and looked up the number of the embassy in Islamabad. He dialed the number quickly, glancing at the closed door. The phone began its odd ringing sound, and he waited patiently for someone to pick up the receiver. Finally a voice answered in English, "United States embassy."

"Administration, please."

"I'll connect you."

Another odd ring commenced, and again Kevin waited. Finally a woman answered. "Renee Williams."

"Renee, Kevin Hayes."

"Kevin, how are you?"

"Not so well. Since I called, I've been read out by my boss for 'interfering' in Asian affairs."

"Truly?"

"Truly. Who did you tell that I'd called?"

"Just the attaché. I . . . can't think of anyone else."

"Must be somebody. It took all of about three milliseconds for her to hear about it."

"Maybe she was listening to your phone."

"Possible. But I don't think so. That would have meant she thought I was doing something *else* that might have been interesting. And I'm not. My Africa stuff is boring as shit. Nobody would spend five minutes listening to my telephone calls."

"So what's up?"

"I know I'm asking a lot. I asked you to look into that guy's background, but I didn't tell you much. The more I think about it, the more I think we have to be very careful with this. I also didn't say why I was asking."

"No. You didn't."

"Go secure," he said.

"Got it," she replied.

They both turned their phones to the encrypted mode that made it impossible for anyone to listen in. All someone who had tapped the line would hear was static.

"It's my brother. He's the acting intelligence officer for a fighter weapons school a friend of his started in Nevada."

"I read about that in the newspaper."

"Yeah. But did you know that four Pakistani pilots are students there?"

"So *that's* it. I knew four pilots had gone to the United States for training, but I didn't put the two together. I thought it was that other school at Mojave. The test pilot school. It came on our screen once a few years ago. The State Department got bent because they didn't have the right visas to be there. This is a different school?"

"Yeah. Like TOPGUN. They fly MiGs and teach fighter tactics."

"Wow. Nice job. So Khan is a student there?"

"Yes. He's the leader. My brother has hair standing up all over the back of his neck. This guy is really bugging him. Brian can't put his finger on it, but he thinks something is up. I learned a long time ago to listen to his instincts."

Renee grew cool. "I learned a long time ago that instincts don't mean anything."

"So let's split the difference and check this guy out a little bit more."

"Kevin, look, I'd love to help you, but I really don't have time to run this guy down. We don't have any evidence of anything suspicious. We can't be spending intelligence assets chasing down every Pakistani Air Force pilot."

"I'm not asking you to chase down every pilot," he said, pushing back against her resistance. She had to do it for him. If Khan was actually up to something, there was no way the ingrown CIA was ever going to get onto it before it happened—whatever "it" was. Kevin's opinion of his employer was that they were much better at explaining why they didn't anticipate something than at actually predicting anything effectively. Typical performance for a bureaucracy. But then he realized maybe that was more a reflection of his own lazy attitude toward the work he considered boring and stupid than of the CIA as a whole. He wasn't privy to much of the work done by the Agency. He also knew if he was to have any hope of staying at the Agency, he needed to distinguish himself—and fast. "I'm just asking you to track down one pilot. Trace him all the way back to where he was born. If he has an ax to grind, if he's up to something, we need to know it now. We're not being told by somebody to do this, we're doing it the old-fashioned way—by getting information *before* something happens, not afterward."

"Come on, Kevin. What do you think is going to happen? You don't have anything."

"One minute the Undersecretary of Defense is against the school opening. Thinks it's stupid. The next minute he's authorizing the school with one stroke of the pen, giving them their license to teach foreign students, then greasing the skids with State for the foreign student visas and making sure the school gets opened with lease terms in place that will make it profitable—*all* conditional on their taking foreign students in the first class, and in particular students from Pakistan."

"Now you suspect the Undersecretary of *Defense* of something? Are you out of your mind?"

He did. But he wasn't ready to make an accusation. Yet. "Somebody's benefiting. I don't know what's going on. But let's find out. And no, I don't know what this guy Khan is up to. But if he has something against the U.S. and is being allowed to fly supersonic jets inside the country, he could do a lot of things. The fact we can't figure it out beforehand doesn't mean we shouldn't try to stop it."

Renee paused. She didn't owe him any big favors, and if she was discovered chasing some crazy theory of his, it could ruin her career. "I'll think about it."

"I'm not going to let you skate on this. I want a commitment from you."

"You're not in any position to demand anything from me. This is a wild-goose chase. I don't have the time or the assets. Who do you think you're talking to?" she asked harshly.

"I'm sorry. I just need your help."

"So now you're begging, all friendly and helpless. Don't try to manipulate me," she said. She thought for a moment. "There are a couple of people I can ask. But I'm not going to do much else."

"That's a start. Thanks. Please let me know what they say."

"If I do tell you something, it's not for your brother."

"He has a secret clearance with the new school."

"Not good enough."

"Okay. Don't worry about that."

"I'll call you," she said reluctantly, and hung up.

14

Luke glanced in the rearview mirror of his Corvette to make sure the tan Taurus was following him down the Nevada highway. Khan was matching his every turn.

Katherine had been unenthusiastic about having Khan and one of his pilots over for dinner, but she was willing if Luke insisted. She had no idea what to fix. She didn't know what Pakistanis ate. Luke had asked the Major what food was acceptable, and he'd said that anything would be fine. Katherine had decided to fix steaks with fresh vegetables.

Luke rounded the final curve and headed directly toward his house. He saw that Brian was right behind the Taurus. He'd run into Brian in the gym at the hangar that morning and watched him fight his deteriorating muscles on the StairMaster. He'd looked as if he were dying, biting the air as he fought his way through every step.

It had been hard to watch, but Luke was glad he'd stopped by. Brian had told him of the efforts Kevin was making to look into Khan. Nothing to report yet, he'd said, but they were working on it. Luke had started watching every one of them carefully.

He turned onto the private road that ran for half a mile off the state highway and passed their house. He pulled into the driveway and activated the garage door opener, then skill-fully guided the Corvette to its spot in the garage. He closed up the garage and went out the side door to show Khan and

Rashim, his lieutenant, the front entrance. Thud was already there.

Katherine got up off the couch and Thud stood from the chair he was in. She kissed Luke and turned to Major Khan to extend her hand. "Welcome. I'm Katherine."

"It is very nice to meet you. This is my lieutenant, Rashim."

"Rashim is a pilot as well. I'm sure I told you about him," Luke said.

"Yes, I'm sure," Katherine said. She looked at Rashim, who was her height and impossibly young. "I'm glad that you were able to join us for dinner."

"It is my pleasure. Thank you for inviting us. I hope it is not too much trouble."

"You both know Brian Hayes," Luke said, acknowledging the obvious, "and Thud. May I get you something? Beer? Wine?"

Major Khan said softly in his deep voice, "We do not consume alcohol. I told you that."

"Right," Luke said. "Sorry. Water? Tea?"

"Tea would be fine."

"Tea it is," Katherine said, heading for the kitchen.

"Please come in. Let me show you around." They started walking toward the family room, Luke next to Thud.

Thud whispered, "Sluf's still nowhere to be seen."

Luke glanced at him. "Where the hell could he be?"

"No idea. He definitely flew in. I confirmed it with the tower. And no one's seen him since. He's missed three flights and two classes. No answer at his condo. He's got one of those tape answering machines where the beep gets longer with the number of messages? It's completely full. Can't even leave a message."

Luke was perplexed. "He can't have just disappeared."

"True."

"What do you think?" he asked quietly as they stopped.

"I don't know. But I think it's time to get the sheriff involved."

"The sheriff?" Luke exclaimed.

"You got any other ideas?"

"There must be some explanation . . ."

"I'm all ears."

"All right. Call the sheriff in the morning."

"Will do."

Luke walked toward the back of the house, pointing out the unique Western and Native American art and furniture. He took them out onto the back patio. Luke had finally finished the shade covering, and the now-sheltered patio looked out over the fifty acres they owned and the thousands of acres that, although indistinguishable, were not their property. It was federal land, as was most of the rest of Nevada. The closest house was at least a mile away and barely visible when he pointed it out.

Khan studied the leveled dirt. "What work are you doing?"

Luke stared at the dirt and his unfinished work. "Building a runway."

Khan and Rashim looked at Luke with surprise. "What for?"

"To buy an airplane to fly to Tonopah every day instead of driving. Or anywhere else I want to go."

"Your own private airfield? Is this allowed?"

"Sure. You have to follow the regulations, but you can fly from your own airstrip anytime."

Khan was stunned. "You own your own fighter squadron, your own private fighter base, and now you will have an airstrip at your own house?"

Luke detected bitterness in Khan's tone. "It's always been a dream of mine. I want to own a biplane. An acrobatic plane that I can just fly in the sky over my house and run out of gas and dead-stick right back down to my backyard. It may sound silly to you—"

"No," Khan said.

"I could fly to work. Take off here, land at Tonopah, fly my MiG, then fly my own airplane home for dinner." He thought about it. "Well, it's not going to happen anytime soon. The plane I want costs too much money."

"What kind of airplane do you want to buy?"

"I was thinking about a Stearman, but I don't know. A good refurbished Stearman would be over a hundred thousand dollars, and they're sixty or seventy years old. I was thinking of buying a new Pitts Special. You can get them brand-new right out of the factory in Wyoming. But they cost even more than a Stearman."

"The Pitts? The one they used to fly in the acrobatic championships?"

"That's the one."

"Small biplane."

"Yep."

"I have seen them before. Very nice."

"If I had a lot of nerve, I would buy a Sukhoi. It's probably the best aerobatic airplane in the world right now. They're a little squirrelly, and maintenance might be tricky, but what an airplane."

"It would be in keeping with your ownership of Russian fighters. You could get your private airplane from the other Russian design bureau, from Sukhoi," Khan said. "I'm sure you never expected to be one of the biggest operators of Russian airplanes outside of Russia."

"Not even close," Luke said.

"How have you liked the school so far?" Luke asked as Katherine handed them each their drinks.

"As you know, we would like more air-to-ground, but the training that we have been getting has been . . . adequate."

Luke almost choked on Khan's description. Adequate? It was at least a hundred times better than anything he'd ever known before. If he paid attention, he might actually leave the school knowing something—knowing how to fight in combat, how to employ his aircraft, how to defend his country. Instead he was more interested in insulting Luke and the school and the United States. "Have you learned anything?" Luke asked, trying to keep the sarcasm he felt out of his voice.

"Like what?" Khan asked.

Never mind, Luke thought. Just never the hell mind. "Don't forget to go down to the flight line tomorrow at 1600," he said, changing the subject.

"Why?" Khan asked.

"Class picture. The first class of the Nevada Fighter Weapons School. It's a momentous occasion."

Khan grew instantly uneasy. "I don't think so."

"Why not?"

"I have set a meeting for my group for that time."

Rashim glanced at him, confused.

"This photo has been on the weekly schedule since you arrived."

"Impossible. Our meeting is extremely important."

Khan was obviously dodging the photo. Luke was tired of letting the little deceptions go by. "I guess we'll have to change the photo to another time. You have any other meetings scheduled?"

"Yes, many. But you go ahead and take the photo."

"Nah, that's okay. We'll reschedule."

"No," Khan insisted.

"Why not?" Katherine asked.

"You would not understand. It is a cultural imperative."

Luke knew he had Khan in a ridiculous corner. He decided to press it. "Tell you what—since you can't make the photo shoot tomorrow, why don't we have Katherine take our picture together tonight, just for fun?"

"No photos."

"None at all?" Thud asked, seeing the concern on Khan's face.

"I'm afraid not."

"Why?"

"Cultural."

"What about your culture?"

"You wouldn't understand."

Thud leaned toward Khan. "Try me."

Khan looked back at him, unmoved. "No."

"It's time to eat. I hope steak is okay," Katherine commented, trying to keep whatever was happening from getting worse.

"Fine," Khan said.

"Let me take your drinks. I have water on the table already." Katherine put all five drinks on a tray and headed for the kitchen.

Khan and Rashim wandered around the expansive family room looking at the decorations and the artwork. The sun had set, and the desert cast a reddening glow over the room through the enormous picture windows that faced south.

Khan had his hands behind his back as he stared at a pottery vase on an end table. He picked it up. "What is this?" He studied it intently, turning it over in his hands, feeling the rough textures and examining the workmanship.

Luke was surprised by his interest. "It's a Paiute pot."

"What is a Paiute?"

"Native American."

"Yes. Of course. An Indian. They are ever-present in my life."

Luke couldn't keep from smiling. "Right. Indians. Columbus thought he'd made it to India."

"Yes. What did they use these for?"

"This one was just ornamental. Sort of . . . art. From

about a hundred years ago. They used to live near Pioche, Nevada, where I grew up. In fact, Pioche was founded when a Paiute Indian showed a miner an ore—"

"Interesting," Khan said, returning the pot to Luke.

Luke placed it back on the table. Khan had the annoying habit of asking about things just so he could dismiss the answer as unimportant or uninteresting.

Hayes decided to ask the question he had been waiting to ask. The more off-the-wall his timing was, the more likely that Khan might actually give him an unfiltered response. "How come you were so shocked by Crumb the other day?" Hayes asked.

"What?"

Luke interjected, "I'm going to go see if Katherine needs any help."

"When Crumb mentioned warheads to you—you know, when he asked you if you wanted a warhead, that hard candy he offered you—you about came out of your skin. Why?" Hayes pressed.

"I didn't understand him. I thought he wanted us to load actual warheads on our airplanes for the school. I couldn't imagine why."

Hayes wasn't buying it. "That's what you thought? Seriously?"

"Yes. That is exactly what I thought."

Hayes drank from his glass and looked at the desert behind Luke's house. "Tell me about life in the Air Force in Pakistan."

"What would you like to know?"

"Where exactly are you stationed?"

"Do you know Pakistan?"

"Not really."

"Then what good would it do for me to tell you?"

"Just curious. Tell me about your career, from training to

where you are now. How does it work there? You know, promotion, job selection, that kind of thing. Where you've been stationed, the kinds of airplanes you flew—all of that."

Khan was on guard. "Why would you care about that?"

"Just curious."

"I am a Major in the Pakistani Air Force and am based at the Air Force base near Islamabad."

"Where were you stationed before that?"

Khan looked at Hayes differently than before. "Why the sudden interest?"

"Just curious," Hayes repeated.

Khan folded his hands behind his back and pushed his chest out slightly. "You are an intelligence officer."

"Was."

"That is your job at NFWS, yes?"

"Sort of."

"Is it part of your job to check out the students? To see whether you trust them?"

"No."

Khan glanced at Rashim, who was concentrating on the smells coming from the kitchen, leaning toward them as if he were about to be drawn to the dinner table against his will. Khan faced Hayes and looked him directly in the eyes. "You don't trust me, do you, Mr. Hayes?"

Hayes was unruffled. "What reason would I have to not trust you?"

"Have you been checking up on me? Have you been asking about me?"

"Why in the world would I do that?" Hayes responded, his mouth growing progressively drier.

"I don't know," Khan admitted. "Just a feeling that I have. Whenever I am talking to someone else, you watch me like you are trying to discover something about me. You have seen others do that sort of thing?"

"I don't know."

"Well, I have noticed it in you. It is disturbing, to be at a school and have the intelligence officer be suspicious of you. You wanted to know what it was like in Pakistan? Well, in Pakistan you don't want the intelligence officers to be suspicious of you—of that you can be sure. If they are, you must do something about it." Khan's eyes bored into Hayes's until Hayes felt as if he were under physical assault. He'd never encountered such energy, such hostility.

Thud watched Khan, afraid he was about to attack Hayes.

Finally Brian answered Khan. "That *would* be bad. It's not like that in the U.S. Intelligence officers just collect data and sit in dark rooms thinking. They're your best friends."

"I think not," Khan replied.

"Dinner!" Katherine called from the dining room.

Brian cursed under his breath. Then he reached into his pocket and turned off the microcassette recorder.

RENEE'S dark skin fitted in well with her look. She had dressed to make herself invisible, wearing a *burkha*. Her face was completely covered, except for her deep brown eyes, deep brown only because of the colored contact lenses she was wearing. She had the look of someone of the lower middle class in Islamabad, perhaps the lower class clawing to become lower middle class. The kind of woman anyone of substance would not even look at even if she spoke to them, a woman with a frayed *burkha* and dirty hands.

She walked into the *mandi*—the marketplace—thirty minutes before the scheduled rendezvous. She looked around carefully for indications of intelligence activities, for someone who might be expecting her, other than her contact. It was an extraordinarily busy square, far from the center of town but near many residential areas. It was where people went to do their daily shopping for produce, as well as to eat—on the rare occasion when they might go to a street vendor.

Renee stood hunched over, working her way down the rows of vegetables while flies circled. She shooed a swarm of them from a bunch of carrots and dropped the carrots into her plastic net bag. She glanced around as if looking for a friend and quickly surveyed where she was to meet her contact. She continued purchasing produce and made her way around several tables, in the process getting numerous wide-angle views of the *mandi*.

After twenty minutes of meticulous shopping she had selected five items and went to the clerk to pay. She pulled out a thin wad of rupees, took two bills, and handed them over. The clerk spoke to her sharply. She replied in a hoarse, tired voice. She put the change in the bottom of her large bag.

She shuffled across the square toward a street vendor who was selling unidentified meat on sticks, and out of the corner of her eye she saw her contact. He didn't recognize her and stood waiting at a table where a woman was selling small rugs. He chewed on a tough piece of meat and sipped a drink as he pretended to examine the rugs. There was a sign on the table telling prospective patrons the woman vendor was deaf.

Renee walked to the end of the table and poked at the cheap rugs. She spoke to the man softly in fluent Urdu. "Thank you for coming."

He replied, "I told you I do not like meetings. Why is this necessary?"

"Did you find anything?"

"Some. Why does this matter?"

"It may not."

"Then why do you want to know?"

"I don't."

The man bit down angrily on the dry meat. "Then why did you ask these questions?"

"Have you found anything?"

"The records go back only five years. Before that, nothing."

"Is that unusual?"

"They're very careful about military records. His are incomplete."

"If you're writing false records, wouldn't you be complete?"

"I would."

"Who is he?"

"An Air Force Major."

"Is there more to it?"

"Not according to the records."

"Where is he from?"

"The records say Islamabad."

She listened carefully. "You don't think so."

"I doubt it."

"Why?"

"I don't know. If you were hiding your origins, you would say you were from here. It is easy to disappear in Islamabad. Our records are poor. We don't have—what do you call them?—social numbers."

"Social Security numbers." She coughed as if she were tubercular, then paused, leaning over the table in apparent pain, still hunched over. Those around glanced at her, then looked away. "But you found other things. What have you found?"

He looked at her in disgust. "Are you ill?"

"No."

He went on reluctantly. "He seems to be well known. He is thought to be many things by many different people."

"Explain."

"Those who are in favor of the government believe he is a threat to the government. Those who are against the government believe him to be a threat to them, and pro-government.

The Islamic fundamentalists believe he is an intelligence agent who will be their undoing. Those who are the secularists, and afraid of the Islamic militants, fear he is an Islamist."

Renee thought about what he was saying. It troubled her deeply. He sounded like a professional intelligence operative. "What do *you* think?"

"I don't know. It sounds disturbing. He sounds like someone that you do not want to be on the wrong side of, and an awful lot of people believe themselves already to be on his wrong side."

"Does he have a particular cause?"

The man finished his drink and wiped his mouth with his sleeve. "If he does, it is unknown. You can find someone who will tell you what he thinks this Khan's cause is, but it will just be whatever the person telling you most fears."

"Any associates?"

"Many associates, but few of them are known. Even fewer are recognized."

"Anything else?"

"One thing." The man fought with himself as he debated whether to tell Renee what he had learned. "It doesn't make sense to me, so I hesitate to repeat it."

"What?"

"He was seen in Karachi recently."

She was surprised. "That's a long way."

"It *is* a long way, and his Air Force base is up here, near Islamabad, flying F-16s, I'm told. He was not in Karachi on behalf of the Air Force."

"What was he doing there?"

"He was seen with other men. Near the docks."

"The docks?"

"Yes. Near some ships loading."

"Why?"

"No one knows. He seemed out of place."

"Do you know when?"

"Six weeks ago."

"Exactly?"

"I don't know."

"Can you find out?"

"I don't think so. Why?"

"He must have been there for a reason. If we know the date, we might somehow learn what he was doing."

"That's all I know. If you want something else, you'll have to get it from somebody else."

"You don't think he's related to the head of Pakistani intelligence?"

"No."

"How can you be sure?"

"I just am."

"Where did you get the information that he was in Karachi?" She waited, but there was no response. She waited, then glanced up and saw that he was gone.

Renee had noticed his growing restlessness and nervousness. She wasn't sure of the cause, probably that he was feeling awkward standing with a woman at a table selling rugs. She did not look for him and did not look up from the table. After a minute or so she grabbed her bag and shuffled out of the *mandi* in the direction of a poor residential district.

15

Luke and Thud leaned on the hangar door as they watched Vlad and Dr. Thurmond climb down from the two-seat MiG-29. They looked for a bulging pocket in his G suit indicating a newly filled barf bag, or that green, peaked look people had on their faces that they tried to smile through to convince others that flying in a jet is really fun. They didn't see anything on Dr. Thurmond's face. They pushed away from the door and walked to meet them.

"How did it go?" Thud asked his father.

"Incredible," Dr. Thurmond replied, a huge grin illuminating his face. "I'd forgotten how great that is."

"Did you let him fly it?" Luke asked Vlad.

"Yes, of course. As soon as we got airborne, I gave him the controls. He did wonderful. Natural pilot."

"How did you think it handled?" Thud asked.

"Great turning ability, incredible acceleration. When I'd get the nose pointed up for a long time at slow speed, I'd get real anxious. If you do that with a 105, you'll find yourself in a hole in a hurry. With this airplane the speed just doesn't bleed off. You can point the nose anywhere you want. Amazing airplane."

They entered the hangar, and Vlad started over toward one of the MiGs that had an engine out of the bay. "I must check on the engine replacement," he said, then stepped under the wing.

Dr. Thurmond pointed toward the paraloft. They walked in while he removed the borrowed flight gear.

"I want to keep flying here. I want to get back up to speed and get checked out in this jet."

"You weren't a TOPGUN instructor, Dad," Thud said. "You can't fly in the syllabus hops."

"No, but what about postmaintenance check flights? Maybe just fly when I feel like it. I own the company, don't I?"

Luke replied, "Yes, sir, you sure do. We'll see what we can arrange."

Dr. Thurmond finished hanging his flight gear, something he was clearly relishing, then turned to Luke. "How well do you know Vlad?"

Luke was surprised. "I don't know, why?"

"He had alcohol on his breath."

"Seriously?" Luke asked, troubled.

"Seriously. What do you really know about his time in Russia?"

"We've got copies of his records. I reviewed them . . ."

"I'd check into him, if I were you."

Luke nodded. "Brian's got the records. He was going to check them."

"I'd follow up."

"Yes, sir," Luke replied.

"Good. Can I talk to Quentin alone?"

"Sure," Luke said, glancing at Thud as he walked out of the room.

Thud was dreading what was coming. He expected another lecture.

Thurmond looked at his son. "Quentin, I think I owe you an apology."

Thud felt awkward and cornered. "Dad, you don't—"

"I've been hard on you. I was against your going into the

Navy. I was against your flying, being a government employee, joining the military—the whole thing. I was putting my Vietnam experience before good judgment, before just allowing you to do what you want to do. Thanks for letting me be part of this."

Thud smiled. "If it had been up to me, you wouldn't be. Luke's the one who thought you might want in."

"Well, he was right. We need to do this thing together. I'll stay out of your hair, but I wanted to let you know I'm behind you one hundred percent."

Thud kept waiting for the other shoe to drop, but it never did. "Thanks."

"Let's go debrief with your drunk Russian."

THE tired-looking freighter crept through the Strait of Juan de Fuca. It was a misty gray morning with the beautiful Olympic Mountains obscured by haze and rain. Water ran down from the sky over the entire ship in one continuous motion—down the bridge windows, the stack, and the rusting sides of the containers secured to the deck.

The tramp steamer worked its way through the beautiful bay to the busy docks of Tacoma. It was the scruffiest of many unattractive ships at the docks, mostly Korean and Japanese container ships stacked with innumerable containers. The ship slowly maneuvered to a stop with the help of two tugs that pushed it gently against the long pier. The captain yelled to the dockworkers to secure the lines and gave the engineer the okay to shut down the propulsion. The pilot made his way out of the bridge as the crane maneuvered the gangplank to the side of the ship. The captain glanced at the clock. They were to be unloaded in one hour. The two containers, the last items placed on the ship, were to be unloaded directly onto trucks. It was unusual for him to carry cargo so time-sensitive that trucks would be waiting, but there they were. He saw the trucks from the company that was on his cargo manifest. He could deliver the containers only to them.

A second crane approached the ship and slung over the cables to grab the container. The deck crew was waiting and hooked the four thick steel cables to the top corners of the container. The cables strained as the container rose slowly off the deck and began a gentle twist. The neck of the crane bent slightly as it absorbed the full weight of the container and slung it away from the ship.

It was lowered directly onto the bed of the waiting truck and secured by the dockworkers. The crane lifted the cables away from the container, and the truck rolled slowly down the pier. The second container was lowered onto the second truck, which followed the first toward the customs shed. Looking bored and tired, the two drivers waited patiently in line for the customs inspectors. They had been driving all night, and it showed in their faces and their attitudes. They didn't understand the need for *them* to pick up these loads. All they knew was that they were to drop them off in a nearby warehouse today. It had to be their trucks, and they had to pick them up immediately upon the arrival of the ship. They couldn't imagine why *they* had to drive all the way up to Tacoma from San Francisco or why some local company couldn't do it. But it wasn't their place to wonder why, just to pick up the containers.

The first truck pulled up to the customs inspector, who regarded the driver carefully. "Documents, please," the inspector said.

The driver handed him the documents he'd brought as well as the bill of lading from the container off the ship.

The customs inspector took the documents and went back to look at the container. The door seal was intact, and the documents were in order. The inspector debated with himself whether to open the container. Only a few were actually opened and inspected. Hundreds, if not thousands, of containers arrived on an almost daily basis in every major port in the United States. If every container were opened and inspected in any detail, the entire system would fall of its own weight. The customs inspectors looked for other things: a nervous driver, documentation that appeared odd or strange, a means of delivery that was different or out of order, or a shipper or manufacturer they'd never encountered before. Every once in a while they would open a container on a simple hunch or just to be arbitrary, so even those who thought they could predict which containers would be opened would be wrong on occasion.

The inspector sipped coffee from a Styrofoam cup, something he wasn't supposed to do while on the line, but he was *cold*. He walked back to the driver, signed the document, handed him the bill of lading, and said, "You're cleared."

The driver, still bored, pulled slowly away from the line. The second truck received the same cursory treatment from the same cold customs inspector.

The trucks threaded through the morning traffic with the mist enveloping the entire scene. It muted everything, as if nothing fast, loud, hot, or flashy was allowed. The trucks, staying together, worked their way down to the row of warehouses that was their destination. The driver checked the address again on the piece of paper he had in his shirt pocket. He drove through the narrow roads until he found the one he wanted and turned left, parallel to the water. The street was set back from the actual waterfront about two hundred yards. He came upon an open space in front of a large warehouse and saw the number on the front of the building in clear block letters. He turned sharply toward the large doors at the front of the warehouse, and the second truck did likewise. As the first truck approached the doors and started to brake, the doors slid open. A man stood in front of him motioning him to keep driving into the warehouse.

The driver released the clutch slowly, and the truck moved

forward through the rain into the cavernous opening. Another door of equal size was open at the other end of the warehouse. A large steel crane hung from the girders above the truck.

Another man stood in front and motioned for him to slow down. The man watched the position of the crane and the truck, waved the driver forward slowly, and finally signaled him to stop. The driver set the emergency brake and got out of the truck with his papers. He handed his clipboard to the man who seemed to be in charge, a small dark man. "Sign for it," the driver said.

The smaller man was of Asian descent, probably Filipino, the driver thought. He looked at the driver for any signs of suspicion or concern. There were none. The man signed with an indecipherable signature, took one copy of the form, and handed him the other. "Any problems with customs?"

The driver shook his head as he took the clipboard and tossed it through the window onto the seat. "You taking the container off now?"

The man nodded and gestured for the crane operator to begin hooking up the container. "It will be just a minute."

The driver stood back, not relishing the thought of some crane accidentally dropping the heavy container onto the cab of his truck.

As the driver watched, the hanging crane rolled into place on large steel tracks on the beam above. He looked around the warehouse warily. He'd never seen a setup like this before. He couldn't account for the huge, empty warehouse and the sterile, concentrated unloading of these two trucks. It didn't smell right. He noticed several brand-new sedans and large Ford commercial trucks, which struck him as odd. He also found it strange that the vehicles were all parked inside the warehouse. Probably because of the rain, he concluded. He turned to the man who was supervising the container. "Whose trucks?"

The man looked at him. "As soon as you pull away from the crane, stop in the office," he said, pointing. "They have your extra pay there."

"What extra pay?" the driver asked, surprised. "We get paid by the company."

"There's a bonus."

The driver frowned, then shrugged.

The crane lifted the first container off the truck and moved it slowly to the side. The truck stood up higher, grateful for the relief from the tons of weight it had been carrying moments before. Once the container was freed from the back of the truck, the driver clambered back up into his cab, started the truck, and drove out from under the crane. As soon as his truck was clear, he pulled to the side, climbed back down, and headed toward the office. The second driver pulled in behind him, right where he'd been, and began unloading the second container. He, too, was told to be sure to pick up his bonus in the office.

He followed the first driver into the office, where they sat down and waited. The small man in charge nodded to two men standing next to the office. They opened the back of one of the new trucks, took out the submachine guns, and strolled into the office. The shots were barely audible above the motor of the crane inside the warehouse.

"You Kevin Hayes?"

Kevin looked up from his computer screen at a man he'd never seen before.

"Yeah. Can I help you?"

The man walked in and sat down in the chair next to Kevin's desk. He was in his early forties and looked authoritative. Not a good sign, Hayes thought. "What's up?"

"I'm Bill Morrissey. Central Asia."

Kevin extended his hand, and the man took it. "Nice to meet you. What can I do for you?"

"You've been talking with Renee."

Here we go again. "Couple of times."

"You had her contact agents on behalf of your brother, who's working for a private company."

Kevin was immediately defensive. "I asked her to look into something that I believe has implications for the United States. My brother told me about it. I didn't think anyone else would consider it a big enough deal to look into, so I did it myself. *How* she was to look into it was her decision, and it was official government business. Why is it that everybody is on my ass for trying to do what we're supposed to do?"

"It looks like you're simply running a job for your brother. But if you're really onto something, I want to hear about it. Tell me what you know."

Kevin did. Then, "It's mostly speculation. The latest stuff from Renee makes me really wonder about this guy, though."

Morrissey thought for a while, then said in a clipped manner, "We really have no indication that he has anything in mind, or even remotely what it might be if he does."

"What about showing up at the docks in Karachi? Don't you find that odd?"

"Very," he replied. "But what was he doing there? Why would he care about shipping? And if he was sending people over to that school, wouldn't they ship over some of their equipment? Airplane parts?"

"I don't know."

"I don't either. We should find out. Find out what's been shipped from Karachi to the United States around those dates, what its destination was, and what has come of it. We could have customs take a look at it."

"Could do. Then there's the whole connection, the whole way that they got into the class. The Undersecretary of Defense."

"What do you know about that?" Morrissey asked.

"Struck me as truly odd. Sounds to me like they're a little too close."

"Meaning what?"

"No way to know. I don't want to accuse anybody of anything. It might pay to have the FBI look into it, though."

Morrissey stood to leave. "They already are."

Good, Kevin thought. But then he wondered what they knew. "Why?"

"They started wondering about him all on their own." Morrissey paused. "Right after he disappeared."

"What?" Kevin gasped. "Disappeared? Are you shitting me?"

"And a lot of money went through his bank account right before he skipped."

"We may really be onto something."

"Maybe, maybe not. I want you to start checking all the shipping records—"

"No way," Kevin said, leaning back in his chair and putting up his hands. "I've already gotten my ass chewed once."

"The witch?"

Hayes's eyes got big. He didn't dare confirm her name.

"She knows."

"It's okay with her?"

"She's on board with you helping me. We've got to get more people on this. That's why I'm here to ask for your help. This one is starting to worry me. A lot."

"Shouldn't we send someone to Nevada?"

"CIA doesn't operate inside the U.S."

"Well, then get the FBI to send someone."

"They're thinking about it."

WIDEMAN'S Gun Shop closed at *exactly* six o'clock every night. Greg Wideman was meticulous and punctual. He never stayed open late. As he turned the sign around on the door and prepared to pull the steel bars home, he felt a push on the door. He looked up and saw four men staring at him. "We're closed!" he said loudly, annoyed. His annoyance was quickly replaced by apprehension when he got a good look at the faces of the four men who pushed through the door and stood in front of him.

They were small men with dark skin and hard, angry looks. They were all unshaven, and their clear leader had a thick black beard. They looked around his gun shop, the largest in Nevada, as if they'd never seen anything like it. The two in the rear were walking backward, looking at the machine guns suspended from the wall above the door through which they had just entered. They continued toward Wideman.

"You the owner?" the bearded man in front asked.

"Yes."

"We need to buy some of your weapons."

"We're closed."

"No, you are not," the man replied confidently as he strolled casually through the store and gawked at the hundreds and hundreds of weapons.

"What did you have in mind?" Wideman asked grudgingly.

"Machine guns."

The owner, who wore a Rueger baseball cap, frowned at the request. "Machine guns are illegal."

"You have semiautomatic, right?" the man continued.

"Sure. All kinds. What did you want?"

"We want the most powerful you have."

"What do you mean by powerful?"

"Largest caliber."

The owner looked at the man's face momentarily. He didn't want to cross him. "We've got several types, nine-millimeter, even a ten-millimeter MAC-10—that's a rare one, can't even get those anymore—and, let's see, an AR-15, that's a .223-caliber, not big around but tremendous muzzle velocity, and"—he turned to look at the rack, which had a steel cable passing through the trigger guards of the guns—"lots of things. Depends on what you want it for."

"We need twelve of them," the tall man said matter-of-factly. "To take now."

"Can't do that. Only three guns per buyer per month."

"Yes. There are four of us. That makes twelve," the man said, unsmiling. The other three were looking around the gun shop for any other patrons, and one was looking for hidden cameras.

"Damned if it don't," the proprietor said. "Which kind do you want?"

"Do you have AK-47s?"

"Nah, those are impossible. Illegal to import them. But I do have a few . . . 'replicas,' " he said.

"Are they automatic?"

"No. Like I was saying. That would be illegal."

"Can they be made automatic?"

The proprietor chortled with his smoker's laugh. "You with the ATF or something? You ask the most direct damned questions. Sure, somebody dedicated to doing it could do it easy. But that would be a *felony*, see. And *I'm* not doing that."

"How is it done?"

"A little kit thing. Just sold as a curiosity. Most people *I* know use 'em for . . . paperweights. But if you get caught putting one of those assemblies into one of those weapons and turning it automatic? You'd go straight to the federal pen. Hell, now you can't even own that. The ATF has taken all the fun—"

"How much are these replicas?" the man asked.

"A lot."

"How much?"

"Where are you boys from?" Wideman asked. "I can't place your accents. You from Nevada? Just move here?"

"Does it matter?"

"Sure. I've got to do a license check. Then I've got to do a felony check."

"Is there any other way?"

The man sighed. "Nope, really isn't."

"You said the guns were expensive. How expensive?"

"Seven-fifty apiece."

"We were prepared to pay a thousand apiece."

"Whoa." Wideman laughed. "That's a lot of money. They're not worth that—"

"We would pay a thousand apiece if they were automatic and did not include a background check."

"I don't think you understand," the owner said as he hitched his pants up quickly over his belly. "I have to do a background check. Where are you guys from?"

"We will pay you twelve thousand dollars for twelve 'replica' AK-47s. We were told they would be available here."

The man's eyes got large. "Who the hell told you that?"

"Someone who knows. Was he wrong?"

Wideman glanced at the door to see if anyone was coming. "No, he wasn't wrong. Let's cut the bullshit," he said as he walked to the front and pulled down the shade that covered the glass front door. "You want fully automatic AKs?"

"Yes."

"I've got them, and I'll sell them to you. None of this trigger kit shit. These are authentic, Russian made. The real things, still packed in cosmolene. I've got a source. Fully auto, *and*," he said, glancing around at the four men, who had come closer, "I've got the ammo for them. *And* there aren't any serial numbers on them, so if you hit something when you're doing your target practice, they can't be traced here. And if you ever get caught for hitting something, you've never been here and I've never seen you. Agreed?"

The leader nodded.

"Fully automatic AKs with no numbers are rare. They will run you more than those replica pieces of shit. They're two thousand apiece. And I'll throw in five hundred rounds of ammo for each and five banana clips."

"Fifteen hundred and a thousand rounds of ammunition for each."

"Two thousand."

"Eighteen hundred."

"Done." Wideman headed to the back of the shop.

The four Pakistani men went out the back door and looked around anxiously as they stood by their trucks while Wideman stacked the crates. The second in command looked at the bearded leader of the group. "Who goes first?"

The leader looked at his digital watch that had the time and date. "You go first. One truck at a time." The four brand-new commercial Ford trucks were lined up behind the gun shop. "We cannot draw attention to ourselves. We don't have much time."

"Leave from here now?"

"Yes," he said, concerned that such a simple plan could be misunderstood. He examined his lieutenant's eyes for fear or panic. There was none. "We stay in the four hotels separately, as I have told you. We will not see each other again until the night before." He watched the crates being loaded. "Do you remember where we meet?"

"The exit on the freeway. Where there is nothing. One hundred miles north."

The one with the beard nodded. "Don't be late."

16

Vlad settled down in front of the television in his BOQ room with a German beer and some sausage on a paper plate. He was fascinated by American television. It was so different from Russian television. Luke had made satellite television available in every BOQ room. Vlad was shocked not only at the number of channels available but at what you could find on the television at any hour of the day. Sports, drama, movies with naked women, Russian-language shows—which he found particularly humorous—anything one wanted was on the television. He especially liked the *Wings* shows; they detailed the history of the development and operation of famous airplanes. Vlad watched every episode he could find. Tonight was the show about the F-117 Stealth fighter. Vlad was excited about seeing it, not only because he wanted to know everything there was to know about the Stealth fighter but also because they had been based at Tonopah when they were still secret, the very base on which he now sat.

He watched the Discovery Channel logo fade in as the music started. He smiled in anticipation. The picture went dark, and one could see a vague, strange shape against the moon in the background. The sound of the lethal jet was coming into the picture from the left. Vlad leaned forward, drinking in the shape, the silhouette, plugging it into his fighter pilot data bank of possible future threats.

He snuck a deep drink from the bottle of beer as he kept one eye fixed on the television screen.

The phone rang in the kitchenette on the wall behind him. "Arrr," he said as he stood up. He slammed the empty bottle down on the coffee table and walked to the phone. *"Da,"* he said.

The voice he heard chilled him instantly. "Vladimir, it has been too long," the man said in Russian.

"Who is this?" he replied in Russian.

"How quickly you forget your friends."

"I don't forget my friends. You're not one of them. Who are you?"

"If not a friend, then at least someone to whom you are greatly indebted, Major Vladimir Petkov."

No one had called him "Major" since he left the Russian Air Force. "What do you want?"

"Did you think your perfect job with MAPS would be without cost to you? Did you think you got to the United States because of your skills and reputation?"

Vlad's heart started beating rapidly, as if someone had placed a noose around his neck some time ago and was only now alerting him to it. "What do you want?"

"It is time to pay the debt to those to whom you owe your entire life, Vladimir."

"Gorgov!" Vlad suddenly realized.

"Ah, you do remember me." Gorgov laughed. "I thought you might. I told you I would get you out of that shithole, didn't I?"

"I would have gotten out—"

"No," Gorgov said tersely. "You wouldn't have. Not ever. *I* am the only reason you got out, the only reason you are where you are."

Vlad didn't reply. He suddenly wished he hadn't just had a beer.

"So. You wonder why I call, no doubt," Gorgov said.

"It is not safe to talk," Vlad said, stalling.

"Of course it is! America is a country of laws! They can't listen to your phone calls without a warrant, and they must suspect you of something first! It is a marvelous country! How do you think we operate so effectively there?"

"You . . . are here?" Vlad gasped. He had felt safer in the United States, away from Gorgov and his type. He assumed they'd forgotten about him.

"My friends are there. How do you think we can be effective businessmen in the United States without being there?"

"Like the Russian hockey players you extort money from."

"You have been reading the American papers again. They accuse Russians of so much." Gorgov laughed, knowing it was completely true. "I am just a businessman."

"What do you want of me?"

"Yes, it does come to that, doesn't it? I will not deny it. I do want something of you. Something in payment of what you owe me for getting you the job you have."

"What?" Vlad grimaced, waiting for whatever it was, which he knew would be unpleasant.

"I cannot tell you exactly. Both because there may be someone listening, which I doubt, and also because your ability to help will be fluid, changing, responding to the moment—"

"Get to the point!" Vlad raged.

"Don't *ever* yell at me," Gorgov growled, then waited to see if Vlad was going to respond. He continued, "Something is going to happen soon. When it does, you will know what you are to do. It will be bad for the United States. Your job is to make sure it happens without interference."

"What bad thing? What are you talking about?"

"You will see."

"Why me? Is it going to happen near here?"

"It is going to happen right there. Right where you are."

Vlad shifted the phone to his other ear and peeked outside in the darkness at the base. Everything was quiet. He had no idea what Gorgov was talking about. "What exactly? Tell me!"

"No. But you will see, and soon. And it will be clear to you what you must do. Then . . . you simply do it. That is all. And if you don't . . . well, then very bad things will happen. You don't want that, do you?"

"I cannot help you if I don't know what you want!" Vlad exclaimed.

"Yes you can, and you will. You will see. *Do svidaniya*," Gorgov said, and the line went dead.

BRIAN struggled against his MS as he fought his way up the unending hill of the StairMaster in the immaculate gym at the south end of the second deck of the hangar. All the pilots were required to keep track of their workouts lifting weights. It had long been recognized that muscle mass helped resist the G forces encountered in flying jets. Although the Navy didn't require a particular workout regimen, Luke did. And he checked the records every week. Brian always had the fullest sheet, the one who'd spent the most time in the gym, fighting the demons that were wrecking his body.

Luke walked in, ready to start his early-morning workout. They were the only two in the gym.

Brian immediately slowed his climbing. He motioned to Luke. "You got a second?"

"Morning, Brian. Fine, thanks. How about you?"

"Sorry. I was thinking about some things when you walked in."

"What's up?" Luke replied.

"I've been thinking about Vlad."

Luke looked at Brian. "What about him?"

"We don't really know all that much about him."

"You're just a suspicious guy. First it's the Paks, now it's Vlad."

"Seriously."

"What?"

"I don't think we got the straight story on why he left the Russian Air Force."

"What makes you say that?"

"I finally dug into his records. They're silent on why he left. They just stop."

"How do you know?"

"I had the records he left with us retranslated. I didn't want to just accept the version he gave us. The translator I found in Vegas used to be in the Russian Army. He said they would *never* just end like that. They always put the reason. Either discharge or retirement—whatever. Vlad has kept some pages from us. We don't have the whole thing."

Luke frowned. "Why would he do that?"

"I don't know." Brian stepped off the StairMaster onto the deck and stood motionless while his legs regained their stability.

"Did I tell you that Dr. Thurmond said he smelled alcohol on Vlad's breath when he flew with him?"

"Seriously?" Brian asked. Luke nodded. "What if he was grounded? What if he was dangerous? What if he's got an alcohol problem? And he's flying as an instructor?"

"The guy's a good pilot. I've flown with him, Brian. He really knows what he's doing. He's a tremendous asset to us here."

"He's sure in tight with the Paks."

"Tight?"

"Yeah. He's given every one of them a flight in the two-seater. I've seen him out there showing them the MiGs. It just seems over the top."

"He was supposed to. We agreed to that."

"I know. But I was thinking about the missile shoot when you came in."

"What about it?"

"It's tomorrow morning. Vlad is getting MAPS to load them up this afternoon. Doesn't it trouble you just a little that we have a Russian MiG pilot here, and Russian MiGs, and a bunch of foreigners who've just learned to fly them, and we'll have four of them loaded up with live missiles? What if they decided to grab the MiGs and go shoot down an airliner?"

Luke froze. "Shit, Brian. Where'd you get that? You been staying up too late watching horror movies?"

Brian wiped the sweat dripping off his chin. "Probably. I'm just saying, if it were me? I'd move the MiGs with missiles off the regular flight line to the back hangars with security around them. Better to be safe."

Luke tossed his towel on the seat of the biceps machine. "I don't know, Brian. Sometimes I think you're paranoid." He thought as he prepared to begin his workout. "I suppose it wouldn't hurt."

"It would give me a little more peace of mind."

"Fair enough."

THE young guard sitting in the large guardhouse behind the high chain-link fence had been there almost every night since the base opened. It had sounded like an easy, exciting job. A guard in the middle of the beautiful Nevada desert at a new fighter base with privately owned jets. It had in fact turned out to be quite boring. As he was the most junior guard, he'd drawn the worst duty. Since he'd started his job as the night watchman at the main gate three weeks before, not one car had come through the gate. Not one person, not one pickup truck, not even a coyote. He'd seen some deer cross the road in front of the gate on the second night, but nothing even as exciting as that since then.

He wasn't allowed to watch television, so he spent most nights listening to the radio, to a show broadcast from a man's house in the middle of the night, and transmitted to the world. His name was Orel Spellman, and he dwelled in the belly of the night talking in hushed tones of conspiracy to those who were still up, alerting them to the growing evidence of UFOs and the government conspiracies to hide them. Orel was really on a roll tonight. The guard was listening so intently to the radio that he was actually staring at it.

Four white trucks drove down the dark, deserted moonlit road just north of the guard. They hadn't seen another car or truck for twenty minutes. It was the darkest, loneliest part of the night in the darkest, loneliest corner of the United States. The nearest Nevada Highway Patrol officer was 130 miles away at a rest stop investigating a pungent smell coming from one of the trash containers.

The lead truck stopped in the dirt on the side of the road until the other three trucks caught up, stopped behind it, and extinguished their lights. They knew exactly what to do. They'd practiced it so many times the plan had grown stale, but now that it was under way their enthusiasm returned. The driver of the lead truck, the one with the beard, watched the digital clock on the dash. They were five minutes early. The other drivers sat motionless with their hands on the steering wheels. Two more men sat to the right of each driver.

Several of the men put on night-vision goggles and adjusted the focus. They wore dark clothing and latex gloves. Each had an AK-47 in his hands.

As the digital clock changed to exactly 4:00 A.M., the lead truck pulled back onto the road. The other three followed carefully, swaying back and forth from their heavy loads. They turned south off Highway 6 at the missile with the sign underneath that announced the Tonopah Test Range Road.

They drove the twenty miles together with their lights off.

The lead truck turned on its lights as it rounded the one curve in the long road, two miles before the gate, careful to control his speed. The other three trucks waited at the curve, trying to stay out of sight. The man to the right of the driver removed his night-vision goggles and scanned the base through a high-powered night-vision rifle scope, looking for any additional security. The security at the gate was obvious, but he could see no other movement on the base at all. He looked for the roving jeep security patrol he knew was there but couldn't see.

In the guardhouse, as Orel warned of a growing conspiracy to combine UFO black programs with NASA, the guard was surprised and annoyed to see headlights approach the gate. Somebody was lost. *Way* lost. No one could possibly be on the road and on his way to the base at this hour. He had a sudden startling thought, that it could be the government working on one of the black programs he'd just been hearing about. This was, after all, where all these things were supposed to happen. He experienced a sudden surge of excitement as he felt himself being drawn into a mysterious event that would take away the boredom of the night.

He turned Orel down slightly and made sure his shirt was tucked in well. He stood up as the truck entered the spotlight beam that shone down from the top of the guard shack. It was a commercial truck, and he could see that the driver was alone. Both his hands were on the top of the steering wheel. The guard relaxed a little and waited for the truck to stop at the gate entrance.

The truck rolled slowly forward. The driver looked confused. He put his hand up to shade his eyes from the spotlight.

The guard stepped out of the guardhouse to speak with the driver. He stood with his hands on his hips, near the handgun in his holster, and looked at the driver through the ten-foot-high chain-link fence.

The bearded driver opened his door slowly, as if ashamed of having gotten lost. He left the door open and approached the fence, holding his hands out as if pleading, as if sorry for having bothered the guard.

Too late the guard noticed rapid movement on the other side of the truck. The passenger door had opened, but at first he couldn't see anything. Suddenly he saw a man running in a crouch around the front of the truck, carrying an automatic weapon of some kind. The young guard unsnapped his sidearm and began to pull out his nine-millimeter automatic. The man with the AK was faster. He began shooting at the guard's legs and feet, assuming he was wearing a bulletproof vest.

The first two shots sparked against the concrete, and the third and fourth hit the guard in the foot. He pulled his leg up in an automatic response to the searing pain and reached for the bleeding foot as he fell to the ground.

It was exactly what the attacker had wanted. He rushed the fence and shot through it at the guard from ten feet away in full automatic. Bullets riddled the guard's legs and thighs, and he screamed out in horror and pain. Finally a bullet hit him in the head, and he jerked back and lay still.

The shooter rushed back to the truck as the driver quickly flashed his lights on and off twice and slid back into the driver's seat.

The other three trucks turned on their lights and drove the two miles to the gate. They pulled up behind the lead, who had backed up to fifty feet from the gate. The driver floored the truck and smashed through the chain-link fence. It bent and then gave, finally springing away from the post as the heavy truck smashed through. The other three followed.

They had memorized the layout of the base from the diagram they'd been sent, right out of the welcome-aboard package by their fellow Pakistanis. They drove straight to the flight line. The other Pakistanis were waiting for them.

The four Pakistani pilots stood by their airplanes in full flight gear.

The night was deathly still as each truck stopped in front of a single F-16. The driver and passengers in the cab of each truck jumped out. One passenger held an AK-47 and wore night-vision goggles. The driver climbed up on top of the back of the truck and unhooked the top while the movable crane was positioned by the first truck. The lid flew open as one of the ordnancemen scrambled down into the truck to hook the lift's cables to the long bomb. The cables strained under the weight, but slowly, surely, the bomb was lifted out of the truck and lowered inch by inch to the waiting dolly.

Major Khan stood next to his F-16 watching the ordnance-men work feverishly to get the fin set and laser-guidance group out of the fifty-gallon drums in the back of the trucks. Men from the trucks stood guard, facing outward with their night-vision goggles on and assault rifles ready, waiting for the attack they expected at any moment.

Khan's bomb was finally ready, with its ominous laser-guidance nose and large fins in the back. The ordies pushed the dolly under the belly of the F-16 and lowered the bomb rack to receive it. It was hooked up, and they cranked the bomb rack, now with its thousand-pound laser-guided bomb attached, back up to the belly of the F-16.

The Pakistanis pushed the heavy lift to the second truck, and the second bomb was slowly lifted out and lowered to-ward the dolly.

Suddenly a jeep casually rounded the corner of the hangar a hundred yards away. The senior guard, the head of the night security detail, was driving the jeep with two other guards in it. He was puzzled when he saw numerous men standing on the tarmac next to the F-16s. He stopped. The guard in the passenger seat stood up and began examining the group with his binoculars.

Khan immediately recognized what was happening and

began shouting at his men who needed no additional encouragement. Several of them began running toward the jeep, firing.

The senior guard threw the jeep into reverse and reached for the radio transmitter as three bullets hit him. He jerked back and then forward and lay dead on the steering wheel as the jeep backed around aimlessly until it slammed into the hangar wall. The other two men in the jeep jumped out with their weapons and began returning fire. The fire from the eight men was too much, and the other two guards were quickly hit. The Pakistanis reached the jeep and ripped the radio out of the dash. They examined each of the guards to see if they were dead, then shot them again at close range to be sure. They turned and sprinted back to Khan.

RAYMOND stared through his binoculars into the dark sky. He'd bought them through a catalog. They were enormous, like something from the signal bridge of a Navy ship. They had hundred-millimeter lenses and were long, heavy, and black—the best binoculars he could find with "low-light" lenses. He'd rigged a camera monopod stand for them so that he could rest their weight on the ground as he sat on his knoll looking up into the sky each night.

Raymond was very pleased with the hill he'd found. It gave him a panoramic view of the section of Nevada toward Area 51 and Groom Lake, as well as a comforting view of Tonopah over his shoulder. He was three hundred feet above the airfield and a mile away.

The wire from an earphone descended into the large pocket of his jacket, where his portable radio was tuned to the lowest position on the AM dial for Orel Spellman. Raymond heard what sounded like sharp crackling over the radio, but he quickly realized he'd heard it in the ear that didn't have the radio earpiece in it. It *sounded* like gunfire, but he couldn't imagine what it really was.

The air base was always quiet in the middle of the night. There was no activity, very little maintenance, and virtually no movement. The pilots who lived off base were long gone before 10:00 P.M., and those who stayed on base had nothing to do outside after 10:00 P.M. Raymond was accustomed to seeing the security jeep drive around the base periodically, and the other lights here and there. But no movement except for the guards. And certainly not the sound of gunfire.

He turned to look at the base but couldn't see much. He wanted to swing his enormous binoculars around to look in the other direction, but he didn't want to move the monopod from the small indentation in a flat rock between his legs, which allowed him to gaze eastward toward Area 51. And the noise he'd heard might not have been a gunshot. It was certainly crisp enough and could have been a hunter of some kind somewhere in the hills—but at night? And multiple shots? Could be some kid shooting at coyotes with a night scope and an illegal automatic rifle. Wouldn't be the first time. But it sounded as if it had come from Tonopah. He decided not to look. He continued to gaze into the sky and at the horizon toward Area 51, until he heard the unmistakable sound of several automatic weapons firing simultaneously. His heart jumped. He pivoted toward Tonopah, pulled his binoculars around and trained them on the airfield. He moved the lever in the middle of his binoculars to bring the air base into focus. He saw several men standing by the F-16s on the flight line near the hangar, then several others running toward the security jeep. He saw muzzle flashes in both directions. His mouth went dry as he realized that the guards were trying to stop someone near the F-16s, but those they were trying to stop were getting the better of the guards. He carefully focused his binoculars to see the shapes in the partial darkness. Most of the light was on the far side of the people, leaving him a view of shadows and darkness. He watched several men run over to the guards in the jeep and shoot them at close range. The sound of the final gunshots reached him long after the vivid picture of the guards' bodies jerking in response to the close-range fire. He nearly vomited. His breath came in gulps.

Raymond's shaking hand reached down to the ever-present cell phone hanging off his belt, one of the large, fat, older-style phones that he liked because they most closely resembled a radio, which gave him some sense of security or authority. He pulled the phone off his belt and hit speed dial "1." He waited anxiously as the phone rang. Finally it connected. "Mr. Henry? Mr. Henry?"

Luke answered groggily. "What?"

"Sir, it's Raymond."

"Raymond who?"

"Raymond Westover, sir, from the air base. The café."

"What do you want?"

"Sir, there's something terribly wrong at the base."

"Like what?" Luke said, sitting up and clearing his mind.

"Somebody is shooting. It looks bad. There are a bunch of automatic weapons being fired."

"What? What did you just say? Repeat what you just said," Luke demanded as the adrenaline coursed through his body, bringing him into a state of instant alertness.

Raymond studied the picture through his binoculars. He found himself whispering. "I don't know. Somebody's shooting. I think the Pakistanis—they're by their airplanes with a bunch of trucks—and they're shooting at the security jeep. They killed the guards, Mr. Henry, sure as hell—"

"What?" Luke cried.

"Looks like they're loading something onto their airplanes. I think they brought something onto the base in those trucks. And more men, with a lot of guns—"

"Can you still see them?"

"Yes, sir. Looks like they're done with the first two airplanes and are working on the third."

"What are they doing?"

"Loading something on the planes."

"Can you tell what? Where are they loading them?"

"Underneath. It's long, has a funny nose, and it's kind of thick at the back."

"Missiles?"

"Can't tell."

"Is it fat or thin?"

"Fat, sir. Way fat."

"Shit, Raymond. Those are bombs!" Luke's mind raced. "Can they see you?"

"No, sir. No way in hell. I'm on a hill off the base. I was just watching the night sky. Like I always do."

"Call Vlad and Stamp—they're at the BOQ—and Thud. Do you have all those numbers?"

"Yes, sir. They're all programmed into my cell phone."

Luke jumped out of bed and began putting on his flight suit. "I want you to listen carefully to me, Raymond. I want you to tell Vlad to find whatever men he can and get the four airplanes set for the missile shoot this morning ready to go. They're already gassed and armed, but we need to get them started. I have no idea where the hell these guys are going, but we've got to stop them. Tell Vlad I'll be there as fast as I possibly can. We may not have much time after these guys get airborne. I'll be there in twelve minutes."

"Sir, I thought your house was twenty minutes away."

"I won't be going the speed limit."

"Yes, sir, I'll call them right away. How can I reach you?"

"Let me give you my cell phone number."

"I have that, sir."

"Call me as soon as you've called everybody else. And let me know what they're doing. Can you still see them?"

"Yes, sir."

"What are they doing now?"

"They're loading something on the wings. Out at the end."

"Are they skinny or fat?"

"Skinny."

"Sidewinders. Shit! Where the hell did they get Sidewinders?"

"Probably out of the same trucks."

"As soon as we hang up, and as soon as you call those other pilots, call me right back. I'll be in my car." Luke quickly slipped on his flight boots and wrapped the laces around them as he cradled the phone awkwardly against his shoulder.

"What's going on?" Katherine asked sleepily.

Luke looked at her quickly. "The Pakistanis are going nuts on us. They're loading bombs aboard their airplanes. They just killed the guards."

"God, no," she said, throwing back the covers and jumping out of bed. "Can I do anything?"

"Yeah. Just a second. You got that, Raymond?"

"Got it. I'll call you right back. And if you need me, here's my cell number."

Luke wrote it down. "Tell Vlad to call me on my cell phone."

"Will do, sir."

Luke hung up. He grabbed his watch and his wallet and turned to Katherine with the lamp now on. "Call the FBI. Call the FAA. Call the Air Force. Call the Navy. Call anybody you can think of who has any ability to get in front of these guys. The Pakistanis have gotten laser bombs onto the base and loaded them onto their F-16s. They have Sidewinder missiles and are going somewhere. I don't know where. Just get the conversations going. Nobody's going to believe you. But I want them to start hearing this so that when I call them on the radio or talk to them on the phone, they'll have heard it first from you. Tell them we are *not* shitting them. Something real bad is going to happen very fast. If there are any Air Force fighters anywhere on alert within five hundred miles of Tonopah, tell them to get airborne with missiles and start looking for F-16 radars. I've got to go."

He dashed out of the room, grabbed his cell phone from the recharging cradle, and headed toward the garage.

17

The Pakistani ordnancemen had finished loading the thousand-pound laser-guided bomb aboard the third F-16 and were putting the last Sidewinder missile on the wing rail. Rashim stood by the fourth jet, the last one in the line. He watched the operations intently and glanced around anxiously every few seconds. They began lowering the steel cables into the fourth truck. The drivers and riders formed a perimeter with their assault weapons, watching for any movement, any new guard. They were well aware that there were other guards on the base who were there to guard the MiGs and the missiles. They expected them to come to reinforce the jeep guards, who might have radioed for help before being overpowered.

It was still thoroughly dark. The Pakistanis were growing restless. They had estimated fifteen minutes to load the bombs onto the F-16s, and they were now approaching twenty-two minutes. Major Khan strode up and down by the F-16s, growing more aggravated and anxious each minute. He knew exactly what time the sun would rise and exactly what time it would start getting light enough to drop. It was at *that moment* he wanted to strike. With each passing minute it would be brighter at the target, and the advantage would go to those who would undoubtedly come to stop them.

The lift bent again under the weight, and Rashim's bomb was pulled from its cradle in the last truck, placed gently on the dolly, and hooked to the bomb rack underneath the F-16. It was slowly cranked up against the belly of the airplane, and the Sidewinders were carefully placed on the tips of both wings.

Khan nodded vigorously at the other pilots as the loading of Rashim's armament was nearly complete. They scrambled quickly into their airplanes and closed the canopies.

RAYMOND speed-dialed Vlad's BOQ number and listened while it rang. It went from the fifth to the tenth ring with no response. Raymond began cursing under his breath when Vlad picked up the phone.

"*Da . . .* yes?" Vlad answered, barely awake.

"Vlad! This is Raymond—"

"Raymond who?" he asked angrily, his head pounding.

"Area 51 Raymond."

"What do you want?"

"Mr. Henry told me to call you. I'm sitting on a hill outside the base, and the Pakistanis are up to something. They've killed the guards and are loading bombs on their airplanes. Mr. Henry told me to wake you up and tell you to get the MiGs with the missiles on them started and ready. He's on his way. We've got to get Stamp and Thud up and go after them."

"What? The Pakistanis? Where did they get bombs? *Chort!*" he screamed. His anger was suddenly aggravated by a chilling fear as Gorgov's words came back to him.

"A whole bunch of guys with assault rifles. They have night-vision goggles and are armed for bear—"

"How did they do this?"

"Sir, I'm just telling you what Mr. Henry told me to tell you. He asked that you get those MiGs started."

"They will hear us! They will send their armed guards over to the MiGs!"

"I don't know about that, sir. I'm just following Mr.

Henry's instructions. I have to call Thud and Stamp right now, sir."

Vlad gathered his wits. "I will get Stamp."

"He's in a different building—"

"I am going over there now."

"Yes, sir," Raymond said. "Here's my cell phone number if you need anything from me."

Vlad hung up.

Raymond wasn't taking any chances. He dialed Stamp's BOQ room anyway.

THE Corvette's tires protested as Luke wheeled onto the highway and accelerated at full throttle heading south. The car quickly passed through eighty miles an hour, then a hundred. Luke's headlights were nearly useless.

He picked up the cell phone lying on the seat next to him and dialed the tower at Tonopah. There was no answer. He hadn't expected anyone to be there but tried on the off chance some of the tower employees who'd be working the missile shoot in the morning might have come in early. He dialed Thud's number. It rang several times, and then Michelle answered. "Hello?"

"Michelle?"

"Luke?"

"I'm headed to the base," he yelled over the loud air rushing by. The top was down, and the wind was thundering past his head. "Is Thud on his way already?"

"Yes. Raymond called him a few minutes ago and told him to get to the base right away. What's going on?"

"How long ago did he leave?"

"About three minutes."

"I'll catch him there." He hung up and immediately dialed another number. It was Vlad's room at the BOQ. There was no answer. "*Damn* it."

He dialed 411.

"Directory assistance, may I help you?"

"Get me the Federal Aviation Administration."

"I'm sorry, sir, I do not have access to Washington, D.C., numbers—"

"Local FAA. Local flight service station. The local anybody affiliated with the FAA."

"I have the Federal Aviation Administration local office in Reno."

"Fine."

"Here's the number, sir." She got off the line as the automated number was read to him by a computer.

He tried to steer while flying along the Nevada highway and dialing the phone. Finally it rang. He watched his lights bounce up and down on the highway as his tires went over minor bumps and changes in the road. The phone continued to ring at the Reno FAA office. A machine picked up after about ten rings: "You've reached the offices of the Federal Aviation Administration. Our business hours—" Luke hung up.

He redialed 411. "I need the number for the Air Force. Try Nellis Air Force Base."

"Yes, sir. Here is the general information number for Nellis Air Force Base." The computer read the number to him. He dialed it as he angled around the sharpest curve of the entire journey. His tires squealed slightly through the turn, but he felt stable. "Come on, come on," he said out loud.

"Nellis Air Force Base, Sergeant Matthews. This is a nonsecure line. May I help you?"

"Sergeant! My name is Luke Henry. I'm the owner of a fighter school at Tonopah. We have a serious problem that you need to get somebody on immediately. Four of the students at my school, Pakistanis flying F-16s, have gotten hold of some laser-guided bombs and are taking off now from Tonopah. I have no idea where they're headed, but they're going to drop them on somebody. It might be Nellis—"

"Is this a bomb threat, sir?"

"No. I don't have a bomb. I'm telling you about some people who *do* have bombs. They're in airplanes. F-16s. We need to get some fighters airborne immediately. You've got to help with this."

"Where are you calling from, sir?"

"My *car*."

"Have you had anything to drink, sir?"

"No, you idiot! I haven't had anything to drink! There are four F-16s loaded with laser-guided bombs and Sidewinder missiles that are going to be launching out of Tonopah soon, if they haven't already, and they could be heading your way. I need your help in stopping them. We need to get your alert fighters airborne, if you have any. Does Nellis have alert fighters?"

"I'm sorry, sir, I'm not at liberty to discuss our alert posture or what steps we might or might not take in response to any threat that does or does not—"

"Shut up! Put an officer on the telephone now!"

"There is no officer here right now, sir. I'm afraid I would have to wake him—"

"Then wake his ass up right now! I'm *ordering* you to do that!"

"Are you a military officer, sir?"

"No. But I was."

"I'm afraid you don't have the authority to order me to do anything, sir. Now, if you'll send me a letter asking me what it is you request from Nellis, I would be happy to pass it on to our public affairs officer. I'm sure she would respond to your request—"

"You've got to be shitting me! Have you heard anything that I've said?" Luke screamed.

"Sir, I don't need to—"

"You listen to me, Sergeant! Get an officer right now, and put him on the telephone."

"The duty officer is not here, sir. I'm the only one here."

"This is an *emergency*!"

"If you don't start controlling yourself, sir, I'm going to hang up."

"If *you* don't start controlling your *brain*, I'm going to have to get somebody who'll do it for you. Get an officer now!"

"I'll see what I can do." The line went dead.

"Hello? Hello? Shit!" Luke yelled. He dropped his cell phone onto the seat as he put both his hands on the wheel of his flying Corvette. The sky was pitch-black. He was on the ragged edge of catastrophe. He was driving much faster than was safe even in his own inflated opinion of his driving skills. His entire professional life was going up in smoke right in front of him, and he didn't know who to call or what to do about it. He needed to get the government officially involved, and he thought that his chances of making that happen by driving the speed of sound on the highway talking on his cell phone to people he'd never met was zero. There were too many nuts out there crying about the sky falling all the time. Still, he had to try. He picked up the cell phone and dialed long-distance information for Washington, D.C.

"What number, please?"

"Pentagon. The duty watch officer."

"Here is the Pentagon's general number, sir." She immediately connected him to the computer-generated number without waiting to find out if that was what he wanted. He listened to the number and dialed it immediately.

"Pentagon, Captain Hargrove. May I help you?"

"Are you the watch officer? Who deals with military emergencies?"

"May I ask who's calling?"

"Luke Henry. Formerly Lieutenant Luke Henry, United States Navy. I now run a private fighter aviation school in Nevada, and four Pakistani pilots—who were approved by the Department of Defense—have laser-guided bombs and are about to take off with them. I don't know where they're going or what they're going to do, but it's bad. We need Air Force help *right now*!"

"I'm sorry, what did you say your name was?"

"Luke Henry. I'm calling from my car, driving in excess of a hundred miles an hour and heading toward that base now to try to stop them myself. I need *help*. I need the Air Force's help. If there are any fighters on alert anywhere in the southwestern United States, they need to get airborne *now* and head toward southern Nevada."

"I don't know that we'll be able to do that, sir. We'll need to authenticate you, your story, your concern, and the risk. We don't simply launch fighters at the request of a citizen on his car phone."

"Do whatever the hell you have to do. Just start doing it. Wake up the person who's going to be *really* mad at you for waking him up. Wake up a General, or an Admiral! Get somebody responsible on this, and get them on it *now*."

"I don't know that I can do that, sir, based just on what you've told me. Who was it you said had authorized it from the Department of Defense?"

"Undersecretary of Defense Merewether."

"I'm afraid he is no longer the Undersecretary of Defense. That doesn't help you."

"What if everything I'm telling you is true? What would you do if you were me?"

"I don't really know, sir. I can't say I've ever been faced with such a situation where I'm responsible for foreign fighters being in the United States ready to attack a target and nobody knowing about it."

"People do know about it! *You* know about it! *I* know about it! I just can't get anybody to *do* anything about it!"

"Yes, sir."

"That's it? That's all you're going to do?"

"I'm sorry, sir. I don't know you, and you're not a member of the military, and you're not with the United States government. I'm afraid I can't help you."

"You asshole! You personally are going to be responsible— What is your name again?" The line went dead. "Shit!" Luke cursed again. The phone rang. He pressed the talk button. "What?"

"Mr. Henry?" It was Raymond.

"What?"

"They're starting their jets. I think they're going to be taking off."

"I'm eight minutes away, Raymond. You stay put. Did you get hold of Vlad?"

"Yes. He's over at the hangar. He was worried they might have people over there waiting for them, or may have already disabled the MiGs."

Luke suddenly recalled Brian's fears about Vlad, about his being in tight with the Pakistanis, about his getting thrown out of the Russian Air Force. And now Vlad was the one getting the MiGs ready to go. "I didn't even think of that. They get those guards, too?"

"I didn't see any shooting from there. They might not have thought to look at the outlying hangar. I don't think they've ever seen you use it before."

"What about Thud and Stamp? Did you get them?"

"Yes. They're both on their way. They should already be on base. Vlad was supposed to talk to them and meet them at the hangar."

"Okay—I've got another call. Later." He pressed talk again. "Yes?"

"Luke? Vlad."

"Vlad! We are in deep shit. Can you get the planes started?"

"Yes. The Pakistanis have started their jets, they will not hear us. The doors of the hangar are open. Thankfully, they face away from the other hangar. I'm going to start the jets in the hangar, which will ruin the hangar where the jet blast hits it, but I don't want to taxi until they make their move—"

"Do it," Luke said immediately. "I'll be there in five minutes. Are Stamp and Thud there?"

"Not yet. They are on their way. I have two mechanics who are helping me start the jets. They will be ready to go when you get here. Wait—I hear the F-16s taxiing. They are moving away from the flight line."

"We've got to know which way they're going. Did you find anybody for the tower? Or to operate the radar?"

"There is no one here. But I did not check every room. I don't want to get shot."

"I'll come right to the hangar." Luke tossed the phone onto the seat. He concentrated on the road, accelerating slightly more, pushing even his own limits. There was more adrenaline than blood in his veins. He felt as if he could rip the steering wheel off the car. He came around the corner, the last curve in the hills out of which he descended toward Tonopah, just in time to see the afterburner of the first F-16 light on the darkened runway. He couldn't see the airplane at all, just a long blue flame as it rolled down the runway for three thousand feet, then lifted off into the night sky. Then a second blue flame illuminated the runway where the first one had been, and then a third.

Luke accelerated still more and drove in furious frustration toward Tonopah. He suddenly knew without any doubt what had happened to Sluf. He'd stumbled onto Khan and his men doing something that morning he had flown in and disappeared. They'd killed him, rather than let him warn the others. Luke's anger grew even hotter. The fourth F-16 lifted off the runway as he approached the gate to his base with its floodlights in his face.

Luke slowed at the gate. He saw the dead guard's bloody body lying where he'd been shot, then run over. He floored the Corvette as he made a hard left and tore toward the southern end of the base and the auxiliary hangar. He could hear the MiGs. Luke ignored all the stop signs, curves, and anything that might slow him when he suddenly remembered there were additional men with assault rifles on the base. They might be setting up an attack force to prevent anyone from going after the F-16s.

His heart pounded even harder than it had been as he thought of a couple of dozen men with automatic weapons charging his MiG as he taxied. He would just have to take whatever came. May as well go out in a blaze of glory, he thought, whether here or in the air. He skidded to a stop next to the hangar and saw Vlad taxiing the third MiG-29 out to the tarmac with its engines running and canopy opened.

Luke jumped out of his car and ran toward the MiG nearest him. The first two were waiting for their pilots with the ladders on the side. The third was about in position and then stopped as Vlad put on the parking brake, hurried down the ladder, ran toward the fourth one, clambered up its ladder, jumped into the cockpit, took off the parking brake, and taxied forward in the darkness. He was about to throw the ladder down on the tarmac when one of the two Russian mechanics appeared from nowhere and stood underneath the airplane waving at him, indicating that they'd handle the ladder.

Vlad had retrieved their flight gear and hung it on the ladders, waiting for the pilots to arrive. Luke saw his helmet on the closest ladder. He jumped into his Russian-made harness and scrambled up the ladder, Vlad right behind him. Luke yelled into his ear over the jet noise, "Turn your radio to squadron common plus point-five! I don't want them monitoring our radios to see if we're up."

Vlad nodded and hurried back down the ladder. Suddenly Thud and Stamp drove up. They jumped out and raced for the other two MiGs. Vlad pointed Thud to the third MiG and

Stamp to the second. They grabbed their flight gear, jumped into it, put on their helmets, and ran up the ladders into the cockpits. The Russian mechanics pulled the ladders down as soon as Thud and Stamp were in their airplanes. The pilots closed the canopies and began to taxi away from the hangar.

THE old man checked his watch, then pushed open the door of his dilapidated Buick. It was still dark, and he was the only one in the entire parking lot just west of Interstate 5. He popped open the trunk and got out his gear. He slipped headphones over his dirty old Dodgers baseball cap and let them rest around his neck. He carried the metal detector in his right hand as he threw his ratty backpack over his left shoulder.

He closed the trunk quietly and began walking to the beach. His gait was painful and difficult, as if he were about to surrender to a lifetime of fatigue, his skin dark brown and deeply wrinkled from years in the sun. He was the first one on the beach that morning, long before sunrise. The moon, now approaching the ocean to the west, gave him just enough light to see his way.

The worn-out leather backpack had a drawstring at the top and shiny edges on the side. His headphones were attached to a device on his belt that had input wires from the long-handled metal detector that searched endlessly for coins and other valuables that had made their way into the sand on the coast of California.

The old man pulled the tired Dodgers cap down over his eyes to protect him from the coming sun. It settled into the comfortable position of a hat that had been worn for years in exactly the same place.

He headed south down the beach, sweeping his detector from one side to the other, occasionally sifting some sand through a can when he came across something. After a mile he turned around slowly, shuffling his bare, flat feet in the fluffy sand away from the hard-packed sand, and pulled his face up as if listening for something. He held the headphones to his ear with his hand as he looked north. He turned south again. Ahead of him, on the water line, he could just make out the two huge rounded shapes outlined against the dark blue sky.

He continued his long, slow walk toward them as he searched for something of value on the way.

18

The canopies came down, and the radios went on. *"Everybody up?"*

"Two."

"Three."

"Four," they said, instantly adopting the positions they'd been scheduled to fly on the missile shoot later that morning. Luke advanced his throttles, released the parking brake, and began taxiing toward the runway. *"I have no idea what they're up to. Get airborne in two sections. Use burner. Fuel is no concern until we catch them. Any questions?"*

"Did you notify anybody?"

"I tried," he transmitted. *"I'm going to keep trying. Stamp, I want you on the radio talking to the FAA about this until you get somebody. Thud, when we get airborne, I want you on every Air Force frequency you can find, particularly Nellis. Talk to anybody who's awake, and tell them what's going on."*

"Roger," they both said.

Luke was taxiing much faster than was safe, particularly in the dark. The taxiway lights were not lit, and he could barely distinguish the black taxiway from the sand right next to it. He was following the faint yellow line in the middle of the taxiway, illuminated by a remnant of moon. He didn't turn on his airplane's taxi lights. He didn't want to draw attention to his position. He had no idea where the rest of the Pakistanis were.

On the other side of the airfield, all the remaining Pakistanis, including the mechanics, piled into the back of the now empty trucks. The drivers and riders climbed into the front and slammed the doors as they quickly started their engines and raced off the tarmac, past the hangar for the gate with their lights off, hoping to escape undiscovered.

Vlad was right behind Luke as they taxied onto the runway in position for a section takeoff in the dark. Luke leaned forward and strained to see the centerline. He looked at his compass and saw that he was heading exactly 260, the precise heading of the runway. He released his brakes and went to full military power. No afterburner—less illumination.

They weaved down the runway, unable to see the centerline, and reached rotation speed. They lifted off the ground and raised their landing gear. Behind them, Stamp and Thud taxied onto the runway and rolled rapidly into a ragged but successful section takeoff.

Luke continued to climb. He quickly took off his oxygen mask and ripped off his helmet. He picked up the cell phone that he'd stuck in his flight suit pocket and dialed the number Raymond had given him. Luke pressed the telephone to his ear, hopeful he could hear the conversation over the jet noise in the cockpit. "Raymond?" he yelled.

"Yes. Who's this?"

"Stick. We just took off from Tonopah. Flight of four. You see us? You still on your hill?"

"Yes, sir. I saw everything. Four F-16s took off, and I saw you after them. I'd say they got about a five- or ten-minute jump on you."

"Which way did they go?" Luke demanded.

"South," Raymond said confidently.

"You sure? Can you give me a compass heading?"

"Positive. I followed them with my binoculars. I watched them as far as I could. I could see right into their tailpipes. They went south, sir. I'm sure."

"You just earned your salary, Raymond. Call everybody you can think of in the world and tell them that the Pakistanis have taken off with F-16s and bombs, headed south from Tonopah. Just tell whoever you can raise—the FAA, the Air Force, anybody," he yelled.

"Will do, sir. Good hunting."

Luke hit the end button on his phone, put it beside him in the map case, and latched the door over it. He had no flight plan and no idea where Major Khan was taking his men and their bombs. He pulled on his helmet and reattached his oxygen mask. *"Back up,"* he transmitted to the other three. He could hear Stamp on guard, 243.0 MHZ, the emergency UHF frequency every aircraft was required to monitor. The FAA and all military establishments monitored guard twenty-four hours a day.

"Mayday, Mayday. This is Nevada Fighter 103. A flight of four F-16s is airborne in southern Nevada with laser-guided bombs. We're unsure of their heading or intended target. Requesting fighter assistance. Mayday, Mayday . . ." Stamp repeated the warning.

Luke cringed. He hadn't told Stamp to use guard. He wouldn't have. It was monitored by everybody, almost certainly including Khan. Now Khan knew that they were onto him, airborne, and coming after him.

Luke pushed the MiGs through five hundred knots toward six hundred. He struggled to figure out what Khan's target was. He thought of all the cities and Air Force bases and Navy bases where Khan might inflict the most damage.

Luke concentrated on his radar. If Raymond was right, Khan should be about fifty miles ahead of them. Luke reached into the map case and moved the phone aside. He pulled out the Las Vegas sectional chart and examined it under the red light on the clip on the instrument panel. He listened as Stamp tried to contact the FAA on guard and Las Vegas approach. He knew they were violating all kinds of

FAA airspace and regulations, and he couldn't care less. He thought it would be just fine if he had a midair with another airplane about now, because he didn't know how he was going to face his wife, his friends, his squadron, or his fellow TOPGUN instructors at Fallon or the rest of the world.

He searched the chart. The Las Vegas sectional didn't go all the way to Southern California. He tried to think of the juiciest targets. Los Angeles? But where? Laser-guided implied precision strike. A particular target, not just to drop on a house or a hotel and kill a few dozen people. And there wouldn't be anywhere that more than a couple of hundred people would be at 5:00 A.M. March Air Force Base? Possibly. Air Force One was there a lot. . . . He jerked his head up as his heart responded to the instantaneous stimulation of adrenaline. He transmitted, *"Anyone know where the President is right now?"*

"Camp David," Thud replied.

Luke was relieved. *"Anybody got them on the radar yet?"*

"I'm getting something," Vlad replied.

Maybe the Navy base in San Diego—32nd Street, or North Island, where the carriers were based. Oh, no, he thought. These guys are going to attack an aircraft carrier, a *nuclear* aircraft carrier. His heart pounded even harder as his mind raced from one potential disaster to another. The MiGs sped on, accelerating through supersonic, violating yet another flight regulation. *"Anybody know if the carriers are in port at North Island in San Diego Bay?"*

"They sure are," Stamp replied. *"Stennis and Nimitz."*

Both nuclear carriers. *"They could be heading there!"* Luke exclaimed.

"That would not be good," Stamp replied.

"Thud, contact Miramar ops. See if the Marines have any alert F/A-18s they can get up between us and San Diego. Stamp, the carriers have any of their own aircraft aboard?"

"Negative," Stamp replied.

Suddenly an unidentified voice challenged them. *"Nevada Fighter 101, this is Los Angeles center. How do you read?"*

Luke jerked to respond. Finally. *"Loud and clear, how me?"*

"Loud and clear. Say your intentions."

"Did you copy the guard transmission?"

"Affirmative."

"We are a flight of four MiG-29s. We have Russian air-to-air missiles with us and are in hot pursuit of four California Air National Guard F-16s that are being piloted by Pakistani pilots training at our base at Tonopah, in Nevada. They killed our guards and have taken off with laser-guided bombs and Sidewinder missiles. We have no idea where they're going. Do you have them on radar?"

"We have a flight of four ahead of you fifty miles, heading south-southwest at thirty thousand feet."

Luke pulled up to climb to thirty thousand feet. *"Request thirty thousand feet. Request you clear the corridor south of them and between us of all traffic. These aircraft are extremely dangerous, and we do not know their intentions. They may try to shoot down an airliner. They have Sidewinder missiles. We don't know what they have in mind."*

"Roger. Are you declaring an emergency?"

"Definitely. I'm declaring whatever is the worst possible thing you can declare."

"Roger, squawk 7733, climb and maintain thirty thousand feet. Switch to 227.6 now."

They did.

"Nevada fighter flight up."

"Roger, read you loud and clear. Sir, how do we know you are who you say you are?"

"You're just going to have to take my word for it. My name is Luke Henry. Call TOPGUN at Fallon, Nevada. They

can vouch for me. We need to get any alert fighters airborne. Whoever would launch in case of a violation of the ADIZ needs to get airborne now, and these F-16s should be treated as a flight that is penetrating the ADIZ without authorization, and they are armed. And be sure to tell them the F-16s are the bad guys and the MiG-29s are the good guys."

"I'll contact the Air Force. I must put you on notice here that you're in violation of Federal Aviation Regulations in that you did not file an IFR flight plan"—Instrument Flight Rules—*"in that you're flying above fly level 180 through the jet routes without clearance, in that—"*

"I don't care if I'm violating every FAR in existence! I'm telling you, these men are about to attack the United States somewhere. I don't know where. Give me their heading! Help me get them. Give me a vector—"

"I don't appreciate—"

"Then get somebody on who's willing to help. I don't need anybody else making it harder."

"Their heading appears to be 190, but that is off raw radar return. Their IFFs are off." The Identification Friend or Foe highlighted each plane's position on the controller's radar.

"Say their speed, and thanks."

He hesitated, then, *"Speed is estimated at 650 knots."*

"Request permission for supersonic—"

"I do not have the authority—"

"What's your name?" Luke demanded.

"I am a retired air controller. My call sign was Catfish."

"Navy?"

"Yes, sir."

"I was with VFA-136, then TOPGUN. We're on the verge of disaster here, Catfish. You've got to help me."

"Stand by."

Luke went to afterburner, and the other three airplanes joined him in the dark, leaving long trails of yellow flame behind them. He checked his airspeed. He was passing through 650 knots to 700. They were supersonic, screaming across southern Nevada, crossing into California. Luke did a quick calculation. If Khan and his men were headed for the California coast, they had about twelve minutes to stop them.

Catfish came back on the radio. *"Sir, I raised the Air Force. They're scrambling a flight of four F-15s. The Air Force controller will be vectoring them toward the F-16s. They are concerned about the rules of engagement and do not believe they will be given clearance to fire, as there has been no hostile intent. They cannot verify your claims nor can they verify that the F-16s are armed. Their instructions are ID and escort—"*

Luke broke in. *"Shooting guards isn't hostile intent? I have an eyewitness that says they loaded bombs and missiles! Just get them up there. Intercept them. Then, if they roll in on anything, that'd be hostile intent."*

"I'll pass it on. Stand by. Sir, I have completed the flight path analysis. They do not appear to be headed toward San Diego. Their current flight path will take them to the ocean well north of San Diego."

Luke was puzzled. He glanced at the other three MiGs and thought for a moment. *"What will they fly over?"*

"Mostly mountains, then Orange County, then to the ocean just north of Camp Pendleton."

"Maybe they're heading for Camp Pendleton. Maybe they're going to attack the barracks or the officers' quarters."

"We will alert Camp Pendleton."

Luke envisioned the area in his mind. He'd been there innumerable times, up and down the California coast—San Diego, Orange County, the beaches, San Clemente . . . *"San Onofre! They're headed to San Onofre!"*

"The nuclear plant?"

"Get on the telephone! Warn them! Tell them to evacuate the place! Shut it down!"

Luke glanced at his gas gauge. His fuel was disappearing at a shocking rate. He looked at his radar for any sign of the F-16s. He had two contacts close together thirty miles ahead. *"I think I've got them, Catfish."* He compared his radar picture to their location and their closing rate. They had 150 knots' speed advantage on the bomb-laden F-16s. It would take them seven minutes to get within a good missile-firing solution. By then Khan would have gone another eighty-four miles—just enough to put them at the coast. "Shit!" Luke yelled into his oxygen mask. *"I don't think we'll reach them in time!"* he transmitted.

"Yes, sir. The F-15s are airborne, but they're as far away as you are."

"Roger," Luke said, checking his airspeed, wishing for more speed, anything to catch Khan. He stole a look at the chart again. *"Do the F-15s have them yet?"*

"Don't know, sir. Separate control."

"Damn it, Catfish! Fix it. Get everybody on the same frequency."

"Yes, sir. I'll work on that. Stay with me for now."

"Do you still have them heading for the coast?"

"Yes, sir . . ." Catfish said, obviously studying the radar information, as minimal as it was. *"Looks like they're starting a descent."*

"Take combat spread," Luke transmitted to his wingmen. *"Acquire any of them you can, and be ready for missile launch, even if outside the envelope. We've got to distract them."*

"Two," Vlad replied.

"Three," said Thud.

"Four," Stamp said.

Luke looked at his three wingmen, who were ripping through the sky with him, anxious to close on the Pakistanis, for the chance to get them before they did whatever they were planning on doing. Vlad backed off Luke and pulled out to his right.

Luke transmitted, *"Vlad, I've got them dead ahead, at thirteen miles. Thud, you and Stamp take a position to the south and west. I want everybody launching on these guys as soon as possible."*

"Don't we need clearance?" Thud asked.

"We can try. Break, Catfish, we need clearance to fire. Get whatever General is in charge on this frequency. We've only got about thirty seconds."

"Sir, there's no authority to do anything yet. They're waking up everybody in the country right now, trying to figure out what's going on. We don't have anybody on the line yet except the Air Force duty officer, and he hasn't given anybody clearance to do anything except take off and investigate. I seriously doubt he'll be saying anything to you, sir. You're a civilian."

"We've got to take them out, Catfish. They're going after a nuclear power plant, and—"

"Sir, I'm showing them approaching the coast."

"They're starting a bombing run! Where are they?"

"Directly over San Onofre. That's restricted airspace—"

"That ought to really matter to them. Get us clearance to fire on them, Catfish!"

"Sir, I work for the FAA. I can't give anybody—"

Luke's transmission ran over Catfish's response: *"Nevada Fighters, I've got four targets. I'm locking on the target second from the right. Vlad, take the lead to the right."*

"Roger," Vlad said. He was nearly overcome by the idea of piloting a MiG-29 in California defending an American target trying to shoot down an American F-16 with Gorgov whispering in his memory. He replied to Luke, *"It is a difficult shot for the missile."*

"We're taking whatever shots we can get, Vlad. Get ready to launch."

Luke could only imagine what would happen if any of the bombs actually hit the rounded domes of the two operating facilities. It would send up a cloud of nuclear fallout that could contaminate all of Southern California. It could contaminate the Pacific Ocean. Depending on which direction the wind was blowing, Los Angeles, San Diego, Orange County, and Palm Springs were all in danger. If it erupted to the same level as Chernobyl, the entire western United States could be endangered by the cloud of radioactive fallout. He pulled his mind back to the fight ahead.

Luke started down as they approached the coast. The F-16s had begun to descend in the darkness toward the coast of California. The horizon behind Luke was just beginning to brighten. Exactly the conditions Khan had wanted. They would be coming out of the east.

Luke looked through the thick, illuminated glass of the HUD, the heads-up display that projected symbols onto the glass in front of him. The missile-launch indicator and the target were moving closer together in the HUD, indicating that his shot was improving with every passing second, but he was still out of range. He knew that Vlad was looking at a virtually identical display.

"I have them on my radar. Request permission to launch!" Vlad insisted. Luke checked his own position and looked at how far ahead of them the F-16s were. It was down to nine miles as they screamed through the black sky at Mach 1.2 in their Russian fighters over Orange County, California. The entire trip from Tonopah to Orange County had taken only twenty-one minutes. The F-15s took ten minutes just to get airborne. He could imagine the F-15s closing on the F-16s supersonic, just as they were, but doubted they'd get there in time, let alone be cleared to do anything decisive. He knew better than most how the military mind

worked. They would much rather hesitate and be wrong for inaction than take decisive action and kill people and be wrong. They can always claim they didn't have enough information to act decisively. They knew they were less likely to be held accountable for doing nothing than for doing something dramatically wrong that would provide pictures of dead, burning bodies.

Luke strained to see the two cement domes of the San Onofre nuclear plant on the coast between Interstate 5 and the Pacific Ocean, dramatically outlined by the morning sun. But there wasn't any morning sun yet, no light for them to see ahead, only a pink horizon behind them.

The radar showed a good lock on one of the jets in front. It was heading down rapidly. He knew that the F-16 was now getting a MiG-29 radar strobe on its radar warning indicator. He prayed it would deter them from completing their task, but held out little hope.

"Fire!" Luke said to his wingmen, taking full responsibility on his own shoulders for whatever came next. He was hanging so far over the edge in so many different ways that it almost didn't matter. He expected to die.

Luke pulled the trigger with the jerking motion he taught his students not to use. He felt the large AA-10 Alamo drop off his left wing. He squinted in the darkness as the rocket motor ignited and lit up the sky all around his Fulcrum. A trail of white smoke followed the blazing yellow light toward the California coastline. A missile flew off Vlad's Fulcrum almost simultaneously.

Luke's weapon selector had automatically cycled to the next Alamo. He held down the trigger, and his second—and last—Alamo fired. He knew he didn't have time to break lock to select another airplane. He simply needed to get some ordnance into the area and hope he hit one or more of the F-16s now hurtling down toward the nuclear plant.

Luke watched the altitude readout on his target spin

through twenty thousand feet, then eighteen thousand feet, then fifteen thousand feet as the F-16s plunged toward the target in a near-vertical descent. They couldn't have planned a more effective way to evade the Russian missiles headed at them. Two of the missiles went stupid almost immediately, clearly not guiding. Vlad's single missile flew straight into the ground. Luke's second missile seemed to be guiding on the target, its motor still rushing to its destination.

Luke checked his radar just as it broke lock and went back into a track-while-scan mode, a fine radar mode of its own but not one in which the Alamo could be guided to a target. "Shit!" Luke yelled to himself. "Chaff? They've got chaff?" Where the *hell* did they get chaff? Damn it!"

On the beach below, the scavenger with a Dodgers cap knelt with his can sifter and grabbed some sand. He glanced around and put the can down. He looked up into the sky at the F-16s plummeting toward the earth with their engines screaming. He pulled off his backpack, grabbed the heavy black laser designator out of his pack. He looked through a gunsight on top of the device to aim it, then pulled the trigger. The invisible laser illumination immediately flooded over the target in eager anticipation of the laser-guided bombs attached to the F-16s above.

Khan pointed directly at the now laser-illuminated target. The two large domes were well outlined in the predawn light.

Vlad's second Alamo flew by the trailing F-16 and was detonated by the proximity fuse in the warhead. The warhead ripped the tail off the F-16, which flipped upside down and headed straight for the ground. The pilot stayed with his plane and fought to regain control, at least enough to drive his bomb-laden aircraft directly into the nuclear plant. His F-16 tumbled slowly toward the dark ocean to the west of the power plant.

Luke switched his missile selector to Archer, the infrared missile considered by many to be the best in the world.

Suddenly a new voice came on the radio. *"Nevada Fighters, this is Eagle 105, flight of four. State your position."*

It was the F-15s. *"Five miles northeast of San Onofre,"* Luke said, struggling to talk, fly, and shoot all at once.

"Roger. Confirm you're flying MiG-29s?"

"Affirmative," Luke yelled, angry they couldn't get there before now. *"The F-16s are the bad guys."*

"Roger. We're twenty miles out."

Luke's heart sank. He didn't respond.

"Say location of the bogeys."

"Directly over San Onofre. They're dropping. The shooting's already started. We've splashed one and are closing on the others."

The Nevada Fighter Weapons School instructors all knew they had gotten there too late but had to limit the damage as much as they could. They charged in toward the F-16s to kill them any way they could—or at least disrupt them. They fired any missile they had, at any distance, hoping it would cause one or all of the F-16s to change their flight path enough to miss.

Luke locked up the lead bogey with his radar. He was outside the maximum range of the Archer, but he couldn't wait. He pulled the trigger, and one of his Archer missiles hissed off the rail toward the lead F-16, which was now pulling up, away from the power plant.

Khan saw the Archer racing toward him at the same time he saw the lead MiG-29. He pulled up and turned inland toward Luke. The missile tried to turn the corner but was just outside the lethal range of its warhead when its proximity fuse detonated it.

Luke suddenly felt panic sweep over him; he remembered that the F-16s had Sidewinders. *"They've got Sidewinders!"* he reminded the others.

"Roger," someone transmitted. The Fulcrums came at the three remaining F-16s in flights of two in combat spread,

with Luke and Vlad in the lead, and Stamp and Thud off their left, to the south. Vlad fired an Archer at the lead F-16, at Riaz Khan.

Suddenly, while Luke watched in horror, a flash diverted his attention from Khan's airplane to San Onofre as the first laser-guided bomb hit directly on the top of a long, flat building just east of one of the domes. The blast was bright yellow for an instant, the concussion visible in the moist sea air. The building was crippled, but the dome was untouched. The second bomb, dropped by Rashim, went in through the now open structure and hit right where Khan's bomb had hit. The rest of the building's flat roof collapsed.

Luke saw an Archer come off Thud's wing and scream toward the last F-16 that was in the middle of its bomb run.

Luke was amazed that they were somehow unable to hit the enormous domes, the home of the active reactors at San Onofre. Whoever was doing the laser designation for the bombs was doing a piss-poor job, Luke thought.

Rashim was right on Khan's wing as they climbed toward Luke and Vlad. A small cloud of white steam began shooting out of the low building behind them, hissing and screaming into the golden predawn of the coast of California. Thud's Archer from the south reached the third F-16 almost simultaneously. The plane never had a chance. The missile tore off both its wings, but it had already released its bomb. The third laser-guided bomb went into a flat building next to the second domed plant and blew a large cloud of dust, debris, and steam into the sky. The third F-16 tumbled to destruction on the beach below.

Khan and Rashim climbed through three thousand feet, heading up toward the MiG-29s that were passing through eight thousand feet on their way down. The F-16 radars scoured the sky in front of them. The MiGs' electronics countermeasures in the humps behind the cockpits were effective in convincing the F-16 radar to look elsewhere.

Luke could now clearly see the waves breaking on the beach behind San Onofre, behind the white steam shooting into the sky. Cars were piling up on the freeway below them.

Vlad pulled to the right of Luke, trying to gain an angle on Khan so he would have to choose to go after one of them. Khan chose Luke, who was straight ahead of him. Luke and Khan raced at each other at nearly twice the speed of sound, now three miles apart. Vlad pulled hard into a high-G turn and tried to get his helmet-mounted sight on Khan. Khan had fought the MiGs enough to know what the outside limit of the helmet-mounted sight was and when he was in danger. He knew that Vlad was nearly to the point where he could fire an Archer. What he didn't know was that Vlad didn't have any more missiles. Khan broke off his attack on Luke to defend himself from Vlad. He pulled hard to his left as Rashim passed him on his right and headed toward Thud and Stamp.

Luke was tempted to fire his last Archer missile at Rashim, but knew that the other F-16, the one in the lead, was Khan—and he wanted him. Luke pulled hard right after Khan's F-16.

Vlad screamed in Russian and pushed his throttles into afterburner to regain airspeed as Khan turned into him. Luke saw his chance. He squeezed the autolock on the radar to find the nearest airplane and lock it up, flooding it with radar illumination, then to slave the Archer missile's seekerhead to the radar. The MiG had too many switches and moves required, though; he had to keep looking into the cockpit.

He pulled hard on the stick and banked to the right to get his nose on Khan, now only a mile away and turning toward Vlad. Luke pulled harder, with his nose only forty degrees behind the tail of the F-16. He pulled through seven Gs, then eight. His face distorted under the force, his cheeks pulled down. His radar suddenly showed a good lock on the F-16 and good missile parameters. He slipped his finger around the stick until it rested on the trigger and he waited for a clear shot, but Vlad's MiG was in the windscreen. The Archer was just as likely to go after Vlad as Khan.

Luke pulled harder still to get a better shot and maybe get Khan to reverse himself and see Luke as the threat. Vlad could escape, or even drag Khan northeast into the low-level California mountains over Camp Pendleton, where Luke could get a clear shot. Luke fought to keep the blood in his head and to keep from blacking out. He noticed he was already seeing in black and white, his vision beginning to get grainy around the edges.

"Eagle 105 flight six miles out. State your posit."

Luke grunted as he tried to speak through the eight-G turn. *"Splashed two. Still over San Onofre. Plant has been . . . ugh . . . hit."*

"We have you. We're right behind you."

Vlad was in a low rolling scissors with Khan that Luke couldn't get into or stop. They were heading toward the ground at three hundred knots as each tried to turn inside the other without gaining any angles.

Luke eased the stick forward and rolled left to see Thud and Stamp. They were two miles south, embroiled in their own 2 v. 1 with the other F-16. Luke watched them for five seconds, to make sure they weren't in trouble. He instantly knew that the F-16 was Rashim. Overly aggressive.

Luke turned back hard right to head down toward Vlad and Khan. As he relocated the F-16 against the dark landscape behind them, a small explosion on Khan's airplane startled him. Too late he realized it was the rocket motor of one of Khan's Sidewinder missiles. It raced across the circle toward Vlad, less than half a mile away. Luke fumbled for the radio transmission button, but he couldn't warn Vlad in the short time it took for the missile to cross the gulf between them. The Sidewinder slammed into the tail of the

MiG-29, and the airplane burst into flames. Vlad immediately pulled the ejection handle, and his ejection seat rocketed him out of the burning wreck.

Khan knew he had the MiG-29 as soon as he launched his Sidewinder. He pulled up, somehow now aware of the F-15s closing on him. Khan was between four F-15s coming from the north and Luke coming from the east.

Rashim had his own problems with Stamp and Thud. He turned into the two MiG-29s, hoping to avoid the combination of their Archer missiles and their helmet-mounted sights. He turned hard, keeping them at bay but not trying to get behind them. He was playing a defensive game, knowing that there were now four F-15s in the mix.

Rashim suddenly dumped his nose and headed for the ground toward the power lines that climbed up the hill from the nuclear plant. He couldn't see the plant from his current position, but he knew the fat wires would lead him right back to it.

He performed a split S as he headed down toward the power lines, hoping to avoid Thud and Stamp as they locked their radars onto his fleeing airplane. He leveled off just above the freeway, crowded with stopped cars, the drivers of which had gotten out to watch the aerial dogfight and gawk at the flames coming from a building on the property of the nuclear power plant, wondering what the screaming sirens meant.

Rashim hugged the ground as he screamed north, then pulled up to climb over the power lines. He was half a mile from San Onofre. He glanced at the growing plume of steam. It was now illuminated by the morning sun and was starkly white and radiant. Rashim pulled hard left and headed toward the steam as he looked over his right wing toward Khan.

On his left, what he couldn't see was that Thud had stayed

at altitude and was racing downhill toward him, rapidly closing the distance. To Rashim's right, Luke was locked in a death fight with Khan.

Luke was on the ragged edge of the aircraft's performance. He reversed his airplane and pulled his nose up to slow down and to slice in on Khan's F-16. He waited for Khan to pull into him aggressively again, as he knew he would. Luke would be ready to cut inside his turn and drill him. Khan had wrestled back, keeping the fight neutral, no one gaining an advantage, countering every one of Luke's moves, but this time, instead of pulling into him, Khan suddenly broke off and headed for the power plant behind Rashim.

Luke was surprised. He leveled his wings, waiting for Khan to commit himself. He saw Rashim with Khan following him. He jerked his MiG over on its back and pulled down toward the ground, his throttles at full throw, accelerating with gravity's help to chase the fleeing F-16s. They were bugging out. Luke made sure his spine was straight so his head wouldn't get buried in his lap by the huge Gs he was about to pull. He yanked back hard on the stick and loaded up the MiG with eight Gs. He went to full afterburner and stayed after Khan, who fell in a mile behind Rashim.

Luke had no idea what Khan was doing, but he was going with him. He eased back on the stick as they leveled out at ground level. Khan tore toward the Pacific. Luke glanced up to his left and saw another MiG descending, much faster than Luke, cutting across toward the lead F-16.

The F-15s finally arrived and crossed from Luke's right to left, above and behind the MiGs, joining in the tail chase of the fleeing F-16s. There were too many airplanes too close together for anyone to lob a missile.

"Thud, that you going after the westernmost F-16?"

"Yeah, Stick. I've got him. No way he's getting away."

Thud was going at least two hundred knots faster than the F-16. Luke watched as he closed on Rashim. Thud had pushed his MiG-29 toward the F-16 nearly supersonic. Rashim stayed low. He knew that Thud was too close for a missile shot and, with the closure he had, was likely to overshoot and expose himself. Rashim was content with that.

Thud rushed in with reckless abandon.

Luke didn't like what he saw. He transmitted, *"Thud, watch your closure."*

Thud didn't reply.

"Thud, pull off and let me have a shot at him. They're bugging out! Thud!"

"I've got him," Thud replied. *"As soon as he sees me closing on him, he'll come back at me. Then I'll have him."*

He had gotten it almost completely right. Rashim was looking over his shoulder. He knew he wasn't going to be able to get away. He'd done what he'd come here to do. Rashim pulled back on the stick, and the F-16 instantly went to 9.5 Gs, as much as the computer would allow. He pulled up and back, directly into Thud.

Thud pulled back on his throttles and tried to increase his distance from Rashim.

Rashim expected that. He kept his eye fixed on the nose of the MiG-29 as he pulled, and flew his fighter right into Thud.

The two fighters collided like cymbals and burst into flames. Airplane and canopy parts littered the sky and fell to the ocean.

"Thud!" Luke cried. He fought the instant nausea that ripped into his gut. "No!" Luke gasped for oxygen through his mask. He pulled back on his throttles and came out of afterburner. He put his head back against the ejection seat. He couldn't do it.

"You want us to take the last one?" the F-15 lead asked.

Luke watched as Khan's F-16 got smaller as it headed out into the Pacific. He waited, then jammed the throttles forward as Glenda spoke in his ear, "Low fuel! Low fuel!" His eyes darted to the fuel gauge. She was right, but it didn't matter. If he had to go swimming to get Khan, then that was just how it was going to be. He'd strangle him to death in the water.

Khan had taken advantage of the midair to make his escape. He was down on the deck, fifty feet off the water. He had a mile head start on the fighters chasing him. Luke and Stamp were right behind him at the same speed. It was a race to the middle of the ocean. He had nowhere to go. The flight of four F-15s flew cover above them, ready to pounce. The lead was ready. *"Nevada Fighter, pull off. We've got a sweet missile shot on him."*

"Negative. I'll take my shot, then you can have him."

"Roger. Fuel state?"

"About twenty minutes. I'm okay," he lied.

Luke was surprised. Khan was clearly planning on running west until he ran out of gas, then crashing into the ocean. But if Khan knew he was going to die, Luke was surprised he didn't want to go down fighting as Rashim had just done.

Stamp was apparently thinking the same thing. *"Any idea on his intentions?"* he asked.

"None."

Luke didn't want to get too close. He settled in one mile behind Khan, waiting for him to commit himself, with the image of Thud's airplane exploding branded into his mind. If he fired a missile now, it would hit the water instead of the F-16. But if he had to wait much longer, Luke would run out of gas and crash into the ocean himself. He had to act soon to have any chance of landing back at Miramar, the Marine Corps air station in San Diego.

As Luke contemplated his options, they reached seventy-five miles off the coast, in the middle of nowhere, with no land in sight. Khan suddenly pulled into a hard left turn, still fifty feet off the ocean.

"Here we go," the F-15 pilot said.

Luke pulled up slightly as the turn took him by surprise. He had closed the distance to Khan too fast. He pulled up quickly into a high yo-yo to keep from overshooting. He looked down at Khan from a high perch position. Khan was in a tight five-G turn right on the surface of the ocean, circling. Suddenly he pulled up into a climbing spiral away from the ocean.

Luke hesitated. He couldn't imagine what Khan was trying to do, but it was the opening Luke had been waiting for. He rolled in and locked up Khan with his radar. He selected Archer and directed his helmet-mounted sight toward the climbing F-16. He heard the growl from the Archer seeker-head. Khan was far enough away from the water to give Luke a clear shot. The F-15s above at ten thousand feet watched in anticipation as Luke pulled hard to line up his last missile shot.

Luke leveled his wings, his breath coming in short, quick gasps. He pulled the trigger, and the Archer hissed off the missile rail toward the F-16. Luke watched in shock as the canopy came off the F-16 and Khan ejected before the missile even arrived. "What the . . ." Luke said to himself. The ejection seat and rocket motor threw Khan away from the F-16 seconds before the Archer missile hit the Viper in the belly and cut it in half. The F-16 rolled over and headed for the water in its two pieces, flames coming out of both ends. Khan floated down gently in his silk parachute as he inflated his survival vest and deployed the seat pan on his ejection seat.

Luke rolled wings level and pulled his throttles back to idle, slowing quickly. He watched Khan float to the ocean. *"Catfish, splash the fourth bogey. The pilot jumped out. Get the Navy out here to take this guy into custody."*

"Roger, copy."

Luke looked down at his TACAN. *"We're on the 298 radial for 98 from Miramar."*

"Roger that."

Luke's heart climbed quickly into his throat and choked off any thought of speaking as he watched Khan touch down and splash into the ocean. A hundred yards away from him, a periscope pierced the ocean's surface. It was barely moving in the water. Seconds later the submarine's sail broke the surface in a bath of white foam. Khan had freed himself from his parachute and swam with a gentle backstroke toward the surfacing submarine.

Two men opened a hatch in the sail of the submarine and came out onto the bridge. They saw Khan and clambered down a ladder to the flat deck behind the sail. They wore life jackets and dark clothes. Luke lowered the nose of the Fulcrum. *"You seeing this?"* Luke asked.

"I'm seeing it, but I'm not believing it," Stamp replied.

This cannot be happening, Luke thought. *"Catfish, we've got a submarine surfaced on the water. They're pulling Khan out of the water. Call the Navy! Get some antisubmarine assets here now!"*

"A submarine, sir?"

"Yes, a submarine!"

"Whose, sir?"

Luke lowered his nose and slowed down to take a hard look at the sub. It was black, in good shape, and almost clearly a diesel. He asked in desperation, *"Anybody got a camera?"*

"No," Stamp said with regret.

"Negative," the F-15 leader replied.

Luke pulled up hard and tried to get out of the way as Stamp followed him down and attempted to get a radar lock on the submarine with his MiG radar to shoot his last missile. The radar refused to lock on to the submarine. It couldn't separate the sub from the rest of the ocean. Stamp fired anyway, hoping against hope that the missile would guide, but he was disappointed. The long Alamo went ballistic as soon as it was launched. It headed straight down into the ocean like an arrow hundreds of yards from the sub.

Luke watched helplessly as the submarine started to dive. "Emergency fuel! Emergency fuel!" Glenda warned. He ignored her. Khan stood on the bridge of the submarine, removed his helmet, and waved at Luke flying two thousand feet above. Suddenly Khan turned and dropped through the open hatch, which closed quickly behind him. The blue ocean closed over the submarine, and the deck was soon awash in white foam and surging water. The sail grew smaller, and the submarine disappeared into the ocean.

Luke reduced his throttles and pulled back on the stick as the MiG climbed away from disaster. Glenda continued to remind him of his fuel state. *"Catfish, I'm emergency fuel. Request bingo profile vector for straight-in approach to Miramar."*

"Roger, Nevada Fighter 101. Fuel emergency. Take heading of 113, climb and maintain maximum-range altitude, and report level."

"Catfish, Eagle flight RTB."

"Roger. Take heading 060, climb and maintain fifteen thousand feet. Break, Nevada Fighter, I've been informed, sir, that the Navy is on their way to get to the submarine," Catfish reported.

As Luke climbed away from the ocean, he glanced back at the vague disruption on the surface of the Pacific where the submarine had been. *"Tell them they're too late."*

19

Luke was on fumes when he landed at Miramar Marine Corps Air Station in San Diego. He barely had enough fuel to taxi to the operations shed, but he wasn't about to be towed; he'd rather flame out. His mask hung down in surrender, exposing his sweating face. He glanced at the operations building and was surprised to see the throng of people waiting for him. He shut down the starboard engine to save fuel. He kept his visor lowered. He didn't want anybody to see his eyes, which were full of frustration and fury. At least the Pakistanis had missed the nuclear plants. Luke was suddenly acutely aware of why Khan had demanded more air-to-ground training.

He taxied slowly, treasuring the quiet, protective shell of the airplane cockpit that kept the world away. Vlad had lost his MiG. Four F-16s had attacked San Onofre and been lost, and his school would be blamed for everything—of that he was sure. He taxied by the windsock. The prevailing wind was from the southeast. It had allowed him to land straight in from the ocean on Runway 6, the opposite direction airplanes usually landed at Miramar. The prevailing wind in Southern California was almost always from the ocean, between 240 and 270. But not today. Today all of Southern California was experiencing a Santa Ana, a wind condition that meant the winds were coming from the east, from the desert. They were hot, dry winds that could easily reach twenty or thirty knots. He was thankful the attack hadn't resulted in a radioactive cloud. He was sure the steam he'd seen meant they'd hit a power substation or the heating plant for the base.

Luke taxied forward slowly to the point where the lineman was indicating, waited until his wheels had been chocked, and shut down the MiG. He waited until his engine had completely stopped and then opened the canopy. A lineman put a ladder in place for him. He unstrapped methodically as he watched Stamp land and taxi toward him.

Luke climbed out of the MiG and down the ladder with his helmet in hand and began walking slowly to the operations shack. A man in a dark blue suit came jogging toward him with three other men on his heels. The man spoke to him from fifteen feet away as he slowed to a fast walk. "Are you Mr. Luke Henry?" he asked, reaching inside his coat for his identification.

Luke stood there with his hands on his hips, his helmet hanging in his left hand, and nodded. "Yeah. Who are you?"

"FBI," the man said, holding his ID out in front of him for Luke to read. "You're under arrest."

"You've got to be *kidding* me," Luke said, suddenly furious.

"Put your hands up, sir."

Luke stared at the man. "Are you shitting me?" he demanded angrily, not moving.

"Put your hands up, sir!"

Luke raised his hands, holding his helmet over his head. The lead FBI agent walked behind him, pulled down his right hand, and put a handcuff over his right wrist. Then he pulled down Luke's left hand and the helmet fell out of his hand, hit the pavement, and began rolling unevenly down the flight line.

"Sir, you have the right to remain silent. Anything you say may be used against you in a court of law. You have the right to consult an attorney—"

"What am I being arrested for?"

"For conspiracy to commit a terrorist act."

"That's total bullshit," Luke replied. "I was trying to *stop* them," he protested.

"Yes, sir, I'm sure you were." They escorted him to the operations office, where the press was already congregating. When reporters saw him coming, they began yelling questions at him. The camera motor-drives were audible as they pushed toward him. Television cameras focused on his face.

"Why did you bomb the nuclear plant?" one shouted. "Do you have a grudge against the United States?"

KATHERINE had gotten dressed as soon as Luke had jumped out of bed. She'd thrown on a loose shirt, gone to the kitchen to make a cup of tea, and sat down at the table with the telephone. She'd called the Air Force, the Navy, the FAA, the FBI, the Department of Defense, and anyone else she could think of. The few times she'd actually spoken to a person resulted in the same response: "Yes, that's very interesting. I'm sure it's terribly important, and I'm sure you're right about what has happened, but I am simply not in a position to do what you have asked . . ."

Always the same. Very nice, respectful, as if they were talking to someone from an asylum, someone who needed the stiff canvas jacket with the sleeves wrapped around her back, and everything would be just fine.

She had kept the television tuned to CNN, hoping against hope that nothing had happened, that nothing would happen, and that Luke would come back with a great story to tell at the O' Club.

Eventually she ran out of numbers to call. Besides, she was beginning to feel ridiculous. She put down the phone and drank the last of her tea. She was about to get up and make some more tea when the morning weather on CNN was interrupted. An ominous screen came up: THE FOLLOW-ING IS A SPECIAL REPORT FROM CNN. "Oh, no," she said.

A man appeared on the screen and began, "Good morn-ing. I'm Carl Allen, and this special report is just in. There has apparently been an attack on the San Onofre nuclear power plant on the coast of San Diego County, California. Four jet fighters attacked the nuclear plant at about five-thirty Pacific time this morning. San Onofre is comprised of three nuclear reactor plants, Units One, Two, and Three. Unit One was deactivated several years ago. The other two units are large domelike structures designed to withstand the impact of a 737 jet flying directly into them from thirty thou-sand feet. As it turned out, the bombs released by the air-planes missed the reactor plants and hit a flat building south of the reactors. Initial reports are that six people were killed at San Onofre by the bomb blasts, and three of the four pi-lots, who were apparently Pakistani, were shot down by the U.S. Air Force. We are just now getting our first pictures from the site. Reporting live from San Onofre is Leslie Mon-teneri. Leslie, what can you tell us?"

San Onofre? Katherine was horrified. She'd never imag-ined that Khan would attack a nuclear plant.

The picture cut to a reporter sitting inside a helicopter fly-ing over the ocean. The sky was light, as the sun had just risen above the horizon. She spoke loudly to be heard over the turbine engine and the vibrating blades spinning over her head. "Carl, the situation at San Onofre is bad. Several peo-ple have been killed. There is a large fire where the bombs hit, with a sort of vapor or dust cloud from the bomb blast curling up into the sky."

The camera swung to the outside of the helicopter. The two damaged buildings were clearly visible, and there was steam and dark dust still rising out of the fire on the ground. "You can see where the bombs hit. Fortunately, they did not hit the nuclear plants themselves. We are told that the plants are intact and undamaged. We're still trying to find out what was in the buildings that were hit, but we've been told that there are at least six people dead and several wounded. The death toll could climb as more information becomes available.

"Carl, as remarkable as the damage itself is, even more remarkable is how this is supposed to have happened. There were apparently four F-16 fighter jets owned by the California Air National Guard that were involved in this attack. They were carrying laser-guided bombs and dropped them on San Onofre.

"According to some people on the ground here, there was actually an air battle over the power plant. American fighters tried to stop them, and many missiles were fired right over this spot by eight F-15s and, according to one source, some Russian MiG fighters, although that report seems unlikely. The Air Force is not known to fly Russian fighters. Several jets were shot down, one of which landed just north of the power plant." The camera zoomed in on burning wreckage that had left a crater in the ground. "We're not sure of the total number of airplanes involved in the air battle or who was shot down. We don't know the present location of the airplanes. One source has told us the F-16s were being flown by Pakistani pilots."

As she spoke, the helicopter's camera continued to show chilling pictures of the power plants, the steam cloud, the traffic jam on Interstate 5, and the burning wreckage of Vlad's crashed MiG.

"There are many many questions that remain to be answered, Carl. How did Pakistani pilots come into possession of four California Air National Guard F-16s? And where were they flying them from? How did they get laser-guided bombs that they could load onto their planes? Who got shot down, and by whom, and are any of the Pakistani pilots alive?

"We will continue following this developing story."

"Thank you, Leslie . . . can you hear me?"

Leslie held her headphones to her ears. "Yes, I can hear you."

"It sounds like there is a siren in the background. Can you tell us what that is?"

She nodded. "Carl, I'm told that at San Onofre there is an automatic warning system, like an air-raid siren system, that goes off whenever there's release of radioactivity. Those who live nearby know what to do, which is essentially evacuate. But some I've spoken to suspect that the alarm was triggered by the bombs exploding and is probably unrelated to the release of radioactivity, especially since the reactors were undamaged."

"So there isn't thought to be any danger of radiation?"

"We've received no response from San Onofre as of yet. There is, of course, an evacuation plan for several miles around San Onofre in the case of an actual radioactive release. As you can see from the freeway, which is completely full of cars heading in both directions, many of the local residents have apparently decided to evacuate based on the sirens. But thus far there's been no call for evacuation. CNN's nuclear expert, Dr. Alfred Boyer, has told us that as long as the nuclear core is not breached, there is no danger of radioactive release. We will continue to get assessments from San Onofre and update you as soon as we have any more information."

"Thank you, Leslie," Carl said as he pivoted in his chair in CNN headquarters in Atlanta. "With us now is Tim Davidson, in Washington at the Pentagon. Tim, what is the Department of Defense saying about this? Have we been attacked by Pakistan? What have they told you?"

"Carl, I must say that the general sense I get here at the Pentagon is one of shock and confusion. When I ask people how F-16s flown by Pakistani pilots came to be operating inside the United States with laser-guided bombs, the answer I get almost universally is variations on 'I have no idea.' The entire Pentagon has been caught completely by surprise. We've asked for an official statement, but so far one has not been forthcoming. I believe they are trying to assess exactly what has happened and how it happened before making any comments. The problem seems to be that there isn't anyone at the Pentagon who knows anything more than what's been on CNN so far this morning. Or if they do, they're not saying. Carl, one confidential source has told me that this may be related to the mysterious disappearance of Undersecretary of Defense Thomas Merewether. I'm not sure what the connection might be, but that was told to me personally by a high-ranking official within the Department of Defense."

"Tim, is the Pentagon talking about this as if we have been attacked by Pakistan?"

"That's a good question. Those I've spoken with—and again, we're still waiting for their official pronouncement— have been talking about the incident as a terrorist attack."

"Thank you, Tim. Tim will be at the Pentagon, and he'll inform us as soon as there is any official statement . . ."

Katherine stopped listening. The images were now back to the orbiting helicopter and the confusion and damage at San Onofre. She tried to remember what had happened to all the airplanes mentioned. There'd been only a vague mention of MiGs, but nothing about what had happened to them. Katherine had a horrible feeling in her stomach.

The phone rang, and she lunged for it. "Hello?"

"Katherine!"

"Luke! Are you all right?"

"Yeah, I'm fine. I'm in jail. On Miramar. The FBI arrested

me for conspiracy to commit a terrorist act," Luke said, glancing at the guard who was listening carefully.

"In jail? Are you serious? They're out of their minds! Luke, what happened? *How* did this happen?"

"Khan smuggled bombs into the country and just forced them onto the base. Killed the security. They loaded them onto their F-16s and flew to the coast—is it on the news yet? What are they saying?"

"It's the *only* thing on television. Everyone is going crazy. But there isn't much that's helpful. The government has no idea what is happening, so they're not saying anything. It's incredible."

"They did miss the reactors, didn't they?"

"Yes, didn't hit either one of them. They hit some low building, thank God. If they'd hit a reactor, they'd have to evacuate all of Southern California. Did they miss because you were there?"

"No. We got there as they were in their bombing runs. At least we don't have a Chernobyl on our hands. Katherine, Thud didn't make it . . ."

"Make what?"

"He was closing on one of the Paks, and the guy pulled back into him and just ran into him. They had a midair. He never had a chance."

"He's *dead*?" Katherine asked, stunned.

"Yeah." He paused. "I saw the whole thing. He didn't get out."

"What about Michelle and their kids?"

"That's just it. We've got to tell them."

"I *can't* just call her . . ."

"This is my one phone call. You have to."

"Oh, Luke . . ." she said, groping for what to say. "She's going to come completely apart. What about his father?"

"You'd better call him, too."

She sighed and closed her eyes.

"Vlad got shot down. Khan got him with a Sidewinder. He jumped out. He's probably wandering around on the beach somewhere north of the power plant. Make sure the government knows to go look for him. Of course, they'll probably just arrest him, too. Stamp is right down the hall in another cell here in the brig."

"This is outrageous. How can they be so incompetent?"

"They've got to find Khan, Katherine. They've *got* to find him."

"He escaped? How? Where did he go?"

"He escaped in a submarine."

"A *submarine*? That hasn't been on the news."

"Khan took his F-16 out over the ocean. I was right behind him. He went to a spot—probably based on a fix from a GPS he must've had with him—and just ejected. I was about to shoot him, and he jumped out. Then a sub came up and grabbed him."

"Wow. Terrorists don't run around in submarines. Who's helping him?"

"Beats the hell out of me."

"Whose submarine was it?"

"I don't know. There weren't any markings on it at all."

"I'm coming down there, Luke."

"No, stay there. You're too pregnant."

"No I'm not. I'll be there by this afternoon. I'm going to get you out. Has anyone tried to question you?"

"Just briefly."

"Don't say anything. They'll use it against you."

"I don't care. My life is ruined—"

"You'd better *start* caring. Your life is *not* ruined. This wasn't your fault."

"I'll tell them whatever they need to know to catch Khan, Katherine. I can't do it myself, so they're going to have to do it."

"I'm on my way," she said.

"You don't have to come—"

"I've already decided."

RENEE climbed into the taxi three blocks from the American embassy in Islamabad. The entire city was in stunned denial and disbelief over what had happened. It had hit them with the same effect the Kennedy assassination and Pearl Harbor had had on the United States, but as the ones responsible, not as the victims. All of Pakistan was glued to CNN International, which was running an ongoing report on the four Pakistani pilots who'd been invited to an elite American fighter school and had responded by borrowing airplanes and secreting bombs into the country to drop them on an American nuclear power plant.

Renee knew there was a deep undercurrent of anti-Americanism throughout Pakistan. She'd become most vividly aware of it in 2000, when she began noticing the widespread display of posters in support of Osama bin Laden around the city, and even in private homes, hailing the terrorist as a hero for standing up to the West. Many parents had named children after him. Some of it was the general sense in many Islamic countries of being disregarded and held in low esteem by the West. Some of it was the perception that the United States treated India and Pakistan differently in matters nuclear. In spite of that underlying inclination to hold the United States in contempt, she saw genuine shock and shame on the faces of the Pakistanis out in public. They couldn't believe that their government had attacked the United States.

The Pakistani government, though, was disclaiming all knowledge of the events and condemning the actions of its pilots as terrorism. As she had expected, the Chief Executive of Pakistan, himself a former General in the Pakistani Army, had gone on the air and condemned the action in the strongest possible terms. He pledged assistance to find and apprehend those responsible. He confirmed there was no Pakistani submarine anywhere near the area at the time and asserted that Pakistan had no idea who was supporting this attack by these renegade former Pakistanis but would leave no stone unturned in the attempt to find out. Renee also knew from her cohorts in D.C. that Pakistan hadn't given any actual help so far.

Renee watched the street carefully. The cars were driving more slowly than usual, many of the drivers bent slightly forward, listening intently to the news reports on their radios. Those in stores and cafés were listening to strategically placed radios or televisions. She spoke to the driver, and he stopped at the intersection. She slid over and got out of the cab near the curb.

She looked for her contact. She'd been on her way out the door of one of her apartments to meet with him when Kevin had called. He'd told her to use her sources, to try to track down the truth. Good old Kevin. They'd been in the same "welcome aboard" class when they both went to work for the CIA five years before. He seemed to believe that gave him the right to call on her at any time to ask for a favor. Like old pals. But now he was working, at least indirectly, for Morrissey. That made Kevin's requests legitimate, and by this time simply confirmed what she would be doing anyway. But Kevin still had to think of it as something she was doing for him. She didn't mind. He'd been the only one in the entire CIA to actually be looking into the men who'd done this *before* the event occurred. Too late now, but Kevin had been onto something, and she'd barely given him the time of day.

Renee had set up the meeting quickly. She knew in her gut that she'd missed a rare opportunity to forestall the attack. If only she'd paid more attention to it over the last week or two. Intelligence matters often start out as minor "see what you can find" missions that sound, and usually are, horribly boring. If anyone knows why a thing is important, the field officers are rarely told, on the off chance that someone might try to get it out of them at the wrong time.

She crossed the street and headed for the train station. Her contact would be standing by the track waiting for the train that was to leave in thirty minutes. He'd told her which post he would be leaning against. She passed through the station out to the throng waiting for that train and glanced around. She counted posts, the ones holding the covered awning next to the train track to protect people from the weather. She saw the post with the out-of-place black paint at the top and maneuvered her way to stand by it. She breathed hard and put out her hand to hold herself up. Finally she leaned against the post. A man stood behind her reading a newspaper, no more than a foot away. He spoke to her in a low, whispered voice. "I cannot believe this has happened," he said in Urdu. "Pakistan is shamed in front of the world!"

She nodded carefully without saying anything, then waited as he came around beside her and stood right next to her.

"This will bring down the government. No matter what happens, it is the end of the current government. I am sure."

Renee thought about that for a moment. It hadn't occurred to her. His newspaper obscured their faces, and the post blocked anyone on the other side from listening too carefully. "We might have stopped him," she replied in her unaccented Urdu.

"I told you what I knew."

"It wasn't enough."

"I didn't know what they were planning. It suddenly explains the attack on the weapons depot a few months ago. Now we know what they took—and where it went."

"You don't think the government could have been behind that?"

"No."

She wasn't so sure. She turned slightly toward him. "If it's the last thing I do, I will find him."

"Them."

"Only one lived."

"Only one *pilot*. But how many others had to be involved—the bombs, the men who were with them? It is *incredible* to me they kept it quiet."

"He escaped on a submarine."

He tried not to look at her. "I heard that on CNN. It must be an error. It is not possible."

"It's true. It almost certainly means some country was involved."

"What kind of submarine?"

"Diesel."

"Many countries have diesel submarines. Russia, China, Iran, India . . ."

"Pakistan."

He looked at her sharply. "You don't really think Pakistan was involved in the attack, do you?"

"Pakistan *was* involved. They were Pakistani pilots. The only question is whether your government was—"

"They were acting on their own! I assure you."

"We'll see about that, I suppose."

"You think Pakistan would accept your country's invitation and then send its Air Force pilots there to blow up your nuclear power plant? You think we're crazy?"

"It was set up by your embassy. They leaned on the Undersecretary of Defense."

"Yes. Yushaf."

"You know him?" she exclaimed.

"Knew *of* him. He was employed by Pakistan. As we now see, he was working for someone else."

"Who?"

"No one knows. Do you know where he is? We do not."

"No. He fled before the attack."

"He has not returned."

"I find that hard to believe. How do I know you're telling me the truth?"

"You don't. But I assure you in the strongest possible terms. We had nothing to do with the attack."

"You may not even know."

"I do. You don't know me as well as you think."

She glanced at him. "What do you mean?"

"I am a member of ISI."

"What?" she said, suddenly aware she was talking to the very people she suspected of conducting the attack.

"I have my fingers in many pies."

"Then why talk to me?"

"Because your country suspects ISI of association with and encouragement of the Taliban of Afghanistan and bin Laden—all kinds of terrorists around the world. You don't know what we do, so you suspect."

"Maybe you should tell me all about it."

"No. I am here to answer your questions."

"Where is he?"

"Who?"

"The pilot."

"Sounds like you should follow the submarine. It must go to some port."

"He could have transferred to a ship, then a helicopter, then another ship, then another helicopter, then a flying boat, then an airliner. He could be anywhere in the world by now."

"So how would I know where he is?"

"Because you would know."

He turned the page of his newspaper.

She waited. She sensed he was considering telling her what he knew. She needed a breakthrough. The attack had sent a shudder through the entire intelligence community, like the feeling under your feet when standing on the deck of a large ship as it runs aground. Once again the CIA had been caught with its pants down in South Asia, just as it had when India had conducted its nuclear testing in 1998 and the CIA learned about it through CNN. The President had been angry then. Now, even though there was a different President, he knew the history and was livid. He'd called in the Director of Central Intelligence and screamed at him. Unless he delivered the Pakistani pilot's head on a platter and found out who was behind this, he was fired. Renee assumed he'd be fired anyway, depending on what certain investigations found out about how four foreign pilots were allowed to operate supersonic fighters inside the United States.

"There have been rumors," the man said quietly now, rustling his paper, making his voice barely audible to her even though she was leaning in his direction. "Those records we discussed. Back five years. Very odd. Why not fifteen years of records? Why not flight-training records? They seemed incomplete. I followed up."

"Yes?" she asked, growing impatient.

"There aren't any records that go back any further."

"What does that mean?"

"There is an entry that says earlier records were lost and cannot be reconstructed."

"Is that possible?"

"Yes."

"So?"

"So my friends in records say that while it is possible, they have never seen it before. Ever."

"Ever?"

"Not ever. It would be a strange coincidence that no one has ever seen such a thing and then the pilot with those very lost records is involved in a criminal attack and disappears."

"What do you make of it?"

"We can't get back into the records now. The entire division is under a total panic, searching all the records of all four pilots. They can't even talk about it. In the records we did get last week, no photo and no identification, no fingerprints, dental records—nothing."

"Do you have anything or not?"

"I think maybe Riaz Khan didn't exist."

"Of course—"

"I mean, there was no Air Force pilot by that name."

"How can that be?"

"With lots of help."

"So who was he?"

"The Air Force is not that big. Pilots are known. Sometimes one group—say, the ones who fly fighters—don't know the ones who fly tankers. So maybe he comes in as being transferred from some other type of airplane, fresh from training in a distant base, and no one knows him. It is possible. And if they didn't know him, and they suspected him, they would just assume he is from the ISI and stay away from him."

"Do you know who he is, or do you not?"

He closed the paper and folded it under his arm. "I don't know. But I am told there was a pilot in F-16s from an Air Force base near Karachi who has been on extended leave to deal with family problems for some time now. The only one it is true about."

"You think it is him?"

He covered his mouth and coughed painfully as he walked suddenly away from her. He was afraid they'd been made. She knew better than to look around. She waited for the train that was approaching and, with the rest of the crowd, boarded it.

20

Katherine listened to the radio all the way to Reno but had learned no new information. There'd been some speculation about a "school" of some sort in Nevada that could account for the presence of the MiGs and the F-16s, but no one could really explain it yet. Katherine drove as fast as she could to the airport to catch the next Southwest flight to San Diego. She made it to the gate ten minutes before takeoff and had been given a yellow plastic boarding pass, numbered 130. She was in the fourth boarding group. She stood on her swollen feet in the closely packed crowd and tried to hear the television that was hanging from the ceiling fifty feet away as a child next to her played with a Game Boy and refused to turn off the sound.

Katherine recognized Carl Allen as the CNN reporter anchoring the coverage, but she also noticed that his demeanor was much less comforting than it had been. Like most of the other passengers in the line, she strained to hear what he was saying.

"We feel it our duty to report that Leslie Monteneri, who had been reporting for us live from the scene earlier this morning, has been taken to the hospital, as have the two helicopter pilots with whom she was flying. At this point we are not sure of the cause of her illness, but we've been told it is most likely radiation sickness. The helicopter that brought you those compelling images live this morning from San Onofre was apparently being bombarded with radiation from the damage inflicted on San Onofre by the Pakistani pilots flying American jets. The exact source of the radiation is unclear.

"We have another helicopter airborne now at the scene, with CNN's nuclear expert, Dr. Alfred Boyer, aboard. He has detection equipment on board to make sure they're safe." The image changed to a shot of the helicopter in the bright California sunshine. "Dr. Boyer, can you hear us?"

"Yes, I can."

The image of Dr. Boyer was horrifying to the passengers waiting to get on the Southwest plane. All conversation stopped. The mother next to Katherine reached down, took her son's Game Boy, and turned it off.

Boyer and the single pilot in the helicopter wore radiation-protection suits that made them look like the evil scientists from *E.T.* Boyer's bearded face was visible through the plastic faceplate, distorted just enough to make him look odd. He was surrounded by a bank of equipment that seemed out of place in the helicopter.

"What can you tell us about reports of radiation?"

"There's definitely radiation coming from the site, Carl. It's almost certain that Leslie and the other crew members are suffering from radiation sickness. I must report that we are very high over the site and using a very large lens to bring you the recent pictures you have before you. As you can see, there are several bodies of firefighters and emergency-response people lying on the ground in the San Onofre compound. They were apparently there to respond to the fire and the damage, and although we shouldn't speculate, were almost certainly overcome by radiation. The speed with which it worked on them and the fact that others have not gone to their rescue indicates to me very high-level, very deadly, radiation. I won't speculate on the cause, but it is clearly not from the reactors themselves."

"That accounts for your appearance in special suits."

Boyer seemed unsure about whether to show the concern he felt or try to be chipper to make the situation seem better than he actually believed it to be. "Um, that's right, Carl. To be abundantly cautious, we've put these suits on." He looked at the baffling array of electronic gear behind him. "We have a lot of detection equipment with us. It's about as sensitive as there is, and we're able to detect radiation in the atmosphere around us. We've been detecting several kinds—"

"You're detecting radiation right now? Right where you are?"

"Yes we are. As you can see"—Boyer pointed—"we have indications of several types of radioactive material—cesium, plutonium, even uranium."

"From a nuclear warhead? Did they drop a nuclear bomb that did not explode but is just slowly melting down?"

"That's unlikely, Carl. Based on what I've seen so far, and without saying too much, it is my belief that the nuclear waste of San Onofre has been compromised. You must keep in mind, Carl, that the radioactive inventory of a spent nuclear rod is about equivalent to that of the bomb that was dropped on Hiroshima."

Carl was staggered. "Where would they find spent nuclear rods, Dr. Boyer? Where would they get nuclear waste?"

"I didn't mean to imply that they brought nuclear waste. I would expect we're dealing with the waste that is stored at San Onofre, on site, as at all the other nuclear plants in the country, but that is speculation on my part."

"How much waste was stored at San Onofre?"

"I'm not sure about that, Carl. I think we'll wait to hear from San Onofre at their press conference on that one."

"Do you expect them to evacuate?"

"There is an evacuation plan, and I'm sure that San Onofre and the local authorities are considering putting that in place. The sirens have been going off for some time now, and the local residents took it as an actual signal of radioactivity, which it turned out to be. They've begun fleeing from the area, but the local freeways are so crowded that we've seen people driving through fences to get to Camp Pendleton on dirt roads to avoid the jammed freeways and city streets of San Clemente."

"Thank you, Dr. Boyer." Carl turned his attention to the camera. "We will keep getting updates from Dr. Boyer. In just a few minutes we expect representatives from the San Onofre plant to hold their first press conference. We'll be carrying it live."

Katherine was jarred back to Reno by the PA announcement. "Southwest flight 1285 to San Diego is ready for immediate boarding. We will accept boarding passes numbered one to thirty at this time."

Nobody moved. Everyone had been listening to the broadcast and realized there was radioactivity in southern Orange County. A burgeoning Chernobyl. They stared at each other. Finally one of the passengers peeled away from the front of the group. "I don't need to glow in the dark. I'm not going anywhere."

Another followed her, then another. Before she knew it, Katherine was standing among a group of perhaps two dozen people who were still intent on boarding the plane. She walked down the ramp and stepped onto the airplane. She hesitated, then turned toward the cockpit. The two pilots were in their seats. "Have you heard anything about San Onofre?" she asked the captain.

He looked back at her. "Sure. What in particular?"

"Is the FAA saying anything about whether it's dangerous to go near to it?"

"There's a large radioactive cloud forming. They're not sure what's going to happen to it, but they're going to vector us around it. San Diego is okay, but they've stopped all flights into John Wayne Airport in Orange County."

"What do you think?"

The co-pilot answered. "We're going to drop you off, then fly to Las Vegas, where we're based. And that's where I'm going to stay until they know what the hell is going to happen. Whatever it is, it's not a good thing."

Katherine thanked them and made her way back to her seat. She had her choice of a hundred or so in the previously sold-out airplane.

"WELL, Cindy," Morrissey said, not needing to say anything else.

She nodded. The entire building in Langley, Virginia, was in shock. No one had ever attacked the United States more effectively. One could say that the attack on Pearl Harbor had done more physical damage, but that was done by hundreds, thousands of Japanese on dozens of ships and hundreds of airplanes. Four men had created the damage at San Onofre, or a couple dozen if you counted their maintenance personnel. And the effects of the attack were now expected to last not just days or weeks, but centuries. "I don't know if it makes it better or worse that we were looking into them. Even active fieldwork. We didn't get to the end of the road in time."

Bill Morrissey closed his eyes. He knew this was it. He would be fired for this. Without a doubt. Pakistan was his area. He was supposed to know *everything* that was going on, even though that was impossible. There'd been an attempt to smuggle a nuclear warhead into Pakistan. He'd made no progress on that whatsoever. It continued to baffle him. Then there'd been an attack on a Pakistani weapons depot, where something had been stolen, but no one knew what. They knew only that the bombs designed to carry nuclear warheads hadn't been touched. Then there'd been this concern about Major Riaz Khan at the school in Nevada. Kevin's little brother had alerted them. But they'd had nothing to go on. Just suspicion. Could have been racism, for all he knew. But now it appeared it was all related somehow—and he'd missed it. The Director had relied on him.

"There'll be plenty of time for them to discover all the reasons I should be fired," he said. "But for now our job is to track this guy down. No stone unturned. No idea unexplored. He snuck into our tent and set the whole thing on fire."

Cindy nodded. Her computer screen was playing streaming video of the San Onofre plant in the California sunshine with the growing cloud of death clearly visible against the blue ocean. "What can I do?"

"We have to figure how he got here, how he got bombs, and who picked him up in the ocean. Way I see it, it's Pakistan until they can convince us it isn't. I just heard that Congress is convening in special session today to determine whether to declare war against Pakistan."

"Seriously?" Cindy asked. "*Seriously?* War?"

"Very seriously. This attack was by members of their military. It was a brilliantly executed military attack, with an escape planned to include a submarine. That means some country was involved. If not Pakistan, who the hell would be prearranged to pick up Pakistani Air Force pilots and help them escape from an attack on the United States?"

"I can't imagine."

"Exactly."

"And the fact you claim no responsibility for an act of war by your military is interesting, but it doesn't get you out of the box. We clearly have enough to declare war against them. And frankly, I don't know which way Congress will want to go with this."

KATHERINE sat across from Luke. Between them was a set of thin metal bars. Her face showed much of the stress she felt, but she was trying to be calm and supportive. She could tell that Luke was at the end of his rope. She replied softly, "It *is* radioactive."

His one oasis of good news, that they hadn't hit the nuclear plant, was quickly eroding. "The plants were completely intact!"

"I don't know," Katherine said, also amazed. "Apparently it was radioactive waste. It was stored on site."

"Waste?" Luke asked, mystified. "Waste? What waste?"

"I don't know. All I know is the experts are totally hysterical. They're saying all kinds of things. On my way here from the airport, I heard that the big issue they're trying to decide now is whether to evacuate Los Angeles."

"Los Angeles? Are you kidding me?"

"No. The cloud is being pushed northwest by the Santa Ana winds. The President has declared an emergency. The Governor has declared an emergency. They're comparing this to Chernobyl. The Nuclear Regulatory Commission is running around in circles, the Navy is searching for an invisible submarine, and the Air Force is looking for anybody in the air who's unauthorized. But the lead story on CNN isn't the attack, it's the fact that the government stopped funding antiterrorism efforts at nuclear plants about three years ago. Too expensive. Everybody screamed how stupid it was at the time. You know how good the press is at 'I told you so.' "

Luke was disgusted. "They didn't find the sub?"

"The Navy isn't saying much, but based on what I've heard, I think the nearest U.S. submarine was about two hundred miles away from where the F-16 went in. They sent out helicopters and P-3s, but nobody has found anything that I've heard about."

"They're long gone. It was a diesel. They're too quiet. If they got even a couple hours' head start, there'll be no catching them." Luke cradled his head in his hands. "I'm really sorry about this, Katherine. You think this was their plan all along?"

"Sure looks like it. Down to the last detail. I'll bet the original plan was to go to TOPGUN. We just walked into it."

Luke was speechless. He didn't know what to do next. "Are we getting hammered in the news?"

"They finally know about the school, the four Pakistani students, the whole thing, but they're not quite sure what to make of us. There's a lot of amazement that a school was allowed to operate in Nevada with Russian fighters and that Pakistanis were allowed to come and operate supersonic fighters in the U.S. Oh, and Pakistan claims to know nothing about the attack. They claim to be equally outraged—"

"Right."

"I'm just telling you what they've been saying. They know the pilots, but say they had no prior history of terrorist or radical activity. They think they might have affiliated with some other group, like the Taliban from Afghanistan, or the Iranians—a lot of possibilities. But nobody knows."

"Can you see the cloud?"

"Yeah," she said, nodding. "It must be ten miles across now and really high, maybe fifty thousand feet. You can see it from here."

Luke leaned back in his wooden chair and closed his eyes. He was unable to clear his head of the shame and anger. He looked at Katherine. "I'm sorry."

"You didn't do anything wrong. You did everything you could to stop him."

"I didn't listen to Brian as much as I should have. He had the scent of these guys. I didn't listen. I looked right by. 'But their security clearances were guaranteed by the United States government. The Undersecretary will look out for—' "

"Yeah, except the Undersecretary disappeared. I heard it on the news."

"Disappeared?"

"Yeah. Vanished. No trace of him."

"We're dead."

"Well, we'll see where all this leads. My first job is to get you out of here. I'll have to hire a lawyer."

"Tell the other guys at the squadron to keep flying. Finish the class."

Katherine braced herself for getting up out of her chair. "They can't."

"Why not?"

She'd hoped not to have to tell him. "The FBI padlocked the gate. The school's been shut down."

"KEVIN," Brian said breathlessly, sick from the developments of the last twenty-four hours and blaming himself, "you've got to help—"

"Where the hell are you?"

"The Mizpah Hotel in Tonopah."

"Brian, I can't even *talk* to you! Everybody involved in that school is a leper!"

"You've *got* to help," Brian repeated, trying not to sound desperate.

"People a lot bigger than me are looking hard, Brian. You can be sure of that. People are looking under every rock. FBI, everybody. Trust me. This is way out of my hands. I can't do anything."

"Yes you can. Call Renee."

Kevin was furious. "Don't *ever* mention her name again! Ever."

"You've got to get back to her. Find out what she knows!"

"Do you really think that with four Pakistani pilots attacking the United States we're *not* going to be exercising our intelligence assets in Pakistan? How friggin' stupid do you think we are?"

"And the Undersecretary. Find out who his contact was."

"We already know!"

"What? Who? I haven't heard anything on the news."

"We don't typically do news releases here."

"So who was the contact?"

"Guy in the Pakistani embassy. His name was Yushaf."

"Is somebody having a chat with him?"

"Seems he anticipated there might be a reaction to his pilots bombing our nuclear power plant. He was on an airplane when the attack was still under way."

"He left *before* it was in the news?" Brian said, thinking.

"What?"

"He must have been in on it. How else could he have known to get on an airplane?"

"I'm not sure," Kevin replied.

"That shows it was Pakistan's plan all along. They pulled their guy from Washington before the shit hit the fan!"

Kevin pondered the implications. "Maybe. Maybe he's just like this pilot. Maybe they're all working *against* their country's interests. Plus, Yushaf didn't go back to Pakistan. He vanished."

"Meaning what? He was working for somebody else?"

"We don't know."

"Where'd they get the bombs? Those have to have come from Pakistan."

"They did. An armory near Islamabad was broken into a couple of months ago. That's probably when they took the bombs."

"You've got to work this, Kevin. There's a radioactive cloud hovering off Southern California, the school has been shut down, and Luke is in jail. Can't you do *anything*?"

Kevin said, "I'll be in touch."

21

Luke and Katherine were ushered into a conference room at the end of the hallway. It was poorly lit but well ventilated, with the thick wire screens over the windows. Luke was still in his khaki flight suit with the Russian wings on his nametag. He felt silly wearing the insignia of a Russian Colonel sitting in a jail on a Marine air station.

They waited patiently; they'd been told that they were to be interviewed immediately. Luke refused to sit. He wanted to fix everything, to make it all disappear. But he knew that the chance to do so was well behind him. The big wooden door opened, and four men and one woman walked in briskly. She was carrying a small black wallet, which she flipped opened and held in front of her. "FBI. Special Agent Helen Li. Please sit down."

"I don't want to sit."

"Sit down," she insisted. He did. She put her identification back into a small shoulder bag, then placed it on the floor next to the chair. She remained standing and leaned against the chair, holding the top of it with both her small hands and looking down at Luke. She was of medium height and very thin. Her straight hair didn't quite reach her shoulders. "Are you Luke Henry?"

"Of course I am."

"I'm here to question you about what happened. There are many things I need to ask you—"

"Aren't you going to give him his rights?" Katherine interrupted.

Helen looked at her. "No."

"He's under arrest, you're here to question him, and you're not going to give him his rights?"

"That's right."

"Then I'm going to instruct him not to answer any questions."

"You may instruct him to do whatever you wish," Helen replied quietly.

Luke looked at Katherine and shook his head subtly. "What do you want?"

"There's a radioactive cloud drifting toward Los Angeles. The entire West Coast is at risk." She let that sink in. "I know that the pilots who conducted the attack were being trained by you in a secret desert airfield for the last three weeks."

"It wasn't secret."

"That's not really important right now," a man said as he stepped forward.

"Right," Luke replied. "Who are you?"

"This is Keith Berger," Li said. "He's with the Department of Energy."

Luke looked at the short, round man, and saw deep pain in his face, like the pain of someone who's just lost a child. "Do you know what happened at the plant? There are only two active plants there. Right? I mean, there are two operating reactors," Luke said. "And they missed them completely. How the hell can there be a radioactive cloud?"

"Yes," he said softly. "They hit another building. Almost certainly by intent."

"What building? What was in there?"

"Nuclear waste."

"Seriously?"

"Seriously."

"A lot of it?"

"Yes. High-level radioactive waste. A lot. The waste from Units Two and Three that has been produced in the last ten years. Even more."

"Wasn't it safe?"

"It didn't have the protection of the two generating plants. And the waste is stored in an open pool of water. I'm afraid the Pakistani pilots knew that."

"An open pool?" Luke asked, his eyes growing larger. "How did they know?"

"They hit the plant at its Achilles' heel. The concentrated radiation in the waste was worse than if they'd penetrated one of the reactors. The bombs were able to penetrate the non-reinforced building. The spent waste was blown up with the water in which it was stored."

"What was it doing there? Why was it stored like that?"

He was obviously distressed. "There's been an argument ongoing for more than ten years within the federal government on where to store high-level nuclear waste. We built a place in Nevada, but then . . . there was concern about earthquakes. Look, we just couldn't get agreement. So the waste has been sitting there—pretty much like it was at San Onofre—at most of the nuclear plants around the country."

Luke stared straight ahead. "This is a disaster," he said to no one in particular. He looked at Berger. "How could the Pakistanis know that?"

"All you have to do is follow the debates on nuclear waste, and you can find where virtually all the radioactive waste in the country is. There are maps all over the Internet. This waste is as bad as it gets, and it's right on the coast."

"But if the wind changes, it won't get to L.A."

"Then it would go to San Diego or Palm Springs."

"So pray for still winds."

"Then it will settle into the Pacific and ruin the coast of California for a couple of centuries."

"Ruin?"

"Kill every living thing in the ocean for miles and pollute the bottom and food sources."

Luke was despondent. "It doesn't dissipate?"

Berger sighed. "Unlike love, radiation is forever. Or at least close enough to forever to count as forever."

Helen leaned toward Luke and put her hands on the table. "We must try to control the impact of what has happened. We must try to prevent this from ever happening again. That's what Mr. Berger is trying to do. But I'm here to find out who did this and why. I need your help. I want you to answer some questions."

"I don't think you should say anything," Katherine interrupted. "We need to get you an attorney."

"I don't want a damned attorney!" Luke exploded.

"Do you agree to talk to us?"

"What are you guys doing to try to catch this guy?"

"Who is it that we should be trying to catch?"

"The guy who *did* this. Major Riaz Khan of the Pakistani Air Force. Do you not know what happened?" Luke asked, looking at Helen, then Katherine.

"I'd like to hear it from you."

Luke was bone tired. Being awakened from a dead sleep to race to his squadron, only to find a catastrophe under way, had begun to catch up with him. The fact that he had just been in the biggest air battle an American had participated in since Vietnam seemed unreal. Instead of throwing back drinks and telling his friends all about it, he was sitting in a brig, explaining why he should be allowed to breathe. He'd done all he could. He'd fought as hard as he could, but it hadn't been enough. Five minutes' more notice, and everything would have been different. Maybe if he'd listened to

Brian a little more closely, he wouldn't be having the self-doubt he felt flooding him. Now he had to try to explain it to people who had no chance of figuring it out. "You know the story . . ."

Helen didn't respond.

Luke debated with himself, then began. "Khan and three other Pakistanis were students of my Nevada Fighter Weapons School. Last night—this morning, actually—a bunch of men in trucks broke into the base. They killed the security guards and brought in bombs. I have no idea where they got them. They loaded their airplanes and took off. I got a call from Raymond—one of my employees who happened to be outside the base—and he told me what they were doing." He sat forward and leaned on the table. "I raced down to the airfield, and four of us climbed into our MiGs. We were under a contract to do some missile testing, and it was scheduled for later that morning. Instead we went after the Pakistanis. We got to the nuclear power plant just as they were—"

"How did you know to go to San Onofre?"

"We didn't. We just took off and chased them down. About halfway through, the FAA guy and I—Catfish was his call sign—concluded that's where they were headed. It should all be on the tape. You can listen to it."

"Go on."

"Like I said, we were too late, but we got all of them but one. Vlad got shot down."

"Is he okay?"

"Yes. He's fine. He landed a couple miles north on the beach."

"Vlad, you said?" Helen asked, acutely interested in this piece of information she hadn't previously heard. "How well did you know this Vlad? He's Russian?"

"Yes. He's with MAPS. The company that did our maintenance."

Helen considered the events from a new perspective. "How do you know he wasn't involved?"

Luke frowned. "*Other* than the fact that he got shot down?"

"Yes," Li replied. "Other than that."

"I guess by the same way I know *you* weren't involved. It's a ridiculous thought."

"How do you know?"

"Because he had no idea the Pakistanis were even *coming*. My hooking up with him was my doing. I'm the one who called MAPS to ask them to work on our airplanes and help us with the upgrades. You're right, maybe he was involved with the Trilateral Commission, or maybe he was on the grassy knoll when Kennedy—"

"You don't have to get sarcastic."

"Well, it's insulting when you ask questions like that."

"Why did they do it?"

Luke sat back and breathed in loudly, then exhaled equally loudly. "I have no idea. He clearly had—"

"Khan?"

"Yeah."

She nodded.

Luke continued. "He clearly had an attitude toward India—that's understandable—and he had some negative things to say about the U.S. But nothing that rose to the level where I thought he would do something like this."

"Did he ever talk about the nuclear testing that Pakistan did?"

"Sure. He thought there was an anti-Muslim bias in U.S. foreign policy."

"Did he ever get more specific than that?"

"No." Luke waited for Helen to ask him another question. She was obviously thinking. Something he'd said had stimulated an idea in her mind. Luke asked, "What about the trucks? And the men who killed the security guards?"

"The trucks were parked inside large hangars at an airfield nearby."

"What airfield?" Luke asked.

"The one at Tonopah."

"Ours?"

"No, no, the one—nearer the town, an old one . . ."

"Right off Route 6?"

"Yes."

Luke shook his head. Of course. They had other planes waiting for them. "Any radar tracks flying out of there?"

"They're checking all the FAA tapes now, but no one remembers seeing anything in that area."

"So you have no idea where they've gone?"

"We'll find them, but we don't have anything yet." Helen sat down at the desk. "There is one thing you may know . . ."

Luke nodded.

"What kind of submarine was it?"

He sat in the chair, his elbows resting on the beat-up table, embarrassed at what his answer had to be. "I'm not sure."

Helen Li glanced at one of the men behind her, who handed her a large folder. "What kind of submarine do you *think* it was?"

"It wasn't a Boomer."

"It wasn't a ballistic missile submarine? You sure?"

"Yes."

"Was it nuclear?"

Luke closed his eyes and tried to regenerate the image in his mind, but all he could see was Khan swimming toward a black structure. "I don't think so."

"Why not?"

"I'm no submarine expert."

"You were in the Navy."

"I was never in submarines."

Helen spoke softly. "I'm told that all Navy pilots are trained to recognize submarines." She was looking at him as if he were lying, as if his inability to be clear about the submarine might in fact be evidence that he was more deeply involved than she had originally thought. "Isn't that right?"

He bit his tongue. "It's been a while."

"So was the submarine you saw nuclear?"

"I don't think so," Luke said, his frustration building.

"Why not?"

"Nuclear submarines have a certain shape. A teardrop, rounded-bow sort of shape. At least I think so. I'm really not sure, but if there are nuclear submarines that don't have that shape, I don't know about them."

"This one didn't have that teardrop shape?"

"No."

"It was a diesel boat?" One of the men suddenly interjected, sitting down next to her.

Luke stared at the man, who was intense and angry. "Who are you?"

"It was a diesel boat? You sure?"

"What's your name?"

"George Lane. Look, we don't have much time. Are you sure it was a diesel boat?"

"I believe so."

"You said you knew Russian submarines. Was it—"

"I said the submarines that we studied were mostly Russian submarines."

"You used to be able to recognize Russian submarines. Right?"

"Mostly nukes."

Lane riffled through a large stack of photographs and handed Luke one. "What is this?"

Luke studied the photograph. He didn't want to get it wrong. "I'm not sure," Luke said. "Maybe a Kilo."

"Exactly," Lane said. "Is that it?"

Luke recalled the image of the submarine again, as he looked down on it from his MiG over the Pacific Ocean. "It might have been. It was just sort of . . . nondescript. Black, the usual diesel look . . ."

Lane put another photograph in front of him. "What about this?"

"Whiskey class? Aren't those things about fifty years old?"

Lane glanced at Helen. "Yes. They are old. But some of them have fallen into hands outside of the control of governments. One of these could be owned by people who don't like the United States."

"Definitely not."

Lane thought for a minute. "What about this?" he said, putting another photograph in front of Luke, a large black-and-white glossy of a submarine on the surface. Luke stared at the photograph. "I don't know. What is this?"

"French. Daphne class."

"Let me see that." Luke held up the photograph and examined it carefully. His eyes raced from one side to the other, the top to bottom. He drank in the entire shape, tried to envision the shape in the ocean behind a swimming Riaz Khan. "I just can't tell. This doesn't look quite right, but I can't say for sure it isn't either. Whose is it?"

"This particular one is French. But the Pakistanis have four of them."

Luke looked at the picture again, harder, longer. He still didn't know. "I'm just not sure."

Lane frowned and gave Luke another photo. "How about this one?"

Luke studied it and shook his head. "What is it?"

"Type 209. German-made."

"Did you ask the Air Force guys? They saw it, too."

"They said it's a sub, and we should ask you 'cause you're a former squid."

"Nice," Luke said, handing the photo back to him. "Sorry."

Lane was growing frustrated. Like Helen, he was beginning to doubt. "How can you not recognize submarines?"

"We never studied French submarines."

He put three photographs next to each other on the table in front of Luke. "What about these? Last chance," Lane said.

Luke studied the photos. "I don't think it's this one . . . What's that?"

"That's the *Hashmat*, a Pakistani Agosta-class sub."

"Definitely not that one."

"What about the other one?"

"The *Khalid*. New Agosta 90B–class Pakistani sub. If you can't tell us what it is, nobody will know what to be looking for. Even if we find a diesel boat in the Pacific now, we have no grounds to stop it. Without a positive ID from you, they have every right to be there and not respond to our request to surface, let alone allow us to search them. They'll just politely say no. We're at a dead end here, Mr. Henry. If you could give us some distinguishing features of this submarine, we might be able to make some progress."

"I just can't tell you anything else. I'm sorry."

Lane put away his file. He looked at Helen, who nodded. He hurried out of the room, clearly to try other sources of information to track down the submarine.

Helen brushed the hair away from her face. "What about these Pakistani pilots?"

Luke sighed. "I know their names. I know they were approved and cleared by the DOD, and their entry visas were authorized by State. I know they were flying California Air National Guard F-16s and that they were flying F-16Cs back in Pakistan. I know the leader—"

"Riaz Khan."

"I never trusted him. But never so much that I could tell him to leave."

"You didn't do any background investigation on them before accepting them to your school?"

Luke tried not to yell. "I've *told* you! They were authorized by Undersecretary of Defense Merewether. He said he'd take care of all clearances and ensure that their backgrounds were properly investigated. I relied on him to do it."

"Did he ever put that in writing to you?"

"They sent us the clearances. You can look at those."

"I already have. They're not standard."

"That's *my* problem?"

Helen looked at him. She backed away from the chair and turned toward the small window, which was dirty on the inside, under the chain screen covering where it was impossible to clean. "We need a picture of this Khan."

"There aren't any."

"No class photos? No welcome-aboard photos? Nothing?"

"Nothing. He avoided photos. He forbade his pilots from being photographed."

"Didn't that strike you as odd?"

"Yeah, a lot. But what are you going to do?"

"What's your opinion on why this happened?"

That was the question Luke had been pondering since he got back on the ground. "It was why they came. The whole reason they were here. But just because he was mad at the U.S.? I guess that could be the whole reason, but my bet is there's more to it. And frankly, I don't know what else there could be."

She glanced at the other two FBI agents, who watched silently. "And for whom do you think he was working?"

He hesitated, studying her face, wondering if he was missing something. "Well . . . Pakistan," he said slowly. "Right? I mean, he was a Pakistani pilot. How could he be working for somebody else?"

"I don't assume anything." Li was thinking about other things. She looked into the distance.

Luke remained silent.

"Did you see any preparation on their part? Anything they did that pointed to this?"

"They asked us to help them plan a strike, but we do strike planning all the time. Nothing really unusual about that. They were focused on air-to-ground stuff, but again, for F-16s that's not so unusual. That's their primary role."

Helen prepared to leave. "I'm having them release you."

"What?" Katherine said, taken completely by surprise.

"The agents who arrested you were overzealous. The irresistible urge to arrest someone for something bad that has happened. It allows you to feel better about yourself." She slipped her purse over her shoulder. "I suggest you go back to Tonopah and think of whatever you can that will help us catch him. Anything at all. Ask all your instructors." She handed him a business card. "If you think of anything, call me. We must work fast. It's my belief that he's not finished."

Luke glanced at Katherine, confused. "What do you mean?"

"He intended to hurt us. But I agree with you. I don't think that was his final objective. I think that was one step in a larger plan."

"What makes you say that?"

"My friends from the Agency believe that very strongly. They're trying to figure out what his end game is, as they call it."

"What could it be?"

"That's the question, isn't it?" she said over her shoulder as she walked out. Then she stopped. "I've told them to re-open your base. We've seen what we need to see there."

22

Renee had collected a lot of intelligence throughout the country of Pakistan for over three years. Thanks to having grown up with a mother who was half Pakistani she had the ability to appear as a very ordinary Pakistani woman, which made intelligence collection almost easy. But she'd never been on a Pakistani Air Force base. They took security very seriously. If she were caught, she would be charged with espionage. At this point she didn't care. She was in a country that had chosen to target her homeland for a brutal attack, killing many workers in the nuclear power plant itself and whoever else they might be able to kill, depending on winds and whatever else might affect the spread of the poison they'd unleashed. It was a malicious, horrifying attack. She was prepared to take extraordinary risks to get intelligence on who had done it.

She shuffled into the back entrance of the officers' mess with the other women who wore *burkhas*. Renee wore hers in the traditional way, with her face completely covered. Her contact lenses bothered her, as they always did. She didn't wear them frequently enough to become accustomed to them, only to change her eye color.

The women worked quietly in the morning darkness, some washing the few dishes that had been left over from the night before. Others prepared the breakfast Air Force pilots would eat before their early flights, mostly breads and coffee with an occasional fried vegetable or tomato.

As the sun lifted over the horizon, Renee stood behind the

serving trays. Her eyes expertly examined every officer who came through. The number of men who came to breakfast was much smaller than she'd expected. Not more than fifty. She would glance at each officer when he first came in, then look away. She would take quick glimpses from different angles. Although it was extremely difficult to identify someone she'd never seen, she was confident she would recognize Khan if he was here. It was the neck. Everyone mentioned the neck. She had the descriptions the FBI had taken from every person in the school in Nevada and the sketch that everyone in Nevada had agreed was a nearly perfect representation of him.

Searching the face of every officer who entered the room was difficult. Pakistani women were not to look directly into the faces of men. Only prostitutes did that. Renee tried to be subtle. She had to look, though, to have any hope of identifying Khan.

Several of the men simply took food and left, while others sat at the table and talked. The tables held eight or ten, and were arranged in long rows on the hard cement floor. As Renee walked among the tables with dirty dishes she had taken from pilots who had finished, she tried to overhear conversations but heard nothing of interest. Several were talking about the attack, but most seemed genuinely amazed at how this Riaz Khan could have done it and how it couldn't possibly have been sanctioned by the government.

The general feel she got from them was outrage. They'd all known that four pilots had been fortunate enough to get spots in this new American TOPGUN school, and they all hoped one day to be able to go to the school themselves. How their fellow pilots could be lucky enough to go to America and then carry out such a brutal attack left them without explanation. They didn't speak of it to senior officers for fear of being implicated in a larger conspiracy. There were whispers of the ISI or of other secret government agendas about which they were ignorant, but Renee heard nothing indicating that anyone seriously believed that Pakistan—as a country, as a government—was involved.

There was much talk of this Riaz Khan, this mysterious pilot none of them could remember meeting. They'd all heard of him, but none had met him. They found this puzzling, because the Pakistani F-16 community was not that large. There were always one or two pilots they didn't know, but for someone of his rank, stature, and reputation, that was simply not possible. They were mystified.

She kept her head down as she moved the plates and cups back to the kitchen for washing, and then she waited for lunch. She stood in the corner of the dining area with a broom sweeping up some dirt, and she waited.

At two in the afternoon the pilots began filtering in from the hot, dusty day, into the cool, dimly lit officers' dining room. This time nearly all the fliers came. Renee's eyes darted back and forth; she looked for anyone who might resemble Khan.

Several pilots saw her looking at them and took it as a sign of encouragement. They smiled at her and tried to catch her eye a second or third time, but she was able to dismiss them. Finally one officer handed her his plate and asked for her to serve him. She noticed that his fingers were strong and thick, and she glanced at his barrel chest. She handed him the plate, knowing he would have to look at it to take it. She used that moment to look into his face. She detected a faint difference in the skin color between his upper lip and the rest of his face. She also noticed that he had a close-cropped haircut, which, based on tan lines, was very recent. As her eyes returned to their normal downcast angle, she took in the bull-like neck, larger than any man's she'd seen while in Pakistan. It had to be him.

She walked over to another of the servingwomen after the rush had died down. She pointed to him, a knowing smile on her face that she knew showed in her eyes, a look implying barely contained lust. "Who is *that*?" she asked. "That is a true man."

The woman lifted her head, annoyed. "Forget it. You would have no chance with him. He is one of the best pilots in the area and sought by every woman who has seen him."

"What is his name?"

"Don't worry about it. He's trouble."

"I just want to know his name."

"Forget it."

"Is he married?"

"He's married to every woman he sees. They all think he's going to marry them, but he never does. He is a wanderer. He is married to his airplane."

Renee waited for the officers at his table to finish. They knew she would clear their dishes, but they were not quite done. She stood back a ways, but near enough the table to try to hear the conversation while looking uninterested and distracted. The man glanced over his shoulder at her with some annoyance. He continued eating. Another officer sitting across the table from him was asking him several questions, to which he was responding.

"When?"

"As soon as . . ." Their conversation was lost in the surrounding din.

She stepped a little closer.

"Three days? Do you have . . . ready?"

"Yes . . ."

". . . airplanes?"

". . . division . . . laser . . ."

"What are you doing?" the head of the cleaning group barked at Renee from behind.

The voice was so close and unexpected that it nearly sent Renee out of her skin. She tried to control her racing heart. "I'm sorry. Forgive me. I was waiting for them to finish so I could clear their table . . ." Renee quickly moved away.

She continued to finish her other work nearby. As soon as they got up, she hurried to their table without looking anxious. She cleared their places and carried their dishes to the kitchen.

Then she went to the head of the cleaning group. "Will I be able to work again soon?"

"Who knows? If we need you, we will call you."

"I would appreciate that. I have enjoyed working here."

The woman was not impressed. "I would say you have. You have been making eyes at every man who has come in to eat. If you came back, you would have to change your ways. This is not a whorehouse, nor is it the place to find a husband," she scolded.

"I'm sorry," Renee said, lowering her eyes. "I just found it all interesting."

The head of the cleaning crew grunted and turned away. Renee closed her hand around the fork in her apron and slipped it into the slit pocket cut into her dress underneath.

"VLADIMIR, Vladimir," Gorgov said in his low voice. He had waited until the middle of the night in Nevada, to get Vlad when he was fatigued and back in his room at Tonopah.

"What?" Vlad replied, his blood racing through his veins. He rested on his side, on his elbow, and reached for the lamp next to his bed.

"It is not possible that you misunderstood me," Gorgov said, declaring the obvious. "You made me look foolish in front of my good friends who gave us a large sum of money." Gorgov stopped and let Vlad listen to the line hiss for a few seconds. "But, fortunately for you, they succeeded anyway. Even more fortunately for you, my good friend, is that there may be another chance for you to make a difference. Because we both know that if you don't . . . things could get very bad, very uncomfortable for you."

Vlad sat up and put his feet on the floor, trying to think his way out of his deepening hole. "Leave me alone!" he yelled.

"And for those you left behind in Russia," Gorgov went on. "Your sister, for example, who is now in Smolensk with her two beautiful young children."

"What do you want from me?" Vlad growled.

"You see," Gorgov said, "this fight is not only not over, it is just starting. There are *many* things left to do, and one piece of it . . . remains undone. You may be able to make sure it happens."

"What is it?"

"Your friend suffers, I think, from the typical American hero complex. I believe it is often associated with another of the actors that Americans worship, a John Wayne. Yes? You have heard this term?"

"Yes."

"Ah. Your friend must be led to believe he is going to save the world. And you will have the chance—the obligation— to make sure he does not succeed. Do you understand?"

Vlad closed his eyes. His back felt as if it were broken. The ejection had been much harder on his body than he'd expected. The ejection seat rocket motor had fired so fast and so hard to get him out of his dying airplane that it had compressed his spine in his lower back. He had pain radiating down to his heels. His crotch felt bruised and sore from where the harness he was wearing had held him in the parachute. All he wanted to do was sleep. But he'd not done what Gorgov had expected him to do. He knew he would be called to account. He wanted to tell himself he didn't care. That Gorgov couldn't touch him in America. But he knew that wasn't true. He took a deep breath. "I understand."

"Well, yes." Gorgov laughed. "There is understanding, and there is *understanding*. I know you understood the words I have said. You are a smart man. You did not become a Sniper Pilot in the Russian Air Force by being stupid or cowardly. I want you to tell me, Vladimir Petkov, whether you understand that when the time is before you, when you have a choice to intervene to assure the success of the goal that will then be obvious to you, whether you will do what I have asked."

"How will I know?"

"You will know."

"How?"

Gorgov's voice lost its friendly tone. "Will you do what I have asked, or will you not? You are free to tell me that you will not. I will understand completely. But then your sister's husband will be very sad indeed, and your mother will wonder how you could have met such a horrible end."

"You are scum, Gorgov. You are a disgrace—"

"Your opinion of me does not matter in the least," Gorgov interrupted. "I want to know whether you will do what you are *told*!"

Vlad was cornered. "Yes, I will do what you ask."

"I knew I could count on you. You are a man of your word. Yes?"

Vlad clenched his teeth. "Yes."

LUKE squinted at the dark brown stain on the concrete in front of the hangar, a dried pool of blood left from one of the guards. He noticed the bullet marks on the hangar door behind the stain, where the jeep had been. Shame washed over him. He'd never even met those guards. Too busy. He'd never even inspected the security in the early-morning hours, as they changed shifts at 0600. Too busy. He hadn't even given a second's thought to the security of having Russian missiles on the base, let alone fighters that could do a lot of damage if united with those missiles. It had never occurred to him. Too busy grading his private runway for his biplane fantasy. He hadn't done his first job first.

Yellow crime-scene tape was draped from one stanchion to another in front of the hangar, around several of the airplanes, and across the doors to the hangar. There were bullet holes in airplanes and in the walls. The FBI had been through the hangar with a fine-tooth comb. They'd searched every computer, every file, every desk, and every residence within twenty-four hours of the attack. According to Katherine, they hadn't found anything, at least nothing they were talking to her about.

Katherine stood next to him, her hands in the pockets of her maternity jumper. "How could they live here for three weeks when they hated us that much?"

"So no one would suspect them."

"I'm really sorry, Luke," she said with deep sadness.

"Like you had anything to do with it."

"I'm just sorry it happened. We had a great thing going."

Her use of the past tense sliced through him like a hot knife. He was about to respond when they heard a car. They turned to look and saw two white sedans pulling up. Helen Li got out of one and walked to them. She looked at the scene, then down at the brown stain Luke had been staring at. She'd already seen it. She nodded and looked at Luke and Katherine. "Morning," she said. "Somewhere we can talk?"

"Hi," Luke replied. "Sure. In the ready room, topside." They all followed him as he headed up the stairs. All the decor, all the aviation paraphernalia seemed somehow excessive and superficial under the circumstances. Vlad, Stamp, Crumb, and Brian were sitting aimlessly in the ready room. They appeared beaten. Vlad looked away from Luke as they came into the room.

Helen went to the front of the room. She was glad they were all there. She wanted them all to hear her. The other three special agents stood at the back of the room. "Let's go over this again," she said. "Everything Riaz Khan did while he was here."

"We've done this."

"And we're going to keep doing it."

"He started out aggressively and went down from there,"

Crumb said. "He was an asshole, which, if he was going to do what he's now done, you wouldn't expect. You'd expect him to try to be nice, at least not to rock the boat. He got here and started being an asshole right away."

"What else?"

"He got us to help him plan his whole strike," Crumb replied.

Helen raised her eyebrows. "How?"

"He came in here insisting that we teach him more about air-to-ground. Dropping bombs. That's not really what we're here for. We're here to teach air-to-air combat. Shooting down other airplanes. He wouldn't hear it. He *insisted* that we do more air-to-ground. So we tried to accommodate him. We even showed him how we do strike planning."

"What planning? What did you help him plan?" Helen asked with intense interest. "Was it the strike on San Onofre?"

Luke hadn't even considered the possibility that not only had he and his crew allowed the Pakistanis to prepare right under their noses, but that they had planned the strike for them. Such a thought was intolerable. "I don't think so. It was in the wrong direction—"

"How do you know?"

"Because we were talking about flying east, or southeast, at sunrise, and the problem of the sun in your face—"

"Go on."

"And the distance was wrong," Luke replied, remembering the planning session as if it were yesterday. "And the attack we were planning was a very low-level attack, against a defended target, in enemy territory, like something into India. They flew against San Onofre at midaltitude, as if they were going against an unsuspecting target—which they were—trying to look like routine commercial traffic."

Helen retreated into a thought she wasn't sharing. A thick silence enveloped the room, full of pregnant implications and fear. She looked up suddenly. "Draw the route you helped plan," she said to Luke.

Luke stood, picked up a black marker, and took off its cap. He turned toward the board to start drawing, then turned back to Helen, who had sat down expectantly in the first row of the ready-room chairs. "What exactly is the point of this?"

"I'm interested."

"All the airplanes crashed. All the pilots but one were killed."

"But Khan himself wasn't killed. The other pilots were expendable."

Luke and the others immediately grasped what she was implying. "You do still think he has something else in mind?"

"Yes, we do."

"You know where he is," Luke said, reading her face.

Helen looked at the other FBI agents. "Maybe."

Crumb asked, "What the hell *else* could he have in mind? He's done more damage than any one person has ever done!"

"We're beginning to believe that San Onofre was part of a much larger plan."

Crumb asked, "Against the United States?"

"We don't know. But against somebody." Helen was fighting with herself about asking them the next question. "What if someone has heard him planning a mission for three days from now that includes carrying laser-guided bombs?"

"What? Where did you get that? You *do* know where he is!"

"We think so."

"Where?" Crumb asked, sitting forward.

"Air Force base just outside Karachi."

"Why don't you get him?"

"Meaning what?"

"Meaning anything. Kidnap him. Kill him. Whatever you

can do," Crumb asked. "Hell, *I'll* go kill him if you'll get me onto the base and make me look like a Pakistani for about five damn minutes."

"He's not there as Riaz Khan. He's there as another Major, which is who he probably is."

"A new identity?"

Helen pondered how much to divulge. "He has resumed his original identity. We think."

"The whole Riaz Khan thing was fake?"

"Probably."

"Then how can the Pakistanis say they didn't know anything about it?"

"The false papers go back several years. Unless they looked into it deeply, they would have no particular way of knowing."

"But all by—"

"The point is, he is a Major in the Air Force, and is apparently about to do something in the next seventy-two hours with laser-guided bombs. We're not quite sure what."

"In Pakistan?" Vlad asked, listening intently.

"We're not sure." Helen looked at the chart of the world on the wall next to the board. "Would it be possible to attack an aircraft carrier with laser-guided bombs?"

"Whose?" Luke asked.

"Ours."

"One of our carriers?" Luke was horrified.

"Yes. Headed toward Pakistan. They were scheduled to conduct a friendly port visit, but now almost certainly won't—"

"You can hit a carrier with a laser-guided bomb," Luke said, "but they'd have to be out of their minds to try. They'd never get close enough. If we even suspected they were coming, they wouldn't have a prayer—"

"*Wait* a minute," Vlad said suddenly, jumping up from his chair. He crossed to the back of the room and started looking through a stack of aeronautical charts until he found one of Pakistan. "Where did you say he is right now?" He was practically panting.

"We're not sure."

"You said you think you have found him. Where is this person?" Vlad said with a demanding tone.

"At an Air Force base. Near Karachi."

Vlad unfolded the chart of Pakistan and began searching for Karachi and the surrounding airfields. He brought it to the front of the room and hung it from the special clips over the board.

"What are you thinking?" Luke asked.

"This man is working with big agenda. He did not want to die here because the full mission is not accomplished. Otherwise he would have turned and fought Luke. I have no doubt. It must have killed him to run away. He is going to do something else."

The others rose to look at the chart over Vlad's shoulder.

"Like what?" Brian asked, his mind spinning.

"He wanted to demonstrate his anger toward America. You did not support them after we—the Soviet Union—left Afghanistan. They turned to France for submarines and airplanes. But I believe his focus is somewhere else. He is—what do you say?—obsession . . ."

"Obsessed," Crumb offered.

"Yes, obsessed with India. We have to look at India." He grabbed a pen, measured three hundred miles from the Air Force base near Karachi, and drew an arc. His eyes darted across the chart until he recognized one area. *"Chort!"* he exclaimed. "Right here!" he said, pounding his finger into the chart again and again. "The Kakrapar nuclear plant! Here, in Surat! It is three hundred miles southeast of a forward-deployment airfield east of Karachi." Vlad looked at the others. "He is trying to start a war between Pakistan and India. There is a large group of people in Pakistan that want a war with India more than anything else. They will do anything to achieve it. It is all about Kashmir. About Islam against Hinduism. Do not forget, there are many hard-line Islam with ties to the Taliban in Afghanistan who have been waiting for this moment for years. This is it!" Vlad exclaimed. "We talked about this all the time in Russia. It was big headache with the countries that border Russia on the south." He was breathing hard, his face full of satisfaction and fear.

"He may be right," Brian said, nodding as he scratched his head. "He may be completely right."

Helen asked, "But how can you know all this?"

"I have flown many times with the Indian Air Force. I was part of the team that delivered the MiG-29s from Russia to India when they bought them. I have spent many days in northwestern India training the Indian Air Force pilots to fly the MiG-29. I heard all the stories of the war that will come between Pakistan and India. They both expect it. It is just a matter of when."

"I need to pass this on to our intelligence people. They will decide whether to pass it on to India or not," Helen said.

Vlad was already headed toward the door. "This man must be stopped. If they go to war, it will be terrible. India has publicly promised never to use nuclear weapons first, and Pakistan has refused to make the same promise.

"Believe me," Vlad said. "The Indian Air Force is no match for the Pakistanis. The Pakistanis have more flight hours, they are better trained, and now Khan has been trained by TOPGUN instructors. They will not be able to stop him."

"India has more airplanes," Brian reminded Vlad.

"Yes, and poorly trained pilots. Plus the Pakistanis have F-16s and new Mirage aircraft. The Indians fly some MiG-29s, but mostly older MiG-21s and -23s. They often fly them into the ground because of poor maintenance."

"So what now?" Stamp asked.

"I don't know," Vlad answered, assuming a position of leadership. "There isn't much time. Seventy-two hours from when?" he asked Helen.

"From yesterday."

"That means we have forty-eight hours," Luke said. "If we warn India, and they start moving their Air Force, Pakistan will claim it as provocation."

"Yes, yes, exactly." Vlad nodded. "They need something much more clever than that." He looked at Helen and Luke. "Perhaps I could call some people I know. They have certain contacts within the Indian government. They might be able to suggest something."

Helen looked at him. She studied his face. "Call them." She then turned to Luke. "One of our most difficult problems, of course, is confirming his identity. Pakistan continues to be outraged at the conduct of its former Air Force officer. We're not so sure. But we need to identify him. Can you think of anything that would help us?"

"He wouldn't let us take any pictures . . ."

"So you said. We went over his room for fingerprints. There weren't any. None. Wiped completely clean. Just like the cars we found in the desert."

"Fingerprints?" Katherine asked suddenly. "Luke, the vase!"

"What vase?"

"The Indian vase at our house!" She looked at Helen. "It's an ornamental Paiute vase. He was fascinated by it and picked it up—"

"What is it made of?" one of the other FBI agents asked.

"Clay."

He looked at Helen, who nodded. "We need to dust your house," he said to Katherine. "Now."

23

Renee opened her eyes to peer at the blue dial of the digital watch she always wore when not trying to look like a Pakistani woman. It was two o'clock in the morning. The knock was unmistakable and insistent. Her heart started to race. She'd never before been bothered at her apartment at night. She quickly reviewed what was in her apartment, what might implicate her in anything, but she knew it was clean. This was just where she slept. It wasn't where she changed before going out into the city; it wasn't where she kept her weapons, or her brown contacts, or dirty fingernails. It wasn't where she wrote down anything in a report, or typed anything that anyone would care about, or had the computer on which she drafted e-mails. She knew she was clean. It was what allowed her to sleep at all.

She wrapped a robe around her nightgown and walked barefoot to the door. She looked through the peephole. "Yes?" she asked, turning on the light. She could see a large man standing at her door, with three others standing behind him.

"Open the door," he demanded in Urdu.

"What? I don't understand," she replied in English.

"Of course you do," he said, still in Urdu.

"What?" she said, ignoring him.

He switched to English reluctantly. "Open the door, *now*."

"Why should I?" she said, implying offense. "It is two o'clock in the morning!"

"Because I have told you to! If you don't, I will kick it in."

"And who are you?"

"Internal Security. Open the door immediately!" The ISI. The Pakistani Secret Police, FBI, and CIA all in one.

She took her eye away from the door and looked around the room for some solution. Her chest heaved. She turned back to the door and yelled, "I am an American citizen! You have no right to enter my residence. I will go straight to the ambass—"

He stepped back and kicked.

She jumped back in time to avoid the door that tore away from the cheap frame and burst open.

"Stop!" she screamed. "You can't do this!"

The man struck her and knocked her down on the floor, her face pressed against the hard tile. He climbed on top of her and pulled her arms behind her. The other three men entered the apartment and began tearing it apart. "You are under arrest for espionage," the man hissed into her ear, his lips touching her hair. "Did you think we were stupid?" he then yelled, handcuffing her and pulling her to her feet.

THE special agents and crime-scene technicians swarmed all over Luke and Katherine's house: the bathrooms, the kitchen, the living room—everywhere.

Luke stood next to Helen watching as one latex-gloved FBI agent dusted the coffee table in the living room. "He wasn't even in this room," Luke told him.

"We do everything," he replied.

Luke shrugged and spoke to Helen without looking at her. "Think it's him in Pakistan?"

"We'll know in just a few minutes."

"How?"

"Our technician has the other prints with him."

"Whose?"

She just watched the tech do his work.

Luke realized she wasn't going to answer. "How'd you get them?" he asked, amazed.

Helen still didn't reply. She reached for her cell phone, which was vibrating on her belt, and put it to her ear. "Li," she said.

Luke watched as she frowned, listening to whoever was on the other end.

"Where is he?" She listened intently. "No, don't wait for me. I'll never get there in time," she said, glancing at her watch. "Pick him up now. If you think he's willing to talk at all, call me, and I'll be there. . . . No, we've got to keep going here. Call me as soon as you bring him in." She signed off, closed the phone, and replaced it on her hip.

"What's that about?" Luke asked.

"Don't worry about it."

"Is it related to this?"

"The Undersecretary."

"Where is he?" Luke asked.

She ignored him.

The FBI technician had set up shop on the dining room table. He had cases opened, special lights set up, microscopes, and a laptop computer. The tapes that he'd used to pull fingerprints off the pot were carefully placed on slides to be scanned, digitized, and visually examined. He typed on the keyboard and brought up two images: the fingerprints he'd just taken off the pot and prints from another location that were already stored digitally on his laptop. He examined the two side by side, then adjusted the size of the new print to match the other one, overlaid the new print on the stored print. The correlation was nearly perfect. He didn't have an entire print from the Paiute pot, but the one they got was 80 percent complete. He glanced at Helen, who was watching him carefully out of the corner of her eye. He put the first slide under the bright light of the double microscope, then put the other next to it in the second slide platform. He examined them together with the double eyepieces.

Luke watched Helen watch the technician. He followed her as she walked across the room, sensing that the technician was almost finished with his analysis.

Helen stood next to him, waiting. He adjusted the focus again, looked at the computer screen, and stood up next to her. She couldn't stand it. "What do you think?"

"Good enough for comparison."

"And?"

He studied the two images and did an automated computer comparison to confirm what he'd already concluded. He waited for the program to complete its analysis, then looked at Helen and said ominously, "It's him."

"Any doubt?"

"None."

"That son of a *bitch*," Luke said, amazed. "How did he get back to Pakistan?"

Helen nodded. "That is a question we will try to find the answer to one day. However, our current job is to get him. Either to bring him back here for trial or . . . some other option. The other options are not in my area."

"Well, who *is* in charge of the other options?" Luke asked.

"That would be the other government agency. The one that begins with a C."

The image of Khan sitting in Pakistan, safe and sound, was too much. "We don't have a lot of time," Luke said.

"Everyone is aware of that." She dialed a number on her cell phone, a digital phone with some additional buttons Luke had never seen before. While it was ringing, she punched in a series of numbers onto the backlit screen. As soon as a connection was indicated, she hit "send" again, and the numbers were transmitted digitally.

"Was that for him? Did you tell the CIA that you've ID'd him?" Luke demanded.

She put the phone back on the clip on her belt and looked at Luke. "You ask a lot of questions."

"So do you."

"It's my job."

"I'm making it mine. I'm not done with him."

"You may be right."

"It's him!" Cindy Frohm said as she burst into Morrissey's office. "They have absolute confirmation that the print on the fork Renee got is the same as the one that was in the house in Nevada."

Morrissey jumped up from his desk. "Renee has outdone herself. Does she have anything else since then? She was going to keep digging."

"She hasn't checked in since we got the print."

Morrissey frowned. "Have you talked to anyone at the DO?" The Directorate of Operations.

"Nothing. They're concerned. The embassy hasn't seen her at all."

Morrissey stopped and stared at Cindy as he thought. "What does that mean?"

"She would disappear now and then if she was on something that required her to stay undercover. But no one knows for sure."

"Think they might have grabbed her?"

"Pakistan claims to be uninvolved in the Khan attack. Why would they go after her?"

"Because she's collecting intelligence on their soil. If you get found doing that, they don't step back and wonder about the final end-of-the-day implications. They just grab you."

"At least we know where Khan is."

"And that he may have something in mind. Did you read what Renee said about something happening in three days?"

"That's less than forty-eight hours from now," she said, looking at her watch.

"Exactly. And what is he going to do?"

"Did you see that estimate from the FBI?"

"Sure." Morrissey felt uneasy. "They think a nuclear plant strike. Based on some Russian telling them what he thinks is the target and his estimate of India's pathetic ability to stop them. I don't know about that."

Frohm waited. "So what now?"

"I need to talk to my counterpart in India. Call in a few chips."

THE man who'd knocked Renee down now sat next to her in a room at a table. She was surrounded by smelly men smoking and leering at her. Renee was still wearing her night-clothes. Her shoulder was throbbing from where she'd strained against his hold, but her wits were completely intact.

He took a long drag from his cigarette, a vile, dark one that produced acrid brown smoke. "So, we have long suspected you are with the CIA." He waited for her reaction. There wasn't one. "Are you?"

"I am with the Department of State. You know that," she said icily.

He smiled. "Yes. The Department of State. Of course. Some kind of—what is it?—cultural person. What is it exactly?"

"It doesn't matter," she replied. "You won't believe anything I say."

"Why do you think that?"

"You broke into my home. You knocked me down. You obviously already have opinions. I doubt I can change your mind. Why try?"

"Why try?" He laughed. He looked at the other men in the room. "Why try?" He grew suddenly serious. "Because I believe you are with the CIA! That's why!" he screamed as he leaned toward her. "And I know that you have been spying on our Air Force base! That's why! You disguise yourself as a Pakistani woman. Your mother was half Pakistani!" Her head jerked toward him. "Ah, you didn't think we knew? You continue to think we are stupid."

"What do you want?"

"I want to know what you know."

"I don't know what you are talking about."

"You have learned information about who attacked your country. It is my belief that you know who it is. I—we—want to know what you know."

"Then ask my country what we know. I'm sure they'll tell you."

"No. Time does not lend itself to such formal requests. They do not trust us. Especially now."

"Can you blame them?"

"Oh, yes. I can blame them. They think they know all about us, and they are mostly wrong. So tell me what you have learned about this pilot that attacked your country. This man, this pilot, has caused greater humiliation to our country than anyone in history. We are more interested in finding him than you are."

"I don't know what you are talking about."

"Do you deny that you were on our Air Force base near Karachi?"

"Yes. I deny it."

He glanced over his shoulder, and a man behind him handed him a photograph. He tossed it in front of her. She continued to stare straight ahead. "Look at it."

She glanced down quickly, maintaining her flat expression as she looked at a photo of herself serving the Air Force pilots their meals.

"Do you deny that is you?"

"Yes."

He reached behind him, and a man put a small case in his hand. He tossed it onto the table. "Do you know what this is?"

She looked at it, trying not to show any reaction. "No."

"It is a set of contact lenses."

"So?"

"They are yours."

"I don't wear glasses or contacts."

He smiled and lit another cigarette with the burning end of the one about to go out. He inhaled deeply and blew the smoke her way again. "You don't *need* to wear glasses or contacts. That is a true statement. You don't need them to see well. But these are brown in color. Can you imagine? Brown contacts? Why would anyone have those? Perhaps if you need them to disguise the blue eyes that you got from your American father so you can look more Pakistani."

"You're out of your mind," she said quickly.

"Can you explain to me why these contacts have no prescription to them? Why would anyone have contacts without any correction?"

"I have no idea. Ask whoever owns them," she said, looking directly at him.

"But we got them from your other apartment. You have no idea how they got there?"

"I don't have any other apartment. I don't know what you're talking about."

"Really," he said.

The first man handed him another sheet. It was a series of photos of her going into the apartment wearing Western dress and coming out in Pakistani garb. "You still deny it?"

"That's not me," she said, dodging. She knew they had her, but she would *never* tell them anything voluntarily.

He sat back and assumed a gentle tone. "You don't seem

to understand what we're doing. We are on the same side of this, you and I. We are trying to find the man who did this to us. The one who has made us look like murderers in front of the whole world. Your country doesn't trust us now and refuses to give us any help in finding the pilot who did this. We have begged for your help, but you refuse to give it to us. We must find this man. We have no idea what he has in mind, but if he is here, we must stop him. Do you understand?"

"Yes. I understand what you've said."

"Then tell me what you know. If you have identified this man, tell me now. Who is it?"

"I don't have any idea what you're talking about."

"We must know!"

Renee looked at him with contempt. "You must know? Why didn't you know that there was someone in your Air Force who had international murder in mind? And theft of bombs or whatever else was stolen from your armory? And what about the attempted smuggling of warhead-grade plutonium over the border? Where were you guys then? So you're left trying to intimidate an employee of the American State Department instead of doing your own good intelligence work?" She shook her head in disgust. "Can I go now?"

"You will tell us what you know!" he screamed as he stood up and leaned on the table.

"I don't know anything," she said.

The man turned in fury to those behind her. "Put her in the dark cell," he ordered. "If anyone asks us about her, we've never heard of her."

"COLONEL," Vlad said into the telephone in his native Russian.

"Vladimir!" Stoyanovich exclaimed, thrilled to hear the voice of his friend. "Where are you?"

"In America."

"Are you near the radioactivity?"

"Not very. It is several hundred miles away."

"Were you involved in that air battle? What happened?"

"Yes, we tried to stop them, but got there too late."

"Your MAPS job has you in that Nevada school where this lunatic Pakistani started all that. Am I right? You are there with MAPS taking care of the MiGs?"

"Exactly. It is the best job you could imagine. It is the dream of a lifetime. And they were letting me fly, Colonel. They made me their MiG-29 instructor, and I fly in the hops with the American pilots who are all former TOPGUN instructors!"

"That is too wonderful, Vladimir. Then you must have your drinking under control. As you said you would. I should never have doubted you. You are so strong. I should tell you, just so you know, that I only intended to keep you away from flying for six months. I told you it was for the rest of your career so you would take it seriously this time. I think it was bad judgment on my part to tell you this. I think you believed me."

Vlad held his head in his hand as he rested his elbow on the counter. If only he had known. But it was too late now. He looked at the open bottle of vodka that sat on a table. "Colonel, I am in some trouble."

"Ah," Stoyanovich said. The enthusiasm in his voice was suddenly tempered. "What is it, Vladimir?"

"I suppose you know how I got here."

"Yes. You were threatened by the Mafia, those thugs, those scum."

"They promised to get me out of the country and gave me this job. There were no strings attached. I just wanted to get out of Russia, and the chance to fly again . . ."

"It is perfectly understandable. But what is your problem?"

"They knew about the attack before it happened."

"The attack on the nuclear plant?" Stoyanovich asked. "How would they know that?"

"That's what I wanted to know. I still don't know. But before it happened, Gorgov—"

"That traitor . . ."

"He told me something would happen, and I was to make sure it came off. He wanted me to make sure this Khan succeeded."

"They were *behind* that attack?"

"I don't think so. I just think they're involved. They've given Khan something. I don't know how or what, I don't know what their role is, but they're involved."

"What did you do?"

"I tried like hell to stop Khan. The air battle."

"I heard."

"We caught them too late. We shot them all down, except for Khan himself, and he got me with a Sidewinder—"

"Vladimir, how could you—"

"I know. But I got out, and I'm okay."

"What is it you need?"

"This isn't over."

"What isn't?"

"Whatever Gorgov and the Pakistanis are doing. They're not finished. He called me."

"He called you again?"

"Yes. Just last night."

"What did he say?"

"He said that there would be another opportunity for me to help. To intervene. To let Luke be—"

"Luke?"

"He's the head of the school. American pilot, former TOPGUN instructor."

"Go on."

"He said Luke would try to be the hero. And when he did, I was to do the right thing."

"What does that mean?"

"We will get a chance to intervene, to save the world. When Luke tries, I am to stop him."

"You couldn't do that."

Vlad choked on his words. "Except Gorgov threatened to kill my sister and her children, and he knows where my mother is."

"They always talk like that," Stoyanovich said, trying to reassure Vlad.

"They mean it. You know that."

"Too often."

"This Khan is at an air base near Karachi. I'm convinced he is planning on attacking the Kakrapar Indian nuclear power plant. They want to start a war between Pakistan and India."

"How can you know this? How can this be? He is still alive?"

"Yes. I can't go into it all, but I'm sure that's what's happening."

"What can I do?"

"You still remember that Indian intelligence man we met when we were in India?"

"Yes. Of course."

"Perhaps you can get one of our people to convince them that what they really need is two highly trained MiG-29 pilots to come to India to help them defend this plant from a guy we know better than anyone else. If India starts moving their Air Force to defend against an attack, it will be seen as provocation, and Pakistan will feel compelled to attack anyway. They've got to stay put."

"Yes, of course. And who would go?"

"Me. Me and Luke Henry."

"Consider it done, but isn't that what Gorgov wants you to do?"

"It is exactly what he wants me to do."

"Then why are you doing it?"

"I don't have any choice!"

"You want me to do *his* work? You want me to help him accomplish his goal? I would rather die!" Stoyanovich protested.

"Please . . ."

"I will do that. Because you asked. But I will also do something else, unless you ask me not to. And if I succeed, maybe you won't have to do anything for him. I am tired of the damage this man and his kind are causing to Russia. I have had enough. I have seen enough. I am going to pay him a little visit. I know where his *dacha* is. Perhaps when he isn't expecting it, I will visit him and show him very clearly what I think of him."

"No, Colonel Stoyanovich. Do not underestimate him. He is a snake, and he is surrounded by other snakes."

"Not always." Stoyanovich smiled. "I will take care of both things. I will call you. It is time that we Russians stood up to the murderers who are ruining our country."

"Please be careful."

"Of course. You should get ready to go to India. It is the right thing for you to stop this Khan. I will take care of everything else."

24

Luke was trying to pretend that things were normal. He was trying to reestablish a routine, even though he wouldn't allow himself to be away from the news for more than fifteen minutes to get an update on the growing crisis in Southern California and the drifting radioactive cloud. There was now a confirmed death toll of fifteen, with several hundred suffering from radiation sickness and a total of two thousand affected. San Onofre was operating cleansing stations twenty-four hours a day and running people through endlessly. They had started holding press conferences every hour, but it all served simply to confirm how horrible things were. Most of the population of Southern California within fifty miles of San Onofre was still trying to get out of the area. The cloud itself was drifting lazily westward, but without much momentum. It was dissipating, but not quickly. Experts were apoplectic. The antinuclear activists were crowing "I told you so! I told you so!" to anyone who would listen, even to those who wouldn't listen, and Luke felt personally responsible for all of it.

He sat in the Area 51 Café and put his bagel with scrambled egg on the table in front of him. Raymond set Luke's coffee next to his plate. "There you go, boss."

"Thanks," Luke said absentmindedly. He looked around the café. He was the only one there other than Raymond and Glenda. "No one else here?"

"No, sir," Raymond said. "Seems most of the instructors

are just staying in their rooms watching their televisions for the cloud and all. No one knows what to make of it. Kind of in shock, I think."

"Thanks for what you did."

"Just doing my job, sir."

Luke nodded and began to eat. The door in the back of the café opened, and Vlad came in. "Hey, Vlad. Join me."

Vlad nodded and sat heavily in the chair across from Luke. He looked at Glenda. "Bread, if you please."

Glenda nodded and reached for the black bread.

Luke stared at Vlad. "You look like I feel."

"What do you mean?"

"Like this is all your fault. Like you really screwed up."

"I did, I think."

"How?"

"I should have known Khan was up to something. I should have figured it out."

"We all should have."

"Perhaps," Vlad said as Glenda put his warmed bread in front of him, along with a cup of coffee.

"Did you call anyone?"

"What?"

"You told Helen you were going to call somebody about Khan. Any luck?"

"Yes. I was able to call some people who will convey our concerns to their friends in India. We will see."

Luke saw something in Vlad that he couldn't explain. "What else? Something else is going on with you. What's up?"

Vlad shook his head. "Nothing, really. I am still hurting from my back, but it will be okay."

"That's all?"

"Yes."

"You sure?"

"I am sure. I . . ."

"What?"

"Nothing. I have other things I have to deal with in Russia. Family things, nothing for you to worry about."

"You need any help? Money or anything?"

"No. I will take care of it myself."

"You know what, Vlad?" Luke said, leaning back.

"What?"

"I want to ask you something."

"Go ahead," Vlad said.

"What happened in Russia?"

"What do you mean?"

"Why did you leave the Russian Air Force?"

"I retired."

"You didn't have enough years in to retire," Luke said.

Vlad frowned. "Yes I did. I gave you my records."

"You gave me the untranslated copies, too. I had them retranslated. The dates were changed."

Vlad slowed his eating but didn't look at Luke. "Must be big mistake."

"Did you change your records?"

"I retired."

"Okay," Luke said. "Nothing else you want to tell me about?"

"No," Vlad said harshly.

Luke watched him eat. They sat there in silence, each keeping to his own thoughts. Luke finally asked, "You ever have an alcohol problem?"

"What?" Vlad exclaimed. "Why do you ask that?"

"Because when Dr. Thurmond flew with you, he told me he smelled alcohol on your breath."

"I must have had drink with lunch, that one day."

"We have a rule, Vlad. I told you what it was. Twelve hours from bottle to brief. Not lunch to brief."

"Sorry. I forget."

"That's all?"

"That's all."

Luke waited, but Vlad wasn't saying anything else. "You did a good job against the Pakistanis."

"I did shit job. I got shot down and didn't get any of them."

"You showed a lot of courage. It wasn't even your fight."

"It *is* my fight. This is *my* school, too. I have bet everything to be here. This is big chance to make different life. He tried to hurt your country—and me."

"Well, I appreciate what you did."

"Yes. You are welcome." Vlad looked at his watch. "I have to go."

Luke nodded as Vlad hurried away. He'd left two-thirds of his cherished black bread untouched.

THE Colonel sat in his Russian government sedan. The heater didn't work, and his dirty officer's overcoat was not keeping out the cold as it once did. But the wait was worth it. As he crushed the last cigarette from the second pack he'd smoked while waiting, he thought of his last fifteen years in the Russian Air Force. It had gone from being the greatest Air Force in the world—possibly the second best, if one believed the American propaganda—to a force that saw its very existence dependent on a corrupt system that sold airplanes and weapons for food. Now the best fighters in the world sat mostly idle, and the pilots struggled to get enough flight hours just to stay competent, let alone capable of defeating skilled Western pilots who would have twenty times the flight hours and bellies full of whatever food they wanted.

The old system was better, Colonel Stoyanovich told himself again, as he did nearly every day. There was respect for authority, there was respect for the Soviet Union around the world, there was food on the tables, and there wasn't the pervasive despair now so common. Well . . . he had to admit to himself, there had been despair even then. Antigovernment despair, despair from never being free to do what you wanted. But the military had been strong, not an assembly of beggars, of second-, third-, or fourth-class citizens.

Now that the government did not assert such authority, were people better off? No. The authority vacuum had been filled not with autonomy, with freedom, but rather with the Mafia, thugs and criminals with their own vicious ambition, not even paying lip service to doing what is best for the country. They did what was best to line their pockets.

Stoyanovich looked up and saw the two young men walking quietly out of the dark woods. They hurried over to his car, nodding enthusiastically. Stoyanovich rolled down his window to talk to them.

The taller one spoke. "He has arrived."

"Is he alone?"

"There is a woman with him."

The Colonel smiled. "Perhaps we should wait a while. Perhaps catch them in a compromising position."

"That would make it too hard to kill only him. Now she will just think it is some Mafia dispute."

"Are you sure you don't need me to go inside the *dacha* with you?"

They both shook their heads. "No. You stay outside. If he kills us both and runs outside, then you can shoot him like a dog. Feel free." They smiled.

Stoyanovich was troubled. "You are taking this too lightly." He looked at their faces. "Has either of you ever killed anyone? It is not easy, you know. To look someone in the eyes and just shoot them."

"This will not be a problem," the other man said. "Let's get this over with. I'm cold."

Stoyanovich pulled the keys from the ignition and struggled out of the small car. He put the keys in his pocket. He took the pistol out of another pocket and chambered a round.

The other two men did likewise with their guns. "Lead the way," he said to the eager man already heading back to the *dacha*.

They tried to be as quiet as they could as they walked through the woods. They could see the lights of the *dacha* half a mile away. The lights were like beacons. Gorgov certainly wasn't trying to hide.

Stoyanovich stopped to catch his breath. He looked around for any signs of activity, any cars or people, but saw nothing. He nodded, and they continued walking. They closed to within a hundred yards of the house, stopped, and knelt down on the hard dirt. He whispered to them, "How many doors are there?"

"Three" came the reply, but not from either of the two men with Stoyanovich.

His blood stopped as he realized that someone was behind them. His head snapped around as he looked. Three men were standing there wearing night-vision goggles and watching them. The one in the middle took off his goggles and shone a light in Stoyanovich's face. "Colonel, what are you doing here, outside my *dacha* with a gun?"

"Gorgov!" Stoyanovich exclaimed. He stood up slowly, as did the other two men, who had panicked looks on their faces.

"Put your guns down immediately, so we can discuss whatever problem you have with me. And please don't move quickly. I have several men behind me whom you can't see. They have rifles with night scopes and will shoot you immediately."

Stoyanovich dropped his handgun next to his foot. The other two men did likewise. Gorgov smiled in the darkness. Stoyanovich could barely make out his face.

"So what is the meaning of this? Who has put you up to this very unwise action?"

"No one."

Gorgov looked puzzled. "No one? You came out here to murder me all on your own? Why? What have I ever done to you?"

"I'm not here to murder you. I am here to talk to you."

"Colonel, I am many things, but I am not stupid. Do you always approach the home of someone you want to talk to by walking through the woods in the dark with a gun?"

"No, not always. Just when I think it is necessary."

"Nonsense. Who sent you to kill me?"

"No one."

Gorgov shook his head. He suddenly raised his gun and shot the man standing to Stoyanovich's left. The man fell in a heap as his life drained away from him.

Stoyanovich blanched as he acutely felt his own mortality. "Why did you do that?"

"Who sent you?"

"No one!"

Gorgov breathed in loudly. "What did you want to talk to me about?"

Stoyanovich's mind raced for anything that was believable. "Major Petkov called me about how to help you . . ."

"What? He called you?" Gorgov asked, concerned. "When?"

"Just yesterday."

"What did he want?"

"He said you had asked him to allow this American pilot to be a hero. He thinks Khan, that Pakistani pilot, is going to attack an Indian nuclear plant."

"They know Khan is alive?"

"I think they suspect it."

"Go on."

"And he asked me to get our intelligence people to contact the Indian intelligence people and suggest to them that Petkov and this American would be of use in defending the Indian plant without too much movement on the part of the

Indian forces. He didn't want to give away that we know Khan's coming."

"They know when he's coming?"

"I think they suspect he—"

The other man with Stoyanovich suddenly dropped to the ground and reached for the handgun he'd found with his foot in the dark. As soon as he moved, four men behind Gorgov opened up on him, and he was knocked to the ground. Gorgov watched his last movements. "I don't think he believed I had others with me. Now, you were saying?"

Stoyanovich looked at his two friends lying dead beside him. He knew he was next unless he thought of some way to remain indispensable to Gorgov in a hurry. "I think they had some indication of timing. I don't know when."

"And?"

"So I did as he asked."

"What exactly did you do?"

"I called our intelligence people and asked them to call their comrades in India."

"Did they do that?"

"Yes."

Gorgov smiled. "Perfect. Then it is all set, isn't it?"

"It appears to be."

"And is Major Petkov planning on doing what I asked?"

"Yes."

"He is."

"Yes."

"Then why are you here?"

"I came to buy his freedom."

"His what?"

"His freedom. Once he has completed the task you have given him, he owes you nothing, and he is free to do as he wishes."

Gorgov had never heard anything like it. "Your offer is rejected."

"But—"

"You called the intelligence people?"

"Yes, I did."

"Thank you," Gorgov said. He raised his handgun to Stoyanovich's chest and shot him dead.

LUKE lay in bed staring at the ceiling. He listened to Katherine's breathing next to him. He couldn't sleep. Too much had happened. Dust on the furniture was all that was left of the FBI's visit. Helen Li was sure they'd found Khan. The idea of him being back in Pakistan, operating as a Pakistani pilot again under a different name . . . But such thoughts couldn't compete with the self-condemnation Luke felt for having let it all happen in the first place.

Luke jumped at the sound of someone knocking on the front door. He slipped on his flight suit that lay on a chair next to the bed, walked to the front door barefoot, turned on the porch light, and peered through the peephole. He recognized the man with the large folder of submarine pictures from the brig at Miramar. There was another man behind him whom Luke had never seen before, carrying a thin briefcase. He had the collar of his blue nylon windbreaker folded up against the cold Nevada night.

Luke threw back the bolt and opened the door. "Yes?"

"Mr. Henry. Good morning. My name is Bill Morrissey. You know Mr. Lane. May I come in?"

"Who the hell are you?"

"I'm with the CIA."

Luke suddenly was able to see Helen Li behind them, standing by the car fifty feet away. For reasons he couldn't explain, her presence reassured him. "You with her?"

"Yes."

"What's she doing?"

"Making sure there's no one else around."

"Who else would be around?"

"You might be seen as someone who knows the most about these Pakistanis. They might not like you talking to people. Don't worry about it, Mr. Henry. It's just a habit."

Luke stood back and pulled the door open wide. They came in and looked around the dark house. Luke then noticed two other people sitting in cars in the driveway. "How many people are with you?"

"Six," the man said, and Helen stepped onto the porch to follow them into the house.

"I think we'd better make some coffee, Mr. Henry," Helen said. "We've got a lot to talk about."

Luke headed toward the kitchen, with them following him. He opened the freezer and took out the ground coffee and quickly set up the filter to make a pot as he watched them make themselves comfortable. "Is your wife here?" Morrissey asked.

Luke looked at him for any hint of any meaning or problem other than the obvious. "Why?"

"We don't want to discuss this with her. Just you."

He felt a chill. "Discuss what?"

"The reason we're here," Morrissey said.

"Vladimir!" the voice yelled over the phone.

"*Da*. Yes?" Vlad answered.

The tone was sinister. "Did you really think you could send a fat Colonel and two stupid men into the woods at my *dacha* to murder me like some kind of animal?"

"What? What are you talking about?" He had never heard Gorgov so furious.

"Your Colonel Stoyanovich was at my *dacha* waiting for me. He and two other men, there to do your work. Rather than do what I ask, you try to kill me?"

"No! I had no idea! What are you talking about? Is this a joke?" Vlad's heart was pounding as his mind raced.

"You betrayed me. I am on my way to get your sister. I

wanted to tell you, so you would know. I will send you pictures."

"No! There has been some terrible mistake!"

"Your beloved Colonel is lying in the woods attracting insects. How did you think you would get away with this?"

"Gorgov, I have done everything you asked."

Gorgov abruptly turned off his rage. "That is a lie. But I was to give you another chance. Now you will have *no* chances—"

"No. You must not do this. I will do what you have asked."

"You are willing?"

"Yes. Whatever you want."

"If you do not . . ."

"I will. You have my word."

There was a long pause before Gorgov spoke again. "It is about to happen. If you fail, your world will be more horrible than you can imagine."

"I understand. I will not fail."

The line went dead. Vlad sat in the dark, completely motionless. He finally took a long drink from the quart bottle of vodka by his elbow.

25

Morrissey put his briefcase on the dining room table and opened it, leaving it open with the top toward Luke. Luke couldn't see what was inside. Helen sat on a stool at the counter watching him pour the coffee.

"So what's this about?" Luke asked.

"We've been talking to some people," Morrissey said. "Thank you," he added as Luke handed him his cup. "Pakistan continues to deny any participation. They would. They have their ISI stir up all kinds of things, then deny involvement. It's a very interesting—and probably effective—way to avoid retaliation. And believe me, there are a lot of people in our government who want some retaliation *big* time. But Pakistan claims to be horrified and outraged. They say they've been had as badly as we have, and although we've suffered terrible damage physically, their injury is worse, because they have an international black eye. They look like vicious murderers, liars, and cheats to the whole world. So they cry and beg for consideration of their terrible condition. Pretty well done. You've seen the politicians on TV . . ."

Luke nodded.

"So that's fine, *unless,*" he said, raising his voice, "unless it's *all* bullshit and they set the whole thing up. See, then all you have to do is have your pilots disappear—three of them being dead—and simply claim they were out of control, aligned with some radical group or other. A very effective way to attack another country, if you have the balls." He looked at Helen. "Sorry."

"You think that's what happened?" Luke asked.

"I don't know. We've been talking to India. They said they've known about this Khan fellow for months. They knew he was up to something but assumed *they* were the target. They say he's tied in with a new superradical group that's supported by the Taliban in Afghanistan." He smiled. "Which, of course, is supported by Pakistani intelligence. You see how tricky this can be." Luke nodded. "Anyway, there are a lot of very smart people looking at this from a lot of angles. But the one angle *I'm* pursuing is getting the man who did this. I will not bore you with the details, but if anyone is going to get this guy other than the military . . ."

Luke replied, not sure what to say, "So what are you doing here? And why is she here?"

"Helen and I are working in parallel. And . . . well . . . a proposal has come our way. A proposal to do something we could not generally do."

"What?"

"The man who works for you. Or maybe this MAPS outfit. Who's subcontracting for you . . ."

"Vlad?"

The man nodded. "He is apparently very well connected back in Russia. He knows many people who seem to know much of what goes on in India."

"Sure, Russia sells arms to India."

"Exactly. Russia wants India to do well, but it doesn't want a war. Others are happy to stimulate a war between Pakistan and India. Russia's not interested. They're scared to death of a huge Islamic state right at their belly. They'd rather keep the 'Stans separate."

"I don't get why Pakistan would go about it so indirectly if they're trying to start war. Why wouldn't they just go at it?"

"The international community would hold it against

them. You can't just go attacking another country. But if India—or someone else—responds incorrectly or improperly to some uncontrolled stimulus, such as an Air Force pilot who's out of control, then Pakistan would of course have to respond to that attack by India, thereby achieving their objective indirectly."

"Must take a lot of training to learn to think like *that*," Luke said. "Is this about Kashmir?"

"Kashmir is only part of it. India and Pakistan have been at each other's throats for forty years now. Pakistan in particular has been looking for an excuse to start fighting again. This may be it."

"An attack on the United States? How does that do it?"

"That might have been the first step. To punish the United States for the way it treated Pakistan, the refusal to deliver arms—"

"Where do they think they got their F-16s?"

Morrissey nodded sympathetically. "Yes, but where do you think New Zealand got the forty F-16s that they're leasing from the United States?"

"I wouldn't know."

"Those were intended to go to Pakistan. But we were annoyed with them, so we blocked that sale, and the planes went to New Zealand. We cut them off for a long time. It was only when Clinton went back and visited Pakistan that we began to reestablish military ties. It's still nowhere near where it was, and the Pakistani military has been bitter about it for a very long time."

Luke rubbed his forehead. "Where does all this take us?"

"Khan is affiliated with an extremely radical group within Pakistan, based in Peshawar, that is intent on stimulating war between India and Pakistan over Kashmir. They think they can beat India and that India doesn't have the will to fight over Kashmir. It will be the first step to a regional Islamic state."

"But why attack *us*?"

"Because not only is he intent on war between India and Pakistan, he despises the secular government of Pakistan. To him they're as illegitimate as the government of India. He wants the current Pakistani government out *and* a war with India. He's trying for both."

"How do you figure that?"

He waved his hand. "I've gone on too long. This is all speculation. But I had to give you some background because of what I'm about to ask you. Based on what you and Vlad told Helen, we believe that the possibility of a strike on an Indian nuclear plant is real. He's probably planning on doing it without any knowledge or authorization of the government of Pakistan."

"Now you believe them?" Luke exclaimed.

"There's a bombing exercise scheduled out of Karachi. F-16s with laser-guided bombs to a bombing range near Karachi. They've done such exercises only twice before, and we believe that Khan—his actual name, we now know, is Major Ghayyur Elahi—will be leading the practice strike."

"It's just unbelievable."

"As I was saying, your friend Vlad has surprising friends in Russian intelligence. They've talked to the people in Indian intelligence, who want to bring huge elements of Air Force into the northwestern part of the country, put out a protective ring of surface-to-air missiles and antiaircraft gunnery, and generally behave as if they're about to be attacked. The Russians were able to convince them that such conduct would simply provoke the very thing they're trying to prevent."

"So what's the plan?"

"Your Mr. Vlad proposed to Russian intelligence—which proposed to Indian intelligence—that you and he go to India—"

"What? What *for*?"

"And fly on their behalf—"

"For what?"

"To defend their nuclear plant."

Luke sat openmouthed. "That's *nuts*."

Morrissey leaned forward. "You know this pilot better than anyone. Do you think you could stop him?"

Luke considered it. "In what?"

"An Indian MiG-29."

"I don't know, probably."

The CIA officer could sense Luke's consideration. "The Indians talk a good game. But they fly about five hours a month. They don't practice dogfighting much, never fire live missiles, and have never flown against an F-16. You've fired live missiles from a MiG-29." He waited for Luke's reluctant nod. "You've fought the very pilot they now fear, in the same aircraft he'll be flying, and have seen his weaknesses. Fair?"

"I suppose. But still—"

"Let me finish," Morrissey said, putting up his hand. "You'd be supported by as many Indian fighters as necessary, up to the entire squadron. More, even. Not too far from the nuclear power plant there's already a squadron of MiG-29s. The Archers." He shrugged. "They might be able to handle it by themselves. But on the off chance that they can't, they're willing to allow you two to be with them if and when Khan attacks."

"Are you serious?"

He nodded slowly.

Luke glanced toward the bedroom to make sure Katherine hadn't woken up. "The last time a government man came to my house, it was the Undersecretary."

"I'm not asking you—"

"Just hold on a minute," Luke interrupted. "Then, when I got back from putting my ass on the line to fight this asshole over San Onofre, another government dickhead *arrested* me. Now, all of a sudden, I'm your best friend? You come to me in the middle of the night because I'm the only one who can stop him?" He shook his head. "I'm not buying it. Let the Indians have their shot at him. If they put up enough airplanes, they'll get him."

"They don't think so," he replied. "Mind if I smoke?" he asked, reaching into his shirt pocket.

"Yeah, I do mind. It stinks up the house. You can go out and sit with the other federales and smoke outside."

He withdrew his hand. "They've asked our government to help them. All on the QT, of course."

"So send some of those crack F-15 pilots who didn't get to the fight in time to make any difference over San Onofre."

"They've asked for you and Vlad by name."

"Why?"

"Because you know the MiG-29, and they think you can beat Khan without starting a war over it."

"What's the official government position? What do you want?"

"It's why I'm here, why we're here," he said, glancing at Helen, who'd been silently watching Luke's face throughout. "We're here to ask you to go. It may be the only way to keep this whole thing from getting out of control."

"It's already out of control!" Luke said, raising his voice and standing. "If you can get his fingerprint while he's on a Pakistani Air Force base, just send back whoever did that and whack him! Just rip his heart out! Why all this covert fly-for-India, Russian-intelligence stuff? Just go get him!"

"We can't."

"Why not?"

"Our options . . . are different than they were."

Luke stared at the CIA officer. He felt trapped. It was asking too much. And where did Vlad get off offering his name to India to come defend them? "What's the plan?"

"What's going on?" Katherine asked from the doorway in her nightgown. She had her glasses on and was straightening her hair. "What are you doing here?" she asked Morrissey.

"Sorry to intrude. I'm Bill Morrissey. I'm with the government."

"Which government?"

"United States."

"What do you do for the government?"

"I'm with the CIA."

She was surprised. She looked at Helen. "What brings you here?"

"We came to talk to Luke. Sorry we woke you."

"You didn't, he did. I tend to wake up when he raises his voice in the middle of the night. What's going on, Luke?" she asked, a frown deepening on her brow.

"They have an idea of how to stop Khan."

"Let me guess," she said. "And you're just the guy to do it?"

"I'm not sure. They were just about to tell me what the idea was. Pull up a stool," he said, motioning for her to sit next to him.

Li glanced at Morrissey, who gave her a reassuring nod and said to Katherine, "We were just talking to Luke about some arrangements that have been made to counter what we think Khan's real plan is. We have to move fast."

"Go on," she said. "Let's hear it."

Morrissey looked at Luke intently. "You leave this morning from San Francisco International Airport aboard Air India Flight 618 and fly directly to New Delhi, where you'll be met by the Indian Air Force. They'll take you to the Air Force base, where you'll be briefed. We think you'll have time for one familiarization flight in the Indian MiG. Then, if the attack is when we think, you'll have about twelve hours to rest and prepare. The remainder of the Indian MiG squadron will be right behind you and will help in any way you want."

Luke rested his elbows on the table and held his head. This was impossible. "If I screw this up, they'll blame us."

"They'll blame you, or the U.S. will blame you—someone will, count on it," Katherine added.

"Your name will never show up anywhere, unless we say it should. If it turns sour, you won't be blamed. They'll go at him with everything they've got if he gets through. Frankly, they're afraid that if you're not there, they won't even find him in time to defend the plant. You're to get the first crack at him." Morrissey waited. He sensed Luke wavering. He played his final card. "I thought you might want the chance to get back at the guy who ruined your school—and your life. And Vlad *is* going."

Luke looked surprised. "You talked to him?"

"The Indians already know him. They know what he can do with a MiG."

Luke glanced at his watch. "I can't get to San Francisco in three hours."

"We'll get you there."

"How?"

"Helicopter."

"There's no helicopter anywhere near here."

"It's hovering five miles from here. It just picked up Vlad and came straight here from Tonopah. They're waiting to find out if you're going. As soon as you say the word, they'll set down on your beautiful, newly paved runway and take you to San Francisco."

"What about the school? You guys shut it down after the attack."

"The government still wants you operating."

"If I go, I want your *word*. The school goes on, with me or without me. Win or lose in India."

Morrissey hesitated. "You have my word."

Luke saw the hesitation. He looked at Helen, who nodded her agreement. "What do you think, Katherine?"

She looked at Morrissey, then Helen. "I'm sorry. I've seen the government at work too many times. They'll lie right to your face if it's to their advantage."

"I wouldn't," Morrissey said, stung by her comments.

Katherine raised her eyebrows. "You're with the CIA and you wouldn't lie to him if you thought it was in the national interest to do so?"

"No. I wouldn't."

Katherine smiled. "I might have been born yesterday, but I wasn't born at night." She looked at Luke. "Unless they put it in writing and *I* keep the document, I wouldn't count on it."

Luke went to the kitchen and took out a piece of paper from a drawer. He handed it to Morrissey. "Put it in writing."

Morrissey hesitated. "I'll have to be vague, at least about what you're doing."

"Just put in there that the school is to remain open and that that is the will of the United States government."

Morrissey's pen hovered over the paper, and then he began writing. When he finished, he handed the document to Luke, who passed it to Katherine without even reading it.

Katherine read every word. Then she nodded at Luke. "This will do it."

"Bring them in," he said to Helen who left quickly.

Katherine was somber. "You don't have to prove anything," she said to Luke.

"I know. But somebody has to stop him."

"India can do it without you."

"Probably. But if they can't, it'll start a war," he said.

"You really think so?" she asked.

"I've got to stop Khan. I didn't get it done here. I'll do it there."

Morrissey closed his briefcase and handed Luke a passport and a ticket. The passport had his picture on it but was in the name of Robert Boswick.

Luke looked at it and frowned. "What's this?"

"We don't want Khan hearing about this. He has a lot of friends. We want him to assume that if we're onto him, all we'd ever do is pass it to India. He has no fear of them." Morrissey's face was dark. "He's much more resourceful than we gave him credit for."

They got up and headed toward the back. As they walked, Luke asked Katherine, "You okay with this?"

"You're taking a risk you don't have to take. India can take care of itself."

Luke shook his head. "It's not about India. It's about Khan. He tried to ruin us, Katherine. I owe him. I owe Thud."

"He's not a threat to us anymore."

He stopped. "I wouldn't ever be the same person if I just let this happen. I'd be cowering in a corner somewhere," he said. "I've got to get this done."

There were a lot of things she wanted to say, but she could tell by the look on his face that none of them would make any difference.

They went to the back of the house. He heard the deep rumbling of a jet-powered helicopter and looked in the direction of the noise. He watched as the dark Sikorsky S-76 settled quickly onto his runway, throwing sand all around on either side. The side door came open, and a man in a flight suit and helmet motioned for him to climb aboard quickly. Luke looked back at Katherine and waved awkwardly before dashing for the helicopter.

26

The special agents pressed their backs against the wall outside Merewether's apartment. They'd been waiting in shifts in their cars for days. No one had tried to enter the apartment since Merewether's disappearance. No cleaning service, no friends, no family—no one. Not even the manager. No lights had come on, the phone didn't ring once—they had it tapped—and no one showed any interest in Merewether at all. It had made for a dull stakeout.

Then, just at dusk, Merewether had driven up in his antique Volkswagen Bug with the rusted bumper and parked on the street. The FBI agents had thought they were hallucinating. They expected *someone* to come at some point, but not Merewether himself. Not in his car, not so obviously.

Merewether had gotten out of his car and gone to the elevator. The FBI agent stationed outside had immediately radioed the others, then hurried to the elevator and to Merewether's floor.

They waited outside his door, their guns drawn. The lead agent knew very well what his instructions were. If Merewether returned, they were to wait to see if he called anyone or tried to make any contact with anyone that might lead them to the Pakistani who'd set up the entire thing— who had himself conveniently disappeared.

The lead agent stood next to Merewether's door. He could hear the television: CNN. Typical Washington, he thought. In D.C. everybody does their work, then runs home to see how much of it was legitimate, determined by how much of it makes it onto CNN. In D.C. if you're not on television, you don't exist.

The agent checked his watch and looked at the other three agents. They were to wait thirty minutes or until Merewether left. Whichever came first. Then they were to arrest him on a list of federal offenses as long as his excuses were sure to be. The lead agent carried the arrest warrant in his suit pocket. He waited a minute and checked his watch again. He knew Merewether wasn't leaving. He must have something else in mind, some specific purpose that would make him come back to this apartment, after being gone long enough to have seen his name in the papers. Whatever it was, he wasn't going to escape. His apartment was on the seventh floor of a high-rise with no way out except through the door next to the agents.

CNN droned on in the background as another seventh-floor resident came out of the elevator and passed the FBI agents in front of Merewether's apartment. He looked at them and their drawn guns and hurried by, quickly turned the corner, and glanced back, horrified and intrigued.

Twenty-seven minutes. The agent had waited long enough. He reached across the door with the back of his right hand and rapped sharply. "FBI, open up. We have a warrant for your arrest!" The agents breathed more deeply, ready for whatever Merewether had in mind.

"FBI! Open up!" he repeated with an insistent, no-nonsense tone.

Still nothing.

"Open up! FBI!" he demanded. No response. He looked at the other agents. They were all in agreement. He nodded. They all knew what the plan was and what each one's role was. The lead agent tried the doorknob. It was locked. He examined the construction of the door. The usual hollow-core apartment door with cheap hardware. One kick, he thought. He went to the other side of the hallway, across from the door, took one quick step, and kicked with all the force of his leg right next to the doorknob.

The door flew open. Merewether had closed the dead bolt behind him, and it tore through the frame and the wallboard as it was forced open. "FBI!" the agent yelled as he moved rapidly into the apartment with his gun ready, looking for any danger. The other three agents flowed into the apartment behind him and fanned out to cover the entire hallway from the living room to the kitchen. The apartment lights were on in all the rooms they could see. The television was on, too, but no one was watching it.

The lead started working his way through the apartment from the living room. He turned off the television to allow them to listen more easily. The silence was eerie. They could hear their hearts pounding. The lead pointed to the kitchen, where one of the other agents looked, then entered. Nothing unusual at all.

The lead agent headed toward the bedroom. The door was closed. He considered his options. He tried the knob, but the bedroom door was locked. It was a thin door with no internal strength. He stepped back, kicked the door open in one motion, and moved away from the opening in case Merewether was waiting for them with a weapon. There was no sound at all. The lead agent glanced around the door and saw a small white television on a dresser playing to an empty room. He turned it off. There was nothing out of order. They searched the room carefully, checking the closets and the bathroom, but there was no sign of Merewether.

"There any more rooms?" the lead agent asked, confused.

"Nope," his second replied.

"Where the hell is he?"

They all looked around the three-room apartment—the kitchen, living room, and bedroom. No Merewether. They quickly checked the bathroom. It was empty. They stared at each other.

"Maybe he jumped," one of them said suddenly.

The lead agent hurried to the balcony off the living room and wrestled with the sliding glass door. He had difficulty pushing the door open. It felt as if the slide rail were made of gravel. He tried to look down to the ground through the white steel railing, but they were too high for him to see the ground immediately.

He noticed in his peripheral vision that a light coming from his left was blocked, then not blocked. He realized that two legs hung in front of him, dangling, lifeless. "Help me get him down!" he yelled as he grabbed Merewether's legs and pushed up. One of the other agents tried to get at the balcony of the apartment above to release the belt that was knotted to the railing. The end was slipped through the buckle, allowing it to cinch tight when pressure was brought to bear, which it certainly was when Merewether stepped off the railing of his own balcony.

The lead yelled, "Get up there and get the belt off!"

"I can't reach the other end!" the second agent protested as he considered climbing up on the railing to reach the balcony above.

"Then get up there and get onto the balcony!"

The second agent ran out of Merewether's apartment and up the stairs to the next floor.

The lead agent and the others tried to keep Merewether from hanging from the belt. They tried not to look at his blue, swollen face.

"Is he still alive?" one asked.

"I don't know. He sure doesn't seem to be breathing. Get an ambulance here!" the lead replied.

Finally they heard the other agent above them and two voices they didn't recognize. "I just need to get onto your balcony," he was explaining as he pushed by them.

"Hey! What could you possibly need out there? We haven't been out there all day!"

He ignored them and leaned down to examine the knotted belt. "Shit, this is tight! Can you get any more pressure off?"

"No," the lead replied.

"I'm just going to cut it," the second said, pulling a buck knife out of its belt holder and slicing through the leather.

Merewether tumbled into the arms of the three agents waiting below.

They laid him on the concrete slab that constituted the balcony and felt for a pulse. Nothing. "We're too late."

The other agents grimaced. They knew that those who had decided to stake out Merewether's apartment around the clock were much less interested in securing a conviction against him than in being able to question him about the Pakistanis. Now they wouldn't get the chance.

"We did it right, boss. Thirty minutes—"

"Shut up." He looked at the body. It was still warm. There was still some color in his hands. They were only a few minutes late. While they were out in the hall, Merewether was ending his life. "We'd better call Li."

"I'll call her," another agent said.

"No, I'll call her."

"It wasn't our fault."

"Doesn't matter. It's not political with her; it's getting to the bottom of things." He finished dialing and waited for the cell phone to connect.

LUKE and Vlad walked through San Francisco International Airport trying not to look conspicuous. Every television continued to broadcast the unending news on CNN and every other news station about the attack at San Onofre. The immediacy of it had subsided slightly, only because the nuclear cloud had not yet decided where to go and was hovering over the Pacific. It was apparently caught in the middle of contradicting weather patterns, which resulted in its staying put, a not altogether unpleasant development, although a marine layer was starting to form and threatened to engulf the California coast in a low-hanging, radioactive fog.

The televisions showed nonstop video of the crumpled San Onofre building, with accusatory reports about nuclear waste. Interstate 5, the main artery that ran along the coast from San Diego to Los Angeles, was closed for the indefinite future.

Luke and Vlad stood in line at the gate. The passengers in front of them spoke of little else. The entire world was transfixed by the attack and by following the drifting, dissipating radioactive cloud. Luke tried to count the number of times he heard the words "Chernobyl" or "Three Mile Island" or "malicious," or some other unflattering adjective applied to the Pakistanis. Luke watched the television out of the corner of his eye, especially when Pakistani officials were answering questions about how their pilots might have pulled this off without governmental assistance. They claimed to be baffled and angry.

His and Vlad's innocuous bags had been checked, even though they contained flight gear, flare guns, and other things that were never supposed to be checked. They'd been assured that their bags would not be inspected or confiscated. All they carried with them were two small Air India flight bags that contained shaving kits and paperback books that looked to them to be particularly boring and ridiculous.

They stopped at the desk to check in with the airline attendant. Luke started to sweat as he stepped to the counter and handed her his false passport.

Vlad was completely unperturbed behind him, in spite of the fact that his passport read "Billy Walters" and listed an address in El Paso, Texas. Luke glanced at Vlad and whispered, "Do you even know where El Paso, Texas, is?"

"Sure," Vlad answered.

Luke tried to look bored and preoccupied. Nearly everyone getting onto the airplane appeared to be of Indian descent. There were very few American passports in the group. "Good morning, sir," the attendant said, taking his passport. She checked it against his appearance, then against the ticket. "We have you assigned to seat 27A," she said in her Indian accent.

"Fine," Luke said, avoiding her gaze.

She handed him his passport and ticket and took Vlad's papers. "Good morning," she said.

"Morning," he replied, trying his hardest to hide his thick Russian accent. He nodded and smiled as she clicked the computer keys.

"There you go, Mr. Walters," she said, giving him his documents. "You're in 27B."

They walked down the ramp into the Indian 747.

They took their seats and put their heads back, gladly accepting a little rest before they would once again be required to fight for their lives.

CINDY Frohm spoke into her phone as she waited for Morrissey's encrypted digital cell phone to connect, "Come on, pick up, pick up!"

"Morrissey."

"Bill!"

"Who's this?"

"Cindy."

"I can't really talk. What do you need?"

"We just got something I think you should see."

"From whom?"

"Go secure."

"Okay. Stand by." He came back on line. "Okay."

"It's from the NSA."

"What is it?"

"Transcript of a telephone conversation in Russian."

"Whose?"

"Between Russia and Tonopah, Nevada. It was the Russian guy at the school out there. The guy who just set up this whole India thing."

"And?"

"And somebody in Russia is involved. He was accusing this Vladimir guy of trying to murder him and of sending a Colonel to try to take him out. They're checking this guy's voice. They think they can ID him. He's with the Russian Mafia."

"What was he saying?"

"It sounds very tense, I'm told. All we have is the transcript. They're checking all the tapes for phone calls between Russia and Nevada over the last few weeks. It will take some time."

"They've already left for India! What are we supposed to do with this?"

"The NSA seems to think Vladimir is working with the other side. It may be under duress, but he may be against us."

"So the whole thing is a trap? Shit!" Morrissey said, trying to think of what to do next. "Get whoever knows about these calls to pull it all together and meet me in my office. I'm on my way."

LUKE'S face had now been on CNN hundreds of times as the one who was in charge of the now famous school where the attack had been launched on the San Onofre nuclear power plant. Everyone in the world was aware of what had happened, and where it had happened from, and who owned and ran the school from which the catastrophe had begun. Yet no one seemed to glance their way as they walked off the 747 into the terminal in New Delhi. They didn't know who was to meet them or what they were to do next. They'd simply been told someone would be waiting.

Luke and Vlad followed the signs to baggage claim. As they were walking down the long hallway, two men began walking next to them. "Follow us, please."

"What about the bags we checked?"

"We've already retrieved them."

"Where are we going?" Luke asked as they walked down

a flight of stairs and out of the terminal into the muggy morning air.

The first man pointed to a waiting Falcon Jet, a two-engine business jet. The engines on the Falcon were screaming with anticipation as Luke and Vlad were ushered inside and the door closed behind them.

"Are you both from the squadron?" Luke asked.

"We're on the General's staff."

"Thanks for meeting us. Where are we going now?"

"To the air base."

"Straight there?"

"Yes, sir, nonstop."

Luke was impressed. "Any developments?"

The first Indian officer, who was doing all the talking, sat down across from Luke. A small table was between them. The man said loudly, "Several of their F-16s have been towed inside the hangar. We think they are being loaded."

"How much time do we have?"

"We don't know. Do you think they'll go during the night or day?"

"You think they'll really do this?"

"We have seen what they did to you."

"Anything else?"

"We're trying to move some air defenses to the area without anyone noticing, but it is extremely difficult. We don't have that many mobile systems, and we don't want them to be obvious in their movement. Have you thought about how to defend the nuclear plant?"

Luke nodded. "We need a lot more information than we have right now. And we'll need to know who's available to go with us, who has experience."

"There is a meeting set up with the commanding officer of the Archers. He's prepared to give you whatever you need."

"If they're loading them now, they could be launching within an hour."

"That's why I asked you whether you thought they would go at night."

"I don't really know whether they have much of a night capability. I sure as hell hope not."

"What if it were you?"

"I'd go at night. Without a doubt. Especially against your fighters. Sorry . . ."

"That's why you're here. Someone else must agree with you. You think they'll come in low?"

"I had assumed so."

"There are many airline routes that fly over Pakistan and India. They might disguise themselves as an airliner, then drop down. It would allow them much greater range and less likelihood of detection."

"That's possible, but I doubt it. My guess is he will come right at us."

The man looked troubled.

Luke looked out the window as the Falcon lifted off quickly from the New Delhi airport, then back at his host. "If we're in time."

THE business jet shut down its engines just outside the hangar and was towed in. Luke and Vlad started to get up but were told to wait until the jet was completely inside the hangar and the doors were closed behind. Someone was being very cautious.

Luke hurried down the ladder behind the two Indian officers. There were ten people waiting for them. One was clearly the leader of the group. The commanding officer of the MiG-29 squadron, no doubt, Luke thought, spotting the yellow Archers patch on his flight suit. He walked directly toward the distinguished-looking man. He was perhaps forty years old, with dark skin and thinning, carefully combed hair.

They shook hands. "Welcome. My name is Prekash. We have been expecting you."

"Luke Henry. This is Vladimir Petkov."

"Yes, I know," the Colonel said as he smiled at Vlad. "How have you been, Vladimir?"

"Well, Colonel. You?"

"Very well. Thank you."

"How are the MiGs holding up?"

The Colonel showed some ambivalence. "Not too bad. We have some maintenance problems, but nothing too horrible. Come this way," Prekash said, pointing toward the back of the hangar.

"Why the closed hangar doors?" Luke asked.

The Colonel glanced at him. "This man who is intent on attacking us, we are told he is very resourceful. He has many friends, even where one wouldn't expect. We are taking all precautions to ensure he doesn't know you are coming or that we are expecting him. We want to show nothing out of the ordinary."

"Towing a Falcon into the hangar and closing the doors isn't out of the ordinary?"

"Fair enough," he replied. "But given the circumstances, we didn't want two foreigners walking off the plane. Better to wonder what's wrong with our jet."

"Have you done any planning? Do you have any charts? Any signs they're getting ready to launch?"

The Colonel indicated a room in the corner of the cavernous hangar. They entered it and closed the door. The room was full of pilots in their flight suits who were obviously waiting for Luke and Vlad. It was a mission-planning room, with charts and flight information on the walls and planning materials on a large table in the middle of the room. "We have everything you need," the Colonel said. "You have your flight gear?" he asked.

"In the bags."

"Excellent." He looked at one of the pilots, who immediately left the room to take care of the flight gear.

Luke and Vlad wanted to examine the charts, to study the defensive situation, and to try to determine how much time they had. The commanding officer of the Indian MiG-29 squadron wanted everyone in the squadron to meet the two pilots. They came forward in what soon became a receiving line to introduce themselves to Luke and Vlad. They all had bright eyes, but Luke detected some resentment. He knew he would be resentful if some foreign pilots were brought in to do his job and defend the United States from attack, implying that those who were supposed to do it were somehow incompetent or, at least, less capable.

Prekash brought the pilots together. "Those who have been asked to be part of the final planning stage are welcome to stay. For the rest of you, please return to your duties."

Those who were being asked to leave headed for the door, while three other officers stayed behind and made their way to the planning table.

Luke glanced around. "We're right here," Prekash said, pointing to the airfield on the chart. "It is my understanding that you believe he'll be attacking here, the nuclear power plant."

"We're just guessing," Luke said, looking at Vlad. "But it's what he did to us, with no warning whatsoever. It's kind of the poor man's nuclear war—if you can't use nuclear warheads to spread radiation, if you don't have your own radiation to drop on someone, use theirs. Hit the nuclear power plants or, as he did to us, their high-level nuclear waste. And if he is truly intent on starting a war between India and Pakistan, wouldn't that be the sure way of doing it?"

"The most sure way I can imagine," Prekash said with an undertone of fury.

Vlad was staring at the chart. "But we should consider other targets. If we were so smart, we would have stopped him before he attacked us," he admitted.

Prekash ran his hand across the chart to flatten it, then looked up at Luke. "You trained this Khan?"

"Mostly in air-to-air," Luke replied defensively. "We did some air-to-ground, but not much. We helped him plan a mission to attack a target from low level about three hundred miles away."

"And here we are," Prekash said. "How do you think he'll come?"

"As low as he can get."

"It does not give us much time to react. If we detect him coming at all."

"Show me where we are in relationship to the target," Vlad said.

One of the other officers pointed to the nuclear power plant. "It is right here. The Air Force base is"—he looked—"here." He took a ruler and showed them the most direct line of flight. "It is a pretty straight shot."

"It looks flat," Luke said.

"For the most part," Prekash said. "There is no real good place to hide, which makes an intercept easier. And that is assuming they don't stage out of one of their forward air bases. A real possibility."

Luke studied the chart. "Where are those?"

"Here, and here, and here," Prekash showed.

"A lot of angles to worry about."

"Precisely."

"How's your radar? Any chance of an early-warning hit on them coming across the border?"

Prekash thought for a moment and stared at the identified air bases and how close they were to the Indian border. "I'd say a one-in-two or one-in-three chance of picking them up. Depending on where they cross the border and how high."

"We told them to attack a target from several directions at once to ensure that some go through." He looked at the chart where Prekash was staring. "I'm sure they know where the radar coverage is the weakest."

"There are some valleys."

"Could you do it without detection?"

"Not with a large flight."

Vlad shook his head. "It won't be a large flight. I'd expect four airplanes at the most. A surgical strike with laser-guided bombs. It's what we recommended."

Prekash and the other Indian pilots studied Vlad and Luke. They still weren't sure what to make of them. They had been ordered to cooperate but didn't feel comfortable yielding. "You make it sound like we will never stop him. What do you suggest?"

"We need to have a complete understanding of your radar system, your early-warning system, and any airborne radar platforms you have available. We also need to devise a plan to get them airborne covering the right places without alerting anyone to increased activity."

"We have some old early-warning airplanes, but they are not very reliable."

Luke stood up straight. "You need to get everything that can detect a low-flying airplane airborne. Even if it looks like provocation, you can argue that it can't be provocation to turn on your own radars. We'll have to have fighters airborne from now until we think the threat is over. And since Vlad and I are to be the first to engage, we need to be in a five-minute alert at the airfield along the most likely threat vector."

"I think you'll see that we have no airfield on the threat vectors. We are as close as there is, and we're a hundred miles away from their most likely route."

Luke and Vlad frowned. Luke spoke first. "That won't do it. With the 29's limited range, we won't be able to get them from here."

"What do you suggest?" Prekash asked, slightly peeved.

"I don't know," Luke said.

A Major spoke. "We might be able to pre-position you at one of our unimproved wartime locations."

"Would it put us on the threat vector?" Vlad asked.

He looked at the chart again. "Yes, it would."

Prekash began to say something, then stopped. He had seen somebody come into the room from behind Luke and Vlad. Luke felt the gaze of the intruder on the back of his head and turned to look. The man was impeccably dressed. He wore expensive casual clothes. He nodded at Prekash, who quickly gave a very subtle and slight bow and left the room with his other officers. Luke and Vlad were suddenly alone with him.

The man came over to Luke and extended his hand. "I am Sunil."

Luke was puzzled. "Luke Henry, and this is—"

"Yes, I know. Hello, Vlad."

"Sunil," Vlad said, surprised.

"Who exactly are you?" Luke asked, perplexed by Prekash's leaving in the middle of their conversation.

"As I said, my name is Sunil."

"Sunil who?"

"Just Sunil."

"So what can we do for you?"

"I wanted to talk to you about what you'll be doing and against whom you will be doing it," he said. His accent was slightly less obvious than the others'. It had a more British, clipped sound to it, as if he'd been educated at Oxford.

Luke nodded without comment. He wanted to get on with their planning.

"We have some very good information that your enemy will be launching his attack either tonight or early in the morning."

"How do you know that?"

"As I said, we have very good information."

"Okay," Luke said. "So what are we going to do about it?"

"We will pre-position your two fighters at a forward strip which is actually a highway. The rest of the squadron will be behind you, in front of the nuclear plant as a barrier. It will be up to you to try to stop them, but if you fail, the others—"

"We won't fail," Luke replied.

"I understand that you do not intend to fail, but failure has a way of sneaking up on you." —

"I don't let failure sneak up on me."

"Yes, well, who intends to?"

"Do you know how many airplanes there will be?"

"I don't think many."

"You sure seem calm," Luke said. "Everyone else around here is on pins and needles. You look like you just got a massage."

Sunil smiled. His teeth were perfect and bright against his dark face and slicked-back jet black hair. "No massage, I'm just confident."

"Why?"

"Because I know our adversary."

"What do you mean, you know him?"

"I've been following him and his group for years. He has been planning this event for a long time, including taking his leave of absence from the Air Force so he could reappear as another pilot with new records."

"How do you know that?"

"I know almost everything there is to know about Mr. Riaz Khan, as you know him."

Luke winced at the mention of the name.

"The man who came to your school, killed your security guards, bombed your nuclear power plant, and now has come here to do the same to us."

Luke put his hands on his hips and shook his head. "Why?" Luke demanded. "If his target is India, why go after us first? Why put a big, sharp stick in the eye of the one country that might actually help him win a war with India? I mean, we've given them a lot of their military gear. I just don't get it."

"Your mistake is understandable. You continue to think that he is working on behalf of Pakistan and that they simply refuse to acknowledge it. In fact, he is working on behalf of an elusive group whose goal is to see one Islamic country in South Asia, including Pakistan, Kazakhstan, Kyrgyzstan, Afghanistan, possibly Iran, possibly Bangladesh, and, of course, Kashmir. Attacking the U.S. undermines Pakistan and will almost certainly topple the current regime, which refuses to go to war over Kashmir and stands in the way of his great Islamic state."

"You must have known all this when he came to the States," Luke asked.

"Of course."

"Why didn't you tell us about him?" Luke demanded.

Sunil took an Indian cigarette from the pocket of his sharply pressed wool slacks, lit it, and inhaled deeply. His gold Rolex watch moved with each hand gesture. "What makes you think I didn't?" he asked.

"You told them what you know about Khan?"

"I told them everything I could tell them without compromising my sources."

"Before he attacked San Onofre?"

"Of course. I told them everything they needed to know. But frankly, I anticipated no danger. I had no idea he would do something to the United States. I always thought Pakistan and India were his targets." He sucked on the cigarette and raised his eyebrows. "I assumed he was in Nevada for training. That is all."

"What did they say?"

He smiled as he exhaled through his nose. "Your intelligence people did not believe me. But finally they believed your courageous agent, who sneaked onto the military base and identified him. She is, of course, now—and will be for a long time—in a Pakistani prison for her efforts."

"What?" Luke said, horrified.

"It doesn't matter. You must get on with your mission. It is up to you to stop Khan."

Luke's head was spinning. "You've been following this guy for years?"

"Frankly, even I did not anticipate the boldness of his moves."

"You are with Indian intelligence, I take it."

Sunil breathed in deeply from his cigarette. "Of course."

"Do we have his target right?"

"I suppose we are about to find out. But I think almost without a doubt that is his target."

"And it's tonight?" Vlad interrupted.

"The airplanes are already loaded with bombs. I do not know what time they will take off, but I am virtually certain it will be tonight."

Luke needed to plan. "Thanks for your help."

"We are grateful that you came here to help us. You did not have to do that." He stepped on the butt of his cigarette with his expensive loafers. He looked at Luke and Vlad. "If there's anything I can do for you—anything at all—let me know. He must be stopped."

"He will be."

27

Luke and Vlad walked out of the hangar with Prekash, toward the squadron's jets. They wore Indian flight suits and boots. Luke thought the Archers squadron patch on his flight suit was worthy of a MiG squadron, but he would have preferred to die with his NFWS flight suit and patch on, and the black star painted on the tail of his airplane.

The Indian MiG-29s were lined up on the tarmac in the bright sunshine. They were in beautiful shape, painted in a green-and-tan camouflage with Indian markings.

Vlad's eyes took in the airplanes and the minutiae that only those who fly them can see. He spoke to Luke, who was walking beside him. "C models. Not much difference. All the latest electronic countermeasures. We should have no problem."

"Sure hope you're right." Luke was too busy having an out-of-body experience, looking at himself walking toward an Indian MiG, wearing an Indian flight suit and boots, being led by an Indian Colonel and assisted by a Russian pilot. All to fly into combat in a Russian fighter in a soon-to-be war he didn't care much about, to stop a lunatic Pakistani pilot. It was one of the more surreal moments in his life. Things were usually clear in Luke's mind, but he found himself unable to recount how he'd gotten to where he now found himself. He could certainly trace the chronology well enough, but that didn't seem to explain it. It was an inadequate way of looking at it. He was more in search of a "why" answer. He felt as Ulysses must have felt in his journey back from Troy to Penelope, when every event surpassed the previous in oddity or difficulty, every monster was bigger and meaner than the last, all calculated by the gods to prevent him from reaching his destination. All Luke had wanted was to fly fighters and start a family. Was that so much to ask? Had he been too greedy? Was there a God so mean-spirited that such a desire was to be met with destruction and death?

All around the base there was a hum of activity. It was clear to anyone watching that combat was imminent. Luke hoped that no such activity would be obvious to someone with a good vantage point to observe it and an inclination to tell Pakistan. He also hoped that if there was such a person, he didn't have Raymond-size binoculars sufficient to identify Vlad and him. But it might not make much difference; Luke was convinced that Riaz Khan would go on his mission regardless of who was waiting for him. He was just afraid that knowing what they were up to might make Khan change something.

Luke stood at the top of the ladder and peered into the cockpit.

Vlad spoke to him from the bottom of the ladder, already having viewed the cockpit. "No problem, right? Just like we're used to."

Prekash walked over to them. "We have decided where you should base your airplanes."

Luke was put out. "What's the plan?"

"We think you should go now. We don't know when he might launch. We should be ready."

"I thought we were going to do a FAM hop first. Get used to your airplanes."

"We don't have time for a familiarization hop. We think you should be in place in case he goes now."

"Okay," Luke said, his uneasiness increasing. He hopped down the last step from the ladder. "When?"

"As soon as you can be ready."

"Anything going on?"

Prekash nodded. "We have some signals intelligence. We have intercepted some communications from the ground."

"I don't see Khan talking on the radio before a strike."

"Not him, others. Fuel trucks and other ground personnel."

Luke nodded. "Where are you going to put us?"

"On a highway."

LUKE sat in his Indian MiG-29 beneath a large tree on the side of a two-lane highway. Vlad's MiG was across the highway inside a large barn. There were a dozen Indian maintenance men around them to ensure that they got their jets started and that their takeoff was uneventful. They waited only for some word, some indication that Khan was actually going to try it.

Luke was uncomfortable with the idea of taking off from a dusty, poorly maintained highway. He'd never done anything even close to that, let alone in a jet. Vlad claimed to have done it several times, but Luke was beginning to wonder how many of Vlad's amazing claims of experience were true. He'd never received any level of comfort on Vlad's probably doctored flight records from Russia. But Luke had been impressed by Vlad's tenacity against Khan at San Onofre. The man had nearly given his life to save an American nuclear plant. Still.

Luke had been sitting in the MiG cockpit so long his muscles ached. The afternoon had passed full of anticipation and excitement. Everyone was ready to launch, but nothing had happened. A telephone had been set up on a portable table for the critical communication. An order to launch would come through the phone, a landline that could not be intercepted by Pakistan's signals intelligence. The plain black telephone looked stark against the high-tech gear all around—the testing equipment, a few spare parts, the hydraulic line charger, and the electric cart that provided nonstop power to the MiGs. Vlad had an identical setup across the road and down a hundred yards. The airplanes had been dispersed in case of attack. One attack couldn't get more than one airplane at a time.

The night had brought strange noises and frustrated traffic from the closed road. The Indian ground crew had gone from unbounded enthusiasm to bored waiting. The hours passed slowly, punctuated only by the activity of Luke and Vlad unstrapping and climbing out of their jets every so often to relieve themselves behind the nearest structure.

Luke found himself fighting unconsciousness. He was exhausted, but he didn't want to be found sleeping when the big call came. It was hard enough to get a jet ready for takeoff from an unimproved roadway. But the problem was magnified infinitely when one tried to get airborne while fighting the fog of recent, deep, satisfying sleep. The result was a fitful, restless existence for Luke, strapped into the confines of a Russian cockpit battling sleep every minute of the night. He would find himself drifting off and shake his head to just short of a headache. He would pinch himself just short of a bruise. Anything to stay awake.

Without any warning, the telephone rang.

MORRISSEY sat in his office with the NSA specialists, numerous transcripts of telephone conversations spread out in front of him. "What do we have?" Morrissey demanded impatiently.

"Several calls. Some from Russia, and a couple to Russia. The most interesting are from this man he identifies as Gorgov."

"Who is he?"

The Russian linguist who had translated them and listened to the originals answered. "We're not sure. He behaves like someone with a lot of power—the kind that comes from holding a gun to your head. He has some control over this Vladimir."

"What about the others?"

"There is a call to a Colonel to apparently take care of this Gorgov. To get him off his back. The Colonel apparently is intending to take Gorgov out."

"And?"

"And then there's a call from Gorgov, telling Vlad his Colonel friend had failed in his attempt to kill Gorgov. He tells Vlad he'd better come through this time, basically. I think he was supposed to make sure the Pakistanis pulled off the attack on San Onofre. Turned out they got there too late to stop them anyway. But there's some other event that's going to happen, and Vladimir is supposed to be in a place to make sure it comes off. It is very unclear."

Morrissey put his head in his hands as he realized what was happening. "Khan is going to strike India. We just sent an American pilot and Vladimir to India to stop them. And the request originated with Vladimir's suggestion to the Russians, who passed it on . . . We are *screwed*," Morrissey declared as he jumped up and grabbed the phone. He looked at a list and dialed a number, then waited for the international connection. Finally someone answered. "Sunil, please."

"I'm sorry, he is not available."

"Find him."

"May I ask who is calling?"

"Bill Morrissey. This is an emergency. Put him on right away," he said.

"Yes, sir, I'll put you through."

Morrissey heard an unusual set of clicks that sounded as if he was being forwarded through innumerable switchboards. Then the unmistakable voice of Sunil came on through what sounded like a digital cell phone. "Yes?" he said.

"Are you secure?"

"Yes," Sunil replied. "Bill Morrissey?"

"Yes. Look, two pilots are on their way there. Luke Henry and a Russian—"

"Yes, I have met them."

"We have reason to believe that the Russian is under the control of Khan, or the Russian Mafia who are helping Khan. He's going to help the strike succeed, not stop it. We've got a lot of other things to do to confirm it, but he shouldn't be on that mission. We can't rely on him."

"How do you know this?"

"We've got some phone conversations that are pretty clear."

Sunil sounded distressed. "It may be too late. They are already in place at a remote road location."

"You've got to stop them!"

"I'll see what I can do, but I am not optimistic."

"Then you'll have to get the other Indian fighters to go after the two MiGs as well."

"To shoot down our own airplanes? How would they know which one had this Russian in the plane?"

"They wouldn't. They might have to take both of them out. Look, we have to stop Khan. If he succeeds, there will be a nuclear war, and you know it."

Sunil was silent. "I will go there myself and inform your pilot. I will let him decide."

"You must hurry!"

28

The ring was amplified and broadcast by a PA system throughout the small area. Luke's heart pounded in his chest as he sat up straight and watched the ground crew scurry around. The officer in charge of the ground crew held the phone to his ear, spoke quickly back, then put it down. He ran to Luke's ladder and climbed up to talk to him. "One of our border guards reported that a flight of jets just flew over him at very low altitude. Very fast."

"Pakistani?" Luke asked as he tightened his lap belts. He looked up at lights from a helicopter that was approaching from the east. The craft's anticollision lights intruded on the otherwise pitch-black sky.

The Indian officer gazed at the helicopter with a puzzled expression, then replied, "Has to be. We aren't flying anywhere near there. They are on their way."

"Your airborne radar planes didn't see anything?"

"I don't know, sir. I am just telling you what they told me."

"Where are they?" he asked, trying to disguise the unsteady voice he heard in his own head. The helicopter continued to approach, making conversation harder.

The officer handed him a chart and shone a flashlight on it. "They were coming through a small pass . . . here." He pointed.

"That's about two hundred miles from here. Heading?"

"He couldn't tell. But he estimated southeast."

"Let's go!" Luke said. "Get this info to—"

"He already has it."

"Then let's get on with this," Luke said, starting to envision a low-level intercept at night. Khan clearly had night-vision goggles and knew how to use them. Luke hadn't even thought about asking for goggles.

Luke was about to close his canopy when out of the corner of his eye he saw a figure jogging toward him from the helicopter. Suddenly Vlad scrambled down from his cockpit with something in his hand. He ran and caught up with the man from the helicopter, who turned slightly to talk to Vlad. The red rotating beacon caught the side of his face; Luke could tell it was Sunil. Strange, Luke thought. What's he doing out here?

He waited to start his engines. They finished their conversation, and Sunil turned toward Luke. He waved, and Luke waved back. Sunil turned and ran back to the helicopter, which was quickly airborne again.

Vlad ran around to the port side of the MiG and scurried up the ladder. As Vlad reached the cockpit level, Luke got a glimpse of what was in Vlad's hand—something long and sharp and metal. His heart jumped. All his doubts about Vlad came flooding back, all Brian's doubts, all Katherine's unwillingness to take Vlad at face value. Luke saw it all before him, as he envisioned himself at Vlad's mercy beneath a tree in Nowhere, India. He was still strapped in and had no chance to do anything about it if Vlad meant him harm.

Vlad stood next to Luke and leaned over toward him. He grabbed Luke by the helmet and pulled him toward himself. Vlad brought his left hand up and showed Luke he had a screwdriver in his hand. He said loudly through Luke's helmet, "I am going to use this. Don't tell our Indian friends. In the left wheel well of our airplanes is a small box that I will open. It will set our engines on their *war* mode. Hotter temperatures and more thrust. It will give us all the thrust this engine was intended to put out. Don't tell *them*, because it will probably also ruin the engines!" Vlad smiled a huge, energetic smile.

"What was Sunil doing here?"

"Don't worry about it. It was about me. I explained everything to him about what we are doing."

"But he was headed over here."

Vlad nodded with understanding. "He thought I was in this airplane."

Luke watched him disappear into the left wheel well, then reemerge after thirty seconds. He gave Luke a nod and a thumbs-up as he ran back toward his own airplane.

Luke quickly lowered the canopy. He shook his head as the first thought that came to him was that Vlad had somehow disconnected the left landing gear or released a fitting in the hydraulic system. As soon as he got up to speed, the MiG would lose the left strut and veer off the road, killing him. He was angry at himself for not trusting Vlad but unable to rid himself of lingering doubts.

He turned on the electrical power from the battery and quickly switched on the auxiliary power unit. It began turning his number one engine as the Indian ground crew watched. Two men stood to the left of the MiG with fire extinguishers in their hands, and a plane captain stood in the grass directly in front of Luke. Luke squinted to see him and realized that his windscreen was covered with mist. Great weather brief. He glanced up at the sky but couldn't see it through the darkness and the tree covering him.

As the engine turned, Luke watched a man by the road working with a box that had a long electrical line coming from it. It clearly wasn't responding as he would like. He adjusted something, and suddenly the highway was lit by a mile-long string of lights on either side, creating a rough, wet, uneven, poorly maintained runway. It was the very kind of strip the MiG-29 was designed to operate from.

The first engine roared to life, and the fuel flow, turbine

inlet temperature, and RPM climbed into normal ranges. He deselected the auxiliary power unit and quickly did a cross-bleed start of the number two engine, redirecting some of the jet air from the first engine across to the second engine to get its turbine spinning. He watched the RPM of the first engine dip slightly as the second began to turn. As soon as the second engine reached 10 percent RPM, he pulled its throttle off the stops, automatically lighting the engine off. The RPM jumped to 65 percent, idle, and he deselected cross-bleed. He turned on all the electronics and prepared to taxi.

The plane captain began signaling for the preflight checks—flaps, control surfaces, and the like. Luke was having none of that and shook his head vigorously. He had to get in the air.

Luke signaled to the plane captain to pull the chocks away from the wheels, and the plane captain signaled the men on either side of Luke's MiG. They removed the large wooden blocks in front of the oversize tires. Luke switched on his taxi light, advanced the throttle, and the MiG-29 rolled down the grass toward the road thirty yards ahead. The MiG drew in the night air from the louvers that were open on the shoulders of the airplane. The large intakes that would feed the hungry engines with the air it needed while airborne remained closed, to avoid sucking anything off the ground and damaging the turbine blades.

Luke looked to his right and saw the light on the nose-wheel of Vlad's MiG bouncing as he taxied forward from his position. As Luke headed toward the road in the pale moonlight that fought its way through the mist, the Indian ground crew saluted him. He returned their salute and turned on his radio. They had agreed to keep their radio communication to a minimum, and only on the frequency that Luke alone would choose.

Luke pondered the idea of taking off from a state highway in the night to intercept an F-16 without the use of any ground or airborne early-warning radar to help him run the intercept. He tried not to think too hard about the fact that the only information they had on Khan's whereabouts was from a border guard. The heading information they'd received was marginal at best, but Luke could imagine the heading, or calculate it, if Khan headed directly for his target. If he didn't, Luke knew he would never find him.

Luke scanned his engine instruments, glowing in the dark cockpit. He turned his MiG to face down the makeshift runway. He looked ahead of him at the narrow road with the lights on either side. It was slightly downhill and curved to the right in the distance where the lights stopped. The lights rose up and down with the road. It gave Luke the impression of trying to take off from a piece of bacon.

He advanced his throttles and moved forward slightly, trying to point his MiG exactly down the center of the road. Then he glanced into his rearview mirror. Vlad was directly behind him. Luke looked at the clock on the dash and knew he had to go. He pushed the throttles to full military power, waited until 100 percent RPM was generated in each engine, did a quick check of the engine instruments and flight controls, and released the brakes on the Fulcrum. The plane sped down the road, the lights disappearing under its wings one by one. The bulbs reflected their white light off the inside of Luke's canopy as if he were dashing into a movie theater.

The MiG accelerated through eighty knots, then one hundred. The road dipped and the nose gear compressed but threw the Fulcrum's nose back up as it headed out of the dip. The airplane almost had enough air over its wings to fly, and the impulse of climbing the small hill nearly threw the Fulcrum into the air before Luke was ready. He pushed the stick forward and held the Fulcrum on the ground waiting for the proper rotation speed.

The curve in the road was coming up too quickly. He

knew he had to be airborne before he reached it. He had disabled nosewheel steering and was able to keep the MiG on the road only by using the rudder pedals to control the big rudders behind him. He put in more rudder and checked his airspeed. He was passing through 135 knots. He hated the idea of taking off with rudder input, but he was afraid of losing control around the turn.

He pulled the stick back smoothly, and the Fulcrum's nosewheel came off the road. The louvers closed and the large engine intake doors opened, sucking in the fresh, moist air. The nose dipped, Luke trimmed it out, and the MiG lifted off. Luke could suddenly feel the crosswind he hadn't even been aware of, having attributed all the side force to the curve. The rear wheels lifted off, and Luke felt himself drifting hard left over the road. He pushed the stick to the right and pulled back on the nose to climb over obstacles, the invisible trees and bushes and wires that surrounded the area. He wanted to get away from the earth as rapidly as he could. He punched in a little afterburner to climb faster, then immediately deselected it to save gas. He raised his flaps, sucked up the landing gear, and pulled away from the road and Vlad behind him.

Vlad released the brakes on his Fulcrum as soon as the lights on Luke's airplane showed him airborne. He rolled down the undulating road, acutely aware of the crosswind he'd seen Luke's plane absorb. He gave himself a little afterburner just before liftoff to avoid the curve he'd seen Luke fight. He was promptly airborne, and he rendezvoused with Luke at five thousand feet over the local navigation aid they had agreed to use.

Luke and Vlad kept their radars off. They knew they had to make the intercept without any help from a ground controller. They would get course corrections if absolutely necessary, but they wanted any communication kept to a minimum to avoid detection.

Luke steadied on a heading of 220 to take them fifty miles ahead of Khan's expected course. He suddenly realized he had no idea how many airplanes were with Khan. The border guard had simply said "airplanes." That could mean two, or four, or six. It would be a rare person indeed who could distinguish the sound of two low-flying jets from that of three or four, especially if they flew directly overhead with their lights off.

Luke increased his throttle until it was at the stops. He pulled back on the stick and climbed to ten thousand feet to save gas and have a better chance of detecting the low-flying Pakistanis with his infrared system.

Luke knew the sensitivity of the F-16 radar-warning indicator much better than Vlad did. He wasn't about to hand Khan any advance warning by giving him a radar strobe from his MiG. Even a passing hit would alert Khan that MiGs were airborne. Luke didn't want Khan to have any idea they were coming until they were on top of him.

Luke turned up the screen of his infrared detector to see the green against black clearly. It didn't transmit anything, it just detected heat sources. He had practiced with it on almost every hop at the Nevada Fighter Weapons School. He found it easy to use and loved the idea of a totally passive intercept, where he would shoot down another airplane without even turning on his radar, without the other pilot even knowing he was nearby. It was a device few American fighters had. The F-16 had no infrared search-and-track system for air-to-air use, nor did the F/A-18 that Luke had spent most of his time flying.

He checked the status of the two Archer and two Alamo missiles he was carrying. It was a decent load, but he would have preferred to carry four Archers. *"Spread,"* Luke transmitted. Vlad took combat spread, a mile to Luke's right. They climbed to ten thousand feet, high enough to hear the chatter on the air-control frequency. The ten Indian MiG-29s

Prekash had ordered to defend the nuclear plant were now airborne and flying low combat air patrol near the plant. Other airborne early-warning aircraft were searching for Khan and broadcasting everything they thought would help identify them to the fighter patrol. Luke was sure somebody would be monitoring the Indian radio channels and fighter control to alert Khan of any developments. Khan would receive any such intelligence over his own radio without disclosing his own position.

Luke checked his chart again and turned toward Pakistan. Vlad was a mile to his right, slightly above him in combat spread. Luke studied the IR image and saw nothing that resembled an airplane. He didn't have much range with the IR system, but he refused to turn on his radar and give himself away.

He looked out toward the dark land below. He could barely see the ground. There were a few headlights on the invisible roads. The waning moon provided some illumination, but not enough to navigate by.

Luke figured they'd beaten the F-16s to this point on their flight path by ten minutes. He turned outbound and headed toward the pass where the guard had heard the fighters. If his estimates were right, he had less than five minutes until he would be on top of the F-16s.

Vlad was getting antsy. *"Nothing."*

"Ditto," Luke replied.

Luke suddenly saw a flash on the left side of his infrared screen. Something very hot was fifteen or twenty degrees below the horizon and far to his left. *"Hard left!"* he transmitted as he threw his stick to the side and rolled his Fulcrum into a ninety-degree angle of bank in the darkness. He headed left and down as his IR system continued to search for and reacquire the target. Luke couldn't see anything and wondered if he'd deceived himself into thinking he'd seen a return. He searched higher and lower. Still nothing. His speed passed through 550 knots as he passed through five thousand feet toward the ground. He rolled out of his turn and pointed at where he thought the targets should be. He couldn't find any signs of any airplanes at all.

He began to doubt himself even more when suddenly he had a strobe, a hint of an IR return on his screen, still to the left and down. Then a second, then a third hit. It had to be them. They were low, and less than ten miles away, still far to his left. If he hadn't caught the initial return, they would already be past him. He would never have seen them.

He pulled into the targets in a descending left turn and accelerated. He tweaked the controls on the IR system to separate out the bogeys. He tried to remember the minimum safe altitude of the area to avoid flying into a hill or antenna tower, but couldn't remember what it was.

Luke heard a buzz in his helmet—the sound of an F-16 radar on his radar-warning receiver. He had a strobe from his one o'clock position, just to the right of his nose. *"I'm getting tickled,"* he transmitted ominously to Vlad.

"So am I."

"I'm going active." Luke threw on the switch for his radar and turned the powerful MiG-29 radar toward the targets tearing across the Indian countryside. He quickly located them and locked up the lead to concentrate the radar's total energy on that one airplane. He was doing 620 knots. Luke was stunned. The altitude readout showed "zero" feet, so low that the radar couldn't tell they weren't on the ground. Night-vision goggles, Luke concluded. That gave them a big advantage he hadn't anticipated.

He broke lock on the radar and went into track-while-scan. He saw two other targets immediately, and then a third came up tentatively on the screen. Abruptly the third target started turning toward him and coming up after him. Luke hesitated as he suddenly realized that Khan had done the very thing Luke had told him not to do—he'd brought fighter escort. Two light F-16s, unencumbered with fuel tanks or bombs, peeled off Khan's formation to come after Luke and Vlad.

They had speed, they had good position, and they had American forward-quarter-firing AIM-9 Sidewinder missiles. Luke knew they had to act immediately or they would be dead. *"Two free fighters coming up after us, Vlad. I'm going low."*

"Roger. I'm going up, then. Over," Vlad responded quickly.

They extinguished their anticollision lights.

Luke pushed the nose of his MiG-29 over, to pass by the climbing F-16s and race toward Khan. The lead F-16 anticipated his move. Luke suddenly had an F-16 radar locked on him from the right side of his MiG. Luke had to turn into him to defend himself or he would never be able to intercept Khan. But if he did, Khan would slip away to his left. Luke had no choice.

He brought the Fulcrum around hard right and looked up through the windscreen with his helmet-mounted sight toward where the F-16 should be. He couldn't see him in the pitch-black sky. Luke tried to get the Archer missile to search for it, to give him the growl he yearned to hear, but there was no sound at all from his heat-seeking missiles.

He strained against the high G forces as he continued around to the right. He slaved his radar to the right toward the F-16, but still nothing. He still had a hard strobe on his radar-warning indicator. The F-16 had him locked up. Luke dumped some chaff to try to break the radar lock but had no success. He was trapped. The F-16 was coming uphill at him. It had a radar lock and almost certainly a sweet infrared shot. Luke had nowhere to go. Suddenly he remembered to activate the electronic jammers in the hump of his MiG, the jammers designed and installed just to defeat American-built radars. He reached and quickly threw the switches. He waited for the flash of the AIM-9 missile coming off the rail, but so far he had seen nothing. Then the F-16 radar was gone, deceived by the electronics of the MiG. Luke grunted. Good old Russian engineering.

The two fighters raced toward each other at twelve hundred miles an hour, neither able to see the other, both following the vaguely remembered strobe of the F-16 radar, which had broken lock seconds before. Luke suddenly noticed a return on his infrared receiver and slaved the seekerhead of the Archer missile to it. The Archer missile picked up the heat signature of the F-16 as it climbed away from the land. The missile seekerhead growled in eager anticipation. Luke fired immediately, reduced his throttle to idle, and turned back hard to his left to stay on Khan's trail.

He saw a flash out of the corner of his eye. The second F-16 had taken a shot at Vlad.

Vlad transmitted, *"I've got one coming directly at me!"*

Luke saw another flash to the right and behind him as Vlad fired a radar missile back at the F-16, which he almost certainly couldn't see. Vlad made a hard left turn to follow behind Luke and went to afterburner and dropped several hot burning flares to draw off the Sidewinder missile.

Luke saw Vlad scream by in full throttle toward Khan and his wingman as they in turn headed toward the Indian nuclear power plant. The Sidewinder chasing Vlad slammed into one of the flares Vlad had dropped and blew it into a bright orb like the one at the end of a fireworks show.

Just then Luke's Archer missile reached its target and flew into the engine intake. The invisible F-16 exploded in a ball of flames and tumbled toward the ground. Luke saw two bright plumes of afterburner ahead of him. It had to be Vlad—the F-16s had only one engine.

Luke wanted to kick himself. He had flown an intercept on the lead F-16 with fighters in cover behind. If one of his students had done that at NFWS, he would have given him a "down" for the flight. He stole a look toward the other F-16, or where it should be, but couldn't see anything. It was like a knife fight in a dark closet.

Luke's radar was on, as was his infrared search-and-track. His plan for a secret intercept of the F-16s to a nice rear-quarter Archer shot had gone up in missile smoke. He pulled back on his stick, deselected afterburner, and climbed to three thousand feet, well above the F-16s somewhere below him.

He was also now in the position of being to the side of the attacking F-16s with no ability to pick them out of the clutter of the ground. He raced toward his expected intercept point but was losing confidence with every second. *"Did you get that bogey?"* he asked, wondering if Vlad's first missile had hit its target.

"I don't know. Didn't see impact," Vlad replied.

Luke's radar-warning receiver was clear. The F-16s had not reacquired him.

"Where are you?" he asked.

"I don't know," Vlad replied. *"I've got them three miles ahead of me."*

"Hit your burner," Luke said.

He saw a burst of two afterburners ahead, then darkness again. *"Got you,"* he said. Luke pulled hard left to get back on the F-16s' course. Now he was chasing them from behind, but there was an F-16 somewhere behind him that probably hadn't gotten shot down.

Suddenly the voice of Prekash, the Indian squadron commander, came on their frequency calmly. *"Let us know if they get through."*

"Wilco," Luke transmitted with supreme annoyance.

He glanced up at the moon to see which side of the airplane would be illuminated. He wanted to be up-moon of the F-16s so they would see only his shadow. Luke accelerated as he began searching the air in front of them with his radar. *"Still have them?"* Luke asked Vlad.

"Lost them. Too low!"

"Still searching," Luke said.

"I've got them!" Vlad transmitted. *"They are three miles ahead of me. On the deck. Heading 130."*

Luke pulled to his left, took up a position of combat spread off Vlad, and redirected his radar toward Khan. Luke's track-while-scan radar picked up the targets quickly this time. They had a hundred knots of closure on the bogeys, not enough for Luke. *"Push it up,"* he said. They closed on the two F-16s. Luke glanced at the navigation aid they'd been using, then the chart on his kneeboard, and noted they were seventy-five miles from the nuclear plant. Fifty was their limit. If they didn't get Khan stopped by fifty miles, Prekash would take over with the rest of his squadron. Luke was tempted to let them do it, to break off the chase and leave it to the Indians, where it belonged. But he wasn't there to help India.

A red glow began to illuminate the horizon, and the rest of the countryside was now almost visible, even though still in mostly dark grays and black. Luke strained to see his enemy through the windscreen. He glanced down at his radar picture. *"I'm showing them in tight formation,"* Luke transmitted.

He had no doubt Khan knew they were there. He was certainly getting a radar strobe from the MiGs. But now Luke *wanted* Khan to know they were behind him. He wanted Khan to pull up, to do anything that would stop his progress toward the target. *"Alamo!"* Luke transmitted to Vlad as he pulled the trigger on the stick and the heavy radar missile dropped off his wing. One second later the rocket motor ignited, nearly blinding him with its intense yellow flame, as it headed for Khan's flight of two jets.

Luke heard a buzz in his headset, the sound of a radar locked on to him. He glanced down to his radar-warning receiver screen and saw a strobe from directly behind him.

Shit! That other F-16 had caught up with them. The missile launch had shown him where they were. *"I've got one on my tail!"* he transmitted.

Vlad immediately broke into a hard turn to cover Luke's tail. *"Looking."*

The radar-warning receiver couldn't tell the range, only the direction. The strobe showed just that the bogey was directly behind him. It could be a mile back, or ten.

Luke's eyes were fixed on the ball of fire ahead of him that was still heading toward Khan. Khan hadn't jinked or moved up at all. He watched the missile hit the ground a full half mile before the fleeing jets. Luke yelled to himself, "Damn it!" as he smashed his fist into the canopy. "Stupid damned Russian missiles couldn't hit the ocean if you dropped them off a pier!"

Vlad continued to pull hard left a thousand feet off the ground, with his radar searching for a target behind where he knew Luke must be. His radar was in auto-acquisition mode, and it locked onto a target a mile and a half behind Luke. He didn't have any time at all. He slaved one of his Archer missiles to the radar to point in the direction of the bogey and fired before he even had a good tone or could see the bogey. He was looking into the black sky to the west, well aware he was presenting a nice silhouette for the bogey as the sun approached the horizon behind him. The Archer screamed off the rail, and Vlad squinted and turned back toward Luke.

The Archer wasn't to be fooled. It angrily bore down on the bogey, hitting it directly on the tail, just forward of the exhaust. Then it exploded, cutting off the entire back half of the airplane. The pilot ejected as the F-16 slammed into the ground.

"Stay behind me and high. I've got to close on these guys."

"Roger," Vlad said as he pulled his Fulcrum up to five

thousand feet and scanned the sky for any other Pakistani fighters. No more surprises.

"You need help?" Prekash transmitted.

Only Vlad heard it, as he was high enough to catch the transmission. He replied, *"Negative. Will keep you posted. Splash two F-16s."*

"Roger. How many remaining?"

"We think two."

"You need support?"

"Recommend you vector a flight of four out now, heading"—Vlad looked quickly at the chart with the nuclear plant marked—*"290. If the F-16s are still airborne by there, we'll need a lot of help."*

"Roger. Flight of four outbound."

Luke heard Vlad's transmission. He assumed that Vlad was talking to Prekash, who no doubt was watching a radar picture of two bombers inbound to his nuclear power plant with the two world-class fighter instructors chasing them from behind. Not how it was supposed to go. ·

Luke noticed that his fuel was lower than he'd hoped. He didn't have much more time to complete this intercept. The F-16 had more fuel than the Fulcrum could ever hope to have; the F-16 had only one engine. He had to get Khan now, or he'd be out of gas. He went to full afterburner and accelerated toward Khan and the infrared signature he had. He again worked his radar onto Khan's jet. He fired another Alamo, his last radar-guided missile. He didn't have much faith in the large Russian missile by now. He had yet to see it hit anything, not at San Onofre, not here.

The morning air was clear and smooth as he started to see color in the landscape. It was the same patchy color as the camouflage scheme on his Indian MiG. He could make out a few trees or an occasional road as he raced across the countryside below him. He watched the Alamo speed toward

Khan and knew that Khan was getting the radar-lock indication on his radar-warning gear.

Luke almost smiled, as he could see Khan's face in his F-16 trying to decide whether he was safer by pulling up and doing a hard turn into the missile or staying low and fast and hoping the missile would hit the ground. He'd stayed low last time, and he might again. But it was going to be harder. Luke was closer, and Khan had to know that. It took a special coolness to take no evasive action when a missile was tearing up on you from behind.

Luke had closed to within a mile of Khan and could finally see the two F-16s as they danced over the Indian countryside. He could get only occasional glimpses of the airplanes, since they blended in with the darkness, but the missile had a very clear picture. It was getting radar return off the F-16s that guided it beautifully toward them. Luke saw small flashes on the underbellies of the two F-16s as they dropped chaff behind them to try to deceive the missile. The Alamo headed right toward them in a downward line like an arrow, when suddenly Luke's radar broke lock.

Khan went even lower, literally at treetop level, still running for the nuclear power plant. As much as he would have loved to turn and fight the two Indian MiGs he was sure he could defeat, he was determined to get to the target.

"Shit!" Luke yelled inside the noisy Russian cockpit as he watched the Alamo fail. He had only one Archer missile left.

Luke closed to within three-quarters of a mile of the fleeing F-16s and reacquired them with his radar. He selected Archer, the fast, infallible, maneuverable missile that he'd taught everyone to fear. He slaved the seekerhead to the radar, heard that growl, and fired. The hungry heat-seeking missile went right at Khan. Its motor burned brightly in the morning, illuminating the white smoke trail it left from Luke to the bogey. Khan knew what was coming. Flares dropped from the F-16s like rain. They burned at different intensity from a jet engine, a different color. The Archer chose one of the flares and blew it to hell.

What? Luke thought. The Pakistanis have a flare that will beat the Archer? When did they get it? It suddenly occurred to him for the first time that he might not be able to get Khan. He had failed to shoot him down with the best maneuvering missile in the world. He was out of missiles and options. The Indians were going to have to take care of him themselves.

He suddenly heard the buzz of a radar that had him locked up. His heart jumped. He looked down at the radar-warning receiver. It was a MiG-29 radar. *"Vlad, you've got me locked up!"*

"Vlad!" he transmitted. *"I'm Winchester. Get ahead of me and take a shot!"* He continued to close on Khan, now only half a mile ahead. As he tore his eyes away from Khan to glance over his shoulder at Vlad, Luke noticed to his surprise that his thirty-millimeter gun was fully loaded. Bullets! But he'd never fired a Fulcrum gun. He wasn't even sure how to interpret the gunsight. He slaved the IR system to the radar and saw the hot signature of the F-16s against the cool ground. He selected laser, and the laser range finder showed one thousand meters to the F-16. He selected the gun and wrapped his finger around the large trigger on the back of the stick. He studied the gunsight picture in the HUD. He had almost two hundred knots of closure. He pulled hard left and back to the right, to allow himself to pull lead on Khan and have a downward shooting angle. *"Vlad, hold off! I'm going to guns."*

Again there was no reply.

Luke pulled back around hard to the right, with the buzz of Vlad's radar ever-present in his mind. Luke was finally close enough to begin his gunnery run, although he was nearly supersonic—much faster than he wanted to be—but the F-16s weren't slowing down for anything. Luke pointed his nose directly at the lead F-16 and watched the pipper—the aiming point—march toward the dark figure streaking across the ground.

The laser range finder and IR system were on target. Luke pulled the trigger, and the thirty-millimeter cannon spit the huge bullets out the front of the MiG. He watched the tracers arc toward Khan and fall just behind him. He pulled hard left to pull more lead on Khan.

Khan knew he had to move. If he continued straight ahead, he'd be dead. He pulled hard left as his wingman broke hard right, in a controlled, disciplined turn. They stayed low to the ground, not giving up the safety of their altitude.

Luke tried to pull lead, but the turn was too tight to saddle in, and too low. If he continued ahead, he would overshoot and fly into the ground. *"Vlad, take the one in the right turn!"* he transmitted with some difficulty through the seven-G turn. He leveled his wings and pulled up to avoid the overshoot. At least he'd gotten Khan to turn from his target, and he was burdened with whatever bomb he was carrying, not a help in a dogfight.

Khan continued to turn hard right next to the ground, making it almost impossible to get a shot on him as he waited for a chance to pull his nose up and take a snap shot at Luke.

It was a clever tactic, Luke acknowledged, but not clever enough. Luke had three dimensions within which to work, and Khan had two. Luke leveled his wings and pulled up away from the earth, the nose of his Fulcrum pointing anxiously into the purple darkness above. He looked over his shoulder to see if Khan was going to follow him up. Khan continued to fly in his tight circle until he saw Luke almost completely vertical, then turned back to his original heading and accelerated away. It was what Luke had been waiting for. He pulled the Fulcrum down and pointed the nose of the Russian fighter toward Khan's F-16. As he plummeted toward the earth, he saw the flash of the missile out of the corner of his eye as Vlad fired.

Luke's heart stopped. Vlad's radar was still on Luke. He waited to see if the missile was heading toward him and saw it was going toward Khan's wingman. Luke finally realized that Vlad was keeping Luke on his radar to make sure he *didn't* shoot him. He'd fired an infrared missile and had slaved the missile seekerhead to the IR receiver instead of the radar. Leave it to Vlad to come up with that, Luke thought.

Luke pulled the trigger as soon as his pipper was near the F-16. It was a bad shot, but he wanted Khan to know he was still around and wasn't going away. Khan would have to fight or go down. In his peripheral vision Luke saw Khan's wingman coming back to support Khan. He was higher than Khan and in afterburner, trying to regain some of the speed he'd lost turning with Vlad. Vlad was behind him about a mile. Luke's tracers arched in front of Khan again, daring him to keep flying straight.

Khan's wingman never saw Vlad's missile. It hit him in the canopy and spiked the F-16 into the ground like a tent peg.

Khan couldn't take any more. He pulled up hard away from the earth toward Luke. Luke quickly selected radar and locked on to the climbing F-16. He placed Khan directly in the middle of his windscreen. The radar grabbed the reflected return from the metal airplane climbing away from the diminishing clutter and held on.

Khan pointed his nose directly at Luke. Khan's bomb limited his ability to maneuver, especially nose up as he now was. Luke heard the buzz from an F-16 radar lock as Khan got his radar onto Luke, then fired one of the Sidewinder missiles on his wing rail at Luke.

"Low fuel, low fuel!" the Indian woman warned Luke.

Luke dropped several flares and headed toward the ground at the same time Vlad did. The Russian-made flares were calculated to defeat the known enemy of all Soviet-bloc airplanes, the AIM-9L Sidewinder. The version the United States had sold to Pakistan was the older model Sidewinder. The Russian-made flare was exactly the right infrared frequency and deceived the Sidewinder into thinking that it was a jet exhaust in afterburner. The Sidewinder slammed into the small burning flare, its warhead exploding two hundred feet from Luke's MiG.

Luke and Vlad were both behind the fleeing Khan now, fifty miles from the nuclear plant. Vlad transmitted, *"One left."*

Prekash replied, *"Roger, break off your attack. We have you inbound at fifty miles. We have four fighters ten miles away. Repeat, break off your attack."*

"Stick, did you hear that? They want us to break off."

"I need you down here, Vlad! We've almost got him." "Emergency fuel! Emergency fuel! Land immediately!" the nice Indian woman told Luke in her inimitable voice. He longed for Glenda.

Vlad replied to Prekash. *"Yes, roger that. Luke is closing on him. He is still with him, hold your fire!"* he yelled as he rolled over and pulled toward the ground.

"Are you Winchester?" Luke asked Vlad.

"One Alamo left," Vlad replied.

"Lock him up."

"I'm on my way," Vlad said, selecting afterburner and racing ahead toward Luke, whom he'd again locked up with his radar. Vlad broke the radar lock on Luke and searched for Khan. He rolled wings level. *"Got him."*

"You got a good shot?" Luke demanded.

"Not very."

"Shoot!" Luke insisted.

"Too low! You're between us! It will never—"

"Shoot now! That's an order!"

"Alamo!" Vlad said as he pulled the trigger, and the last missile of their flight dropped off the Fulcrum and tore through the cool morning air.

Luke saw the flash behind him in his rearview mirror and continued to hold Khan on his radar. He had only guessed where Vlad was behind him; he hadn't really known. He'd taken a huge risk in ordering Vlad to shoot past him to Khan, but his method had its own madness. The Alamo flew by Luke's Fulcrum on his right a quarter mile away. It headed directly toward Khan.

Khan could see it coming and went lower to try to cause the missile to hit the ground as all the others had. It was exactly what Luke had wanted. He stayed in afterburner and closed to gun range. If Khan stayed straight and level, Luke would have him. If he pulled up, the missile would get him.

Luke pulled lead and placed the gunsight pipper on the nose of the F-16. It danced around in the bumpy airstream, but Luke could hold on the nose of the bogey. The laser range finder instantly gave the MiG computer the firing solution it needed. He pulled the trigger, and the thirty-millimeter rounds pounded out of the cannon.

With the tracers in front of him, Khan knew he had to make an instant decision. He lowered the nose of his F-16 slightly and descended to the trees. The belly of his plane scraped the tallest trees, and the Alamo came up immediately behind him and tried to get him by going through the branches. One of them was too thick for the fiberglass radome of the radar missile. It shattered the nose of the missile and its radar guidance. The missile went stupid and guided left and down, away from Khan. But it had gotten close enough to Khan to know where he was. Like most airborne missiles, it had two fuses: an impact fuse and a proximity fuse. The proximity fuse measured the range to the target when it got to within a few hundred feet. When the decreasing range suddenly reversed and started increasing, the missile knew it was passing the target and triggered the warhead to explode instantly. It did.

Khan pulled up hard to avoid the tracers at the same time the warhead's proximity fuse sent its message. The high-explosive warhead that sent shrapnel out at incredible speeds took off a foot of the left tail of the F-16. Khan's hard pull-up lost much of its authority, and instead he drifted higher in an arcing left-hand climbing turn. He flew directly into Luke's cannon fire. The first huge, high-explosive incendiary round cut through the center of the F-16. The second hit the back of the ejection seat in which Khan sat. The third shell passed through the fuel tank in the middle of the back of the F-16, and the airplane exploded as it pitched over and slammed into the ground.

Luke and Vlad both pulled up high into the sky as Vlad transmitted quickly on the radio, *"Splash four F-16s."*

"You got them all?" Prekash asked.

Luke could now hear Prekash as his Fulcrum passed through five thousand feet with ease. *"Got them all, Prekash. Four down, maybe one survivor,"* Luke said in his studied casual tone.

"Well done. How's your fuel?"

Luke checked his fuel gauge for the first time in ten minutes. His Fulcrum was out of gas. The Indian woman had apparently given up. She knew that her stupid pilot was going to kill her and had surrendered to the inevitable. The primary weakness of his favorite fighter had been vividly demonstrated. *"I'm out of gas. Request vector to the nearest airfield."*

"There isn't one within two hundred miles. Just put her down," Prekash ordered.

"Say your fuel state, Vlad."

"Zero."

Luke leveled out at seven thousand feet and glanced down below him. There was a straight section of a highway five miles away. *"I think I see our new auxiliary runway below us."*

"I'm right behind you," Vlad said.

"We're going to set down on the highway right below us. Do you have our position?" he asked Prekash.

"We're looking. We'll send a helicopter right away. Good shooting."

Luke took off his oxygen mask and gasped for air. He rolled into a downwind leg approaching the highway as if it were a typical runway. He checked for power lines and traffic and saw neither. He relaxed, lowered his landing gear and flaps, and prepared to land. He lined up on the road, which now looked narrower than he'd thought. He slowed carefully, then flared and touched down on the road. He quickly deployed his drag chute and got on the brakes. He watched his speed drop below 120 knots, then below 100. The MiG was behaving beautifully.

Something to his left caught his eye. He suddenly realized it was Vlad's MiG, in a steep nose-down descent. *"Vlad!"* he yelled. He pushed the transmit button on his radio, *"Pull up! Pull up!"*

There was no response. The MiG plunged into the ground and burst into flames.

29

"**L**ook at this," Cindy said as she gave Morrissey the final report.

Morrissey was so tired he knew he'd never read a report right now. "I don't have time to read it. What does it say?"

"I think you need to read it. It's the final conclusions of Naval Intelligence on the submarine angle."

"Let me guess," he said, sitting back and rubbing his eyes. "They don't know what kind of submarine it was, and the reason is that the people who saw it couldn't tell them. And the reason they couldn't find the submarine, in spite of trillions of dollars spent on antisubmarine warfare in the last decades, is that nobody told them soon enough to get assets in place in time. And because of all of that, they have no idea what kind of submarine it was, and therefore their report can go into the shit can." He looked over at her. "Pretty close?"

"Not even. They think they *do* know whose sub it was."

"Seriously?"

"Seriously."

"Who?"

Cindy knew better than to deliver that kind of news to her boss. She'd seen too many messengers shot in her days at the Agency. "See for yourself."

Morrissey took the report and began reading it quickly. His eyes grew large, and he stopped breathing. He flipped to the last page and read the conclusion. Then he closed his eyes and shook his head. "I've got to go to Nevada. Get

Helen Li on the phone for me. Tell her to pick me up. Get Lane to meet me at the airport. I want him to go over this report with me." He stood and grabbed his briefcase. "If this report is right, we've been had."

LUKE stopped his MiG on the highway and broadcast on his radio. *"Mayday! Mayday! We have an airplane down. Vlad has gone down. Request immediate SAR assistance! Prekash, do you copy?"*

"Affirmative. We'll get someone over there. State your position."

"We're near a road, about thirty miles west of position Lima on our charts."

"Roger. On the way."

Luke felt horrible. Vlad had fought bravely, valiantly. He'd shown what he was made of. Luke set the parking brake. He shut down the engines and opened the canopy. He realized he didn't have a ladder to get down. He didn't care. He undid his harness and stood on the seat. He threw his left leg over the side, then his right, and held on to the canopy rail with his hands. He lowered himself as far as he could, then dropped the last four feet to the ground. He stumbled and fell but stood again, uninjured. He removed his helmet and his other flight gear and began running toward the burning hulk of Vlad's MiG a half mile away. As he closed on the fire, he saw a figure walking toward him, dragging a parachute behind him.

"Vlad!" Luke exclaimed.

Vlad stopped and sat on the soft green ground. Luke knelt next to him. "Vlad, you all right?"

"Yes, I am fine." He tried to stand again.

Luke unfastened the parachute from his harness and helped him remove his flight gear. "What happened?"

Vlad stretched his back, then straightened up. "Nothing happened, really. The airplane was fine. Nothing wrong."

"Did you run out of gas?"

"No, it had gas."

"Why'd you punch out?" Luke asked, perplexed, then looked up to see if another fighter was around, someone who had shot Vlad down.

"I had to."

"What are you talking about?"

"You have been very kind to me, Luke. You have given me everything. Another chance. It is the happiest I have ever been in my life. But I have to tell you: I was not completely honest with you. I was dismissed from the Russian Air Force because I had a drinking problem. I think I have it under control, but it is a constant battle."

"Don't worry about it. We can—"

Vlad put up his hand. "The way I got out of Russia got me tied up with some very bad people. They owned me. They were helping Khan, and they tried to force me to join them by allowing Khan to succeed."

"Are you—"

"Let me finish, please." He sighed. "I did not help him. I would rather die. But now they know I helped defeat them. I have no chance against them. They have threatened my sister, her children, my mother—whatever I have, they will destroy."

"Vlad. I'll help you . . ." Luke protested.

"No. This is my battle. I ejected because you are going to go back to the United States and tell everyone that I was killed. I crashed in landing. Very tragic. Horrible accident, but my name is to be honored. And my Indian friends will tell everyone here that I was killed. Those in Russia who want to kill me will think I am dead."

"What are you going to do?"

"You called for help when you saw me go down, I assume."

"Sure."

"Good. And you sounded distressed and upset?"

"Probably."

"Good. The Indians will send a helicopter, and you will get in it. They have already sent another one to pick me up."

"How did they know to do that?"

"I had a chat with Sunil. I told him what I was doing. He said he had some scores to settle with these Russians, too. He offered his assistance."

"So what are you going to do?"

"I am going back to Russia. I have some things I have to attend to."

"Then what?"

"I don't know."

"Come back to Nevada. Build the school with me."

"Who knows? If I make it out again, who knows?" He extended his hand. They shook hands as the sounds of a helicopter came from the horizon behind them.

LUKE tried to sleep aboard the Air Force transport plane. He was completely exhausted, but his mind couldn't stop going over everything that had happened. The more he thought about it, the more he felt as if he'd been operating in the dark. Others had known things he'd only glimpsed.

On orders from the U.S. government, the transport flew straight in to Tonopah—no customs, no international flight terminal, just a gray Air Force airplane landing in the desert so far away from any population center that no one would know it had even arrived.

Every instructor waited with Brian and Katherine in the ready room. Even Thud's father was there. Bill Morrissey, George Lane, Helen Li, and some other government officials sat in the back of the room. They had arrived unannounced, looking concerned and out of sorts. Katherine had to convince Dr. Thurmond that they could come in. They all stared at the television tuned to CNN.

The President of India was holding a press conference to comment on what had already been reported, that Pakistan had attempted to attack an Indian nuclear power plant but was driven back and defeated by the Indian Air Force. There had been footage of the four downed F-16s, including shots of the Pakistani tail markings and helmets from the dead pilots. The President of India was outraged, telling the world that Pakistan's claim of a runaway pilot attacking the United States might have been believed, but no one could possibly believe that a strike from Pakistani territory with Pakistani jets and pilots into Indian territory was done without the backing of the government of Pakistan, especially the same week as the attack on the United States. It was impossible. Outrageous. But India was going to resist responding to such an aggressive attack, calling instead for international condemnation of Pakistan, including dismissal from the UN and universal economic sanctions until the government resigned and was replaced by an elected group of what he called "rational" people. Pakistan was obviously beholden to the Islamists and other irrational forces, and India wasn't going to let them plunge South Asia into a war, he said.

Finally, Luke walked into the ready room. He was smiling, but it wasn't the smile of a conquering fighter ace returning from the war. It was the smile of someone who was glad to be home, and not in a body bag. Katherine got up slowly and walked to the back of the room. They embraced silently. He kissed her.

Katherine looked behind him. "Where's Vlad?"

Luke shook his head. "He didn't make it."

"What?" Crumb asked.

Luke tossed his flight jacket onto the back of one of the ready-room chairs. "We found Khan. He tried to get the nuclear plant. Vlad had the whole thing figured."

"What happened?" Stamp demanded.

"We staged off a road. Just Vlad and me, with an entire

squadron circling low over the plant in case Khan got through."

"And you got them?"

"Big night fight. Unbelievable. We ultimately got all of them."

"How'd they get Vlad?" Crumb wondered.

"They didn't. We were about out of gas, so we landed on a road in the middle of nowhere. I was rolling out, and before I know it, Vlad's pitched over, inverted, and hits the ground a half mile from where I am."

"He just flew into the ground?"

"There was something wrong. He had to have had a mechanical failure."

"He didn't get out? What about the magical ejection seat?" Stamp asked.

Luke looked at Stamp and could tell that only Katherine and Stamp were able to see his face. He gave Stamp a quick wink, then said, "You've got to eject for it to work."

Stamp got it. "That's too damned bad. He was a great guy."

"How many of them did you get?" Crumb asked.

"We each got two of them."

"You got Khan? You sure?"

"Yeah. I'm sure."

"Archer?"

"Nope. Ended up having to gun him."

"You ever fired a MiG gun before?"

"Nope."

Crumb smiled. "Wish I could have seen that."

Luke looked around the room and saw the instructors, and Brian, and felt at home. He glanced back at Morrissey, whom he hadn't even noticed before. "What brings you here?"

"You," Morrissey said, looking at Helen and Lane. "I

brought a nice, wet blanket." Morrissey walked to the front of the ready room; the instructors watched him. "Congratulations on your flight in India, by the way. Nice job." Morrissey looked at the rest of the room, then turned to Luke. "The submarine. You thought it was probably a Kilo. Right?"

Luke rolled his eyes. "I told you, I told *him*," he said, looking to the back of the room at Lane, "I wasn't sure. I'm still not."

"It was our suspicion, and yours, I believe, that Pakistan had been deceiving us all along and was in fact behind the entire operation. They used the rogue Air Force officer excuse, the Islamic radical excuse, to hide. It allows them to achieve their objectives *and* claim no involvement. It makes our response very tricky, because if we come down hard on them, it looks unfair. Reactionary. Exactly what they would like. But we couldn't be sure. It could have been anybody's submarine."

"We've been through all that," Luke said, glancing in annoyance at Helen Li, who was still sitting in the back of the room.

Morrissey started walking back and forth. "But Pakistan doesn't *have* any Kilo-class submarines. Who does? Iran, of course. So we all chased the rabbit that led to Iran. Maybe *they* picked Khan up off the coast."

"Exactly," Luke said. "That's what India implied. Or at least one guy—"

Morrissey nodded knowingly. "Who exactly?"

Luke was getting an awkward, cold feeling. "Intelligence guy. Gave us the final stuff on when the strike was going to happen. He said they'd been following Khan for years. It was kind of odd. Everybody else left when he was there." Luke recalled the conversation. "He said he'd *told* you guys," Luke said, "but you wouldn't listen to him. He said the United States always assumed that anything India said about Pakistan was full of lies because it's in India's interest to upset our relationship with Pakistan. He said we would never believe what he said. Looks like he was right."

"When did you see him?" Morrissey asked icily.

"The night of the attack."

Morrissey nodded. "Good-looking guy. Sophisticated, British accent—more than usual."

Luke was startled. "How did you know?"

"Sunil, right?"

"How do you know all that?"

Morrissey said nothing.

Lane spoke. "Iran has only two Kilo-class submarines. Both were in port during the attack on San Onofre. The only Kilo not in port was an Indian Kilo."

Luke looked at Brian and the others, who all looked as confused as he felt. "What are you saying?"

"This photograph is of an Indian Kilo."

Luke frowned. "Indian?"

Morrissey nodded.

Brian couldn't stand it anymore. "Why in the hell would an Indian submarine pick him up?"

"The very question I've been wrestling with for the last three days. Then I read the Naval Intelligence analysis," Morrissey replied. "It finally occurred to me, and I checked with several sources—sensitive and highly placed sources we can check with only once. An Indian Kilo was deployed during that time. We thought it was operating off the coast of India. That's what India told us when we inquired. But our sources confirm that it was somewhere far away and was transiting faster than it had ever transited before. No one knew what it was doing, at least no one I could find."

"What are you saying? What the hell are you saying?" Brian demanded.

"It is my belief that Khan was assisted by India."

"What? *India?* Why?"

"Intense and irreparable damage to Pakistan. There are some new people working in Indian intelligence who aren't just sitting back and taking Pakistani aggression anymore. They're becoming much more active, bolder. This is the boldest and most aggressive move I've ever seen, if I'm right."

"They were helping Khan attack *us*?" Luke asked, his head spinning.

"Khan was what we thought. Part of some splinter group." Morrissey shifted his weight, obviously debating with himself whether he was saying too much. "We think this entire thing started when the Chief Executive of Pakistan addressed the UN General Assembly in New York. He told them Pakistan was prepared to sign a no-war pact with India, that they were ready for mutual reduction of forces, ready to agree to a nuclear-free South Asia, and ready to talk to India anytime, anywhere, at any level. Khan and his people saw that they were doomed unless they acted quickly, and dramatically, not only against India but to get rid of a Pakistani government that would utter such heresy.

"Khan thought he had an inside guy. A guy I understand who went by the false name of Shirish. He thought *he* was using Indian intelligence to kill the current Pakistani regime. But Shirish was one of Sunil's agents, an Islamic Indian, I'm told. He convinced Khan they could help him, even to attack the Indian nuclear plant. He promised to alert Khan if anyone was suspicious of an attack and warn him of preparations. If there were no suspicions, Khan would succeed in his attack and certainly start a war between Pakistan and India. There were already hundreds of men strategically placed by Khan's group in Kashmir—dressed as both Indian and Pakistani belligerents—to fight in both directions so each side could claim the other started it. They know that the next time there's fighting over Kashmir, it won't stop." He studied their shocked faces. "President Clinton didn't call Kashmir the most dangerous place on the planet for nothing."

"And it was all a *trap*?"

"Sunil lured Khan into a very *deep* trap. He used him to disgrace Pakistan and—you've seen what the President of India is saying—avoided the very war that was inevitable if Khan succeeded. Pakistan has lost its credibility for fifty years. He made sure you were waiting for Khan when he came. He took out perhaps the greatest threat to peace in the region. They were prepared to defend their nuclear plant on their own, but when Vlad offered to help—passed on to India by the Russian intelligence people—Sunil must have laughed out loud. Perfect symmetry. Use an American and a Russian to stop the Pakistani. He didn't even have to risk an Indian pilot."

Luke sat down and put his head back. The others in the room simply stared at Morrissey, who continued, "But there's one thing I need to know."

Luke didn't know what to say. His mind was spinning. "What?"

"Did this Vladimir Petkov try to do you harm in India? Did he try to prevent you from stopping Khan?"

Luke shook his head. "No. He kept me from getting killed. Why?"

"We had developed information that he was controlled by the Russian Mafia. And they were tied in with Khan somehow. It's probably lucky for him that he died over there. If he hadn't, I've got a feeling he'd be on somebody's shit list."

Luke continued shaking his head. "I can't believe it."

Morrissey put his hands in his pockets. "So here's the wet-blanket part. Nobody else would believe it either. That's why we can't go public with it. If we did, we'd look completely foolish. You'd look like a dupe, and nobody would buy it. *You* don't even buy it," he said, looking around the room. "India is the big winner. They get to say Pakistan is full of nuts who attacked the United States and then India. They'll say that what happened to the U.S. is terrible, and it almost happened to them, but fortunately, thanks to their skilled Air Force, they were able to defeat the attack by the Pakistani Air Force on their nuclear power plant. They'll rub Pakistan's nose in this for decades. And Pakistan had nothing to do with it.

"As for us, the wind stalled and saved our population centers. But the Southern California coast is ruined for several lifetimes. All because we couldn't get our act together about nuclear-waste storage."

Brian was stunned. "How sure are you of all this?"

"In this business you deal in degrees. But I'm pretty sure. Your brother's pretty sure." Morrissey looked around. "I normally wouldn't tell a group like this all of that. But I know that each one of you has held a top-secret clearance in the past—except Katherine. I'm asking all of you to keep this to yourselves. We can't handle a public discussion of this, and if I didn't tell you what was behind it all, you wouldn't have listened to me; somebody here would have talked to the press, to proclaim your greatness and your role in restoring world peace. Hell, *I* would have if it were me. But you can't."

Brian replied, "I didn't know India's intelligence operations were that . . . I don't know . . . sophisticated."

Morrissey smiled ironically. He hesitated. "Well, it's been changing."

"How?"

He scanned the room. "In the summer of 2000, the head of Mossad and General Security Services of Israel went to New Delhi." He let that thought sink in. "The Indians turned to Israel to help them combat Pakistan's border incursions and terrorism. In exchange, they agreed to share nuclear information with Israel."

"The *Mossad*?" Luke asked, incredulous.

Morrissey nodded. "I'm afraid the Indians were good students." He reached into his briefcase pulled out a stack of papers, and started passing them around. Those in the room began to read as soon as each got one of the sheets. "What you have in front of you is a nondisclosure agreement. If you sign it, you agree to keep everything you know about the Indian operation to yourselves forever. You can never speak about it, or write about it, or even hypothesize about it, without the prior written consent of the United States government." A couple of the pilots put the documents on the seats beside them.

"Why should we sign this?" Luke asked, still reeling.

"Because if you don't, I'm afraid Ms. Li has been instructed to conduct an extensive investigation into this school and its operations, beginning this afternoon. It would require the school to be closed for at least three months, and if she finds *anything* out of the ordinary, the MiGs will be confiscated and the school will be closed permanently. But if you sign, you are free to return to full operation. Immediately."

Luke stood up and looked at the other officers, then at Morrissey. "We risk our lives, and all we get from you is a threat to close us down? You *promised*!"

"And my promise is still good. If you sign."

"*I'm* not signing," Crumb said. "Stick, how many did you get in India?"

"Two."

"Hell. We've got to be able to paint them on the wall at the O' Club! And Thud's kills? We've got to be able to put it up."

"What do you want us to do?" Brian asked. "It's your school."

Luke looked at Katherine. He looked around the ready room and the school they had built.

"Sign it," Dr. Thurmond bellowed from the back of the room.

Helen stood and walked to the front. She looked at Luke and nodded slowly, telling him to sign.

"I'm not exactly eager to tell the world we got duped by an Indian intelligence puke who got us to fight his fight for him. Let's do this," Luke said, pulling a pen out of the shoulder pocket of his flight suit.

The rest of the officers went along. Morrissey collected the papers and deposited them in his briefcase. "Thank you. There are a lot of things yet to be done," he remarked as he put on his suit coat. "But your work is done. We appreciate it."

Luke smiled. "Sure," he said, tired of Morrissey, and the government, and the world of intelligence and all it stood for.

Morrissey walked out of the room with Helen and Lane and the others.

The rest of the room watched as Dr. Thurmond stood and came up to the front. He turned and looked at them, then spoke. "When Luke came to see me about starting this school, I warned him. I told him that when your existence is dependent on the government, you are at risk. But even I didn't have in mind that foreign governments would target us. They have. And we got had. But frankly, I am proud of the way this school responded. I wish Quentin were here to talk with us about it. I am so proud of him . . ." He fought the emotion that charged into his consciousness. "Thud would have wanted this school to go on. It's the first thing he has ever wanted on his own. But you need some leadership. You need someone who can push back when the government pushes. I want to be a part of this school. Luke," he said, "I think it's time I took over as CEO. You be the chief instructor, I'll run the day-to-day operations. Okay with you?"

"Sounds good to me," Luke responded.

"And we should rename the O' Club after Thud," Crumb said loudly as he stood. "Thud Alley."

The others nodded.

"Let's go over to the O' Club now," Thurmond insisted. "Enough of this."

Luke pulled out a videotape and tossed it to Crumb. "You wanted to see it?" he asked.

Crumb caught the tape and stared at Luke. "What's this?"

"Khan."

"You've got Khan's shoot-down on *tape*?"

"Gun-camera film," Luke replied. "Splice it into the O' Club tape."

Acknowledgments

I would like to thank Rob Young at the National Air Intelligence Center at Wright-Patterson Air Force Base for showing me the MiG-29s the United States bought from Moldova. I would also like to thank the Navy Strike and Air Warfare Center in Fallon, Nevada, and TOPGUN in particular, for their kind hospitality. Commander Bill Sizemore of TOPGUN and the other officers there were extremely helpful. I took some license with things at TOPGUN, such as ignoring the contract each TOPGUN instructor signs, promising not to get out of the Navy. I am hopeful they will not hold it against me.

I am grateful to my friend Don Chartrand for his support and suggestions and his shared interest in the problem of nuclear waste.

Mark Juergensen was a great help to me in understanding nuclear fallout and radiation exposure.

I want to thank my editor, Henry Ferris, for his guidance and insight. He made this a better book.

I also want to express my deep appreciation to my agent, David Gernert, for his continued support and wisdom.

Lastly, I want to thank my wife, Dianna, and my children for putting up with my long hours and for giving me their undying support and love.

James W. Huston
San Diego, California

Coming in hardcover
in June 2002
from William Morrow

THE SHADOWS OF POWER

Lieutenant Ed Stovic stared at his name on the flight schedule in his squadron's ready room aboard the USS *Harry S
Truman.* He was listed as the wingman for Commander Pete
Bruno, the squadron Commanding Officer. Stovic hardly
ever flew on Bruno's wing. His eye quickly scanned over to
the mission—covert escort of an EP-3, the big, slow EP-3
was to fly down the Mediterranean coast of Algeria and "listen." Collect intelligence. There had been some talk that the
Algerians were getting testy about the American battle
group crossing into Algeria's newly claimed two-hundred-
mile economic zone. It was just the sort of thing that might
stimulate a response from the new Algerian government.

Stovic tried to contain his surprise as he looked around
the ready room. All the other pilots were watching, some
smiling, some giving him looks of feigned anger for having
scored the only good hop on the schedule. They were to
launch before the official first launch.

Stovic briefed with Bruno and manned up. The excitement was noticeable in the crisp movements of everyone involved in the special launch of the two fighters. It came off
beautifully. The two F/A-18E Super Hornets rendezvoused
with the tanker above the carrier to top off their fuel tanks.
They pulled off the tanker and flew low and fast to their rendezvous point, a random latitude and longitude in the middle

of a lonely section of the Mediterranean Sea where the EP-3 waited for them, orbiting a thousand feet over the sea.

The EP-3 wagged its wings on seeing the Hornets across the rendezvous circle. The Hornets closed on the EP-3 from the left and slightly behind. Stovic studied the ungainly plane. He had never seen an EP-3 close up. He had never wanted to see it close up. It wasn't a fighter, so he had never thought much about it. But now he noticed the bulges and antennas all over it, like body piercings, defacing its otherwise clean body. Stovic watched Bruno carefully, waiting. Bruno glanced at him, raised his left hand above the canopy rail, then closed his fingers and thumb together like grabbing a sandwich to indicate he was about to open his speed brakes. Stovic moved his finger to the speed brake button. Twice, three times Bruno made the signal, then he moved his head forward and quickly back to signal execution. They deployed their speed brakes simultaneously and their closure on the EP-3 slowed even more.

The EP-3 was flying at two-hundred-twenty knots, slow for the Hornets, but manageable. Bruno moved up close to the EP-3, up to the cockpit where he could see the pilot who waved at them. Bruno nodded. He looked over at Stovic who was tucked comfortably under his left wing. Bruno backed off, dropped under the EP-3's left wing, kissed off Stovic leaving him there, and crossed under the EP-3 to the right wing where he took up his own position. They tucked up close to the larger plane, now invisible to any radar that might be looking.

CHAKIB Nezzar glanced ahead as his flight lead lifted off the runway. He pushed his throttles all the way forward. Brilliant flames roared out the back of the enormous engines of his MiG-25 Foxbat as his huge Russian-made fighter raced down the runway outside Algiers. Nezzar raised his landing gear and climbed after Hamid to join him as they headed out to surprise the American spy plane.

They climbed through fifteen thousand feet, careful not to use any of their electronic equipment. The American plane could detect any electronic signal they might make, and they almost certainly had Arabic linguists aboard listening to any radio communications. It was nearly impossible to surprise one of the United States Navy's EP-3 intelligence gathering airplanes, but they were sure going to try.

Nezzar heard the first intercept transmissions. *"Bearing 350, distance 300."* It was in the blind, requiring no acknowledgement. He knew it was for him, and he was to add ninety degrees to whatever heading they transmitted, and subtract one-hundred-fifty kilometers from any distance. So the American plane was 080 from them at one-hundred-fifty kilometers away.

They increased their speed, pushing through the sound barrier, through Mach 1.2, and headed directly for the unsuspecting American plane which was ten thousand feet below them.

KENT Rathman used his new CIA badge to open the door to the CounterTerrorism Section on the first floor of the enormous office building in Langley, Virginia. He was surprised it actually worked. The first time was always iffy. He walked down the hallway, looking for Don Jacobs, the Director of CounterTerrorism at the Agency. They were to meet in a conference room, but he always liked to do things differently. He spotted Jacobs' office across a large area full of cubicles, and walked around to approach it from the side without the window so his approach couldn't be seen. He looked through the crack behind the door where it stood open, and saw Jacobs still sitting at his desk checking his watch. Rathman stepped silently through the door. "Morning, sir," he said quietly.

Jacobs jumped, catching the expression on his face before

it could fully develop into the shock he felt. "What are you doing in here? Are you Rathman?"

"Yes, sir."

"We're supposed to meet in a conference room. Didn't you get my message?"

"Yes, sir, but there wasn't anyone there. I thought I'd come find you and save you the walk."

"We're still going to the conference room." He started walking down the hall, then stopped. "We need to get one thing clear right away. I don't like games. If you like games, you're in the wrong place. You got that?"

Rathman tried not to smile. "Sorry, sir."

They reached the conference room. Jacobs grabbed a carafe and poured coffee from it. He held it up, asking Rathman if he wanted any.

Rathman took a cup gratefully. "Thanks."

"You come highly recommended."

Rathman said nothing.

"Have you met Carpenter?" Craig Carpenter was the Deputy Director of Operations, the number two in the DO, the Directorate of Operations. The Directorate of Operations consisted of several subdivisions, including the CAS, the Covert Action Staff for political and economic covert actions, the PM for paramilitary covert action, and the Special Operations Unit, for counterintelligence. Within the Special Operations Unit was the SAS, the Special Activities Staff.

"Yes sir. We've gotten to know each other pretty well."

"Why did he pick you to set up a new SAS team?"

"I think I was just available. He interviewed me, and thought I'd be a good liaison between the SAS and your people."

"So that's it. You're now a member of the SAS. At least temporarily."

Most people talked about the SAS in hushed tones. It was

odd to hear Jacobs asking about it in full voice, not caring who was listening. "Yes, sir."

"What do you know about them?"

The SAS was one of the least well-known special operations units in the country. The Special Activities Staff. A nice vague name for a very pointed, deadly group, was responsible for covert action undertaken by the Agency. Rat had done his homework. He wasn't about to accept his current assignment without learning everything there was to know about the SAS. "I've gotten a lot of good information, but would always like to know more."

"You have a lot of experience," Jacobs said watching Rathman's face. "You were involved with the French special forces in Bosnia. You nabbed several of the most wanted war criminals."

Rathman controlled his surprise. "Who told you that?"

"And after the World Trade Center bombing your Navy group, Dev Group, was given a pretty free hand. We heard you were personally involved in several missions."

Rathman paused. "I can't really talk about much of that."

"I've read all the op reports. You think I'd let you be the liaison with my counterterrorism people without checking up on you?"

"I assumed you had," Rathman said.

"One thing makes me wonder though."

"What's that?" Rathman asked, sipping from his coffee but not taking his eyes off Jacobs.

"If you're so good, why did the Navy let you come on temporary duty to the SAS? Why would they let you go?" Jacobs didn't want to say what he thought. The SAS hadn't done as well as had been expected in the War on Terrorism. This was a clear attempt on the part of the Special Warfare Community to cross-pollinate those who had done spectacularly well into the CIA. Jacobs resented it.

"I was due to rotate and my detailer was sending me back

to BUDS." Basic Underwater Demolition and Seal training, in Coronado, California. It was where all Navy SEALs were trained. "They were going to make an instructor out of me. My Dev Group CO thought that was a waste. He set this up." Dev Group, or DEVGRU, The Development Group, as it was known, was the Navy's counterterrorism SEAL team. The elite of the elite. The Navy didn't even acknowledge its existence. They would talk of a certain SEAL Team, its predecessor, but not DEVGRU. The group was elusive, unidentifiable, able to work both under cover and overtly; and deadly.

Jacobs stared at him. Too pat. "Nothing else?"

"No, sir."

"Sure?"

"Yes, sir."

"You haven't been sent here to 'show us how to do it,' or something, have you?"

"Not at all. I asked for another operational billet, and they asked me if I'd be interested in going TAD to the SAS." That was mostly true. They had begged Rathman to go to the SAS. They needed more people operating at the highest levels. They needed to expand the American Special Forces capability wherever they could. And somebody had big plans for the SAS.

Jacobs smiled. "So have you been able to set up your corporation?"

"All set, sir. International Security Consultants, Inc. I've already got rental space in D.C., Virginia Beach, and New York, and a whole bunch of employees. Even a few contracts. We even have a couple of weapons evaluation contracts from the U.S. Government. Business is good."

"It had better be. This has to be a going concern. You have to actually get business and fulfill contracts."

"We're all set."

Jacobs drank from his cup as he looked over the top of it

at Rathman, the one they called Rat. "I understand you're good with languages."

"Some. I can't do oriental languages, but I can handle a couple of others."

Jacobs stood. "Where'd you learn them?"

"Monterey." The Defense Language Institute was in Monterey, California. They could make someone speak like a native if they had him for long enough.

"Where will you spend most of your time?"

"Here in Washington. This will be my main office. The Virginia Beach office is a good second bet. I don't plan on going to New York much."

"How many people do you have working for you? I understand they're all part of the package." He said "package," with some sarcasm, as if he wasn't quite sure what was in a package that had just been handed to him. The SAS usually operated in teams of twelve, sometimes two teams together.

"Well, yes, sir. I thought all your people interviewed and cleared all of them. At least that is what I was—"

"Yes, yes, we did. How many?"

"It's a flexible number, frankly. They have their own operations here and there, unrelated to whatever I'm doing, but in a push, I could get probably twenty-four or so together for anything you needed."

Jacobs liked that answer. "I look forward to working with you Rat." He said "Rat" with the vague distaste he felt for someone who was just outside his grip. "By the way, why do they call you that?"

"Just a name thing. Based on my last name. Rathman— RAT-man. It started at Annapolis. I look forward to working with you too, sir." Rat meant it. He was stepping into a different world. Operating with DEVGRU had been his life, covert overseas operations, raids, kidnappings . . . other things . . . all in support of the longstanding, smoldering, War on Terrorism. They had had success, but there was much still to be done. Rat was enthusiastic to go after terrorists from a totally different angle, with different tools and objectives. Whatever it took. It was a dirty war, but a war nonetheless. "I hope I can help you succeed."

Jacobs face broke into a wrinkled, reluctant, ironic smile. "I need all the help I can get. I'll be in touch—"

A young man in a white shirt and tie and a CIA identification badge dangling from his neck rushed into the room. "Mr. Jacobs, you said you wanted to know if that Algerian thing got hot."

"What's up?" Jacobs asked, glancing at Rat.

"The Algerians have launched fighters and are going after the EP-3."

"How many?"

"Two."

"Did we do the escort?"

"Yes, sir. Two Navy F/A-18s are under the wings."

Jacobs put down his cup. "This could get interesting." He looked at Rat. "Come on. Let's see what the Algerians do when they find out our unarmed intelligence plane isn't so unarmed."

THE E-2, operating two hundred miles away, broadcast through its encrypted radio to the two navy fighters: "*Gulf November 103 flight, you have two bogies approaching from the west. Angels unknown, estimated speed, Mach 1.5.*"

Stovic felt a rush of adrenaline as the transmission sunk in. He ensured his radar was off, as was his radar altimeter and anything else that would send electronic signals out of his airplane. They hadn't said a word on their radios since starting their jets. As far as anyone else could tell, they weren't even there. Their radar signature would blend in with the EP-3 which flew five feet above their heads with its four large turboprop engines turning methodically.

Inside the EP-3 Chief Petty Officer Jerry Kenny pressed

his earphones to his head. He squinted at the screen in front of him as he dialed the frequency in more carefully. He finally took his hands away, nodded to the linguist next to him, and pointed to the frequency. He started the tape. He switched the large screen display in front of him to the radar repeater mode, and saw the two targets that their air controller was watching. It showed two targets, bogeys, as they were being called, fifty miles behind them.

The Chief, an Arabic linguist, looked at the radar return and compared it to the heading and distance information being undoubtedly transmitted to the fighters he was following on the screen. He watched the computer triangulate the GCI, ground controlled Intercept, transmission that he was listening to, and confirmed it was coming from the Air Force Base outside of Algiers that had launched the fighters thirty minutes ago.

Kenny nodded again and spoke through his lip mike into the ICS so that only the other linguists who had his channel selected could hear him. "They're sending their fighters range and bearing data, but are adding 90 degrees to the bearing and subtracting 150 from the range. Pretty basic. Everybody got the fighter channel?"

The three men to his right nodded. "Okay. Sprague, see if you can find any other traffic we haven't seen yet. Thompson, get on the HF and see if they're getting any help from anybody else. Amad, check the ground crew transmissions again. See if anyone else is turning on the ground."

They all nodded their agreement.

"Come on down," Kenny said to himself as he smiled and watched the two MiG-25 targets approaching them at an ever increasing speed.

A similar picture was right in front of Stovic. The E-2C was transmitting its radar picture via data link to the airborne fighters. All Stovic and Bruno needed to see where the MiGs were was electrical power. Stovic's screen showed the symbols for two data link bogeys—inverted chevrons. He shook his head, moving his oxygen mask back and forth slightly. The MiGs were coming out to intimidate the unarmed EP-3 and probably thump it—fly underneath it, then pull up directly in front of them to startle and intimidate the Americans. Instead they were about to get a rude surprise of their own.

The American radios were deathly quiet now. Everything that needed to be known was being transmitted by UHF data link. And it was always transmitting. No one who was listening to the UHF transmission would be able to make any sense of it—it was all data and was all encrypted—and the volume of transmission didn't change if things got more interesting. There was simply no way to know what the Americans were looking at or whether they were even tracking the MiGs.

Suddenly Stovic's AN/ALR-67(V)3 radar warning receiver jumped to life. It was the unmistakable sound of a fighter radar. He tore his eyes away from his visual cues on the side of the EP-3 to glance at the display. MiG-25. Bigger than hell. He'd never seen this radar indication before. Few Americans had ever flown against the vaunted MiG-25. The Russians rarely sent them out, and the Algerians never did. It was the fastest jet fighter ever built. It was the gorilla of Russian fighters—big, fast, and mean.

Stovic watched the MiG radar. It was unusual for them to illuminate a target from forty miles away. They liked to sneak up on targets, illuminate late in the intercept, then be right on top of them. In this case, no doubt because they were confident the American surveillance plane was flying alone, they wanted the Americans to know they were coming, to be concerned and worried, and possibly do something they would never do if they kept their cool.

He ran through his combat checklist. His AIM-120 AMRAAM missiles were ready, as were the AIM-9 Sidewinders. His gun was fully loaded. He checked all his switches, and held off only on the Master Arm switch, which would make his trigger hot as soon as he selected a weapon. Fifteen miles.

"MR. President," Sarah St. John said softly.

The President put down the *New York Times*. His favorite thing to do every morning when he was at Camp David was to read the paper. He knew that his National Security Adviser wouldn't interrupt him lightly. "What is it?"

"They're all airborne. You said you wanted to know."

The President drank from his orange juice.

"The Algerians are coming out?"

"Yes, sir. MiG-25s."

"How many?"

"Just two."

"That's a pretty big fighter isn't it?"

"Yes, sir. Biggest one they've got. Very fast. Capable of Mach 3."

President Kendrick sat back. "Think they know what we're up to?"

"We don't think so." She replied.

"You still having doubts?" the President asked.

"This decision has been made, sir. I just think if something happens, it will look like we set them up."

He rolled up the *Times,* tossed it to the middle of the table, and stood. "Get everybody. Let's go over this one more time. Could we still call off our fighters?"

She nodded. "They're escorting the EP-3, but nothing has happened yet. We've only got a few minutes though."

"Get everybody into the conference room."

She hurried out of the room. It wouldn't take long, since they were all eating breakfast in the guest dining room in the next building. It was only his Chief of Staff, the Secretary of Defense, and Sarah St. John, the National Security Adviser. They gathered in the newly refurbished high-tech briefing room just off from where he had been eating. The table he had been sitting at had been quickly taken away, and the room had been restored to a family room with a large brick fireplace.

They looked at St. John with a curious look as they entered the large room. What could have happened in the last thirty minutes since they had received the security brief?

President Kendrick stood against the wall in a loose-fitting polo shirt and khakis. "Go ahead, Sarah."

"We've talked about this. We agreed to send the *Truman* battle group into Algeria's new two-hundred-mile limit—"

"We *had* to, Sarah," Stuntz said. Howard Stuntz was the Secretary of Defense who was forever nipping at her heels, trying to impress her with his superiority. She had learned to deflect most of his comments. "We don't let countries just shut down international waters. And here, it's right by the Strait of Gibraltar."

"Of course," she replied. "But the EP-3, with fighter escort, could be seen as provocation. I just wanted to make sure we were all on the same page."

Stuntz rolled his eyes. "I hope it *does* provoke them. I mean really, a two-hundred-mile economic zone? No ships or airplanes allowed? It's ridiculous. What did they think we were going to do? Just say okay, close off the western Mediterranean? Libya did the same thing with their 'Line of Death.' Same deal. Same result. We sent in carrier battle groups until they made some stupid moves, lost some boats and airplanes and relented. The 'Line of Death,' " he said with mocking tone, "suddenly went away."

She looked at the map of Northern Africa that someone had called up on the huge projection screen in front of them. It had the positions of the forces in place, including the carrier battle group, the EP-3 and the F/A-18 Super Hornets with it. Approaching from the west were the two symbols representing the Algerian fighters. "I just don't want another China incident."

Stuntz grunted. "We've got to protect the EP-3."

Kendrick interrupted. "Look, all that has happened is the Algerians have launched a couple of fighters. That's what we expected. There's nothing new. If they go out there and see the escort, they should turn around and tell all their friends maybe the American intelligence planes aren't such easy targets. Right?"

St. John replied, "Yes, sir. That's why we're doing this. I just wanted to keep the bigger picture in mind. The new regime in Algeria has been on the sidelines on the War on Terrorism, but they're sympathetic to the wrong people. They haven't done what we feared. I'm just concerned this could push them over the edge."

The Chief of Staff, Dennis Arlberg, a lifelong friend of the president, watched the president as the others spoke. He jumped in, "Look, the EP-3 is a national asset. The NSA and everybody else care a lot about what happens to it. This new regime in Algeria is borderline irrational. They come from people who used to kill civilian villagers in their own country for 'intimidation.' They don't come from the same kind of thinking we do. *They* are the ones who came up with the two-hundred-mile limit. Not us. And they had to know we always challenge restrictions on international waters. Always have, always will. No matter who is president.

"The only thing different about this is the escort. But if you think we should troll up and down the coast of Algeria in their new two-hundred-mile limit without protecting an unarmed, slow airplane, you're out of your mind. If they make something of it, it's at their peril, and we have a carrier battle group right there in case they do."

Kendrick asked, "Is the MiG-25 a problem for the Super Hornet?"

Stuntz shook his head. "Anything can happen, of course, but it shouldn't be any problem."

"Anything else?" Kendrick asked. No one responded. "Keep me posted."

Riveting Military Adventure from
New York Times Bestselling Author
James W. Huston

"If you like Tom Clancy,
Huston is a good step up."
Washington Post Book World

FALLOUT
0-380-73283-1/$7.99 US/$10.99 Can

FLASH POINT
0-380-73282-3/$7.50 US/$9.99 Can

THE PRICE OF POWER
0-380-73160-6/$6.99 US/$9.99 Can

BALANCE OF POWER
Mass Market paperback: 0-380-73159-2/$6.99 US/$8.99 Can
Audio cassette: 0-694-52515-4/$9.99 US/$14.95 Can